HURRICANE
PUNCH

TIM DORSEY

HURRICANE PUNCH

WILLIAM MORROW
An Imprint of HarperCollins*Publishers*

HURRICANE PUNCH. Copyright © 2007 by Tim Dorsey. All rights reserved. Printed in the United States of America. No part of this book may be used or reproduced in any manner whatsoever without written permission except in the case of brief quotations embodied in critical articles and reviews. For information address HarperCollins Publishers, 10 East 53rd Street, New York, NY 10022.

HarperCollins books may be purchased for educational, business, or sales promotional use. For information please write: Special Markets Department, HarperCollins Publishers, 10 East 53rd Street, New York, NY 10022.

FIRST EDITION

Library of Congress Cataloging-in-Publication Data

Dorsey, Tim.
    Hurricane punch: a novel / Tim Dorsey.— 1st ed.
        p.   cm.
    ISBN: 978-0-06-082967-4
    ISBN-10: 0-06-082967-2
    1. Storms, Serge (Fictitious character)—Fiction. 2. Serial murderers—Fiction. 3. Psychopaths—Fiction. 4. Florida—Fiction. I. Title.

PS3554.O719H87 2006
813'.54—dc22

2006049513

07 08 09 10 11 WBC/RRD 10 9 8 7 6 5 4 3 2 1

For Steve Genest

It's only funny until someone gets hurt—then it's hilarious.

—ANONYMOUS

ACKNOWLEDGMENTS

I owe deep gratitude to Nat Sobel, Henry Ferris, Lisa Gallagher, and Eryn Wade for continuing to put up with me.

HURRICANE
PUNCH

PROLOGUE

Editor's Note—In cooperation with local authorities, *Tampa Bay Today* is seeking the public's help in identifying a serial killer using this unprecedented hurricane season as cover for his string of grisly homicides. The following letter was just received by one of our reporters:

Dear Florida,
I am the one you seek, borne on the curling wisps of ghostly madness that crawl onshore at midnight and seep over the swamp. My glorious evil rages north from the Everglades, the living fury of the land welling up. Flushed birds fill the black sky; reeds yield as one in genuflection. I stalk across the turnpike as you sleep in your new six-bedroom abominations with screened-in pools, blissful sheep ignorant of the million alligators beyond ridiculous canals you've scarred into the sacred ground. I am the pressure drop in your soul when you finally accept, bound and gagged, that you are in The Place of No Hope, with your last breath, pitifully whimpering for the impostor

that is mercy. My next sacrifice will be offered when the barometer dips below twenty-nine inches.

                                  —The Eye of the Storm

Editor's Note—In cooperation with local authorities, *Tampa Bay Today* has decided to publish a second letter in connection with the recent rash of homicides. Based upon evidence they cannot disclose, police have confirmed that the author is responsible for at least some of the murders. However, investigators are uncertain whether this new correspondence is the work of the same person writing in a different state of mind or evidence of a second, copycat killer. A word of caution: Certain language may offend sensitive readers, but we are leaving the letter intact to increase the chance that someone might recognize the writer's syntax.

Dear Letters to the Editor,

This is the third time this month I've gotten a wet paper—what the fuck? You can fill the building with Pulitzers, but it doesn't mean dick if the guy delivering your product is on the pipe. Don't bother trying to contact me to apologize or deliver replacement papers, because I stole them off someone's lawn. All I can say, sirs, is that the residents of 3118 San Luis Obispo have every right to be prickly with your level of service.

    Next: What's with giving that retardo-bot serial killer credit for every unsolved murder in this state? He doesn't possess nearly the intellect or wit to conceive the imaginative technique that police aren't divulging in the Fowler Avenue case (if, hypothetically, I knew anything about it, which I don't). But you have to admit, it was pretty funny, especially if you were there (which I wasn't). And then, what on earth were you thinking publishing his letter last week? Could you believe that trite prose? What a bunch of self-important, freshman-philosophy drivel!

Sure, I went through the same idealistic phase about the encroachment of rampant development on our stressed ecosystems. And yes, people need to be killed, but not *randomly*. That's just wrong.

Plus: What's with letting the guy name himself? "Eye of the Storm." Give me a break! The guy's a serial killer! At the very least, his punishment should be he doesn't get to choose his own nickname. On the other hand, it's better than the dumb stuff the media always comes up with. Like a few years back when they started finding those bodies in Yosemite National Park, and you guys called him something lame like "The National Park Killer." Hey, there's no law that says you can't go back and improve a serial killer's nickname, so here's my gift to you, what he should have been dubbed in the first place: "Son of Yosemite Sam."

Finally: Why don't you run bridge anymore next to the crossword? When did *that* stop? Personally, I hate the game and all who play it, but seeing those little hearts and clubs in the paper each morning was a reassuring cultural anchorage. Now I constantly feel off balance, like when you take a really sound nap in the afternoon and wake up just before sunset and for a brief, terrifying moment you don't know what part of day it is: "Jumping Jesus! I've been drugged and kidnapped!" And you start checking for signs of anal violation. Know what I mean? Please run bridge.

Dissatisfied in Tampa,
Serge A. Storms

AUGUST, MIDDLE OF THE SEASON, BETWEEN HURRICANES #3 AND #4

Traffic was heavy on Tampa's main north-south artery. Several cars were flying little satin flags declaring respective allegiance to the Bucs, Lightning or Gators. A unique flag snapped in the wind from the antenna of one vehicle: a large red square with a smaller black square inside. Storm warning.

Bump. Ba-bump. Bump. Ba-bump . . .

Serge and Coleman sat through one of those ultra-long, four-way traffic lights at the corner of Dale Mabry and Kennedy. Coleman was driving so Serge could practice his new electric guitar. It was a pawnshop Stratocaster. Serge just *had* to have a Stratocaster because he was going to be "like Clapton, only better." He tuned the D string and began strumming unplugged.

Coleman held his joint below window level. "What are you playing?"

"Classic Dylan." Serge cleared his throat and inflected the distinct nasal twang. *"This is the story of the Hurricane . . ."*

Bump. Ba-bump. Bump. Ba-bump . . .

Serge stopped. The tuning was off; he twisted a knob again. "Can't tell how glad I am it's hurricane season again. I'm so pumped! I relish preparing for each new storm the way other people get ready for big football games, especially the tailgating."

Coleman took a hit from the roach secretly cupped in his hand in a way that looked even more suspicious. "Why's that?"

"Because I *love* hurricanes!" He test-strummed a chord and twisted another knob. "Everything about them. History, science, the way the community bands together in the collective memory of a common experience, which stopped when we got Internet porn. As a bonus, TV provides gavel-to-gavel coverage from those insane weather reporters on the beach. What a scream! No matter how hard you try, you can't stop watching. It's worse than crack. I just surrender and sit there for hours, like when PBS runs those Labor Day marathons on bacteria."

Coleman looked sideways at Serge.

"What?"

"Nothing." Coleman faced forward.

"No, you were going to say something."

"Don't want to judge. Just sounds like you're hoping for tragedy."

"Easy mistake to make," said Serge. "It appears ghoulish on the surface, but an obsessive interest in hurricanes actually saves lives. The more you know, the easier to react and recover."

"You're saving lives?"

"When am I not?" Serge tried another cord. "If only more people had my ungoverned curiosity. Some politicians should be going to prison for New Orleans. Remember when that FEMA wimp said he didn't know that people were stranded at the convention center until *Thursday*? Imagine being so incompetent that your performance rockets a thousand percent if someone tells you, 'Okay, stop absolutely everything else you're doing and just watch a motherfuckin' television."

"I want that job."

"You're overqualified."

The light turned green. They drove. Serge's hurricane flag fluttered in the breeze. "Nope, nothing would make me happier than if every storm this season obeyed my psychic commands and spun harmlessly out to sea."

Coleman stopped at another red light on the corner of Cypress. "How did you first get into hurricanes?"

"Was imprinted as a kid by Charles Chips."

"The trucks that used to deliver?"

"They'd drop off those giant, yellow-and-brown-speckled metal tabernacles of potato-chip goodness," said Serge. "Another casualty of progress."

"What's that got to do with storms?"

"Hurricane Betsy, 1965, Riviera Beach. Had a can all to myself, practically as big as me. It's how my parents bribed my hyper little butt from running around the house near the windows getting blown in." Serge tuned another string. "Ate the whole thing in the hallway while wind howled and candles burned down and a tree crashed through the garage roof. After that, hurricanes and Charles Chips went together like tonsillectomies and ice cream."

Another stoplight. Serge released the tuning knob. "There we go. . . . From the top. One and-a two and-a . . . *This is the story of the Hurricane.* . . . "

Bump. Ba-bump. Bump. Ba-bump. Bump. Ba-bump . . .

"Why'd you stop playing?" asked Coleman. "I was getting into it."

"That sound's drowning out my song. Where's it coming from?" Serge stuck his head out the window and looked up at the sky. "Are we being bombed? Is a building under demolition?"

Coleman pointed at the rearview. "I think it's that car back there."

Serge twisted around. "Where?"

"Coming up from the last light."

"Can't be." Serge rolled up his window. "That's at least a half mile. How is it possible?"

The other car grew bigger in the back window.

Bump. Ba-bump. Bump. Ba-bump . . .

Their whole vehicle shook. Metal seams hummed. Coleman tightened his grip on the vibrating steering wheel. "How far?"

"Two hundred yards and closing."

The other vehicle pulled up in the next lane and stopped at the light.

BUMP. BA-BUMP. BUMP. BA-BUMP . . .

Serge and Coleman turned to see a sunburned man with a shaved head, Fu Manchu and Mr. Clean gold earring.

"What kind of car is it?" yelled Coleman.

"Datsun," shouted Serge. "Standard package: Gothic wind-shield lettering, chain-link steering wheel, fog lights, chassis glow tubes, low-ride tires, thousand-watt bazooka amplifier, and those shiny, spinning hubcaps that glint in a manner saying, 'I have no investments.'"

Coleman grabbed his cheek. "I think I lost a filling."

"It's untuning my guitar." Serge's voice warbled as he gestured toward the next lane with an upturned palm. "The Death of Courtesy, Exhibit Triple-Z."

The light turned green. Squealing tires and smoke in the next lane. The Datsun raced four blocks and skidded up to another light. Serge and Coleman took their time. The music pounded louder again as they approached the intersection.

"I haven't heard this song before," said Coleman. "The only words I can make out are *fight the oppression* and *pump that pussy.*"

"He's getting on my final nerve."

"But I thought you liked rap music."

"When it's played by rappers. The genre organically sprang forth from a culture of adversity and fortitude. I can respect that. But it also fucked up some Caucasian DNA and spawned an unintended mutant."

"Mutant?"

They eased up to the light and Serge tilted his head. "The Hip-Hop Redneck."

"Now that you mention it, I've been noticing them in disturbing numbers."

"They should work on their own sound."

"What would that be?" asked Coleman.

"More cowbell!"

"If he's going to play so loud, why does he have the windows down?"

"It's his mating call." Serge rolled down his own window and waved. "Excuse me?"

The other driver couldn't hear him.

"*Excuse me!*"

The driver looked around and noticed the passenger in the next car.

"Yoo-hoo!" shouted Serge. "I sure would appreciate it if you'd crank down the tunes. I believe I speak for the bulk of society. . . . No, not *up*, down. . . . Down! *Down!* . . . That's *up* again! . . ."

Serge rolled his window shut. He faced forward and counted to ten under his breath.

Coleman leaned and looked across Serge. "He's giving you the finger."

"Just ignore him. The light's green. Drive."

Coleman started to go. "But you never ignore guys like that."

"My psychiatrist says I must learn to walk away from this kind of negativity. So I focus on enjoying the future he's limited to."

Coleman glanced across Serge again. "He didn't patch out this time. He's staying right with us. . . . Now he's yelling something about your mother."

"Turn in this parking lot. Let us go our separate ways."

Coleman pulled in to Toys R Us. "He's following."

"Park here," said Serge.

The Datsun screeched up alongside. The driver jumped out and grabbed the locked door handle, banging on Serge's window. *"Open up!"*

Serge rolled his window down a crack. "You look like you could use a big hug."

"I'll fuckin' kill you!" He hopped on the balls of his feet, throwing punches in the air. *"Come out here, you wuss!"* He ripped Serge's hurricane flag off the antenna, threw it to the ground and began stomping.

"Coleman, you're a witness. Didn't I try to walk away?"

"That you did."

"Just so it's noted in the official record." Serge grabbed his door handle. "Okay, I'm coming out. . . ."

MIDNIGHT

Police cruisers and flashing lights filled the parking lot of a budget motel on Busch Boulevard. The Pink Seahorse.

Agent Mahoney was getting out of his unmarked vehicle when a newspaper reporter drove up in an oil-dripping '84 Fiero.

"Got here as fast as I could," said the journalist. "What do we have?"

"Someone's ticket got punched, and it wasn't a round-trip."

They headed for the open door of a room that was the source of all the attention.

"That motel sure is pink," said Jeff.

"It's the Pink Seahorse."

A stout police officer ran out and became ill in unpruned shrubs.

They went inside. The reporter caught a brief glimpse and jerked away. "Oh, dear God! What kind of madman . . ."

The victim was still tied to a chair in the middle of the room. Blood aggressively streaming from every natural orifice. No wounds.

Mahoney offered a hanky.

"Thanks." The reporter wiped his mouth. "What the heck happened in here?"

"Serge is what happened," said the agent. "Watch your hooves."

The reporter looked down. The entire floor was a spaghetti plate of electrical cords and cables. Miles of wire, tangled and snarled and plugging together an eclectic menu of raw electrical components and cannibalized acoustic magnets bolted to the walls.

The lead homicide detective shouted into a cell phone and slammed it shut. Mahoney approached. "What's the skinny?"

"A horror show." The detective marched toward one of his subordinates. He signed something official and handed it back. "Usually when we get a Hip-Hop Redneck in a motel room this involved, it's a meth lab. Except there are no chemicals. Just all these wires and magnets. Doesn't make any sense."

Mahoney pointed. "Why's plywood bolted over the window?"

"Haven't figured that either," said the detective. "Got our best guy on the way."

"Anyone in the other rooms hear anything?"

"*Every*one. Shook the whole motel. And the strip mall across the street. Dozens came out to rubberneck, but nobody saw anyone leave this room. That's how we know he was alone when it happened."

"Explosion?" asked Mahoney.

"Music," said the detective.

"Music?"

"Witnesses said it sounded like the Stones, but their statements differ on the album." Another aide approached with something else to sign. "The press is going to have a field day. . . ." The detective happened to notice something over Mahoney's shoulder. "You brought a reporter in here?"

"It's copacetic. He's a friendly."

"He's contaminating the crime scene."

"Jeff's hip not to paw anything."

"No, I mean he's literally contaminating it. He's throwing up."

A police officer who did not look like the others entered the motel room. He was Dipsy the Hippie Cop. Tie-dyed T-shirt, gray ponytail halfway down his back, sandals manufactured from recycled tire treads. General appearance regulations did not apply to Dipsy, because he was the department's technology wizard.

"Whoa!" said Dipsy. "Someone's been busy!"

"You know what happened?"

"Abso-fuckin'-lutely." His smile broadened as he surveyed the room. "I definitely want to rock with these cats!"

HURRICANE #1

CHAPTER ONE

TAMPA

The consistently inventive positions of the hurricane-flung bodies validated the chaos theory, particularly those equations involving trajectory, procrastination and trailer parks. Certain corpses seemed purposefully arranged, the rest very much not. Some appeared to have been scattered by mortar strikes, others peacefully reclined like stuffed pandas on a child's bed, still others looked like sick practical jokes being played on the recovery crews. The disturbing circumstance of one particular body, the next to be discovered, was no accident.

But wait, we're getting ahead of ourselves. Let's back up. . . .

June 1.
The opening day of the Atlantic hurricane season was like any other: dire predictions in the media and cheerful sales at the home-improvement centers.

How people ramped up for hurricanes depended on experience. If you'd been through a direct hit, you didn't fool around. Plywood, gas, go. Those with small children were the first to bolt, followed by seasonal residents, who had more options. The old-timers went one of two ways: Most had developed keen instincts and knew precisely when to pull the trigger; the crustier stayed put no matter what and were interviewed on CNN. Newer residents forgot to charge up cell phones; the wealthy scheduled unscheduled vacations; families gathered family albums; insurance executives canceled coverage. Prescriptions and sandbags were filled. Some believed in the power of hoarding canned meat; others lost faith in electricity and withdrew massive amounts of cash from ATMs. Door-to-door entrepreneurs purchased chain saws for the brisk post-strike downed-tree business. There were the tourists, who stared bitterly at unused portions of multi-park passes; sailboat owners, who spiderwebbed vessels to docks; the motor-oil-baseball-cap people standing in the beds of pickup trucks, making everyone wonder by loading the heaviest, most worthless shit; and college students, whose hurricane preparation consisted of not knowing a storm was coming.

The memories of 2004 were supposed to greatly improve public awareness. *Charley, Frances, Ivan, Jeanne.*

Since then, authorities found less trouble getting residents to heed evacuation orders. But not a lot less. The culture of complacency had deep roots in nearly four decades of borrowed luck. There was one ten-year period from 1975 to 1985 when but a single hurricane made landfall in Florida. The next seven years saw only three more. Meanwhile, thousands of new communities and condos sprouted along coastlines with the growth-speed and sturdiness of spring-shower mushrooms.

Then 2004. As many hurricanes that had struck during seventeen years pummeled the state in less than six weeks.

A lot of residents learned their lesson and installed the latest storm shutters. Others drank beer.

Then 2005.

Dennis, Katrina, Rita, Wilma.

Another wake-up call. Someone hit the snooze alarm.

Hurricane shutters were already up on an old theater in Seminole Heights. It was now a low-rent professional building. A clock ticked on the wall of an upstairs office, postmodern feng shui. Two people sat in white leather chairs, facing each other twenty feet apart. Only one could see the clock. That was by design.

A self-assured woman with pulled-back strawberry hair folded her hands on top of a small notebook. She smiled with genuineness. "What are you thinking about?"

"It's dark in here."

"The shutters are up," said the psychiatrist.

"I know," said Serge. "A big one's already on the way, and it's only the beginning of June. It's all I've been able to think about."

"The anxiety's perfectly normal. Especially after the last few years. I've been seeing a lot more patients—"

"Oh, I'm not worried," said Serge. "I'm cookin'! I *love* hurricane season!"

Her expression changed. "Why?"

"Potato chips."

The doctor took a deep, poised breath and looked down at her notebook. "I didn't think I'd ever see you again."

Serge slouched in his chair. "I was in the neighborhood."

"I just moved to this office. That means you had to look me up."

"Happened to be reading the Yellow Pages."

"Give yourself more credit. The last time we saw each other, you were involuntarily committed. This time you came on your own. You're taking steps."

"See? And you wonder why I've been away so long. You still think I'm crazy."

"That's an unfortunate term we don't like to use."

"*I* like to use it," said Serge. "You want to talk about crazy? I knew this caseworker who was checking on a guy in a St. Pete transient hotel. One of those beautiful old places with the striped awnings over the sidewalk. But that's another tragedy, another day. My friend knocks on the door and doesn't get an answer, so he tries the knob. Unlocked. He goes in, and there's shit everywhere. I don't mean trash or PlayStations. I mean real shit. The smell hit him like a shovel. The guy he's looking for is sitting in the middle of the floor wearing nothing but one of those hats with the moose antlers, singing Peter Gabriel—*Shed my skin!*—playing with more turds, sculpting little bunny rabbits. He's got a whole bunch of them lined up on the floor in an infantry formation like some kind of Easter-morning nightmare. My friend says, 'Tito, you haven't been taking your medication, have you?' Then he gets hit in the chest with a shit-bunny. But he tells me he likes his job because it's something brand new every day. In my thinking, there's *good* brand new and *bad*. Know what I mean?"

"And this story is important to you how?"

"*That's* crazy. I just want someone to talk to."

"Then let's talk. How have you been? Do you recognize the improvement?"

"Not really."

"I can," said the doctor. "When we first met, you were wearing a straitjacket."

"Since then I've learned to dress for success."

"What about your medication? Have you been taking it?"

Serge squirmed into a different slouch. "Those pills made my head thick. I was turning into my friend Coleman. You know how you are the first few seconds after waking up in the morning? He's stretching it into a life."

"We can adjust the dosage." The doctor got out a prescription pad. "There's a drugstore one block over."

"Maybe next week," said Serge. "I'm busy revising my global strategy for the president."

"Listen to what you just said."

"What?"

"The president. Global plans. Don't take this wrong, but doesn't that strike you as a bit . . . delusional?"

"Oh, like I can do any worse. You watch the last State of the Union? Talk about delusional."

The psychiatrist handed him a slip of paper. "Please get this filled."

"I'm telling you, I don't need it."

"Just look at your body language. All the fidgeting."

"I can't see the clock. That's no accident."

"But you have a wristwatch."

"I need the official time. I have to know The Deal."

"This is why I want you to get that prescription—"

"Tom Cruise says it's a crock. *Born on the Fourth of July* is a classic, so I'm forced to side with him on this one."

"Those were some uninformed interviews. Did a great disservice."

"Remember the one with Matt Lauer? I thought Tom was going to pop him. Matt acts all nice, but underneath he's a snake. I'm on the edge of my seat: Come on, Tom, you can do it. His guard's down, quick left jab. Knock that fuckin' smirk into next week."

"You're still having violent urges?"

"I hope so."

"Why?"

"You should know," said Serge. "Any behaviorist will tell you it's a healthy condition of the animal kingdom, how all living things are programmed for survival. But your medication deadens those urges. And if an animal stops having them, it means his wiring's crossed, and he ends up doing something unnatural like beaching himself and flopping in the sand, making shrill clicking noises, and then the lifeguards ask you to move along because you're 'frightening the children.' . . ."

"Serge . . ."

". . . Ever observe insanity in the wild? Even if it's something small, it'll freak you out. I once saw a squirrel lose its mind at the Lowry Park Zoo. . . ."

"Serge . . ."

". . . Jumped on one of the gorillas. Just didn't give a fuck anymore. . . ."

On the other side of the wall from Serge was another office. Another psychiatrist sat with an unlit Dr. Grabow pipe. This office had a couch.

A law-enforcement officer lay on it. He was out of uniform. Black slacks and lime-green dress shirt. A crumpled fedora rested on his stomach. His necktie had martini shakers.

The psychiatrist studied the patient's folder. "Forgive me, but I'm not familiar with this condition. I've heard of *paranoia*, but not *noir*."

"Mickey Spillane, Raymond Chandler, *The Maltese Falcon*, diners, dames, dime novels."

"Are these things real to you?"

"Of course not," said Agent Mahoney. "It's pulp. Like I told the shrinks at the drool farm, I'm over that now. I can separate reality."

"What about your wardrobe?"

"What about it?"

"Seems you're still in this 'pulp' world. Like that tie."

"Doesn't mean anything."

"So you're saying that sometimes a tie is just a tie?"

Mahoney turned slowly and stared stone-faced.

The doctor grinned. "Thought I'd lighten the mood. That's a psychiatric joke. You know how Freud—"

"I get it."

"You're not laughing."

"It's one of those think-about-it jokes. I'm enjoying it inside."

"You are?"

"*That* was a joke."

"Oh. . . . Ha, ha, ha, ha . . ."

"When I just said that was a joke? That was sarcasm."

"I see, okay . . . ahem . . ." The doctor nervously rustled papers.

Mahoney maintained his glare. "You're not very good at this, are you?"

"Not really."

"Didn't think so. Heard you were working off a narco beef, writing scrips to yourself. Just got your license back."

The doctor recoiled in his chair. "Where'd you hear that?"

"What do you think I do for a living? It's how I picked you."

"You did?"

"Saw your rap sheet. Makes our understanding easier."

"Understanding?"

"You keep signing off that I'm making progress, and I make sure no crooked flatfoots plant any silly pills, if you catch my drift."

"I do."

"Good. Look, I like the way I am. Hell with everyone else. Sometimes I'm noir, sometimes I'm contemp."

"How can you tell?"

"My threads, how I jaw."

"Interesting."

"No it's not. I'm going to do some reading now. . . ." Mahoney opened a dog-eared paperback with a hard-boiled broad on the cover. She had stiletto heels, a whiskey sour and the road map to Trouble Town.

The psychiatrist tapped his notepad. "Excuse me . . . ?"

"Are you still here?" asked Mahoney.

"I'm not comfortable—"

"Jesus!" He slammed the book shut. "Would this go more jake if I just gave you the goofballs I was going to plant, and you can do up?"

"No, I mean, I'm not going to cause any trouble with the progress reports, but it would make me feel less awkward if we at least went through the motions."

"Would it?"

"It would."

Mahoney sat up and cracked his neck. "Shoot."

The doctor clicked open a pen. "So you're only occasionally living in this *noir* fantasy world?"

"I prefer to think of it as an alternate lifestyle," said Mahoney. "Society hasn't caught up."

"How's that?"

"Today it's a sickness, tomorrow you get a pride parade. I've started working on my float."

"Help me with the concept," said the doctor. "What's your fascination?"

"Back then a cop was a cop. Black and white. You needed to lean on a twist, slip hopheads a yard, throw lead, no one snooped."

"And now?"

"Everything's sensitivity training."

"You don't agree?"

"Fuck sensitivity."

"That's a new way to put it." The doctor wrote something.

"It's the straight dope," said Mahoney. "They're never going to catch Serge without turning the big screws."

"Serge?" The doctor flipped back to the front of his notebook. "Isn't that the case that first landed you in the, um . . . *hospital*?"

Mahoney stuck a toothpick in his mouth. "Sharp cookie. The department doesn't understand what it's like inside his noodle."

"And that's why you've come back to Tampa?"

"His stomping ground. I can feel him. He's real close."

"But according to your file, you're supposed to drop this whole Serge obsession. One of the terms of reinstatement."

"They don't have to know."

"But . . . that doesn't sound like you care about getting better. How am I supposed to treat you?"

"Like I said, we're tripping for biscuits. So why don't you just button it and validate my parking?"

The psychiatrist tapped his mouth with the pen. "Okay, let me try coming at this from a different angle. Say I'm a new partner you're breaking in, and we're looking for Serge together. I'm on your side."

"Are you?"

"No. What makes you think you can catch him this time?"

"He's reaching that age. Serial killers have a poor shelf life. Burn out, slip up. Or worse: Their personalities split, and we think we're now tracking a second killer when it's the same guy."

"What's our first move?"

"He's been quiet. Too quiet. We flush him out."

"How?"

"Go to the fish wrappers—"

"The what?"

"Newspapers. Find a reporter willing to play ball. Then we bait the hook."

On the other side of the wall from Mahoney: a third office. Another psychiatrist sat in a chair. His suede jacket had leather elbow patches to make up for an inferior college.

Someone was weeping in the chair across from him. A young newspaper reporter named Jeff McSwirley.

"I can't take it anymore!"

The newspaper didn't provide trauma counseling, and it didn't pay much, so Jeff was forced to seek budget mental-health care.

"You're really on the cop beat?" asked the doctor.

The reporter nodded, hands still covering his face.

"Ever seen a dead body?"

"I always get there too late."

"Darn."

"I tell my editors I'm bad with directions, but I'm really doing it on purpose." Jeff raised his head and sniffled. "I keep seeing their faces."

"The dead people?"

"Survivors. Hundreds of them. Even when I dream."

"What are they doing?"

"Crying. Some grab for me." Hands covered his eyes again. "I can't take it."

The psychiatrist looked down at a brimming folder of newspaper clips. Death, death, death. The top article was about a landscaper. The psychiatrist whistled. "Shoving palm fronds through the grinder and finger got caught, sprayed into the mulch cart." The doctor raised expectant eyebrows. "Did you get to see it?"

"I was late."

The doctor frowned and looked back down. "Here's another landscaper article."

"Routine in Florida. I've covered seven." He lost composure again. "I can't take it anymore."

"But it's the job you wanted," said the doctor. "It's what you went to school for."

"Not *this*. I trained to do investigative work. But all reporters have to pay their dues. They said the cop beat shouldn't last more than six months, twelve tops."

"How long's it been?"

"Three years."

"Why don't you request a different assignment?"

"I have."

The doctor stroked his goatee. "This is clearly taking its toll. You might consider a different line."

"But it's all I know how to do." Jeff blew his nose. "I was hoping to hang on until they transferred me to the government beat, but it doesn't look like they're ever going to let me off cops."

"Why not?"

"They say I'm good at getting interviews."

"Are you?"

"Yes."

"How good?"

"I scoop everyone. People who've slammed doors in all the other faces—I get in. Circulation's way up."

"Listen, I don't want to suggest anything unethical," said the doctor, "but what if you tried *not* to get interviews?"

"That's how I get them."

"I don't understand."

"At the scene of every tragedy, reporters swooped like vultures. Survivors screamed to be left alone. Some even took swings. I detested myself for being part of it. But I didn't want to get fired. You have to at least ask for an interview or you'll get in trouble back at the office. So I asked. And that's when the problem started. Guess my anguish made me look sympathetic. Got invited inside while they kept the rest at bay on the front lawn. The more interviews I landed, the sicker I felt, which meant more exclusives. That's when I started the sabotage you mentioned: 'I really don't think it's right to be bothering you, but I'm supposed to ask or I don't eat. So now I've asked. Sorry for your loss. Bye.' Just made it worse. I was practically yanked into living rooms."

"Perfectly understandable," said the doctor. "Certain psychological types withdraw in grief; others need a shoulder."

"I don't want to be a shoulder," said Jeff. "You should see these people, showing me baby photos, telling incredibly private stories that rip your heart out. I'm starting to gain weight."

"How's that?"

"They keep giving me casseroles."

Full circle, back to room one.

"Serge, please look at me."

"Wait. . . ."

"You can't just keep staring back at the clock."

"Yes I can."

"If you turn around, we'll talk about your hurricanes. You mentioned it was something that made you happy."

Serge turned around. "You're manipulating me."

She smiled and shrugged. "It's my job."

"I'll bet you got straight A's." Serge reached in his pocket and unfolded a piece of paper. "Just received this year's list of storm names. Aren't they the weirdest? You'll never hear such a combination in the real world unless someone's taking attendance at a wine tasting: Alex, Bonnie, Cristobal, Danielle, Esteban, Fay, Gaston, Hermine, Isaac . . ." He twisted in his chair. "What's the clock say? How much time do I have?"

"Forget the clock."

"You deliberately put it back there and then say forget about it?" He grabbed his head and rocked manically in distress. "Another conspiracy! The clock. You thinking I'm crazy. Mail-in rebates that are like applying to fucking law school . . ."

"Serge, we're off the clock. I'm here to help. I'm your friend."

He covered his face. "I'm at the end of my rope."

"What's the matter?"

"I can't keep it in any longer." He stopped rocking. "There's something I need to talk to someone about. It's extremely private and embarrassing."

The doctor leaned forward. "You can tell me."

"I've been wanting to buy a Porsche."

She sat back in puzzlement. "You want to talk about a car?"

"No, it's the oddest thing. I don't even like Porsches. And I *really* hate Porsche people, and people who can't afford to be Porsche people so they buy Porsche sunglasses, and people who can't afford those and buy counterfeits, and the whole pronunciation debate. . . ."

"What do you suppose triggered this?"

"I feel sick just thinking about it. I . . . turned forty-four."

"You're entering mid—"

"Don't say it!"

"It's completely natural."

"It's completely stupid. I'm not going to turn into one of those male-menopausal freaks with a sports coat over a black T-shirt and the barely legal girlfriend."

"How do you explain the Porsche?"

His shoulders fell. "I can't."

"Serge, I wouldn't worry about getting old. You should be more concerned about growing up."

"What's *that* supposed to mean?"

"Like a job. You have one?"

"Yes, but it's not recognized."

The doctor wrote something in her notes. "I think it would be constructive for you to find full-time employment. Something with a regular paycheck."

Serge bit his lip. "That's not original."

"Your life needs the structure." She looked up from her writing. "By our next appointment, I'd like you to have at least submitted some applications."

"Can't waste the time," said Serge. "Mortality's breathing down my neck. I've starting doing all kinds of desperate things."

"Like what?"

"I sort of began looking into . . . *religion*. Doc, what's wrong with me?"

"Nothing." Her voice filled with encouragement. "That's very positive. Faith has provided many people with a lot of answers."

"I'm just getting more questions."

"What denomination?"

"My parents raised me Catholic, so I'm starting there. In order to cleanse my mind of physical illusion, I've decided to become celibate."

"Like priests?"

"If you're just going to make jokes . . ."

The doctor smiled. "Go ahead."

"I was thinking of celibacy more from an Eastern aesthetic, or when you're a young Catholic boy and can't get any—until you hook up with the right Catholic girl. Shazam! Don't be fooled by those plaid skirts. You would not *believe* when the floodgates of repression finally blast open. . . ."

"Serge . . ."

". . . Every hole's a party!"

"Serge!"

"What?"

"You're getting off track again. How long have you been celibate?"

"What's today? Tuesday?" He looked at his watch. "Eight A.M. and—no, wait, after breakfast and again on the roof. Ten o'clock? Let's call it an even ninety minutes."

"Hour and a half? That's it?"

"Didn't realize it would be this rough."

"You mind me asking how old the woman was this morning?"

"I don't know. Nineteen? Twenty? Real sweet kid. The entire stripping thing is completely out of character. Made me promise to call her this afternoon. That's when the celibacy started. Think she'll buy it?"

"Let's get back to religion," said the doctor. "Besides not wanting to call this girl, have you been having any other spiritual feelings?"

CHAPTER TWO

TAMPA BAY

The mandatory evacuation order had just been issued.

The problem with mandatory evacuations in Florida is that everyone knows they're voluntary. The orders have no teeth. Authorities don't possess nearly the resources to knock door-to-door, and the best they can manage is canvassing barrier islands in emergency vehicles, broadcasting last-chance pleas from rooftop bullhorns. During these final passes, the civil-defense trucks have the roads to themselves; anyone stubborn enough to still be there ain't budgin' now. Then the bridges are closed, and nobody can leave even if they want to.

That time was rapidly approaching.

A lone vehicle rolled down an overcast residential street near the Gulf of Mexico. Madeira Beach to Indian Rocks. The empty lawns usually saw a smattering of egret and heron, but nature had given them intelligence. An amplified voice echoed off waterfront houses:

"You are under a mandatory evacuation. Proceed at once along designated routes. This is your final warning. Shelters are open. You don't want to be like those pinheads who held a party for

Camille and the sole survivor floated out a third-story window on a mattress. Do not panic. Bring necessary medication and dietetic provisions. There's still time. Or maybe not. The hundreds who washed to sea in the Labor Day Storm of '35 thought they had several more hours. So I could be way off. . . ." Cars screeched backward out of driveways and raced for safety. The antique bullhorn strapped to Serge's roof continued blaring: ". . . Six thousand vanished in the Great Galveston Storm of 1900. Entire city blocks erased. . . . Serge's Disaster Fun Fact Number Fifty-three: The word 'hurricane' comes from the Mayan god of wind and rain, Hurakan. . . . Another two thousand lost in the un-named storms of '26 and '28. Whole houses flicked off foundations like bugs. . . . Serge's Hurricane Tip Number Sixty-two: Public shelters are generally icky. Top-shelf alternative? The international airport. Open twenty-four hours, even in storms, for stranded out-of-towners who have to curl up on the floor waiting for runways to reopen. You're not supposed to use it as a shelter, but they're not allowed to kick you out either. Just pack evacuation supplies in American Tourister and pretend you're from Akron. . . . Donna peaked at two hundred miles an hour, over-whelming morgues. . . ." More cars sped by for the mainland. ". . . Don't forget to bring playing cards and board games. Remember Operation? I loved that one. 'Remove wrenched ankle.' . . ."

LANDFALL

A cold, gray wind howled up the soulless mouth of Tampa Bay. No more time. Direct hit.

Everyone was inside. Just the satellite trucks and reporters in bright rain slickers lining the lips of the bay at Fort DeSoto and Anna Maria Island. Their job was to illustrate why nobody should be where they were.

If power was still on, so were TVs: color Doppler in repeating loops, Egmont Key under the pulsing, orange-and-red radar blobs. The upper-right rotation of the storm's forward path shoved a massive tidal surge toward downtown. Leading rain bands churned straight for the Sunshine Skyway. Rogue waves crashed against the bridge's pylons, sending columns of white spray hundreds of feet.

The bands passed, and the bridge broke into the eye. Shafts of deceptive sunlight hit the yellow, string-art suspension cables and swept down the bridge's apron to the causeway. An engine started.

A dark SUV pulled out from behind the windbreak created by a dense nest of Australian pines. It eased onto the road and accelerated toward the Skyway. Ahead: flashing amber lights and concrete barricades. Bridge closed. The vehicle took a service road to Maximo Park and the fishing pier, also blocked off.

The driver got out, black scarf concealing his face to the nose arch. Matching black gloves opened the vehicle's back doors and wrestled to remove a device that was cumbersome, complicated and unrecognizable. He wheeled it to an open stretch of shore near the anti-erosion boulders. A series of levers deployed arrays of spring-loaded kickstands. Other buttons swung out the actuating arm and sighting mechanism.

The driver returned to the SUV. One of the passenger doors opened. Black gloves grabbed a pair of rope-bound ankles. The hostage hit the ground sideways on his rib cage. The trailing eye wall passed over the mouth of the bay, and the wind returned.

FOWLER AVENUE

It looked like a river, if you didn't already know it was a street. A lone Jeep Grand Cherokee drove blind through the flood, creating a generous wake. Wide four-by-four tires sent twin cascades of water up past window level.

Bang.

The driver jumped. "What was that?"

"Something hit the door panel again." The front passenger lit a joint. "I'm hungry."

"Still looking for a place." The driver leaned over the steering wheel for a closer view of the rain.

Bang.

"Left fender," said someone in the backseat, reaching for the jay.

"Maybe you should turn on your hazards."

The driver pressed a button on the steering column. Taillights began flashing. The bumper had a University of South Florida parking sticker.

Another passenger took a hit and looked out the side window. "Nothing's open. Is it a holiday?"

"Don't think so."

The vehicle fought its high-profile tendency to lane-drift with wind gusts. The driver slowed at the next intersection.

"What are you doing?"

"Where's the traffic light?"

"There it is. Sitting on that curb next to all those sparks."

The driver sped up again. "It's almost as if something's going on that we should know about."

Smash!

Heads jerked back. Large cracks snaked across the windshield. "What the hell just hit us?"

A passenger pointed at a glass-repair shop. "Another windshield. That's like irony."

"Shut up."

"I wouldn't get mad." The joint was offered. "There's no deductible for windshield replacement. Insurance companies believe it's ultimately more expensive to let cheap people drive with busted glass."

"I forgot to pay my premium," said the driver.

"Then there's a deductible."

Bang.

"Why can't we find someplace that's open? There's a hundred restaurants on this street."

"Wait," said the driver, snapping his fingers. "I got it. The one place that'll definitely be open." He accelerated.

Sure enough. Five blocks later, light from a yellow-and-red

sign filtered though the sheeting rain. The Jeep's occupants saw the first evidence of life since leaving their dorm. A line of idling vehicles wrapped around the side of the building. It alternated between students ordering takeout and news trucks interviewing the kid in a safety-orange poncho working the drive-though window.

A radio-station van pulled up. A waterproof mike poked out. *"Why are you still open?"*

"The owner wants to make money."

The Jeep parked in a handicapped slot a few feet from the front door. They were drenched before they got inside.

The driver wrung out the front of his shirt on a welcome mat. "I told you they'd be open."

"And it's a buffet!"

The buffet was the reason the restaurant was always jammed, being so close to the university. Football weekends were big, but that was nothing compared to tropical storms and hurricanes, when it became the only option. Employees double-timed it restocking stream trays. Others mopped up student drip trails. More kids arrived; the one at the cash register was paying with loose change organized in separate dollar stacks on the counter.

A small frame hung on the wall behind the cash register. The first dollar bill the owners had made. It was that kind of bar. Lots of faded photos over the liquor bottles: a onetime mayor, other semi-famous customers and the Little League team they'd sponsored in 1983. Shriners gumball machine. A red lamp with fringed paper shade. The lamp flickered. Then the thunder.

Serge turned a limp newspaper page and waved for the bartender. "Could you turn up the TV?"

The man threw a towel over his shoulder and aimed a remote control. Serge leaned forward on elbows.

Coleman peeled the napkin off the bottom of a frosty mug. "What are you watching?"

"Hurricane coverage."

Coleman pointed another direction. "Why don't you just look out the window?"

"Because hurricane coverage is hilarious," said Serge. "These idiots stay out far too long. Theoretically all their clothes get ripped off in a category four."

Coleman scooted his stool closer. "Do they have that hot chick from Channel 2?"

"Yeah, but don't get your hopes up. Usually they're miles off target and have to *act* like they're taking a beating."

"Who's the other guy out there behind the reporter?"

"Where?"

"Left side of the screen," said Coleman. "The homeless dude drinking a beer."

"Gotta love this state," said Serge. "Once I saw a Geraldo-type screaming bloody murder into the camera like his arms were being torn off, and then this old lady from one of the condos strolls behind him walking her poodle."

A plate of food sat in front of Coleman. He popped a sesame-battered shrimp into his mouth and chased it with a swig of Tsingtao beer. "Serge?"

"What?"

"How'd you know this place would be open?"

Serge cracked an egg roll. "Chinese restaurants never close during hurricanes."

"Where'd you hear that?"

"Watch storm coverage. Reporters are constantly driving around looking for interviews at the last business still open. And it's always a Chinese restaurant. *Always.*"

"Why's that?"

"Because the Chinese are an impressive people. They just took up capitalism a few minutes ago, and they're not stopping for anything. Notice how they've already zeroed in on America's fat-ass weakness for buffets."

"Chinese buffets are my favorite," said Coleman. "Everything's fried."

"They have our number. We better watch out."

Coleman's teeth ripped the skin off a wing. "How come we're alone at the bar? The rest of the place is packed with students."

"Because there are no three-for-one well specials, beat-the-clocks or hand grenades. Just real-world drink prices."

"What's that mean?"

"We will not be bothered by academia."

The TV showed slow-motion replay of a reporter in a motorcycle helmet taking an ugly spill from a pier.

"That station's boring." Coleman chomped another wing. "I want to see the Channel 2 chick."

Serge got the bartender's attention again. The remote clicked. Next station: a Chinese restaurant on Fowler Avenue. *"Why are you still open? . . ."*

"Keep going," said Serge. The remote clicked again. A beach scene and a woman in a bullfight-red parka. The jacket was open halfway down the front to expose her shirt, soaked and clinging, the way it had been since they'd sprayed it with a hose before the rain started.

". . . Steve, the storm's really beginning to pick up. It's extremely dangerous out here now. The only people left are emergency management officials patrolling the streets in amphibious military half-tracks. . . ."

"Look!" yelled Coleman. "It's the Party Parrot! It's the Party Parrot!"

A man in a parrot costume had run out behind the newswoman, jumping up and down and waving a WPPT-FM bumper sticker over her head. Network technicians tackled him. The screen abruptly went to test pattern.

"The Party Parrot cracks me up!" said Coleman. "Don't you just love him?"

"We now return to our regularly scheduled programming,

already in progress." The TV cut to a man in a three-piece suit sitting at the front of a boardroom. *"You're sacked!"*

"What's this program?" asked Coleman.

"The Mogul," said Serge. "British knockoff of Trump's show."

The program segued to another scene. The man from the boardroom was now waving out the pressurized window of a space-age teardrop hanging from the bottom of a rapidly ascending experimental rare-gas balloon.

Coleman signaled for another beer. "What's going on now?"

"That's the premise of the show," said Serge. "He fires people, then does an expensive stunt."

"Why?"

"The direction of society. We worship rich people who buy celebrity."

"I don't recognize him."

"Neville Gladstone?" said Serge. "He's the media tycoon buying up everything in the state. That's what really pisses me off. Never even set foot here, then he grabs Florida Cable News and slices coverage in half so he can add a bunch of stupid shows: *The Mogul, Xtreme Poker, Gotcha!"*

"I love *Gotcha!"* said Coleman. "Did you see that one prank where this bum's in a mall and pulls a dirty diaper from a trash can and starts licking? It had been planted with melted chocolate or something. All these shoppers got sick anyway. You have to be really smart to think up stuff like that."

"This has been a production of Gladstone Media. . . . Stay tuned for Florida's Funniest Surveillance Videos . . ."

CHAPTER THREE

Welcome back to our *Storm Team Five Special Hurricane Report, your one-stop information source for complete landfall coverage, with continuing live broadcasts from Kirk in Clearwater, Wade in Sarasota, Chad in Fort Myers, and the rest of the Storm Team: Mary with the shelter roundup, Biff with canceled sports, Flip down in the Channel 5 Weather Bunker, and Ernie driving the Hurricane-Buster Mobile Command Unit. . . . Let's go to Ernie at the mouth of Tampa Bay. . . . Ernie?"*

"Alex is really blowing now! Despite our vehicle's heavy armor, he knocked us off the road like a toy and down into this ravine."

"Can you get a video shot outside the Hurricane-Buster?"

"Negative. The wind won't let me open the hatch. We're trapped."

"Doesn't sound like much is happening. . . . Let's go to Chad. . . ."

"Hank, it's a beautiful day at the beach as the hurricane completely missed Fort Myers. I was almost in danger."

"How close were you to death?"

"Less than a hundred and fifty miles."

"Better go back inside. . . . Mary?"

"Order was restored this morning at the downtown shelter. As you can see behind me, just the usual scuffles—"

"Hold on, Mary. Ernie's back. . . . Ernie?"

"I got the hatch open. I'm sticking my head out. . . . Wow! Did you see that sheet metal?"

"Way to duck, Ernie. . . . Ernie? . . . We just lost Ernie. . . . Biff?"

"No games on tap."

"Flip?"

"Check out this excellent graphics software we just bought! I can rotate the 3-D map on every axis. And these buttons make cool animated tornadoes. Look at 'em all!"

"Flip, how many tornadoes has the hurricane spawned?"

"None. I was just showing you the buttons. Want me to crash them into something?"

"Wait, we've got Ernie back. . . . Ernie, what's the latest?"

"Hank, this is an unbelievable display of nature's fury. I'm using all my strength to raise the camera out of the hatch. . . . Any second now you'll be seeing the first historic footage of Alex's landfall. . . ."

"We see it, Ernie, absolutely incredible! Try to get an interview with that shirtless guy drinking a beer. . . ."

Serge stared up at the TV and grimaced.

"What's the matter?" Coleman wiped beer foam. "Thought you liked hurricane coverage."

Serge rubbed his leg. "It's not that."

"Your knee again?"

"Acts up in this weather."

"You said you were glad to have it." Coleman waved for the bartender. "Helped you track hurricanes."

"I was making lemonade."

"It starts in the joints."

"I am *not* getting old!" said Serge. "Jesus! You're just like my psychiatrist!"

"What did your psychiatrist say?"

"That I have to come to terms with the aging process. . . ."

"Sounds like a good psychiatrist."

". . . And I should get a job."

"I'd get another psychiatrist."

"No, as much as I hate to admit it, she's right on both counts. But like she also said, forty-four really isn't *that* old."

"Forty-four!" yelled Coleman. "Holy shit! I didn't know you were forty-four. That's almost fifty, which is almost sixty, which is almost dead."

"Thanks, Mr. Sunshine. How old are *you*?"

"I'm . . . I . . . I don't know."

Serge gave him a dubious glance.

"Hey, getting old bothers me, too," said Coleman. "Know how I handle it?"

Serge returned to his newspaper. "You get fucked up?"

"Near the end they give you morphine. I'm looking forward to that."

Serge turned another page. "You might want to bottle some of that excess ambition for the afterlife."

"You're awfully cranky today."

"Sorry." He closed the paper. "Didn't mean to take it out on you."

"What's the matter, buddy?"

"Everything lately. My birthday, the psychiatrist, the knee, Porsches." Serge gazed toward the buffet and a room full of sprite youth. "On top of all that, they say I'm losing my edge."

"Who is?"

"I hear talk."

"What kind?"

"That I'm mellowing out, not killing motherfuckers as fast as I used to."

"People can be cruel."

"What did I ever do to them?"

"But that's just talk," said Coleman.

"It's also in print." Serge lifted his newspaper to reveal a magazine underneath. *Florida Law Enforcement Quarterly*. It was folded over to an unsettling charcoal illustration of a faceless humanoid trapped in a box. The figure was grabbing its head, which had storm clouds in the brain region.

Coleman leaned. "What's that?"

"Article warning about the psychological perils of profiling serial killers. The writer just got released from a mental hospital in Miami after obsessing about a suspect and getting too far inside his head."

Coleman tapped a spot in the body of the type. "It mentions you by name. . . ." His lips moved as he read. He stopped and sat back. "Wow. I can see why you're so sore."

"What the heck does he mean, lunatics like me don't have a good shelf life? Our abnormal brain waves age us twice as fast?"

"It means you're"—Coleman stared painfully into space—"almost seventy."

"Thanks. I know what it means."

"Why don't you just kill a few people and make them happy?"

Serge pounded a fist on the bar. "That's the whole problem: Everyone has the wrong idea. I don't *want* to do what I do. I need a very good reason. Unfortunately, people in this state keep providing them. *But I am not a serial killer!*"

Coleman pointed at an info box in the magazine. "Says here you're number twenty-six all-time, just about to pass Dahmer. And you're way up to eleven on the active list."

"This isn't about keeping up career stats."

Coleman read on. "What's 'sexual dysfunction'?"

Serge pounded his fist again.

"Look at the writer's name on the top of the article," said Coleman. "It's Agent Mahoney. Isn't that your old friend?"

"Not after this hatchet job." Serge snatched the magazine back and shredded it. "I'm going to show them. I'm going to show them all!"

"What are you going to do?"

"Remember the *Elvis Comeback Special*?"

"You're going to be Elvis?"

"The Elvis of comebacks!" Serge stood quickly and threw currency on the bar. "They ain't seen nothin' yet!"

Coleman chugged the rest of his beer and ran after him. "Is that what the guy in our trunk is for?"

Serge accelerated toward the front door. "I'm tired of driving people around like that. They think I'm their fucking chauffeur."

Coleman jogged to keep up. "But I don't think he wanted to come with us."

"Should have thought of that before he broke the social contract." Serge burst outside into the driving rain. The door closed behind them, and the power went out.

THE NERVOUS HOURS

No idle chatter. Everyone huddled tight wherever they were, staring up at creaking beams. The hurricane spun west over the lifeless landscape. It rattled empty roller coasters at Busch Gardens and ripped canopies from ticket booths. Torrents raged down water slides. A brief twister skipped across Rhino Rally.

The storm continued its unnegotiable course, sweeping over the University of South Florida. Landscaping surrendered. A diverse stew of debris from unsecured dorm balconies sailed over the campus: patio chairs, potted plants, pristine textbooks, name-brand laundry. Fast-food signage shattered in chain reaction down Fowler Avenue. McDonald's, Wendy's, Taco Bell, Domino's, the trademarked fonts broken down to individual letters, swirling together and forming a ransom note in the sky. The last to go were the yellow-and-red Asian characters above a popular buffet. Inside, electricity was out and air stagnant, the storm growling and hissing all around like a living thing, no natural predators, alone way atop the Florida food chain. Students filled cold plates in the dark.

Four freshmen who'd arrived in a Jeep Grand Cherokee finished their third helping and headed back for more.

"Let's smoke another joint first."

"Where?"

"Outside."

"Don't you see what's going on?"

"We'll stay close to the building."

"The dope will get wet. *If* we don't get killed first."

"Look!"

The dining room suddenly brightened. Everyone turned. The rain had stopped. Residual drops teamed up and trickled down the front windows. The scene outside had gone from perpetual motion to still life.

"The storm's over. Let's get high."

"It's not over. It's just the eye."

"Cool. We'll get *high* in the *eye*."

The level head in the bunch was outvoted, and they tiptoed past the restrooms to the service door.

"This is going to be so excellent!"

They glanced around one last time, then clandestinely opened the door and slipped onto the receiving dock.

"Who's got the lighter?"

"Yo."

"Fire it up!"

That's when the first of them saw it. His horrible scream directed the others to the ghastly sight. They scrambled back inside. The eye left, and the wind resumed.

CHAPTER FOUR

FIVE HOURS LATER

The back side of the hurricane was long gone, somewhere out over the map near Kissimmee.

The streets of Tampa had come back to life, busier than ever with added emergency-response activity, like a stepped-on anthill. Urgent, efficient movement in every direction. Police, fire, EMTs. Power-company people in cherry pickers repaired sagging tension lines. Officers in reflective vests directed sightseeing traffic through lightless intersections. The water level on the flooded side streets continued rising. Someone zipped by on a Jet Ski.

Four college students shivered on a receiving dock behind a Chinese restaurant. They sat bundled in coarse government blankets. Cops everywhere. A uniformed officer handed them cups of hot cocoa. Detectives in suits took notes and evidence. Others lifted the sheet over the facedown victim for more photographs.

"I've never seen anything like it," said a homicide veteran.

"I have," said his partner. "But it happened to a tree."

"You drinking again?"

"Remember that famous photo from Hurricane Andrew?

Two-by-four smack through the trunk of a hardwood like it was a banana. People have no idea the power these storms generate, or they'd never risk going outside."

"Like our friend over there." The detectives looked back at the white sheet rising above the deceased like a circus tent. A third detective joined them and shook his head. "Two-by-four clear through the chest. That had to smart."

A white Lincoln with blackwall tires pulled up. The chief of police got out with a carload of assistants. The detectives unslouched.

"How are we coming?"

"Still working on it, sir."

"Any more witnesses?"

"Just those kids over there who found the body in the middle of the eye. But they didn't see anything."

"What were they doing out in a hurricane?"

A detective reached into his pocket and produced a clear evidence bag with a soggy dropped joint.

The chief shook his head. "Wonderful." He bent down and lifted the sheet. He was about to drop it when something stopped him. "This guy looks familiar. Who is he?"

The chief didn't get a response. He looked up. They were all staring away.

The chief quickly straightened with authority. "Okay, spill it."

"Just got the victim's ID."

"You going to tell me anytime soon?"

A younger detective glanced nervously at the others and cleared his throat. "Sir, remember that sex offender who was in the news after getting released from prison?"

"Which?" said the chief. "I need a daily racing form to keep track."

"The one who claimed the community kept harassing him and sending death threats? Then somebody sent that video to the TV station of the guy lurking around an elementary school, which should have violated his probation. But his lawyer successfully argued the school was closed for teacher training. The guy didn't know that, but it still worked."

The chief's eyes were closed. He was massaging his temples. He opened his eyes. "I want this wrapped up fast. The press is going to have a field day."

"No problem." The lead detective opened his notebook. "Already have preliminary cause of death. Think I can rush it through and get the M.E. to sign off by sunset. All kinds of debris flying around a hurricane. Just a coincidence who the guy was."

"You're saying this was an *accident*?"

The detective nodded. "What else could it be?"

A new voice: "Murder."

Everyone turned. A thin man in a rumpled fedora walked toward them. His necktie had jazz instruments.

The chief's patience left town. "Who the hell are you?"

The man flipped open a wallet with a gold badge and just as quickly returned it to his jacket. "Agent Mahoney."

"Fantastic," said the chief. "The state wants in. That's at least another news cycle."

"Listen," one of the detectives pointedly told Mahoney. "We *would* appreciate the help, but we *don't*. Do yourself a favor and just go back—"

Mahoney brushed past them, leaned down and lifted the sheet. "Just as I thought. Here's your accident." He raised the victim's right arm and twisted it to display the underside of the wrist.

"Ligature?"

Mahoney dropped the arm and stood. "Looks like you got a joker in the deck." He stuck a wooden matchstick in his mouth and leaned against a post. Except it was the two-by-four in the chest. He crashed over.

"Look what you did!"

Mahoney jumped up and wiggled the board back into the victim. "No harm, no foul."

A detective grabbed his arm. "Just leave it."

"I'm here to help."

"You've helped enough."

"You'll need my street sense if you want to nail this collar." Mahoney gave him a business card. "You have no idea who you're dealing with."

"And you do?"

"Instinct, hunch, gut feeling . . ."

"Wait, now I know who you are," said another detective. "Yeah, you're that cop they sent to the loony bin."

"I got better."

"You're a fruitcake." He gave Mahoney a two-handed shove in the chest.

Mahoney produced a set of brass knuckles. The detective pulled a drop weapon from his sock. They squared off.

The chief jumped between them. "All right, you two. Cut it out."

Mahoney stowed the knuckles and eyed his rival. "You're the one I'm going to bond with. This is how it always starts. Initial suspicion, physical confrontation. Then we're getting drunk together in an Irish corner bar named O'Malley's and helping each other through on-and-off relationships with women who genuinely care but don't understand that being a cop isn't something you can just leave at the office."

"Psycho."

"Buddy."

A uniform rushed over to the chief. "Sir, university had a burglary. Hurricane-research center."

"A lot of looting goes on after a storm. Why are you bringing this to me?"

"Might be related to this case."

"How's that?"

"The burglary was *before* the storm. And you're not going to believe what they took."

"Which was?"

He told them.

"That can't be right," said the chief. "Who'd want one of those?"

Another officer ran up with a small metal box in his hand. "Sir, we located a new witness. One of the students from the restaurant. Just discovered his Hummer H2 was stolen. . . ."

"How rich are these kids?"

". . . Happened almost the exact same time of the victim's death."

"What makes you think that?"

"The distance the H2's traveled. It's got a LoJack transmitter." He held up the portable monitor. "See? They're almost to the turnpike."

The chief summoned a factotum. "Call the Okeechobee sheriff."

One of the detectives grabbed the device from the patrolman. "Wait a second. I've seen this before."

"What do you mean?" asked the chief.

The detective tossed the monitor back to the officer and ran to an unmarked car. He quickly returned with a sheet of paper.

The chief studied the page: a tracking map with a dotted line jitterbugging diagonally across the state. He compared it to the handheld display. "How'd you get a printout of the stolen car so fast?"

"I didn't. That's not the route of the H2. It's the hurricane. Notice how all the time coordinates match."

"But how can that be?"

"I don't know electronics," said the detective. "The receiver must be picking up transmissions from the National Weather Service or a TV network. Some kind of mistake."

"It's no mistake," said Mahoney.

His nemesis sighed and squared off again. "I'm getting just a little tired of your attitude!"

Mahoney pointed up the street. "There's this great Brooklyn sports bar. I'm buying the first round. My ex is filling the kids' heads with crazy ideas about me." He put a hand on the detective's shoulder. "What about you? Wife sleeping around? I can do some checking."

The detective swatted his arm. "Get the fuck off me."

Another uniformed officer hurried over, finishing a conversation on his walkie-talkie. "Sir . . ."

The chief smacked himself in the forehead. "Now what!"

"Pinellas has another crime scene on the other side of the bay. By the Skyway."

"So?"

"So you're not going to believe this."

CHAPTER FIVE

LANDFALL PLUS SIX

The police were wrapping it up, but the media was just getting started. The first TV truck arrived behind the Chinese restaurant. EYEWITNESS 5. A reporter jumped out and hit the ground running. The others weren't far behind. ACTION NEWS 7, EYEWITNESS ACTION 4 and ACTION EYEWITNESS NEWS 12. Then the big network satellite trucks. Telescoping antennas ascended with an electric whir, acquiring magic signals from orbit.

Blood was in the water, literally. The press corps stampeded to the coroner's wagon, cameras and microphones through the back doors. The medical examiner slammed them shut. "Nothing to see here."

They drooped momentarily, then brightened. "There's the chief!"

He saw them coming. "Oh, no." Thoughts of escape, but it was too late. Surrounded. A bank of lights.

"Why are the police dragging their feet?"

"Who bungled the case?"

"Will there be an internal investigation?"

The chief shielded his eyes. "No comment."

The reporters noticed four students wrapped in blankets on the receiving dock, talking to cops with open notepads.

"Are those kids under arrest?"

"Why'd they do it?"

"Was it a devil-worship ceremony?"

"I said, 'No comment.' This is an open investigation. We'll give you everything as soon as we're done."

The wolf pack raced over to the loading dock. The chief could tell by the students' excited gestures that it wasn't going to play well on the evening news. "How can this get any worse?"

This is how:

The next of kin arrived, a multi-generational, overly extended family that lived within two miles of each other near a toxic-waste site of their own making. They consistently defended the innocence of their pedophile brother/uncle/son even after the taped confessions and DNA.

"You killed him! You *all* killed him!" shouted the family's self-appointed spokesman, a self-tattooed second cousin whose résumé had been prepared by the Department of Corrections. "You never gave him a chance!" He put an arm around the shoulders of the hysterical family matriarch. "It's okay, Grandma. Don't cry. Here, have a cigarette."

The press ran over. TV lights shone in faces.

"How's the grieving process?"

The spokesman stepped forward. "We're not talking to no fucking reporters! Not after all those lies you told!"

"Did he deserve to suffer more?"

The spokesman punched a camera lens. "You're as guilty as anyone! It's just like you pulled the trigger yourselves!"

"He wasn't shot. A two-by-four ripped through his chest, bursting major organs."

The matriarch wailed. The spokesman lunged. "Why, you son of a bitch! I'll rip your fucking head off—"

Police jumped in. He continued taking swings over their shoulders. "I'll kill you! You hear me? Every last stinking reporter!"

A luxury sedan rolled up.

"Look! It's the mayor!"

"Are you going to resign?"

The chief of police threw back aspirin and crumpled a Dixie cup. The department's media-liaison officer walked over. They stood together watching the public-relations disaster unfold.

"We need to hold a press conference," said the liaison.

"That's the last thing we need," said the chief.

"No, we have to get out in front of this thing. Otherwise it's a train wreck."

More reporters arrived and fed the fray with the relatives.

The chief slowly began nodding. "I guess you're right."

"I'll start courting my contacts."

"Look." The chief raised his chin. "It's quieting down."

The family spokesman had composed himself and told the officers he was okay now. They released him. He lunged again. Cops jumped back in. Great footage. All the journalists surged forward.

Except one. A lone reporter stood on the far side of the parking lot, losing his breakfast in a storm-water ditch.

The liaison canted his head. "Isn't that McSwirley?"

On the other side of Tampa Bay: another industrious crime scene with another white-sheet circus tent. This one at the foot of the Sunshine Skyway bridge.

Investigators sipped coffee and milled in small groups. *"Talk about your shit luck"*—a detective tapped himself in the breastbone—*"two-by-four right through the sternum. Just like that photo from Andrew."*

Someone with latex gloves tweezered fibers into Ziploc bags.

Someone else from the county CSI unit waited for plaster to dry in a tire track.

A burnt orange '61 Coupe de Ville pulled off the highway and drove through the wet plaster. Mahoney jumped out and flashed a badge. "Who's in charge here?"

The Tampa chief of police glanced across the parking lot. "Yeah, that looks like McSwirley."

"I'll start with him," said the liaison. "See if we can't steer this thing."

"Good thinking," said the chief. "He's one of the few I trust."

"Know what you mean," said the liaison. "Most reporters think it's not a story unless they can embarrass the department. Not McSwirley. He just wants the facts."

"Actually, what it seems he really wants is to be somewhere else."

"That's why he's so good. This stuff gets to him. The others almost take delight."

"But it's the same with cops," said the chief. "The best are conflicted. The ones who seem a little too happy, you gotta watch."

"He stopped throwing up. I'll be right back."

The liaison strolled over to the ditch and offered a handkerchief. The reporter thanked him. Jeff McSwirley, three years out of journalism school, the cub crime-beat reporter for *Tampa Bay Today*. His hallmarks were the quick smile, a fierce pacifism, and difficulty dressing himself: unironed shirttail hanging out, belt not threaded through one of the loops, wide brown tie knotted in the yet-to-catch-on style with the thin length in back hanging longer. A blue ink stain had signed a long-term lease for the bottom of his breast pocket. He blended in with the rest of the print media.

McSwirley was the least experienced and most effective crime reporter in the bay area. Green on the law, naïve with sources, grammatically suspect. What set him apart was the interviews. Scooped all the best. It wasn't technique or trickery. It lay in a single, God-given trait: McSwirley was one of the most likable people you'd ever meet. The other reporters hated his guts.

The toughest interview hands down was surviving relatives, made even more difficult by journalists' unsanded personalities. At best, they crashed about fragile emotional arenas like drunken orangutans. At worst, they . . . Well, like several years ago, when a jetliner went down. The first reporters in the terminal were thrilled to have beaten crisis counselors to unaware loved ones still waiting at the arrival gate.

Microphone and lights. *"What's your reaction to the plane crash?"*

"The what?"

It was hard to fail against that yardstick, but McSwirley did much more. He excelled. Jeff's specialty was the ultrasensitive Barbara Walters sit-down. Except in McSwirley's interviews, *he* was the one who cried, and the next of kin had to console *him*.

Or the job fell to cops, like now. The media liaison placed a hand on McSwirley's shoulder as the reporter hung back over the ditch.

"Going to be sick again?"

McSwirley stood up. "False alarm." He wiped his mouth and turned toward the fracas with the victim's relatives. "I better be getting over to talk to them."

On the other side of the parking lot, the family spokesman broke free again. *"I'll kill all you motherfuckin' reporters!"*

The liaison felt obliged. "I'm not exactly sure this is the ideal time."

McSwirley shook his head. "Believe me, there's nothing I want less. But my editor will have my head if I don't at least make the effort. He always asks."

The liaison watched sympathetically as the reporter headed over with ungainly strides.

Moments later, a typical scene: police holding other reporters back while the victim's family gathered around McSwirley, giving him so many quotes he couldn't flip notebook pages fast enough. He was also slowed by having to rewrite stuff because his tears made the ink run.

"There, there," said the family spokesman, arm around Jeff's shoulders.

"But it's just so sad."

"It'll be okay. Have a cigarette."

"Don't smoke."

The matriarch clutched his hand earnestly. "Let me make you a nice home-cooked meal."

Two men watched in the background.

"I'll be," said the chief.

"Never ceases to amaze me," said the liaison.

"How does he do it?"

"Sometimes he cries. Sometimes he gets sick . . ."

The relatives suddenly jumped back as the reporter jackknifed over.

"Sometimes both."

A new detective approached the chief with the department's technology wizard. He held up the LoJack monitor. "Sir, Dipsy checked this thing out thoroughly. Said the receiver isn't malfunctioning. In fact, it's working perfectly."

"So it really is tracking the stolen Hummer?"

"Within three meters," said Dipsy. "But they're working on something insane that'll go under eighteen inches."

"Is it still following the eye?"

"Straight down the pike."

"How's that possible?" asked the chief. "Hurricanes don't follow highways."

"The tracker shows he's been zigzagging like crazy on county roads and others that aren't on the maps. Has to be someone who knows Florida like his own skin."

"Even so, it wouldn't give him enough to stay in the eye. Especially in that remote part of the state."

"He's also crossing fields. The Hummer has four-wheel drive."

The chief reached for the receiver. "Where's the storm now?"

"Almost to Jackass Crossing," said Dipsy.

"Jackass Crossing?" asked the liaison.

"Real name's Yeehaw Junction," said the chief, studying the display. "Truckers call it the other on the CB."

"How'd you know that?"

"Great-granddaddy used to drive cattle through there."

"But you're black," said the liaison.

"You're kidding," said the chief.

"I mean, the guys who drove the cattle—weren't they called *crackers*?"

"That's right. Sound of the whips as they ran herd."

"The name doesn't bother you?"

"Should it?"

"I thought it was an insult. I'm guessing even more so if you're . . . you know, not a cracker."

"That's Mississippi. Totally different etymology in Florida. Proud name. My family's sixth-generation."

"Sir, shouldn't we call some of the departments over there? Let 'em know what's coming?"

"Definitely. Except it's not going to do any good for a while. They can't run out in the middle of this storm, and the roads will be blocked for hours afterward. Have to clear 'em first with chain saws and bulldozers." The chief looked down at the display again and rubbed his chin. "What on earth are we dealing with?"

"Whatever it is, we need to keep it out of the papers," said the liaison. "Can you imagine the headlines?"

"Vividly," said the chief. "Not only do we have a psycho killer on the loose, but he's tooling around in the middle of a hurricane."

"That's the only silver lining," said the liaison. "Press doesn't know about the tracking device yet."

"And we need to keep it that way," said the chief. His eyes followed the slow-moving green dot cutting across southern Osceola County. "Who *are* you?"

A TV reporter leaned over the chief's shoulder. "What's that?"

CHAPTER SIX

TWENTY MILES WEST OF
THE FLORIDA TURNPIKE

Wooooooooo-hoooooooo!

A late-model H2 bounded across an open field of tall swamp grass. Above: a tight hole of clear, blue sky.

"Look at that eye wall!" said Serge. "Isn't she beautiful? Perfectly stratified."

"What are you doing?" yelled Coleman. "We're heading right for it!"

Serge steered with his elbows so he could shoot video out the windshield. "Coleman, uncover your face. You're missing the convective chimney and shotgun debris field . . ."

"We're on a collision course!" Coleman's hands shook as he popped a beer.

". . . I've only seen this in photographs from the hurricane-hunter planes. Check that cloud bank curving miles straight up. It's even more inspiring than I'd hoped."

"But you said we'd avoid the eye wall."

"That was just to get you in the car. Sometimes we have to play chicken with the wall in order to pick up the next road. Then, at the last second, we reach pavement, make a hard turn and pray to outrun."

"Will we make it?"

"Who knows? She's a fast one, twenty miles an hour. And we're closing at sixty from forty degrees. . . . Coleman! You're spilling beer on the laptop!"

"Sorry." Coleman wiped the keyboard with his forearm.

"Is it still working?"

Coleman nodded.

"You idiot. Just hold that thing still. Without it we're dead."

Coleman killed the beer and tossed the empty over his shoulder. He squeezed the laptop with both hands to steady it against the severe bouncing. Serge looked sideways at the stolen computer with the live-GPS-mapping software he'd installed. A tiny cartoon car ticked across the screen on an empty part of the map. A perpendicular black line lay ahead. Serge faced forward and strained his eyes. "Come on, where's that road?"

The vehicle became quiet, both of them realizing the wall was moving in too fast from the right. A thousand yards, eight hundred, six hundred . . . Serge accelerated as fast as he dared in the uneven, spongy terrain, but it wasn't enough. . . . Four hundred yards, two hundred . . ."

He glanced at the laptop again. The cartoon car was right on top of the black line, passing to the other side. "Where's that stupid road?" One hundred yards, fifty . . . The dense, gray monster gobbling real estate. "Uh-oh," said Serge. "Grab something!"

The wall didn't overtake the car as much as crash down upon it—a surfer losing his board in the tube. They took an extra-hard bounce, and Coleman bonked his head on the ceiling. "Ow! What was that?"

"Just hit pavement!" Serge cut the wheel fast to the left, the back end skidding out in an expert quarter spin, lining up with the eastbound lane. He practically stood up on the gas pedal, four thick tires blowing steam before gripping the slick blacktop. Seconds later the H2 punched out of the eye wall and into the clear.

They sped across State Road 60, adding cushion between them and the pregnant darkness filling the back window. Finally Serge released a breath and let off the fuel. "We need to find a motel to put up."

"I thought you wanted to ride it all the way to the coast."

Serge pointed at the laptop. "Storm's changed course. Very slight, but enough to take this road out of play. At the current rate, that left side of the eye will be on us in ten miles."

"So turn on another street like you've been doing. Or a field."

"Can't. We're in swamp country now. This is the only road. Just lakes and deeper bogs on both sides."

"But it's the middle of nowhere. Where are we going to find a motel?"

"In the middle of nowhere."

The eye wall was almost to the road again when Serge swung into the parking lot of a lifeless inn with lost power. It was hard to tell whether the motel had been abandoned for the hurricane or in general. Serge grabbed a crowbar and ran to the door of room number three.

Coleman brought up the rear toting a cooler. "Why don't you just use a credit card?"

"Locks are too old." The door popped, and he ran back to the vehicle, grabbing a duffel in each hand. "Help me get our stuff inside. We don't have much time."

Coleman looked at the sky over the motel roof. "Oh, shit!"

They made several unloading trips at battle speed. Almost done. Coleman stood at the back of the SUV. "Serge, what about this . . . whatever-you-call-it that you stole from the university?"

Serge's hair blew straight back, and the sun went out; he looked directly up into the act of God. "Too late. We'll get it in the morning." A sudden gust whipped through the parking lot, and Coleman went tumbling. Serge grabbed the luggage rack, working his way along the side of the vehicle. "Give me your hand!"

Coleman crawled and reached up. Serge leaned acutely into the wind. "Stay low."

"Not a problem."

Stinging rain and sand. Nearly there. A tree gave way with a loud crack. Only a few more feet, now on their bellies. They slithered across the threshold, slammed the door and uprighted mattresses against the window. Seriously dark. Serge used waterproof matches to light a candle, and Coleman used the candle to light a joint.

TAMPA POLICE DEPARTMENT

Shortly before midnight. The chief sat at the head of a long conference table for a closed-door meeting. He checked his watch as the last arriving division heads took chairs. "Looks like everyone's here. Let's get started. We've got the Pinellas sheriff on the speakerphone. . . . Sheriff, you there?"

A faceless box in the middle of the table: *"I'm here."*

"Good." The chief looked sideways. "You all know Collins. I'm going to turn it over to him."

The department's media liaison finished reviewing his talking points. He pushed back his chair and stood. "We've all had quite a day. Tomorrow gets worse. Chief's scheduled a press conference for noon. He wants me to make sure we're all on the same page."

A premature hand went up from Robbery Division. "I heard a crazy story about the cause of death behind the restaurant."

"That's why we're meeting." Collins looked to his left. "I'm going to let Homicide explain the forensics. It's a little technical. Gillespie?"

The head of homicide laid it all out from the confidential, eyes-only report. It wasn't a pleasant task. He finished without fanfare and took his seat.

Murmurs shot around the table. "What kind of sick bastard . . . ?"

"That's not all," said Collins. "We have the additional complication of an identical crime scene on the other side of the bay." He looked down at the speaker on the table. "Sheriff?"

"Our lab boys arrived at the same place."

More murmurs.

"Gentlemen," said Collins, "there's more. It looks like we have a serial killer . . ."

The talk grew louder.

". . . Maybe two . . ."

Open revolt.

"Pipe down," said the chief. "Collins, show 'em the tape."

The liaison walked to a rolling media center at the front of the room. He turned on the VCR. "This is from a surveillance camera at the university. It's down the far end of a hallway outside the hurricane-research center, where the murder weapon or weapons were stolen. Twelve frames a minute. And they had an old tape. That's why the quality's so bad. Okay, here's our first guy." A vaguely human figure walked across the hallway in choppy time lapse. "Now he's busting out the window in the door and reaching through to unlock it." The figure disappeared from view. "I'll fast-forward. . . . And here he comes back into the hall with a hand truck before leaving the building."

"That's not much to go on," said Robbery.

"Gets stickier." Collins advanced the tape again. Another blurry figure came back into the hallway. The screen went static.

"What happened?"

"He shot out the camera," said Collins.

"That doesn't make sense. It only helps if he shoots it out at the beginning."

"It makes sense if it's a different person," said Collins.

"Is it?"

"That's our problem. Two crime scenes on opposite sides of the bay, far enough apart that it's unlikely the same person could cover the ground, especially in that kind of weather."

"But not impossible?"

"Right," said the liaison. "And it might be two people on the tape. Or one."

"You mention 'weapon or weapons,'" said Vice. "How many of those things did the university lose? That should tell us."

"They think two."

"'Think'?"

"Or one," said Collins. "They don't keep good records."

"Jesus," said Narcotics. "Did anything break our direction?"

"No," said the chief. "Either way it's a nightmare. We got one serial killer. Or two working as a team."

"Or dueling serial killers?" suggested Robbery.

"Don't even think that," said the chief.

"The press will be asking a lot of questions," said Collins. "We need to no-comment this all the way, 'active investigation.' . . . Sheriff?"

"I just gave the instructions."

The chief finally stood. "We might be wrong and can't have this city in a needless panic. Until we know what we're dealing with, none of this leaves the room. Not the tiniest, most innocent fact about the case is to get out. That's an order!"

NIGHT DESK, *TAMPA BAY TODAY*

The metro editor sat in front of a green-and-black computer screen, slowly scrolling through tomorrow's top story. The reporter who wrote the article watched over his shoulder. The official newsroom clock said midnight.

"Incredible," remarked the editor. "You've outdone yourself again, McSwirley."

"I really didn't do anything but get those interviews."

"Take credit." The editor tapped the cursor. "Cops aren't giving anyone squat, but you got the whole story. And more."

"Thanks."

"The only thing that worries me is this confidential source of yours."

"Agent Mahoney?"

"What do we know about him?"

"Florida Department of Law Enforcement," said McSwirley. "He's a profiler."

"Get his badge number?"

McSwirley nodded.

"I can't see you nodding back there."

"I got his badge number."

The editor scratched his head. "Something's not right. Local police are circling the wagons, but this Mahoney's blabbing his head off."

"I recorded him," said McSwirley, patting a microdevice in his pocket.

"What about that video from the university break-in? We get a copy?"

"No," said the reporter. "Department's not releasing it. But he let me watch the whole thing. It's just like I wrote."

"You're solid on this Mahoney?"

"Hundred percent."

"That's good enough for me." The editor kept tapping down through the story. "It just gets better and better. He really gave you all this?"

"He did."

The editor whistled. "I'll need to get in early tomorrow to take the calls. Chief's going to be pissed."

CHAPTER SEVEN

YEEHAW JUNCTION

The storm roared around the motel and shook the trusses, a counterpoint to the stillness inside.

Serge's luminous expeditionary wristwatch said midnight. The candle on the dresser had melted to a stub. He lit a new one, turned it over to drip wax, then held the base in the hot pool until it hardened.

Coleman lay on the bed with the red tip of a joint. Serge opened a well-worn hardcover to a bookmarked page. He sat down at the dresser and began reading by the flame.

THC adjusted the tint, contrast and brightness knobs on Coleman's eyesight. He looked across the room at a dim portrait of Serge's face in the wick's warm, orange glow.

"Serge . . ."

He kept reading. "What?"

"This is eerie. I'm getting scared."

"You should be." He turned a page. "We're riding out a major hurricane."

"No, I mean the dope. It makes everything eerie. Once I had to run out of *Shrek 2*."

"I'm trying to read."

"Sorry." Pause. "What are you reading?"

Serge showed him the book's spine.

"I can't see it in this light."

"Florida guide written by Roosevelt's Works Progress Admin-
istration. This edition was published in 1939."

"Serge . . ."

"*What!?*"

"How'd you know this motel would be out here? We would
have been doomed."

"Rule Number One: Wherever you are, always know the coolest local hurricane shelters. Not to be confused with official. Besides, this is the Desert Inn. I've *always* wanted to stay at the
Desert Inn. National Register of Historic Places. Since 1880—"

"That's almost before people."

". . . Originally a way station for early timber railroads, Indian traders and cattlemen driving herds south from Kissimmee,
now just a remote trucker crossroads with two gas stations, this
motel and a theme-park ticket hut trying to lure tourists off the
turnpike. A few times a year, they have excellent biker rallies and
a bluegrass festival." He pointed east. "Still serving turtle and gator tail in the restaurant."

"But what town is this?"

"Not a town. Yeehaw Junction, aka Jackass Crossing. It's
what I'm reading about right now. We're in the old stomping
grounds of Coacoochee, the great chief during the Seminole Wars.
Says here the U.S. Army wanted to hold peace talks, so the chief
and his band showed up in, quote, 'colorful garb, taken from the
wardrobe of an American theatrical troupe they had attacked
and killed.'"

Coleman tapped an ash. "Talk about your harsh reviews."

Serge closed the book. He picked up a clipboard and handed
it to Coleman.

"Checklist time," said Serge.

Coleman uncapped a pen. "Ready."

"Checklist."

"Check."

Serge began unloading duffel bags with precision. "Candles and waterproof matches."

"Check."

"Weather radio, flashlight, batteries . . ."

"Check, check, check . . ."

"Hurricane-tracking chart, potable water, freeze-dried food, can opener, organic toilet paper, sensible clothes, upbeat reading material, baseball gloves, compass, whistle, signal mirror, first-aid kit, snake-bite kit, mess kit, malaria tablets, smelling salts, flints, splints, solar survival blanket, edible-wild-plant field almanac, trenching tool, semaphores, gas masks, Geiger counter, executive defibrillator, railroad flares, lemons in case of scurvy, Austrian gold coins in case paper money becomes scoffed at, laminated sixteen-language universal hostage-negotiation 'Kwik-Guide' (Miami-Dade edition), extra film, extra ammunition, firecrackers, handcuffs, Taser, pepper spray, throwing stars, Flipper lunch box, Eden Roc ashtray, Cypress Gardens felt pennant, alligator snow globe, miniature wooden crate of orange gumballs, acrylic sea-shell thermometer and pen holder, can of Florida sunshine . . ."

"Check, check, check. . . . What about my inflatable woman?"

"Natural enemy of the trenching tool."

"You popped it?"

"She was just holding you back."

"Serge, I can't write anymore. The paper's all damp."

"From the hurricane."

"But we're inside."

"Amazing, isn't it?" Serge dropped to the floor for a set of high-speed push-ups. "The general public doesn't realize how humid it gets in one of these. People think they're perspiring, but you could lay clothes on a bed and they'd grow mildew by dawn."

Coleman tried to take a hit. Nothing but air. He looked at his hand. "My joint went out."

"Dry it over the candle." Serge switched to one-handed push-ups. ". . . Three . . . four . . . five . . ."

"What are you doing?"

"Staying in shape. . . . Eight . . . nine . . . ten . . ." He changed hands. "I've decided to put myself on the sixty-minute workout. An hour a day and stay fit for life." Serge jumped up and went over to the window.

"That wasn't an hour," said Coleman.

"Who knows how long I'll live? Can't waste it exercising. So now I'm on the one-minute workout. That'll buy me tomorrow." Serge peeked around the side of a mattress. "Think it's too risky to go to the car?"

"Listen to that wind. We're getting the worst of it now."

"I know, I know," he said reluctantly. "But I have a cool new gadget I can't play with."

"It'll still be there in the morning."

Serge took another peek outside. "Did you see that trash pile at the end of the parking lot when we pulled in?"

"What about it?"

"Notice what was on top?"

"No."

Serge got that look in his eyes. "Two-by-fours."

NIGHT DESK, *TAMPA BAY TODAY*

McSwirley hovered over his editor's shoulder. The front-page scoop had already been vetted. Just housekeeping left. Pronoun agreement, transitions, inverted-pyramid fact flow.

The editor cut and pasted a paragraph. "You need to get the first quote up higher. Bring it alive."

"I keep forgetting."

Newsrooms have open floor plans: a sea of desks with no partitions for instant, shouted communication. A large, official clock hangs somewhere visible to the entire room, so there can be no argument over whose watch is right. Because every minute counts in this business, especially on the night shift.

The clock in this newsroom had red digital numbers. Now: 12:10. Twenty minutes to first deadline. Fifty to press start. No-nonsense time.

Earlier in the cycle, a different story. Newsrooms are notorious day-care centers for adults. High jinks and all-purpose farting around. But you wouldn't have to see the staff in action to figure that out. The big tip-off was workplace decor. Toys everywhere. Slinkies, fortune-telling Eight Balls, plastic palm trees with Christmas lights, radio-controlled race cars. A life-size promotional cardboard Batman looked down over the movie reviewer's computer. One of the columnists had an HO-gauge train set circling his desk.

But on deadline everyone grows up. Foolishness gives way to a rapid-fire clattering of keyboards.

12:12.

The front wall of the newsroom held a large, washable map of the state. Grids for latitude, longitude. A wobbly red line traced the current hurricane's path from landfall at the mouth of Tampa Bay to the turnpike exit at Yeehaw Junction. Someone walked up to the map with a fresh printout from the National Weather Service. He uncapped a marker and made dashes toward the Atlantic Ocean, stopping shy of Vero Beach.

12:14.

The copy staff's desks formed a large, interconnecting H configuration. The metro editor sat in the center, typing last-minute polish. A second reporter joined McSwirley in hovering. The editor reached the end of the article. The last line said "-30-."

"McSwirley, how come you keep typing 'thirty' at the end of every story?"

"In J-school they said it was tradition."

"We don't do that anymore." He tapped the delete key and hit *spell check*. "Fine work, McSwirley. You did it again."

"Uh, thank you?"

"Don't say it like a question." The editor added an *r* to "embarrass."

"Sorry."

"And don't apologize." The editor hit *file* and swiveled around to face them. He leaned way back in off-deadline posture. "On second thought, forget that. Stay the way you are. It's how you succeed."

"Excuse me . . ." said the other reporter.

"What is it, Justin?"

"I think I should get a byline, too."

"I gave you a contributing tagline at the end." He pointed back at the screen. "See? Right here. 'Justin Weeks.'"

"But sir, it's my story, too. I worked just as hard—"

"Get over yourself," said the editor. "McSwirley landed both main interviews: the confidential source and the victim's family at the Chinese restaurant." The editor adopted a sarcastic edge. "You *do* remember that family, don't you?"

Weeks didn't say anything. His black eyes did.

"Plus, McSwirley even stopped to get great footage with his camcorder for our sister cable network—even though I still think that idea stinks."

"Sir," said Justin, "there's still time to put my name at the top."

"Justin?"

"What?"

"Shut up. Let's talk about tomorrow. It's our story now, but we'll have to hit the ground or someone will take it away from us." The editor reached for a Slinky on his desk. "Obvious follow-up is talking to the family of the victim at the Skyway, the guy who ran the Internet scam for Katrina relief."

"I'll go," said Justin.

"Let Justin go," said McSwirley.

"Not a chance." The editor undulated the Slinky between his hands. "This is McSwirley's strength. You need to let those shiners fade."

"Sir, I don't want to go," said McSwirley.

"He doesn't want to go," said Justin.

"And that's exactly why he *is* going." The editor put the Slinky down and picked up a slingshot. "Don't think I've forgotten how you handled that plane crash." He stuck a gumball in the sling-shot's pocket and fired absentmindedly in the direction of the photo lab. "Had to run a front-page apology."

"But you've got to give me something," said Justin.

The editor thought a moment. "Jeff, what was the name of that suspect Mahoney kept yammering about?"

"You mean Serge?"

Someone came out of the photo lab rubbing his arm. He looked around, went back in.

"Justin, check the archives and call Tallahassee," said the editor. "See if you can't find out more about this Serge character."

CHAPTER EIGHT

THE MORNING AFTER

Hurricane Alex left the state overnight. The exit wound was Vero Beach. The rising sun flirted with the Atlantic horizon. The storm was somewhere below it. Looking seaward from the calm shore, you'd never have known there'd been one. Looking inland, there was no doubt.

Cops directed traffic as heavy equipment cleared trees from major roads. The electric company found itself at the spearhead of civilization, racing everywhere to head off mob rule. With power out, society was breaking down and re-forming at the same time. Police couldn't be at every intersection, and some motorists took advantage with tribal aggression. Others worked things out with improvised hand gestures and a rediscovered civility that had been forgotten since driving had become cell-phone time. There were price gougers and good Samaritans, looters and citizen patrols, whiners and volunteers.

The Acropolis of this new world was the local Wal-Mart. Truckloads of donated goods arrived from faith-based charities across the Midwest: winter coats, musical instruments, butterfly nets. On the other side of the parking lot sat a disciplined row of semis. The National Guard stood in the trailers' open back doors, distributing federal relief.

One of the Guardsmen tossed down a ten-pound sack. "That's the last of the ice."

On the west side of town, just past Interstate 95, a column of police cars idled with all the lights flashing. A sergeant stood outside the driver's door of the first vehicle. "Hurry up! We have to get through!"

"Almost there . . ." Workers in city-issue hard hats chain-sawed a massive tree blocking the only route to Yeehaw Junction. A bulldozer plowed the middle section of trunk off the pavement, and the cruisers shot through the narrow gap, speeding west with a LoJack receiver and an all-points bulletin from Tampa.

YEEHAW JUNCTION

The air in the parking lot was uncommonly still.

A motel door opened. Coleman came out with bed hair and a just-popped, sixty-nine-cent Natural Lite Ice. No sign of Serge. Typical. Serge always rose hours earlier, and Coleman had to go hunting.

He walked into the silent lot and chugged half the sixteen-ounce. He looked around. Moonscape. Snapped trees, downed lines, corrugated aluminum crumpled like typing paper. No Serge.

He ventured to the edge of the empty highway. More trash. Antifreeze jug, tar paper, ground glass. He finished the beer. Silence was broken. A vehicle appeared. A tractor rig way up the bend. It slowly grew larger on the long straightaway toward the crossroads, finally reaching Coleman and blowing by with a violent wind that kicked up a dense haze. Coleman blinked dust from his eyes. Brakes hissed. The driver pulled in to one of the gas stations just beyond the motel, learned it was closed and accelerated away in a diesel cloud.

It was quiet again. Coleman gave up the search for his pal and started back to the motel room. Something caught his eye. He looked up over the roof. A two-by-four sailed like an arrow and arced into the woods with a crash of branches.

Coleman moseyed around the end of the building. He turned the last corner in time to see Serge pull a lanyard.

"*Yeeeeeeee-hawwwwwwwwww!*"

Another board took flight. Coleman strolled over to his bud. "Morning."

Serge stood beside a contraption that looked like a combination table saw and industrial clay-pigeon launcher. "Watch this." He kicked a large rock out from under the front legs, lowering the firing line.

"See that abandoned school bus by those trees?" Serge loaded another board and pulled the cord. The stud flew horizontally across the field, piercing the side of the bus like an antitank round.

Serge took off running. Coleman took off walking. He came around the back of the bus and found Serge holding the board triumphantly over his head. "Went right through both sides."

"That's nice."

Serge returned to the machine and folded spring arms. "Isn't she a corker?"

"Don't know. Never seen one before. Where'd you hear about it?"

"That big hurricane expo at the convention hall." Serge began rolling the device back around to the front of the motel. He reached the H2 and opened the rear door. "Between state regulators and licensed contractors, there was growing demand to establish a more precise hurricane-rating system." Serge reached into his pocket and flicked open a multi-tool. He removed the carpeted panel over a hidden storage well and began unscrewing. "These stud launchers are used to bench-test storm shutters and window safety film. You get an insurance break." Serge removed a small metal box from the chassis.

"What's that?"

"LoJack."

"You knew it was there this whole time?"

"Had my suspicions. I only accept quality rides."

"But the police could have caught us."

"Doubtful." Serge walked toward the gas station next door. Another diesel sound grew louder. "Nobody's crazy enough to come after us in that storm."

A semi rig with Georgia plates rolled into the station. The driver got out, placed hands on hips and looked around in futility. He was wearing a plaid flannel shirt and a baseball cap that indicated he had yet to accept the outcome of the Civil War.

Serge stepped up to a newspaper box in front of the station. He was about to insert a quarter.

"Hey, buddy!" yelled the driver. "Know any place I can get gas around here? All the stations are closed."

Serge threw up his arms can't-help-you style. "Power's out from the storm. No pumps work."

"But I'm almost empty."

Serge went over to the driver. "Got a map?"

"Right here." The driver reached under the front seat of his cab.

Serge unfolded it. "Okay, here we go. . . ." He ran a finger across the county line. "Take the turnpike north—that's the entrance ramp right over there past those trees—and get off on Exit 242. Lots of gas stations. They were outside the damage cone. Unless you're bone dry, shouldn't be a problem."

"Appreciate it," said the driver, shaking Serge's hand. He climbed back into his cab.

"Don't forget your map." Serge slipped it under the seat.

The driver slammed his door and leaned out the window. "Thanks again."

Serge waved as the truck pulled away. "Welcome to Florida!" He returned to the newspaper box. In the distance a long line of speeding, wailing police cars crested an overpass.

"At that hurricane expo, the university had an exhibit from their new storm-research center . . ." A quarter clanked down into the news box. ". . . They unveiled a revolutionary super stud launcher with three times the p.s.i. of anything from Underwriters Laboratories." Serge opened the squeaky door and pulled out a paper. "One look and it was love at first sight. I said to myself, I gotta get me one of those!"

The convoy of squad cars raced toward the gas station. Serge began going through his paper. "It has to be in here somewhere."

Flashing blue lights flickered off Serge's shirt as the first cruisers screeched into the parking lot.

"What are you looking for?" asked Coleman.

"Coverage of my comeback." He turned pages quickly. "How could they ignore it?"

Police tires squealed a few feet in front of Serge and Coleman. The lead car executed a sliding U-turn and sped off in the opposite direction. More cruisers skidded into the lot, more noisy turns, all reversing course and following the first car up the turnpike's entrance ramp.

"This is so unfair!" Serge flipped to the next section and looked at the top. He smacked the paper with the back of his hand. "Of course! It's yesterday's paper. They didn't deliver because of the storm. I should have known from the day-old tracking chart of the next hurricane."

"Another hurricane? But we just had one. Don't we have to wait till next year?"

"There can be more than one a year."

"I thought it was like Miss Universe."

"Not remotely. Hurricanes are now so frequent it's completely changed the way we live in this state. From June to November, one storm's just left, another's about to hit, and three more are forming, a tropical backbeat that's so constant, residents don't even raise a pulse anymore. They just bring in lawn furniture like people in Quebec shovel driveways all winter."

"So that's what's been going on?"

Serge nodded. "It's the New Florida Lifestyle: Put up the plywood, take down the plywood, rent a movie, get your dry cleaning, plywood up, plywood down, time to make the dough-nuts."

"But, Serge, when will it all end?"

"I'm afraid it's only getting worse. The weather craziness of the last few years actually began in the early nineties. Meteorologists are split between a permanent upward trend and interdecadal cycles. The twenties and thirties were particularly bad. So were the sixties. Unfortunately, most of Florida's population and construction came during the last down node."

"I have no idea what any of that means."

"It means back off the weed. There's a category two bearing down fast on St. Augustine. That's why we have to hurry." Serge threw the newspaper in the trash. "I'm sure there'll be a big spread about me when we reach the coast. Let's rock."

Coleman looked around. "What did you do with the LoJack?"

"What? Oh, I slipped it under that trucker's seat with his map."

CHAPTER NINE

VERO BEACH

The chief of police stood next to a semi trailer in the Wal-Mart parking lot. He was on the phone. ". . . No, we don't think the truck driver was involved. The killer must have slipped it under his seat. . . . Who knows? He could be anywhere by now. . . ."

Serge walked past the chief and up to a National Guardsman with embroidered stars on the shoulders of his camouflage fatigues. "General, you can relax now. We're here to help."

The general was preoccupied with a new shipment of generators and blue roof tarps.

Serge coughed. Nothing. He tapped his arm. "General!"

The general noticed Serge for the first time. "Did you say something?"

Serge saluted and clicked the heels of his sneakers. "I place myself and Coleman under your command!"

More distraction. Someone handed the general a clipboard; he signed quickly and handed it back. "I'm sorry, what did you say?"

"When do we get uniforms?"

"I'm very busy. Please." The general began walking briskly.

Serge ran up alongside. "The whole problem with society today is 'me, me, me!' But not the National Guard! My hat's off
to the whole operation. You've really bounced back since Kent
State."

The general ignored him, barking orders as he passed the head-
quarters tent.

"Yes, sir, the Guard's got a whole new image," said Serge.
"Thanks to Bush, you're on the front lines with the real soldiers,
whether you want to be or not. Completely different mind-set
since when the president was AWOL. He's transformed the Guard
from the *door to a draft dodge* to a *back-door draft*. I thought that
up all by myself. I could write your press releases."

The general continued ignoring him and marched purposefully.

Serge kept pace. "I hear there's been looting. I can save manpower there. Just loan me a sniper rifle."

The general stopped and turned. "What?"

"Or a machine gun if you're in a hurry—"

"Shut up!"

Serge stopped. The general was rubbing his forehead.

"What's the matter?" asked Serge. "Pressure headache?"

The general took a deep breath and signed another clipboard.
"If you want to be useful, get over in that line handing out
MREs."

"*Meals Ready to Eat?* I love those!" Serge stepped back and
saluted smartly again. "You won't regret this! Do you have the lasagna? Those little heating packets really are something, aren't
they?"

But the general was already walking away.

"Coleman, come on!"

The pair arrived at the back of a semi; Serge aggressively
threaded his way to the front of the crowd. He saluted a lower-
echelon officer. "We're here on special orders from the general,
which I'm not disposed to discuss if, in fact, such orders did exist.
Our uniforms haven't arrived yet. The general's a great man, but

he's gotten himself into a quagmire. We briefly considered the option of sniper fire, but he dismissed it because, after all, this is the new National Guard: 'Be all that you can be!' Wait, that's the army. What's the Guard's slogan? 'Sorry about Kent State'?"

The officer was a veteran of the 2004 season. Florida street loons didn't faze him anymore. "Stand in that line over there and just pass whatever's handed to you."

Another salute.

Soon they were rapidly unloading cardboard boxes. "Hey, everybody!" yelled Serge. "Did you see *Full Metal Jacket*? We should all sing! After me, children first: *I don't know but thought I'd ask . . . Will Hurricane Alex kiss my ass? . . .* "

Coleman passed a carton of military rations and panted. "Serge, what are we doing here? I thought you wanted to get up to St. Augustine."

"Liberty isn't free."

A local resident walked around the back of the trailer and called up to the Guardsman inside. "Any ice?"

"Ran out an hour ago. Try another trailer."

"They're all out."

"Check the other distribution sites?"

"Everyone's out. Except for all price gougers on U.S. 1. Why aren't you doing anything about them?"

The Guardsman passed down another heavy box. "Hands full here."

The bucket brigade fell into a finely tuned, civic-duty rhythm. Except Coleman. Perspiration pasted the shirt to his stomach. He gasped for air as Serge tossed him another case. "I don't think I can last much longer."

"Hang in there," said Serge. "Let's finish emptying this trailer. Then we book. I have something planned."

"What?"

"Complete my religious journey." Serge checked his wristwatch. "I've blocked off noon to twelve-thirty."

"Is that enough time?"

"It'll be tight, but I want to go sightseeing later."

Coleman grunted and heaved another box. "I don't get it. You've always been turned off by religion."

"That's because of religious people. What do *they* know about religion?"

"Why the sudden change?"

"Another birthday. Decided it was time to place my bets on the afterlife. But there are so many choices. You got your Catholics, Protestants, Hindus, Buddhists, Zoroastrians, Wiccans, your Santería, your voodoo, your tarot cards, that guy on the corner of Highway 92 in the sandwich board with his day-and-night diatribe on all things great and small. Plus every kind of cult you can imagine—they're the spiritual microbreweries. I'm sure I'll find a brand I like."

Coleman passed another case of rations. "You should drop acid."

"That's not a religion."

"Oh, it's a religion, all right. I've seen God many times." Another case. "Once he told me to spray-paint my legs silver. But after the LSD wore off, there no longer seemed to be a point."

"He was giving you a test, like Abraham." Serge held out his hands for another box, but it didn't come. He looked up. "Coleman, the trailer's almost empty." He walked to the bumper; a Guardsman was climbing down. Serge pointed. "What are those last cases?"

"Lasagna," said the Guardsman. "Everyone hates it. Even in disasters."

"Lasagna's my favorite!"

"You want 'em, they're yours."

"Don't move." Serge ran to the H2 and backed it up. They loaded the cases.

Serge had just begun pulling away when he noticed a row of news boxes. He threw it into park. "Coleman, wait here."

TAMPA

The historic neighborhood juke joint sat on the back side of Palma Ceia Liquors. It was called the Crow's Nest because it used to be upstairs. But now it wasn't. McSwirley stopped crying. He grabbed a bar napkin from the Cutty Sark promotional dispenser and blew his nose.

"That's the way! Get it all out!" Mahoney slapped him hard on the back.

"Ow!"

"I'm here for you," said Mahoney. "We're going to be inseparable. This is how it starts. Natural adversaries. The tough-as-nails cop and bleeding-heart reporter who come to respect each other and share problems from home. My daughter's a tramp."

Jeff picked up his ginger ale and sagged on the high-mileage bar. He gazed out the propped-open back door at a quiet residential street. There was a sudden spike in noise from the opposite direction: someone entering the bar from the package store. Jeff turned and squinted at bright fluorescent light and a brief glimpse of heavy traffic on Dale Mabry Highway. The door closed. Coziness resumed.

"Barkeep!" yelled Mahoney, pointing at a Crock-Pot next to the cash register. "Boiled peanuts for my compadre, another Bombay Sapphire here."

McSwirley broke into light sobs again. A bowl and cocktail arrived.

"Thanks, Al." Mahoney pointed up at the TV. "Anything besides *Celebrity Justice*?"

The bartender aimed a remote control. Channels changed. Courtney Love was replaced by a card game.

"*. . . Gladstone Media presents another breathtaking round of* Xtreme Poker!" Four people sat motionless around a green felt table. "*It's high-stakes card action like you've never seen*

before! Taken to the edge and beyond! . . ." The people sat still.
". . . It's . . . Xtreme!"

Mahoney raised his drink and nodded down toward the bowl.
"Jeff, get some of those up in you. Boiled peanuts always stopped
me from crying. Of course, I was five."

McSwirley tore open a soft shell. "I don't think I can do this
anymore. Never thought I'd say it, but I'm seriously thinking of
quitting."

"You can't do that," said Mahoney. "We need each other. You
help me catch Serge, and I'll make your career."

The TV: *"Coming up next, a wild shoot-out from the bad
boys of Scrabble!"* A bearded man in a black cowboy hat placed
a small wooden tile on the table. FUNGIBLE.

"I'm having nightmares," said Jeff. "It's so sad."

"I can't believe you actually feel sorry for those dead guys."

"Not them," said McSwirley. "The survivors. Even jerks have
moms."

"Those people yesterday really got to you?"

"No, three years of people got to me. Ever talked to the parents of a murdered child?"

"A couple times."

"Forty-six," said McSwirley.

"You keep count?"

"Want to hear their names?"

On it went, an afternoon of peanuts, gin and despair. The TV
showed grainy footage of a pickup truck crashing through the
front windows of a convenience store.

Mahoney rattled ice cubes around the glass in front of his
face. ". . . Then my daughter moved in with a Portuguese punk
band and got the clap. . . ."

TV: The pickup's occupants leaped from the truck to steal
beer, but the vehicle was still in gear and pinned them against the
cooler until police arrived.

"Hey, look." Mahoney pointed at the television. "It's *Florida's
Funniest Surveillance Videos.*"

CHAPTER TEN

TAMPA

There was a war on.

Not in the Middle East. In Tampa Bay.

It was a newspaper war, and the fighting was fierce, house to house.

The *Tampa Tribune* and *St. Petersburg Times* had been going at it for years, with no sign of letting up.

Newspaper wars in America are an endangered species. Most have long since been settled by exterior economics. With the advent of cable, dual-income 24/7 lifestyles and the Internet, readership in most communities dwindled to natural-monopoly levels where only one paper could remain viable. No capitulation; the clock simply ran out.

In Tampa Bay, however, geography created natural bulwarks on both sides of the bridges. The papers occasionally made incursions into enemy territory with satellite news bureaus and sports-arena naming rights. But the bloodiest battles were in the past. It was now a cold war.

Then, shortly into the millennium, a new player. It came in the form of journalism's latest innovation. Bias.

Ground was broken near the Trump condos in downtown Tampa for another screaming office tower. One year later a third major paper hit the newsstands. British media tycoon Neville Gladstone (the Younger) had diversified an electronic empire into print, launching his U.S. flagship, *Tampa Bay Today*.

Papers began flying off the presses with a proud new slogan: "Fair, unbalanced journalism."

Copy editors quickly pointed out that this probably wasn't the sentiment they were reaching for, but the stationery had already been ordered, and management said, "Our audience will get it."

They were more than right. The upstart instantly stole massive circulation chunks from both traditional papers due to a variety of farsighted promotional gimmicks that left the other two giants with their dignity. Coupons, contests, giveaways, publicity stunts, Klieg lights, and the dancing *Tampa Bay Today* Front-Page Bombshells in newsprint bikinis with black-and-white pom-poms.

Oh, and guided tours. Very big with the community. Retirees, elementary classes, dignitaries. The schedule was jammed, with a new group leaving every fifteen minutes throughout the day, and they still had a three-month waiting list. Because this wasn't some arm's-length experience—it wound right through the heart of the newsroom, every department, all hours, circling desks for close-up snapshots and eavesdropping. A rare opportunity to view the inner gears of a daily metro at work. But mainly it was the complimentary hot dogs, sodas, coffee mugs and umbrellas.

This particular morning, a combined group of seniors and second-graders assembled in the rotunda. "Please keep together." The spunky tour guide distributed visitors' passes and binoculars.

They headed down the main hallway. A long line of frames on both walls. "Please note the famous front pages of *Tampa Bay Today* from key dates throughout history."

The group was impressed. Pearl Harbor, the JFK assassination, man on the moon.

A child's hand went up. "Did the paper exist back then?"

"No. And now we come to the magazines. . . ."

They stopped to admire blown-up cover photos of Neville Gladstone. *Newsweek, Forbes, Editor & Publisher, Military Diorama Monthly.*

You had to be under a rock not to know who Gladstone was. If the billion dollars and bestsellers weren't enough, there was the new wife, the reality show, and another new wife. In addition to his recently inaugurated newspaper, Neville held controlling interest in three hundred radio stations, a cable network and a growing list of hit syndicated TV shows.

A tiny, white-haired retiree from Sun City craned her neck in curiosity. "Is Gladstone here right now?"

"Not right now."

Another hand went up. "When will he get here?"

"Actually, he's never been to Florida."

"Where is he?"

"On location with the film crew for his honeymoon. . . . Please follow me."

The tour took the elevator to the next floor, and the guide assembled them in the hallway beneath an On Air sign.

"And this is one of Florida Cable News's finest state-of-the-art sets. Let's take a peek inside. . . ." She opened the door to a cavernous room with flickering monitors.

Stage lights bathed two people sitting behind an anchor desk. Idle staff in headphones waited beside large studio cameras. The desk had bold, lighted lettering across the front: HARD FIRE.

A retiree in a mobility scooter raised his hand. "What program is this?"

"Our new political-argument show. We're just in time for rehearsal."

"They rehearse arguing?"

"Let's listen. . . ."

"*No! No! No!*" shouted the show's director, stepping out from behind the cameras.

"What's wrong?" asked the host.

"I understood your guest."

"But—"

"You didn't talk over him! I could make out every word!"

"I was letting him—"

"Interrupt!"

"But I was—"

"Don't interrupt me!" The director stepped back into the shadows. "From the top . . ."

The host and guest faced each other.

"God—!"

"Values—!"

"Liberal—!"

"Nazi—!"

"F—!"

"M—!"

". . .!"

". . .!"

"Again!" yelled the director. "Tighter!"

Back to the elevator. Next floor. They entered the newsroom. It was overwhelming at first. All the desks, the dramatic digital master clock, the giant washable state map with the path of the season's second hurricane on a collision course with St. Augustine.

"It's so big."

The guide smiled. "Biggest in the bay."

She led them down an aisle. The white-haired woman tapped the tour guide and pointed at someone working on an upcoming computer terminal. "Oh, my! Is that the famous humor columnist?"

The guide smiled again. "Yes it is."

"But I thought he was with the *Trib*."

The guide smiled wider. "Was."

In a preemptive air strike to soften up the competition's beachhead, *Tampa Bay Today* had recruited several of the *Times*'s and *Tribune*'s most respected scribes. They had all balked at first, because of Gladstone's reputation, but the money was absurd. Now the birth of regret.

The retiree was beside herself. "Heavens! He's my favorite columnist. Is he actually writing?"

"Sure is."

"I just love his stuff. He's so funny!"

"Would you like to pet him?"

The tour continued up the aisle. The columnist was lost in concentration, numerous ideas spinning like dinner plates on tall poles. As happened so many times a day, he sensed the group's approach with his neck hair. One of the plates began to wobble.

The spunky tour guide arrived. "Hi, Dan!"

"*Hi.*" Eyes still on the screen.

"My group has some questions they'd like to ask you." A plate fell.

"What are you doing?"

"*Trying to write.*"

"Is it hard?"

"*Currently.*"

"How'd you learn to be funny?"

The rest of the plates crashed. The columnist angled back in his chair. "*Talking to idiots.*"

"What do you mean by that?"

The guide jumped in cheerfully. "Look! There's our cartoonist!"

The group filed by. The columnist felt an old woman's hand on his shoulder. Then something on his arm. He looked down. A drop of mustard. He looked up. A camera flashed.

He bit his lip until they were past. ". . . *like trying to write in a fuckin' theme park . . .*"

A child raised her hand and pointed behind them. "He said a bad word."

The guide chuckled. "I'm sure you heard wrong."

The little hand stayed up. "It began with an *f*."

"That couldn't have been—"

The little hand waved. "Is he going to hell?"

"*No!*" shouted the columnist, standing quickly and stomping away. "*I'm already in it!*"

The guide clapped her hands a single time and grinned hard. "Well! Wasn't that special? A genuine taste of gritty journalism in action! . . . Now, if you'll come with me . . ." She reached the end of the aisle and outstretched her arm. "Please direct your attention toward that big conference table on the other side of the newsroom."

The table was surrounded by cushy chairs and ill-fitting suits. Against the wall stood a long, five-hundred-gallon saltwater aquarium to reduce stress and pad year-end figures. The aquarium was installed and maintained by a service-contract company that tended office plants in downtown high-rises and had recently branched from flora to fauna. But the firm was still new to coral-reef species compatibility, and the tank had become a daily source of small-scale drama.

"That's the budget meeting," said the guide.

"They're talking about money?"

The guide laughed politely. "No, it's a newspaper term: the meeting where all the top editors decide what stories will go in the paper. . . . What do you say we pay them a visit?"

VERO BEACH

"Woooooo-hoooooo!" Serge ran back across the parking lot, waving the local/state section of a newspaper. "It's in here! I made it!"

"What's it say?" asked Coleman.

"My big comeback! The wire service picked it up from Tampa. I'm all over the state, probably the country. They're calling me an 'insane genius'! They— Wait, what the heck's this?"

"What?"

"I didn't croak that dude at the Skyway. This isn't adding up. . . ." His eyes raced down the article. "Okay, here we go. The Chinese restaurant and . . . no! . . . *Son of a bitch!*"

"What's wrong?"

"They're calling me a copycat killer! They're giving all the credit to some other guy at the bridge!"

"I choose never to read anything." Coleman lit a joint. "That's how I stay happy."

"At worst it's a tie!" yelled Serge. "For a copycat there has to be some kind of time lag so the idea-stealer can first hear about it in the news. Doesn't this writer know anything?"

"Pretty sloppy reporting."

"And it's spooky to think there might be other people wandering around Florida on my wavelength."

"Almost makes you too scared to live here."

"No shit. . . . Hold on. What's this? A videotape?" Serge continued reading. "So that's what happened! Someone was following us at the university. That's how they ripped off my idea!"

"I didn't see anyone," said Coleman.

"This was supposed to be my big comeback! Someone's going to pay! Who's saying these awful things?" He checked the byline at the top of the article. "'Staff writer Jeff McSwirley.'"

Coleman exhaled a pot cloud. "What kind of name is Mc-Swirley?"

"A dead man's!" Serge began screaming at the paper. "*You hear that, McSwirley? You're dead! . . .*" Serge's peripheral vision inadvertently caught something down in the body of the type. "Of course. Now it all makes sense."

"What does?"

Serge punched the paper. "Confidential police source. And I have a pretty good idea who it is. That explains the copycat business. He's manipulating some naïve young reporter to plant lies." Then back to yelling at the paper. "*You're a dead man, Mahoney! You hear me? Dead! . . .* No, stop. Get a grip. Don't take the bait."

"Bait?"

"He's trying to flush me into the open." Serge nodded with a grudging smile. "So that's the way it's going to be, eh? Just like old times? All right, I'm up to a little spirited competition. You zig, I zag." Serge glanced up from the paper and scanned the horizon.

"What are you looking for?"

"An asshole."

CHAPTER ELEVEN

TAMPA

"Fourteen, corner pocket." Mahoney bent over the lone pool table in the Crow's Nest. Balls clacked. "Damn. Jeff, your shot. . . . Jeff? . . ."

Jeff stood with a cue stick, shoulders bobbing, his face covered with blue chalk from wiping tears.

"There, there." Mahoney placed a reassuring hand on his back. "Maybe this will cheer you up. Did I tell you about my ex setting all my clothes on fire in the front yard?"

Jeff wiped more chalk on his face. "I've never lied in print before!"

"You didn't lie. *I* lied. You quoted me accurately."

"But I knew what you were doing."

"That's right. I'm catching Serge. That copycat stuff we planted must be driving him nuts about now." Mahoney circled the table, considering balls and trigonometry. "Someday you'll look back and tell your children all about this. Unless they won't accept collect calls from bars after midnight, the ungrateful brats."

"So you really don't think there's a second killer?"

"Not a chance."

"But how can you be so sure?"

"Because I know Serge. Classic textbook case, reaching the end of serial-killer life expectancy. He's about to disintegrate, if he hasn't already. Can I take your shot?"

Jeff nodded. "What happens then?"

"Any number of things." Mahoney walked around the end of the table and lined up the thirteen. "Blaze of glory, suicide, but in this case I'm taking the short money on identity fragmentation."

"Fragmentation?"

"Strong split-personality vibe in the air." The lamp over the pool table had a Tampa Bay Bucs helmet. Mahoney ducked under it with his stick. Clack. "Probably talking to himself in different voices, committing murders he doesn't even remember."

"You got to be kidding," said Jeff. "That's what you're basing all this on? A *vibe*?"

"Sixth sense. From getting inside Serge's noggin. I can't explain it, and the department isn't buying." Mahoney picked out a yellow-striped ball. "Fifteen, side. . . . It started just before they locked me in the rubber room." Clack.

"This is getting too weird for me," said Jeff. "I should have my head examined for ever agreeing to your plan."

"And don't think I won't appreciate it. No, sir. Not Mahoney. As soon as I catch Serge, you get the big exclusive. Now, here's what we're going to do next. . . . Ten, corner . . ." Clack.

TAMPA BAY TODAY

"It's settled," said the balding man with a British accent, seated at the head of the conference table. "Front page, top position, Hurricane Cristobal. Second slot, McSwirley's serial-killer follow." He turned to the metro editor. "When can we expect it?"

"Don't know."

"What do you mean, you don't know?"

"I can't get a hold of Jeff," said the metro editor. "He's supposed to be interviewing a confidential source, but his phone's turned off."

"Find him! We have a deadline to make! We're murdering the competition!" He flipped a page on his computer printout.

A tour group wound its way around the table, forming a tight peanut gallery. A small child looked into the five-hundred-gallon saltwater aquarium. A clown fish looked back. The child smiled and waved. "Nemo!" The spunky tour guide narrated from behind. "And this is the budget meeting I was telling you about. . . ." Cameras flashed.

Actually, it wasn't *the* meeting. There were several throughout the news cycle as stories' respective stock rose and fell. The paper had started with three meetings a day but was now up to six. Two cultures were present: hard-core news people who had no use for meetings. And higher-up corporate types, which meant they only attended meetings. The second group prolonged the meetings with discussions to add more meetings.

The balding man at the end of the table jotted something quickly and raised his head again. *"Let's take it around the horn."*

The title of the person in charge of the meetings traditionally would have been "managing editor." Managing editors were the boots on the ground that actually put out a paper, while publishers accepted plaques at United Way luncheons. Except at this conference table the top cheese was now called "maximum editor." The complete title was Maximum Editor for Life and Vice President, Gladstone Florida Media Group. The broader label was required to command a more tentacled operation. After Gladstone finished hammering together his diverse media holdings, the "enhanced" budget meetings coordinated hydra-headed coverage from print, TV, radio and the Internet. The goal was to share scoops and cut costs.

Gladstone had personally chosen the perfect man for the job, Maxwell Begley, the hugely popular British television personality whom the tycoon enticed across the pond to launch his stateside juggernaut. Begley had risen to fame a decade earlier as host of numerous daytime confrontation shows. London's own Jerry Springer. The success would have continued, too, but after a third guest was murdered in the green room, it was time for a change. And that's how he came to be sitting at the head of a table in Tampa, Florida. Maxwell Begley. Max Ed Max.

"International desk?" said Max.

A man with a green eyeshade read from notes. "Foreigners hate us. People blow themselves up far away. Two Americans die in plane crash in Indian Ocean, and three hundred other people—"

"National desk?"

"Borders aren't secure. Congress hates one another. President solves botched hurricane response with national day of prayer—"

An abrupt splash in the aquarium. "Nemo?" A large fish had replaced a smaller fish. A child began crying.

"State desk?"

"Drugs, shark attack, riptide. Bodies stacking up in funeral homes because they can't bury in hurricane-soaked ground. Update on the new feeding-tube case—"

"Metro?"

"Vaseline-covered guy with sixty empty jars arrested for ten-thousand-dollar damage to Vaseline-covered motel room—"

"Special sections?"

"Sixteen-page blowout. 'One Year Later: Family Begs Media to Be Left Alone'—"

"Features?"

"Human-interest on owner of flattened mobile home who didn't have insurance—"

"I got an idea," said the photo editor. "How about finding the mobile-home owner *with* insurance?"

The photo editor wilted under the glare of the maximum editor. *"Photo?"*

"Yes, sir?"

"Anything besides more aerials of flattened mobile homes?"

"We have . . ." He thumbed a photo log. He sat back in his chair. "No."

"Graphics?"

"Topographical tracking charts of the hurricane and Brad and Angelina's vacation."

"Lifestyle?"

"Power-outage cooking with pizzazz."

"Money sense?"

"The business of suffering."

"Corporate guy?"

"What about adding another meeting at six-thirty?" He looked at his watch and stood. "I'm late for a meeting."

"Which brings us to convergence . . ."

This part was something new. "Convergence" was free-lunch-seminar jargon that stood for the previously mentioned media fusion. As the electronics age unfolded, many newspapers were forced into partnerships with local broadcasters, through either outright ownership or arranged marriage. Neville Gladstone again set the pace by teaming his newspaper with both TV *and* radio. He already owned a pair of heavy players in the market—Florida Cable News and WPPT-FM—which were promptly relocated into the newly christened Gladstone Tower. They gave the broadcast people laptops to write stories, and they gave print reporters camcorders in case they stumbled across telegenic misery. . . . The budget meeting continued. . . .

"Florida Cable News?" asked Max Ed Max.

"Sir, I have a complaint," said the FCN programming director.

"What is it?"

"It's WPPT radio. Every time we try to do a live broadcast, they sabotage it."

"How do they do that?"

"The damn Party Parrot! He keeps running out on camera!"

"We *are* the Party Parrot!" said the WPPT station manager, wearing a Hawaiian shirt and blinking sunglasses. "Our partying will not be denied!"

"You're screwing up all our remotes!" yelled the cable director.

"Hey-hey-hey! Party! Party! Party!"

"*Gentlemen!*" said Max. "*I expect you both to behave like adults. This is about professional ethics. Each division must remain completely independent for journalistic integrity. We all have our roles to play*"—he turned toward the TV director—"*and yours is to produce the finest cable-news coverage in Florida!*"

"What's the Party Parrot's role?"

"*To disrupt that coverage.*"

"This is insane!"

"*Comes from the very top. New ratings just arrived. Everyone's tuning in to see what the parrot will do next.*"

"Why can't he disrupt the competition's broadcast?"

The editor shook his head. "*Then* they'll *get the ratings. You'll just have to work something out.*"

"The Party Parrot rules all!" said the radio chief. "Bow to the awesome partying power of the Parrot! . . . *Party! Party! Party!*"

"You son of a bitch!" The TV director dove across the table. A sports editor grabbed him from behind; Features pried fingers from the radio manager's neck. They ended up rolling down the mahogany table in a snarl of limbs, scattering water carafes.

"I'll fucking kill you!"

A child's hand went up in the tour group. The guide clapped sharply again. "What do you know? We're behind schedule. If you'll come with me and direct your attention toward those double doors on the other side of the newsroom . . ."

The doors flew open. In came the Front-Page Bombshells, singing and high-kicking in a chorus line: "*What's black! . . . And white! . . . And read! . . . All over! . . .*"

CHAPTER TWELVE

VERO BEACH

A black H2 sped north on U.S. 1 toward the Sebastian Inlet.

Coleman was in the passenger seat mixing a drink. Bourbon and Coke. Except he was out of Coke, so he used more bourbon. "I've never been to St. Augustine before."

"You're pulling my chain," said Serge. "Florida's Cradle of Civilization?"

Coleman shook his head.

Serge slapped the dash. "This calls for the A-tour! You're going to remember this the rest of your life!"

The H2 passed a commotion on the side of the highway. A noisy crowd surrounded a man standing in the bed of a late-model Ram pickup. Serge's head swiveled as they went by. He hit his turn signal.

The scene had grown even louder by the time Serge and Coleman walked up behind the mob in the parking lot of a defunct Sunoco station. Serge stood on tiptoes and saw the oversize cooler in the pickup's bed. He tapped the shoulder of someone in front of him. "How much is he asking?"

"Ten bucks," the man grumbled. "We're trying to talk sense, but he's being a dickhead."

Coleman tapped Serge's shoulder. "What's going on?"

"Price gouging. Bags of ice. Third-degree felony."

Serge circumnavigated the crowd and came up on the side of the Dodge. He looked over the lip. The cooler was even bigger than he'd originally estimated. One of those two-hundred-gallon, deep-sea-fishing jobs. For now the lid stayed closed. The man standing next to it featured sunburned shoulders, a Hard Rock tank top and That '70s Porn Mustache. He openly relished presiding over the crowd. *"Ten bucks."*

"It's an outrage!"

"You want ice?"

"You're taking advantage of misfortune!"

"Ten bucks."

A woman cradling an infant pushed her way to the front of the crowd. "But I have baby formula!"

"And I have ice. Ten bucks." He sipped an ice-cold lemonade.

"Excuse me," said Serge. "I'd like to buy some ice."

"How much you want?"

Serge pulled a thick roll of bills from his pants. "All of it."

The crowd jeered.

The sunburned man stepped back and narrowed his eyes. *"You a cop?"*

"What's it look like?"

"Like you're a cop."

"I'm not a cop."

"Then what are you going to do with all that ice?"

"Drive up the road and sell it for twelve bucks."

The sunburned man laughed. *"You're my kind!"*

Serge handed over the money. The mob became a lynch mob. Shouts, elbows. Someone shoved Serge into the side of the pickup. He caught his balance and spun on the crowd. "Hey! Free enterprise!"

They weren't having it. Serge slammed into the truck again. He turned again, this time with a gun in the air. Much different reaction.

"That's better." Serge tucked the pistol into his belt and looked at the man in the pickup. "Locals are getting a tad cranky. Might be best if we conduct business elsewhere. My car's around the corner."

The man vaulted the side of the pickup. *"Meet you there."*

Five minutes later the pickup reappeared from around the corner and rolled back into the parking lot. Serge was driving.

Someone in the crowd pointed. "It's him!" They wanted to charge but remembered that gun.

Serge opened the driver's door and jumped down. "I don't know how it slipped my mind. You know what today is?"

No answer.

"Why, it's Free Ice Day!"

Confused expressions.

Serge walked to the bumper and dropped the tailgate. "Go ahead, grab as much as you like."

Something was wrong. Some kind of trick.

"What's the matter?" asked Serge. "The iceman cometh!" He climbed up into the bed and opened the cooler, hoisting a sack with each arm. "Who's first?"

Nobody moved. Serge read their minds. "Okay, I'll unload my gun." Click. "There's the magazine." Click. "And there's the one in the chamber. Happy?"

He'd barely gotten the words out when they swarmed.

"Take it easy," said Serge. "Plenty to go around. . . . And a bag for you, and one for you, and you. . . . Please pass this one to the new mom in back. . . . And one for you. . . ."

"Gee, thanks, mister!"

"Really appreciate it!"

"Mighty neighborly!"

"Where'd the other guy go?"

THAT NIGHT

A table sat under the dim blue glow of a television with the sound off. The screen showed radar sweeps of a major hurricane two hundred miles east-southeast of St. Augustine and closing. A single sheet of stationery sat on the desktop. Childlike ballpoint handwriting slanted to the left.

Two hands in surgical gloves folded the page in thirds and slipped it into an envelope, along with a Polaroid of the crime scene taken before police had arrived. One of the gloved fingers dipped into a glass of water and ran along the envelope's gummed seal.

The right hand instinctively picked up the pen again. It switched to the left and began printing an address.

JEFF McSWIRLEY
STAFF WRITER
TAMPA BAY TODAY . . .

CRISTOBAL

CHAPTER THIRTEEN

ST. AUGUSTINE

A black H2 passed the base of a bridge. Coleman had his head out the window like a Labrador. "Serge, I see two big animals."

"The Bridge of Lions. Very historic."

Coleman pulled his head inside and quickly rolled up the window. "They're growling at me."

Serge glanced dubiously at Coleman, now clawing the roof of the silent vehicle. "Where's that music coming from? It's like a sitar, except rockabilly."

"What's gotten into you?"

Coleman raised a clear, candy-red-filled sports bottle. "Hurricane Punch."

"Another of your signature concoctions?"

"Figured since you were getting into the storms with your science and history, I should contribute with my expertise. . . . Where *is* that music coming from?"

"Pray tell," asked Serge. "What is in this cocktail of champions?"

Coleman stretched his neck in several directions for the source of the sound. "Remember Torpedo Juice?"

"Red Bull and Everclear, if memory serves."

"Thought that was a little bland, so I added cranberry juice, grapefruit juice, pineapple juice, light rum, dark rum, amaretto, blue curaçao, orange passion fruit, a wedge of lime, a leaf of mint, a squirt of triple sec, a splash of Grand Marnier, a dash of grenadine, a pinch of coconut, a sprinkle of sugar, shaved ice. Oh, and a whole bunch of mescaline. You really can't hear this song?"

"No, but I think I remember the words: You're going to fuck up our trip."

Coleman set the sports bottle down and popped a Schlitz. Then another.

"*Two* beers," said Serge.

Coleman looked at the can in each hand. "Wow. I had a feeling I just opened one. Or was it an hour ago?" He began chugging.

"Now you're going to get wasted," said Serge. "You'll miss all the history like every other time."

Coleman finished one beer and raised the other. "I'm just taking the edge off. I think I OD'd again. We're driving down the back of a big black snake."

"In these parts, it's called a road."

"It has snake qualities." The passenger window rolled down again; a bulbous head went back out. "St. Augustine is cool! Look at all this rusty shit. Every sign says it's the oldest everything. Oldest house. Oldest store. Listen to my voice. It's like the thunder of the gods! . . . *I am the Great Coleman, king of the funky people!*"

The H2 continued north on U.S. 1, Coleman waving and hollering out the window. He suddenly retreated back inside and curled up in his seat. He timidly peeked over the dash. He ducked back down. "Serge, there's a big conquistador fuck out there swinging a sword at us!"

"It's just a billboard."

They turned in to a parking lot and passed the entrance sign: FOUNTAIN OF YOUTH.

Serge led the way to a ticket window and opened his wallet. "Two adults. I say that loosely."

The man in the booth made change. "Don't know how long we're going to be open. And the train's not running. Because of the storm."

"That's okay," said Serge. "I naturally absorb history at an advanced rate."

They went inside. Serge was true to his word. He already had the attraction's map and attack plan preloaded in memory sectors from past study. His 35mm wide-angle Pentax continuously fired on motor drive as they whipped through exhibits in quick succession: Indian burial ground, saltcellar, springhouse, Timucuan artifacts, cross of twenty-seven stone slabs Ponce de León laid to mark the spot. Serge bellied up to a concession stand and changed film. "Coke, please."

"Souvenir cup?" asked the girl inside.

"The souvenir cup is required."

The girl smiled and began filling a plastic tumbler under the CO_2 spigot. "Hate to say it, but you might have to cut your visit short because of the storm."

"Actually enhances my visit, because St. Augustine is *all about* hurricanes. One completely changed the course of this city. All of Florida, for that matter. I speak no lies. France established a foothold at Fort Caroline just north of here."

The girl topped off the cup. "Never heard of it."

Serge slapped the counter and made her jump. "Because of the hurricane! France wanted control of the peninsula, so they set sail to attack that Spanish fort just up the road from the Circle K. But the Spaniards could read Florida's weather. The great hurricane of 1565 wiped out the French fleet, while a Spanish division circled inland and sacked Fort Caroline, securing dominance over the entire state."

Serge pointed at the sky. "I was going to take advantage of this storm to employ the same military tactic, but I decided the U.S. was too entrenched."

She smiled politely again.

Serge appraised her for the first time. Zappa T-shirt (WEASELS RIPPED MY FLESH), far-off emerald eyes, sandy blond hair decorated with a single innocent wildflower over her right ear. Serge recognized the bloom as a rare state species illegal to pick. He decided not to report her.

"Where are you from?" asked Serge.

"Earth."

"How old are you?"

"Now."

Serge rolled his eyes. "Nice talking with you." He walked away and dumped his drink in the first bush.

Coleman ran up from behind. "Why'd you pay all that money for a soda if you were just going to toss it out?"

"Soda rots your teeth. I only needed the cup." Serge's internal tracking system picked up a small stone building. He made a beeline. Coleman caught up again, and they went inside.

"Excellent," said Serge. "Because of the storm, we have the place all to ourselves, just the way I like it."

Coleman spotted the building's centerpiece on the other side of the room. "Now I know why you needed that cup. It's the whole reason we drove up here. You're going to drink from the fountain, aren't you?"

"Got a problem with that?"

"Nope. I just don't know why you keep denying you're having a midlife—"

"I am not!"

"Sure you are. We're both getting old. You especially."

"I'm only forty-four," said Serge. "You know how old Ponce was when he discovered Florida?"

Coleman shook his head.

"Fifty-three."

"How old when he died?"

"Fifty— Shut up." Serge approached a grotto of coquina rock. "There she is, eternal vigor."

Coleman's eyes shifted around the empty room; he torched a fattie. Serge looked down into the well. "Deeper than I thought. Coleman, grab my ankles."

"You're not really going down there. . . ."

"Just grab 'em, okay?"

Coleman clenched the joint in his teeth and began threading his pal down through the dark hole. "You're heavier than you look."

"I'm almost there," echoed Serge's voice. "Whatever you do, don't let go."

A voice from behind. "I smell pot!"

Coleman let go.

"Coleman!" Splash.

Coleman spun around and hid the joint behind his back.

"Are you smoking dope in here?"—the girl from the concession stand.

"No, I'm not."

"You just hid it behind your back."

"No I didn't."

"Don't worry. I'm not going to tell. I just wanted some."

"*You* smoke pot?"

"Gimme that thing."

Coleman passed the number. "But you look so innocent."

"This is nature." She pinched the end.

Serge climbed out of the well and dripped on the stone walkway.

The girl pointed with the joint. "Hey! What the fuck are you doing in our fountain?"

Serge spread his arms. "Do I look any younger?"

"Twenty minutes," said Coleman. "How do you feel?"

"Lied to." Sneakers squished as he walked. "I didn't want to say anything and jinx this, but natives putatively told Ponce to seek the well at 'BeeMeeNee,' which some scholars argue is Bimini in the Bahamas."

The girl tapped Coleman on the arm and handed him the stub of a burned-out roach.

"You smoked the whole thing!"

"Got another?"

Coleman fished one from his wallet and grabbed his Bic.

She snatched both. "I'll blaze it." Serge and Coleman watched in amazement. She finally passed the half-gone bone, holding her breath. " 'Ere."

Serge looked down at her bare feet. "You're a regular wild child."

"It's society that's wild. I actually have very strong beliefs about the planet."

"And I noticed you got a little tattoo like all the other kids," said Serge. "So you're a conformist."

A smiling green gecko poked out the neck of her shirt. Thunder rumbled in the distance.

"That's the outer bands," said Serge.

"They're going to close the park," said the girl. She grabbed the joint from Coleman and began walking. The guys followed.

"So," said Serge, "I never caught your name. . . ."

TAMPA BAY TODAY

The maximum editor was running late. He rushed in and took his chair. "Let's get started. . . . Wait." He noticed a new person at the table: the guy in the crumpled fedora and a necktie with bongo drums. "Who the hell's he?"

The metro editor whispered and pointed at the visitor's badge clipped to Agent Mahoney's shirt pocket: CONFIDENTIAL SOURCE. "I see," said Max. "New slant on the story?"

"You could say that." The metro editor angled his head toward the center of the table: a single sheet of paper in a clear evidence bag. "The serial killer wrote McSwirley a letter. Enclosed a crime-scene Polaroid for proof. Calls himself 'The Eye of the Storm.' "

"What's the letter say?"

"Serge's usually ranting," interjected Mahoney. "Living fury of the land Florida ecology mumbo jumbo."

"Serge?" said Max.

"Been tracking him for years. That letter just might be our break."

"How so?"

"The next stage of my plan to flush him into the open. You run the letter and let me plant certain quotes in the accompanying story. He'll blow sky high. Then you'll *really* have a story."

"I like your thinking," said Max.

"Sir," said the metro editor. "There's something we haven't considered."

"What's that?"

"He specifically wrote McSwirley. This is a dangerous game you're playing. We could be risking his life."

A tour group encircled the conference table. "That gentleman at the front is the maximum editor," said the spunky guide. "Most of the others are department heads. The guy in the hat is a confidential source."

A camera flashed.

THE NATION'S OLDEST ECONOMY MOTEL

Rain whipped. Trees bent. Lightning streaked. Cristobal. The second landfall hurricane of the young season.

A transformer blew with a shower of sparks, and all the signs went dark on St. Augustine's budget-motel strip.

Candles again in one of the anonymous rooms. "I'm hungry," said Coleman.

"Grab an MRE," said Serge.

"A what?"

"Meal Ready to Eat. Those military rations from the National Guard. I got six cases."

Coleman ripped open a carton and rummaged through brown plastic bags. "They're all lasagna."

"If you don't like that, you can fill up on the side dishes. They got all kinds of cool stuff in there."

Coleman tore open bags and dumped camouflaged contents on the dresser: Wheat Snack Bread, Beverage Base Powder (Grape), Mixed Fruit, Cheese Spread, Cocoa Beverage Powder, Vegetable Cracker, Strawberry Jam and the accessory pack. "Hey, Serge, everything's little. Tiny iodized salt, tiny nondairy creamer, tiny bottle of Tabasco. They even got a tiny pack with two Chiclets. . . ."

"War gives you bad breath."

". . . Tiny Taster's Choice, tiny packet of toilet paper. . . . Serge, what's this thing?"

"The heater pack," said Serge. "That's the neatest part. Just rip the top and add a little water."

"How can that make it hot enough to cook?"

"I was skeptical, too, until I tried it. Amazing breakthrough. Water activates a chemical pack at the bottom of the pouch and generates a ferocious amount of heat you wouldn't believe. Just lean your selected food packet against it, and in five minutes soup's on!"

"I'll try the lasagna."

"Good choice."

Coleman went to the sink and filled a plastic cup with water. He came back to the dresser and poured it into the heating pouch. "Nothing's happening."

"Give it a second."

"Wait, I think I see bubbles." He stooped to eye level. "Yeah, something's definitely starting." The bubbles gave way to full boil. A plume of hot vapor gushed from the top of the pouch.

"Coleman! That's hydrogen! Get it away from the candle!"

Coleman grabbed the pouch. He snatched back his hand and shook it in the air. "Ow! It burned me!"

"You used too much water."

"It didn't seem like much."

Flash.

"Coleman! How am I going to explain that scorch mark to the management?"

"I think my eyebrows are singed. Can you check?"

"Don't you see I'm busy here?"

"Sorry."

"And it's not polite to stare."

"*Oh, God, yes! Faster, faster. Don't stop! Fuck me harder! . . .*"

Coleman faced the wall like he was in time-out. "So you like her?"

"I don't *dis*like her. . . ." He thrust again. "Take *that*, Mahoney!"

"*. . . Harder, faster, harder, faster. Oh, God! Fuck the living shit out of me! . . .*"

Coleman ran a finger through the carbonized mark on the wall. "She seems fond of you."

"What makes you say that?"

"*. . . Oh, God, I'm coming. I'm commmmmmmmmmm-iiiiiinnnnnngggggggg! . . .*"

"You going to start seeing her?"

"Don't think so," said Serge. "Got her qualities, but she smokes too much pot. Why am I always attracted to the naughty types?"

"They fuck."

"There's that," said Serge. "The clincher was when she told me her new spiritual name: 'The Fountain of Youth.' Figured it had to be a sign."

"*. . . Oh, God, here's another one. . . . Oooooohhh, yesssss! . . .*"

"How do you feel?" asked Coleman.

"Truculent yet melancholy."

"*. . . I'm there! Oh, God, I'm there. . . . I'm there again. . . . Don't stop. Another one's coming. . . . Here it is! . . .*"

"What's she talking about?" asked Coleman.

"Multiples."

"Multiples?"

"Orgasms. The lucky can have a few, but this one's a friggin' Gatling gun. Meanwhile I have to keep my powder dry or it's a lengthy retreat to reload the antique musket."

"Doesn't seem fair."

"... *There goes another one! Oh, sweet God! That's seventeen! Don't stop!* ..."

Serge kept thrusting. "Now she's just rubbing it in."

"How old?"

"Twenty-two. Why?"

"No reason."

"I know what you're thinking."

"I wasn't thinking anything."

"I told you. I am not one of those guys!"

"... *Fuck me harder! Here comes a big one!* ... *Eighteen!* ..."

"What are you reading?" asked Coleman.

Serge turned the page of a magazine on the pillow next to her head. "*Speedboat Illustrated.* I'm thinking of getting a Scarab."

"... *Nineteen!* ..."

CHAPTER FOURTEEN

McSWIRLEY

Journalism gets into your blood, like disease, addictions.
Heroin is the closest comparison: stop seeing friends, keep strange hours, borrow money all the time, look like shit.

Many cub reporters cut their teeth on the cop beat. And most soon move on to more coveted positions. Some get particularly good at it and want to stay. Others are bad at it and are forced to stay. Jeff McSwirley carved his own category somewhere in between.

The "cop" beat is part misnomer. There's the expected crime and law-enforcement reporting, but it's also a bigger tent covering fires, accidents and miscellaneous brainlessness from the consequence-impaired fringe.

People outside the business who heard what McSwirley did for a living always asked the same question: "Ever seen a dead body?"

And they were always disappointed. McSwirley was the exception that way. Three years on the beat and not a single stiff. The closest he'd gotten were the lumpy white sheets. What McSwirley *did* see was far worse. The people who always asked about the bodies wouldn't have been interested, which was fine, because McSwirley didn't want to talk about it.

The survivors.

You were required to interview them—or at least make them turn you down. And in journalism, time is the coin of the realm, so you had to ask as soon after the tragedy as possible, a cheese grater to raw emotions. It required equal parts psychiatrist, spiritual adviser and instant friend, but there was no training for the Grief Patrol.

Jeff fell into the deep end his first week on the job. Way out in the county. Young woman in labor. Family of six racing to the hospital. Logging truck. Took three coroner's wagons. McSwirley arrived as they closed the last door. All gone just like that. The trembling logger was still on the scene. McSwirley's legs became lead as he walked over.

Following week: Nursing-home staff didn't check bathwater before lowering an eighty-seven-year-old to her scalding fate. Two hours later McSwirley sat on a plastic-covered couch, surrounded by distraught relatives passing Kleenex. Then the hometown eighteen-year-old soldier who stepped on a land mine. The mother of five who timed her jump off the overpass with the Mack truck. The picked-on high-school student who immolated himself in the middle of the basketball court. Infants left in hot cars, pit-bull maulings, prom-night collisions, rave-club overdoses. And murders. Absolutely the worst. Especially children. After three years, they were too numerous to count, and McSwirley remembered every one. He thought of them each day and dreamed about them every night.

Jeff got an expected number of doors slammed in his face, but others sincerely wanted to talk. They believed a newspaper article meant loved ones hadn't lived and died without the world taking notice, even if the interest only resulted from a stray bullet, smelting accident or waterskiing in an unmarked channel at night on cocaine. They needed McSwirley as much as he needed them; it was an expensive emotional transaction on both sides of the ledger.

The previous cop reporter, Justin Weeks, was a cocky piece of work who had perfected the technique of being run off property. He was yanked from the beat following enough screaming complaints to the newspaper's switchboard. After that, McSwirley was unexpected fresh air. Not only were there no gripes, but the paper actually began receiving *positive* calls. Half thanked them for genuine concern. The rest wanted to know if Jeff was all right.

The answer was no.

"I'd like another beat, please."

"Sorry."

"But I don't like this one."

"It's your strength."

"I didn't get into journalism for this."

"Who did?"

Jeff's best ally was his immediate supervisor, the metro editor, Thomasino Guzmaniczheck. Or, as colleagues generally preferred, Metro Tom.

Tom was old-school newspaper and old-school neighbor. He didn't pull journalistic punches, but he also didn't sell out friends. Which meant he didn't fit in at *Tampa Bay Today*.

Metro Tom came to Tampa via a stint on an east-coast paper as State Editor Tom, where he was fired for refusing to fire someone. True story. One of his hardest-working reporters married an editor at a competing paper, and management couldn't have scoops leaking across the pillows. They told Tom to fudge the next performance report and send her packing. Tom refused. So they fudged Tom's performance report.

And that's how he became Metro Tom, supervising a pod of greenhorns, including his favorite. Tom hid a personal affinity for Jeff, because he believed it would undermine the toughening up that the young reporter obviously needed. Behind the scenes, however, the editor was steadfastly protective of McSwirley. He felt the cop beat was something Jeff had needed at one time, just as Jeff now needed a change. Each week McSwirley dutifully filed his standing transfer request, which Tom promptly signed and personally delivered. "Anything for Jeff yet?" "Not yet."

They were now at 157 weeks and counting, so a transfer was the last thing on Jeff's mind when they summoned him to the budget meeting.

"You wanted to see me?"

"Jeff, have a seat," said Max.

McSwirley grabbed the empty chair. He looked around for his editor. "Where's Tom?"

"Doing something. Listen, how'd you like to get off the cop beat?"

"Really? Yes! When?"

"I'm speaking conceptually," said Max. "But we have an idea that could go a long way in that direction."

"Anything," said Jeff.

"That's the spirit," said Max. "We'd like you to do an exclusive interview. Could be your biggest yet."

"Who?"

Mahoney removed a toothpick from his mouth. "We're inserting a coded message in the paper. Arrange contact."

Jeff turned back toward the head of the table. "I . . . don't follow."

"Your pen pal," said Max. "We might be talking Pulitzer."

"You want me to interview a serial killer?"

"We're hoping you can submit written questions," said Max. "But he may insist on meeting face-to-face. What do you say?"

ST. AUGUSTINE

The current hurricane season seemed to have a thing for bays. Cristobal blew straight up the mouth of the Matanzas. He was a real mover. Five to ten miles an hour's average; fifteen's fast. This one briefly flirted with twenty-five. If you're on the right side of the counterclockwise swirl, add it to sustained wind and you bump up a category. That's where most of the town was.

The coastline correspondents didn't even go through the motions. After a few minutes in the strike zone, they got religion and booked. The storm raked Flagler College, pummeled Ripley's and pounded the Alligator Farm. The Museum of American Tragedy had recently closed down, or it would have been tragic.

The only remaining citadels of confidence were the lighthouse and Castillo de San Marcos. The sixteenth-century masonry fort had been Serge's original choice to ride out the hurricane, but the girl from the Fountain of Youth developed a sudden personal rule against catacomb sex.

"But catacomb sex is the best!" said Serge.

Lost cause. That was ten hours ago. The wind howled around the quiet, dark motel room. Coleman stared down at the motionless body on the bed. "Is she okay?"

The girl stirred with a loud snore.

"Just pooped," said Serge. "That was the plan. I poured it on at the end because I've got a lot on my mind and didn't want to chat afterward."

The room flickered, then stayed bright.

"Power's back!" yelled Coleman. "TV! We're going to live!" Coleman sat at the edge of the bed with the remote and clicked the set on. A research ship lowered a large egg into the sea. "What's this show?"

Serge sat next to him. "Looks like the end of *The Mogul*." Neville Gladstone waved farewell and went searching for the coelacanth off Madagascar in a bathyscaphe.

The next program started, and Coleman raised the remote.

"Stop," said Serge. "I want to watch this."

"*Welcome to a special edition of* Hard Fire. *I'm your host, Colin Becket. . . .*"

"Don't tell me," said Coleman. "Another of your boring political shows?"

"No, *Meet the Press* is a boring political show. This is a runaway news truck."

"*. . . Tonight we have a special guest, the Reverend Artamus Twill, leading candidate in the Thirteenth Congressional District on the Gulf Coast of Florida. . . .*"

"Always a pleasure, Colin."

Coleman got an odd look. "Do you hear a banging sound?"

"I hate this show already!" said Serge.

"Want me to change it?"

"No! . . . I can't believe this guy's going to be one of our next congressmen."

"How can you be so sure?"

"Reverend, what do you think your opponent has against God?"

"I'm praying for him."

Serge hung his head.

Coleman looked around. "I'm definitely hearing a banging sound."

". . . To what do you attribute your tremendous groundswell of support?"

"It's a grassroots response to the pro-death lobby attacking my faith with anti-family smear tactics. This country won't stand for that kind of meaningless labeling."

Serge punched the air in anger. "I can't believe this shit still works!"

Bang, bang, bang. Coleman began walking around the room. "You don't hear that?"

Serge was on his feet now. "The worst of it is that this guy has no experience whatsoever. All he's ever done is write a bunch of books for the Divide America industry and compulsively gamble away the royalties."

"In case our viewers don't know it, you have quite a bit of experience, writing such bestsellers as My Courageous Journey *followed by* A Virtuous Life: My Journey Continues *and your latest,* How Other People Should Behave. . . ."

"The ones I really blame are journalists . . ." said Serge.

Coleman twisted his neck. "Where *is* that sound coming from?"

". . . The media lets these yahoos hijack the language so that intolerance and bullying are now 'values issues.' "

"... I understand you're polling quite high on values issues."

"America wants someone who will stand up to the radical homosexual agenda."

"Which brings us to our next guest, speaking in opposition ..."

"All right, finally we get our say," said Serge. "Usually our side self-destructs because we can't play the word game as well. But this Twill asshole is so completely mean and wrong, there's no way we can lose in the court of public opinion."

"... In rebuttal to the same-sex-marriage ban, we welcome Graham Espy, regional field coordinator, Fear the Queer Action League. . . ."

Serge began banging his forehead on top of the TV. "No! No! No! . . ."

Bang, bang, bang.

Serge stopped banging his head. "Do you hear that banging sound?"

"That's what I've been trying to tell you."

"Sounds like it's coming from over there." They turned and looked at the closed bathroom door. The sound got louder.

"Whoops," said Serge. "How could I have forgotten?"

"Can't believe he stayed out this long."

"I conked him pretty hard." Serge opened a suitcase, removing scissors and rolls of duct tape.

"They won't be able to call me a copycat this time."

"What are you going to do?"

"My comeback special." Serge went to the corner and dragged a two-hundred-gallon boat cooler across the carpet. He opened the lid. "Five bags of ice left. Perfect."

Thirty minutes later a bound and gagged price gouger was crammed into the bottom of the insulated chest. "I knew he'd fit the second I saw this thing in the pickup. Coleman, ice."

Coleman handed him a bag. Serge ripped it open and poured cubes in an even distribution on top of the hostage. "Can you believe your luck? It's another Free Ice Day!"

Serge dumped the remaining four bags, then knelt next to the cooler. "All right, here's what's going to happen. . . ." He cleared a little hole in the ice and whispered. Cubes began popping into the air from panicked thrashing. Muffled cries were silenced by the closing lid. Serge then wrapped the cooler innumerable times with the tape. He stood and rubbed his palms impishly. "Now it's in the hands of science." He grabbed a towel and began wiping down the room for prints.

"That's your comeback?" said Coleman. "You're going to freeze him to death?"

"Please," said Serge. "A first-grader could think of that."

CHAPTER FIFTEEN

LANDFALL PLUS SEVEN

The storm was gone. Havoc remained. Young eyes fluttered open in an economy motel room near St. Augustine. A head of matted blond hair rose and looked around.

"Serge? . . . Coleman? . . ."

She checked the closet and bathroom, then the parking lot. The H2 was gone. "That bastard!" She returned to the room. "What's this?"

The two-hundred-gallon cooler looked familiar, but where'd all the duct tape come from? She placed a hand on the lid. That's odd—warm to the touch. She peeled up the end of a gray strip and began unwrapping.

TAMPA BAY TODAY

Top of the morning. A newsroom waking up.

Agent Mahoney had an appointment. He tapped fingers and checked his vintage Mickey Mouse watch. Ten minutes early. He looked around the empty conference table. Nobody but the tour group. More tapping. The washable map of Florida showed a downgraded hurricane passing through Gainesville. The Party Parrot walked by with a cup of coffee.

Editors began trickling in. Metro Tom arrived with two reporters, Jeff and Justin, who took seats on each side. More editors in a bunch. Stragglers filled out the remaining chairs. Finally the maximum editor. "Let's get started. . . . What's that?"

A blue-and-red cardboard envelope sat in the middle of the table.

"Jeff got another letter," said Mahoney.

"He FedExed it?"

"Must have been in a rush."

"What's it say?"

"He's upset we let the 'other' killer pick his own nickname, and because we stopped running bridge on the crossword page."

"What?"

"Gibberish," said Mahoney. "He's unraveling fast, so we have to move faster." The agent pulled several sheets of paper from his briefcase. "After our last meeting, I took the liberty of composing the secret message for Jeff to reestablish contact. You can insert it in tomorrow's classifieds. I made copies for each of you."

The agent passed them around the table . . .

> RIDING lawn mower, 72", good cond., low miles, 14.5 hp Briggs eng. $2,500 obo. If you're the killer, please write or call Jeff McSwirley at (813) 555-7392 for lunch or dinner. Not seeking commitment. I like walks on the beach and Turner Classic Movies. Pets OK.

Metro Tom fell back in his chair. "I don't even know where to begin. When Jeff first told me about this, I thought maybe you were playing some kind of joke on me."

Max handed his sheet to an assistant. "Get this in the next edition."

"No." Metro Tom extended a protective arm across McSwirley's chest. "I'm not going to let you put one of my reporters in that kind of jeopardy."

"I'm sorry to hear you don't like your job," said the maximum editor.

Justin piped up. "I'll do the interview."

"Let him do it," said McSwirley.

Tom and Max in harmony: "No!"

"We'll have a SWAT team standing by," said Mahoney. "And I'll be using my ninja cloaking technique, never more than ten feet from Jeff."

"You've both lost your minds," said Metro Tom.

"Listen," said Max, "we're just as concerned for his safety as you are. So Agent Mahoney and I have devised a fail-safe backup plan to get him right out of there if anything starts to go wrong." He turned to Jeff. "First sign of trouble: Run."

"That's it?" said Tom.

"You want him not to run?"

"I don't want him to go at all!"

"He'll be wearing one of our bulletproof vests from the photography department," said Max. "Actually, bullet-*resistant*. We got a break on the price."

"You really don't get it," said Tom. "You have no idea what you're dealing with. I had Justin look into the background of this Serge. . . . Justin, tell them what you learned."

Justin beamed in the newfound spotlight and opened his notebook. "Incredible stuff. Goes back a decade. Serge A. Storms, actively sought as a 'person of interest' in at least a dozen homicides. . . ."

"At least," said Mahoney.

". . . Police have been close many times, but he always manages to escape. Meanwhile there've been sightings all over the state, from the Keys to Jacksonville. He ran a tour service in Miami, worked on the governor's campaign and delivered a commencement address at USF." Justin looked up. "Apparently they didn't do the proper résumé check."

"But with all that visibility, how is it possible he hasn't been caught?" asked Max. "The odds must be incredible."

Mahoney took a swig of mud coffee. "He beats the odds by being so crazy he doesn't even know there *are* odds. At any given moment, one out of five stupid criminals is still at large by sheer luck. And Serge isn't stupid. He usually slips away in plain sight, camouflaged with utter confidence. Remember the ray-gun fight in *Star Wars* when R2-D2 and C-3PO stroll unscratched across the spaceship's hallway through intense crossfire? That's Serge, except he's the one with the guns."

"You see now?" said Tom. "Is that what you want to send one of your reporters up against?"

"We're all aware of the hazards in this business," said Max. "Everything is done to minimize physical risk, but we also have to weigh the other side."

"What other side?"

"Sweeps week."

A cell phone rang. The theme from *Dragnet*.

"That's mine." Mahoney reached into his pocket. "Hello? . . . What! . . . Where did this happen? . . . I'm on my way right now."

CHAPTER SIXTEEN

ST. AUGUSTINE

Serge cradled a hard black sphere the size of a grapefruit. He shook it vigorously. Liquid sloshed inside. He turned it over and held it to his face. He didn't like what he saw. He began shaking it again. He turned it over again. More disappointment.

"Serge," said Coleman, "why'd you buy an Eight Ball?"

"My religious journey. I now have eternal faith in its power." He closed his eyes and shook it again. "Almighty Eight Ball, can you put me in touch with the one true living God? I have some suggestions." He stopped shaking and turned it over: *Try again later.*

"What happened?" asked Coleman.

"Busy signal."

Coleman looked around the interior of the tiny, dark booth. "Serge?"

"What?"—shaking the ball.

"Why'd we come to confession?"

"Religious journeys begin at your roots, and I was raised Catholic." He turned the black orb over again. "I'm hedging my bets in case this Eight Ball business is as stupid as I'm starting to suspect."

"But you just said you had eternal faith."

"You have to say that in every religion even if you're not sure. It's like a job interview. 'I promise I'll work hard'—but who knows? Both sides understand that."

"What *I* don't understand is how you can just pop back into confession. You haven't been Catholic for years."

"You never stop being Catholic. It's like the Mafia or Amway. And when you finally return, the first place you're *supposed* to go is confession."

Coleman shifted his weight. "This is starting to hurt. Why do we have to kneel so long?"

"It's part of the torture package, like Guantanamo, so they get a full confession."

Coleman fidgeted again. "How much longer?"

"Hang in there." Serge had his ear to the wall. "The guy on the side's got a long list, but I think he's almost done. . . . Jesus, I can't believe some of the shit I'm hearing."

Coleman put his own ear to the wall. "What's 'bestiality'?"

"Shhhh! Here's the sentencing. . . . What! Ten Hail Marys? That's an outrage!"

"It is?"

"Quiet," said Serge. "I think he's coming."

THE OTHER SIDE OF TOWN

A local 911 operator had fielded the hysterical call from an economy motel. "Slow down. I can't understand you. . . ."

Six minutes later, the room was crawling with police. A young girl sat on the curb outside, clutching herself tightly. A cop filled out a report.

She wiped her nose. "Fountain of Youth."

"No, not where you work," said the officer. "Your name."

Inside: photo flashes, evidence bags, disgust. Someone took scrapings from a scorch mark on the wall. Detectives sported large perspiration stains on the backs of dress shirts from leftover hurricane humidity. The homicide chief dabbed his forehead and stared down into the open cooler. "That poor girl's messed up for life."

A forensic tech came over. "Looks like they wiped down the room."

"Damn. No prints."

"I wouldn't say that just yet. They wiped the room, but they didn't wipe what they *wiped* it with." He looked toward the dresser.

"You can lift prints from a bath towel?"

"Long shot, but there's this new computer program that subtracts fabric patterns. I hit it with the light." He waved a hand-held violet fluorescent tube. "Something's there. I called for an epoxy vapor kit."

A man in a rumpled fedora entered the room and flashed a gold badge.

"Who the hell are you?"

The badge closed. "Agent Mahoney. Tallahassee." He walked to the cooler. "Well, well, if Serge isn't back to his old tricks."

"You know who did this?"

"I'd bet your pecker on it," said Mahoney. "Signature technique."

"We don't even have a cause of death yet, let alone technique."

"I already know the cause of death," said Mahoney.

"You barely looked at the victim."

"I knew *before* I looked at him," said Mahoney. "From the contents of this room."

"You're full of shit," said the detective in charge. "I got six veterans in here, and everyone's stumped."

"That's right," added another agent. "Nobody's ever seen a freezing victim look like that before. We're still waiting for the M.E. to take a blood sample."

Mahoney leaned down for closer inspection. "Going to be kind of difficult."

"Why do you say that?"

"Because he didn't freeze. He cooked." Mahoney stood back

up. "Hard to draw blood, but plenty of juices. You can carve him like a Thanksgiving turkey."

"You're wearing out your welcome," said the lead investigator. "Shoot straight or get the hell out of here."

Mahoney moved across the room. "Got to hand it to you, Serge. One of your masterpieces, regular *Mona Lisa*."

The detective was red-faced. "How did he do it?!"

Mahoney picked up a piece of brown plastic. "Know what this is?"

"MRE bag. From a military meal. National Guard's been giving them out."

"They're all over the room," said Mahoney. "Fifty or sixty."

"So they ate a lot. So what?"

Mahoney tossed the bag aside. "If I know Serge, he told the guy right before he closed the lid: 'Just wait for the ice to melt.' When you pull him out of there, you'll find dozens of activated chemical heaters at the bottom."

The detectives began buzzing. Mahoney leaned against the dresser. "Dang, it's hot in here." He wiped his face with a bath towel.

CONFESSION

Serge and Coleman heard a wooden panel slide shut on the far side of the priest's compartment, then another slide open in front of them. An ominous silhouette appeared on the thick cloth screen. "Yes, my son?"

"Okay, I think I remember, but you might have to feed me a line here and there." Serge made the sign of the cross. "Bless me, Father, for I have sinned. Yada-yada-yada. It's been thirty-three years since my last confession. Wait—thirty-*four*. I remember because you guys gave me fifty Hail Marys just for touching myself. And it was incidental contact, too. Remember when you were ten years old and you'd get a woody for no reason? I was in my bedroom putting the finishing touches on a one-thirty-second-scale Spitfire, when all of a sudden: 'Hello! Look who's making a guest appearance. I better check it out.' But Father Cabrini wouldn't listen and threw the book at me—we called him the Hanging Priest. I said enough of this nonsense. That was thirty-four years ago. Then, later on, I read where Father Cabrini got arrested! Turns out the whole time we're getting maximum penance, he's playing 'beat the bishop' with Jimmy O'Toole—"

"Son!"

"Oh, sorry. That slang's probably offensive in here. Heard it from George Carlin—he busts me up! I'll use 'spank the monkey' or 'burnishing the German helmet.' Fair enough? I just turned forty-four, so I thought I'd give this outfit another chance. But I'm beginning to get the picture that little has changed. Father Cabrini gave me fifty Hail Marys—and that was in 1973 Hail Marys. Then you let that last guy off with ten. He diddled a cocker spaniel, for heaven's sake!"

"You were listening?"

"Not on purpose. He was talking pretty loud. I could almost hear him without putting my ear to the wall. I'll bet he's a big donor or maybe top dog at the Knights of Columbus."

"The sanctity of the confessional! That's a mortal sin!"

"There we go again. Mortal sin, the whole fear factor. That's what my mom said when she caught me in the bedroom. Dragged my ass right out to the car and off to confession. Told me if I died with a mortal sin on my soul, it's straight to hell, and I'd better pray she didn't get in an accident before we got to the church. I'm screaming the whole way over, 'Mom, you're driving too fast!' 'Mom, watch out for that bus!' . . ."

Coleman tugged Serge's shirt. "This is creeping me out."

"I told you not to get high first."

"Who's that?" asked the priest.

"Just Coleman."

A beer can popped. "Hey, Padre."

"Someone else is in there with you?" asked the silhouette.

"It's okay. Anything you can say in front of me, you can say in front of him."

"This is completely inappropriate!"

"I know he's not Catholic. I've been trying to convert him, but he's heard the rumors. Thought I'd let him experience it first-hand."

"No, I mean there's only supposed to be one person in the confessional at a time."

"Let's be honest," said Serge. "Membership isn't going anywhere but south. You want to fill those collection plates or not?"

"I'll have to ask you to leave the confessional."

"You can't do that."

The silhouette stood up. "It's obvious you're not here for the sacrament."

"Yes I am. You didn't let me get to my sins yet. I might have killed this guy the other day. He was still alive when I left him in that cooler, but I'm pretty sure . . ."

The silhouette sat back down. He was a good priest. Sheep return in many ways. A troubled soul could account for the shaky start. "My son, have you taken life?"

"Hate to admit it, but yeah." Serge whistled. "And how!"

"Son, are you truly sorry for these horrible acts?"

It was quiet.

"Son?"

"I'm thinking."

"You must be sorry, or you wouldn't have come back to the church."

"How about, 'I'm sorry he was a real jerk'?"

"You must feel at least some remorse?"

"I'm not sure. Hold on. . . ." Serge turned the Eight Ball over. "Sorry, Father. Put me down for a 'probably not.'"

"But you won't be absolved. You'll go to hell."

Another pause. "The Eight Ball begs to differ."

"Eight ball?"

"Kids' toy. Very big at birthday parties. Everyone's all excited asking it lots of questions for five minutes until they lose interest and take suction cups off darts for eye injuries."

"You're putting your faith in a toy?"

Serge theatrically waved an arm in the air. "Like that's any more far-fetched than invisible angels flying around preventing mishaps. No offense, Father, but the malarkey factor has been pushing me away ever since the nuns."

"You were taught by nuns?"

"Yeah, I seem to remember a little teaching going on between all the whippings. It's like they singled me out for persecution."

"Why do you think that?"

"Because nuns are *messed up*. Horribly sadistic to little kids and way too sensitive about the nicknames. My first-grade teacher *really* hated the one I gave her."

"Which was?"

"Cunt."

"What!"

"Beat me all the time for no reason." Serge suddenly became quiet and leaned forward with a different voice. "Say, you're not going to tell anyone about the dead guy. I mean, just because I ain't sorry. Not making any threats, but I can't be around all the time to stop every accident from happening, if you get my meaning. . . ."

The priest began stuttering. He quickly got up and opened his door.

Serge opened his own door. They faced each other behind the last pew. The priest was ashen.

"Just joshin' you. I'd never hurt a man of the cloth." Serge poked him in the stomach with the Eight Ball. "But don't forget the sanctity of the confessional. You'll go to hell."

The priest ran for the rectory, and Serge and Coleman walked out the back door into the sunshine.

CHAPTER SEVENTEEN

JUSTIN WEEKS

Public-opinion polls consistently tout Walter Cronkite as the most trusted man in written history. Yet, curiously, those same polls place journalists, as a class, down with politicians, attorneys, used-car salesmen and ex-cons.

The media has no one to blame but themselves. They're the media, after all. They're in the image business. It's like a chef dying from food poisoning.

Still, the burden is largely undeserved among rank-and-file beat reporters. They fulfill an indispensable civic function, casting light where the rich and powerful would prefer to transact by slippery feel. In a fair world, these journalists would be rewarded with parades or one of the minor holidays where everything stays open.

It was occasional bad apples, if you will, that made the going rough for everyone else. Pollsters weren't altogether wrong about several questionable individuals at Gladstone Media. In one particular case, they were right on the money.

Journalists have many reasons to be called to the profession. Justin Weeks had his. He liked to inflict misery. He *truly* liked it.

Weeks began his journalistic career as a small child in his backyard. Interviewing lizards and frogs and bugs. *No comment? I set you on fire!*

As he moved through grade school, Justin embraced the roles of hall monitor, crossing guard and fascist. But it wasn't until joining the high-school paper that he fully appreciated the joy of provoking from cowardly distance. This continued, more or less, through college and his early professional years bouncing around a series of entry-level community newspapers in the Florida Panhandle and south Georgia. The "community" part meant small town, which meant positive stories about the paper's biggest advertisers. To Weeks, however, it wasn't a real story unless there were fire-code violations, civil unrest, sexual perversion and hopefully all three. Unfortunately for Justin, small town also meant small-town power structure. Mayors and sheriffs and newspaper publishers getting drunk together. Weeks made the healthy decision to move on.

He headed south and got his big break. Three, in fact. The first two were with the *Tampa Tribune* and the *St. Petersburg Times*, very reputable papers on constant alert for the Justins of the profession. Their early-detection radar sounded both times; he was summarily fired for absence of accuracy and presence of malice. Justin took a short drive across town to Gladstone Tower, where the same stories that had gotten him dismissed prompted the hiring editor to remark, "Nice clips."

A news style that had no place in the business found a home at "fair, unbalanced journalism." The paper needed an attack dog, and they got a pit bull. All the biggest stories were his for the picking. Justin's smirking face was featured prominently in TV ads and Florida Cable News special reports. He was getting famous, and he was getting laid. It wasn't enough.

Weeks had to lord it over the rest of the newsroom. For important phone interviews, Justin not only used his loudest voice but actually stood on top of his desk. He harassed the female reporters and demeaned the males. But his best was saved for the path of least resistance. All day long humiliating McSwirley. Joke after belittling joke. Jeff just smiled and went back to work.

Nobody approved of what Justin was doing, but an interesting psychology started to develop. Many subconsciously began resenting *McSwirley*. His submission made them uncomfortable about something in themselves. Why didn't he stand up for himself?

One person, however, finally had heard enough. Metro Tom yanked Justin into a private office. Literally, by the arm.

"Leave McSwirley alone!"

"Fuck off, old man!"

"What's he ever done to you?"

"I can have your job." Weeks stormed out and slammed the door.

The editor steamed in silence. He knew that Justin was right. There was rank, and there was revenue. Weeks was untouchable.

Then two things happened. First the airport.

A Florida Cable News cameraman scrambled through the terminal to keep up with Justin, who raced past the grief counselors. "What's your reaction to the plane crash?"

"Plane crash?"

An avalanche of complaints poured in. Phones rang nonstop. Even a viewing public responsible for the rise of tabloid TV couldn't stomach this. Gladstone Media wasn't sorry, but they said so anyway. They lowered Justin's profile. They told him it was temporary.

Coincidentally, McSwirley picked this serendipitous time to nail his first big interview. Then another. And another. He hit his stride like Secretariat. Cards and letters poured in. Baked goods from a concerned public. Central Florida had a new media darling. More and more exclusive interviews, leading up to the seemingly impossible: a living room full of plane-crash relatives, whom McSwirley persuaded to accept the career-rehabilitating, on-air apology from Justin.

Ratings blew through the proverbial roof.

Gladstone Media was beside itself. The suits called both reporters into a penthouse conference room for the big announcement. From now on, they were a team, good cop, bad cop. Weeks was clearly the better-looking, in a rugged way, almost to Hollywood standards. But McSwirley wasn't to be written off. He countered with what they call intangibles. It was like pairing Russell Crowe with Tobey McGuire.

Weeks was an ass, but no dumb-ass. He smiled and shook McSwirley's hand. "Sorry about the stuff I said before. Looking forward to working with you."

"Thanks," said McSwirley. "Really appreciate it."

Weeks smiled again. *I'm going to fuck you so bad.*

He was still thinking that as he sat next to Jeff in the budget meeting. The next letter had just arrived, the one responding to the classified ad setting up a meeting with the serial killer. Weeks stared down at the evidence bag. *How can I screw Jeff with this?* He thought some more. An energy-saving lightbulb went on over his head.

"It's all set," said the maximum editor. "Midnight. Hillsborough River State Park."

"Tactical team and sharpshooters standing by," said Mahoney.

"He's not going," said Metro Tom.

"I'll go," said Justin.

"Shut up," said Tom.

"Jeff," said the maximum editor, "we wouldn't ask if we didn't think this was perfectly safe. But it's your call. Could get you off the cop beat. Will you do it?"

"Don't do it," said Tom.

"I'll . . . do it," said McSwirley.

"That's my boy," said Max. "Now, just a few ground rules. You can promise him anonymity, but under no circumstances do we pay for an interview. Okay, we do, but if he asks, try getting him down from his original price. And make sure you bring your camcorder."

"Except he's not going," said Tom. "I don't care if you intimidated him into it—"

A news clerk approached the table and handed Tom a slip of paper. "Your three o'clock job interview. Already in your office."

The editor checked his watch. "Shoot, we ran long." He looked up. "I have to take this. I'll be right back. . . . Jeff, no matter what they say, don't go anywhere without talking to me first."

Serge and Coleman sat side by side in a pair of chairs. The chairs faced a desk. The puzzled man on the other side read a single sheet of paper.

The metro editor took off his glasses and set the page down. "You do realize that job interviews are usually one-on-one."

"Usually," said Serge. "But Coleman and I are a team. Like Evans and Novak. I know people expect to start at the bottom, which is why the competition is most crowded down there. That's why we're shooting straight for the top! Our groundbreaking column demands your attention and begs for syndication. It's all things to all people: poignant, humorous, informative, now! Give us ten minutes, we give you Tampa Bay! I'll hit the road like Charles Kuralt, scavenging for strangeness and insider tips: The best time to view the Mennonite colony in Sarasota is at dusk when the air's cooler and they wander out like miniature deer in the Keys. Did you know Sarasota High School actually has a circus team? Trapeze and everything, because John Ringling used to live there. I don't know how they find other schools to compete against; must be national champs every year. Got a million like that trapped in my head and banging to get out." Serge handed a photo across the desk. "This is our twin mug shot until you can take one of your own. Just crop those flames in the background. It wasn't my fault." Serge sat back and grinned.

Metro Tom hid his thoughts: How'd these guys get past security? He picked up the sheet of paper again. "This résumé just lists hobbies—and some other stuff that I'm guessing are hobbies. Photography, music, urban archaeology, historical loitering, guerilla raconteur, oil painting in the third person, nonmaterialist-for-hire . . ."

"I'm very well rounded."

"But where have you worked?"

"Self-employed. I help people. Unless you're part of the problem. Then you won't like it."

"Yes, but do you have any actual journalism experience?"

"Absolutely none! That's my strongest point: I'm completely free of bias."

"Our classified ad said at least three years' experience on a daily. Didn't you read it?"

"I read between the lines," said Serge. "You don't want lemmings. You need people with practical life experience. Have I got some stories to tell you!"

"Look, I don't want to waste your time—"

"And I don't want to waste yours!" Serge shot back. "So what do you say? Let's get started! I can take the desk right over there."

"That's our human-interest columnist."

"He's through," said Serge. "Have you read his stuff lately? Sheesh! Seventeen inches on following his dog around the house. My psychiatrist says I need structure."

"You're under psychiatric care?"

"Don't worry. I've stopped taking my medication. She objects, of course, but I'll need a clear head to pound out the kind of timely insight your readers demand and deserve!"

The editor sniffed the air. "Do I smell beer?"

Serge pointed sideways with his thumb. "Coleman's power lunch. I'll be carrying him at first, until he completes your chemical-dependency program. I hear you have great insurance." Serge leaned forward and winked. "It's not a preexisting condition if they don't know about it, right?"

Coleman reached for the desk. "Are you going to finish that Danish?"

Serge slapped his hand. "The man might get hungry later. He's very important."

"I'm hungry now."

"Don't make me . . . !" He turned to the editor. "Sorry. He always does this in front of company." Serge stretched out his right leg and struggled to retrieve something from the bottom of his hip pocket. He handed the editor small, thick squares of paper the size of matchbooks.

"What are these?"

"My first two columns."

The editor began unfolding a sheet of paper that had been creased eight times. Tiny handwriting and coffee stains filled the page.

"Told you I know this business," said Serge. "Applicants who want to be taken seriously come prepared with professional writing samples."

"This looks . . . interesting." The editor set it down. He pressed a secret button under his desk.

"You didn't have time to get past the first sentence," said Serge. "I worked hard on those things. At least read the first one. It's a transcript from a meeting I secretly recorded. You can either run it in the religion section or your annual income-tax supplement."

The editor smiled awkwardly and began reading:

> God Talk with Serge
> Today, I'd like to chat about the people pushing Creationism. I know what you're thinking: They must be fucking idiots! That's what I thought, too, and boy was I wrong! Honest mistake. At first glance, teaching Creationism in science class makes as much sense as demanding that the school band include air guitar. Then the brilliance of it hit me like a baseball bat. You see,

they're not really serious. It's all a super-intellectual satire on atheists. Because who's dumber than atheists? (Although they made great Cold War foes. Remember the comfort of having an enemy with a theological self-interest *not* to blow themselves up?) Anyhoo, atheists are so dumb they say, "I believe in evolution instead of God." So Creationist jokesters say, "I believe in God instead of evolution." Get it? See how they turned the whole thing on its head to mock stupidity? It never dawned on me until I boiled their argument down to its essence: "We worship an omnipotent deity whose technique in creating the universe is limited to the level of my intelligence." Even accounting for blunt trauma, no brain performs that badly. That's how I realized it was all a put-on— that's when I saw the genius! Because what thinking person can look out upon the infinite palette of churning life and not be blown away? I actually have to force myself to *stop* marveling at God's work, or else I'm endlessly wandering fields, running fingers through blades of grass and tripping on the interrelationships all around: oak trees, flocks of crows, raccoons, yeast, telemarketers, and then it's weeks later and I'm waking up in another state without identification. And at least once each winter I catch a cold and lose whole months contemplating viruses. Aren't they ridiculous? So small, but a bitch. If there's no receptive host organism, they just mutate and change their own DNA, like evolution's drive-through window. Fuck *that* recombination! So before each flu season, I spend a few days in meditation changing *my* DNA. Why should the doctors get rich? Then I blinked and it was the new millennium, yet another of God's wonders: time! One minute you're at the prom, the next you haven't filed tax returns for ten years. And that's why I'm sitting in your office today, just a little nervous, because working for the IRS like you do, I'm sure you've heard every bat-shit excuse in the book. Normally ten years would be way out of line. Except in my case I've been booked solid working on Big Truths. But if I can comprehend it, it can't be the answer, because God's infinite. In other words, I have to comprehend something I can't comprehend. Am I getting through? Stop writing in my folder and listen! Okay, let's try this: About ten years ago, I started my own church, which I don't need to point out is tax-deductible. It's based upon intellectual curiosity and vigorous self-questioning—so much so, in fact, that you're supposed to think it's the stupidest religion in the world. It seems to be working too well, because I'm still the only member, and Coleman won't let me baptize him. Despite his aggressive lifestyle of constant impairment, he's a slippery fuck when you try dunking his head in the sink. Just keeps splashing and screaming crazy talk, like, "Why are you trying to kill me?" I tried explaining that I only wanted to make sure he went to heaven, but, looking back, this apparently just reinforced his initial misconception, and then he broke off the faucet and water's gushing everywhere, which is how they found out the building's fuse box was out of date, and the owner drives up right after the fire engines and screams, "My apartments!" I pat him on the shoulder: "God's will." And that's why I haven't been able to file those returns. So what do you say about an extension?

Next Week: Pimp My Dogma

Tom set the page down and manufactured a smile. "Shows promise. How about I keep your résumé on file in case anything opens up?"

"That means, 'No, I'm going to throw it away as soon as I get these bozos out the door.'" Serge pumped his eyebrows. "See? I don't need experience to be a good journalist. I can spot bullshit over the horizon. We get the job?"

"I can't make a decision until I've interviewed all the applicants."

"Let you in on a little secret," said Serge. "We went to the *Times* and *Tribune* first. But don't think you were our last choice. More like saving the best. And they weren't nearly as polite. Actually, they threw us out. I learned there's a secret button they can press. . . ."

Four bulky security guards arrived in the doorway.

Serge looked back at the men, then the editor. "You must have a secret button, too. . . . Hey, let go of my arm! . . ."

The guards rushed them down to the ground floor and out the back of the building. They added a final, insulting shove because of unrelated personal issues.

Serge stumbled and caught his balance, but Coleman sprawled into shrubs framing the corporate sign. He got up and pulled sand spurs from his palms. "That could have gone better."

"I didn't realize how hard it was to become a syndicated columnist." Serge produced a scrap of paper from his pocket and crossed something off.

"What do we do now?"

"Work our way down my list." He tapped a spot on the page. "Next-best thing to being a syndicated columnist."

CHAPTER EIGHTEEN

TAMPA

Five minutes before midnight. McSwirley was drenched in the perspiration of dread. He had trouble commanding his legs to move down a dark, remote hiking trail in Hillsborough River State Park.

A nearby bush: "Jeff, it's me, Mahoney. I'm right here. I won't let anything happen to you."

Silent commandos in black uniforms and face paint filled the woods. Tactical rifles swept the perimeter with night-vision scopes.

Jeff continued walking like a child just learning to. Bushes rustled alongside.

"This doesn't make sense," said Jeff. "He has to know the police will be waiting."

"I told you he was getting sloppy," said Mahoney.

"Darn it," said Jeff.

"What is it? What's the matter?"

"My camcorder battery's almost dead. Better turn it off and save the last few minutes."

"Forget the camcorder," said Mahoney. "You need to stay on your toes. Serge may be getting sloppy, but he's still Serge."

McSwirley came to a trailhead. He checked the Xerox with

the killer's instructions: *right at fork, forty paces*. He began counting. "One, two, three . . ."

Bushes rustled. Night scopes panned. ". . . Thirty-eight, thirty-nine, forty." The reporter stopped and looked around, straining his eyes against the darkness. He suddenly jumped.

"What is it?" whispered Mahoney.

"My cell phone's vibrating." He pulled it from his pocket. "Hello? . . . Uh-huh. . . ."

Mahoney leaned his head toward a pinhole microphone on the shoulder of his camouflaged jumpsuit. "Condor's getting an incoming call. You picking up anything?"

A half mile away, two police technicians with headphones sat in a black, windowless van down one of the park's service roads. They glanced at each other. "Condor? What's this guy's problem?" One of them looked over at a green oscilloscope. It was flatlining. He picked up his own microphone. "Negative. 'Condor' must be in a dead spot."

"Roger. Tell the units something's going down."

"That's a big ten-four, Mongoose." The van guys cracked up.

"Jeff," whispered Mahoney. "What's happening?"

Jeff waved for him to shut up and held the phone closer. "Yes, I'm still listening. . . . But that's not the plan we agreed—" He stopped and returned the cell to his pocket.

The bushes: "What'd he say?"

"Changed locations," said Jeff. "Quarter mile from the next fork. Then he hung up."

"Trying to get surveillance to reveal themselves," said Mahoney. "Not as sloppy as I thought."

"I guess that's it." Jeff started walking.

"Where are you going?"

"Back."

"No, we're going to the new location," said Mahoney.

"You just said—"

"You'll still have me," said Mahoney. "And maybe a couple of the snipers if they can flank."

"But I'm scared."

"We don't have much time. Let's get moving." Mahoney led the way, quickly rustling unseen along the side of the trail.

Jeff suddenly realized he was alone. "Don't leave me!" He ran to catch up.

Twenty minutes later they were waiting at the new rendezvous point.

"Jeff," whispered Mahoney. "Everything okay?"

"I want to go home."

"Just a little longer."

The reporter checked his watch. "He's late."

"They always are," whispered Mahoney. "Serial killing makes you run behind schedule. Or he might already be here, watching us right now to make sure you came alone. Act like you're not whispering to me."

Precious time passed. An owl hooted. "He's not going to show—"

A twig snapped. Their eyes swung to the other side of the trail. A dark form appeared.

"Jeff! Behind you! Watch out!" Mahoney leaped from concealment, brandishing one of those heavy metal flashlights. He swung with all his strength.

The form thudded to the ground.

Jeff looked down at the motionless person sprawled across the trail. "Is he dead?"

"Just cold-cocked him." Mahoney bent over. "So Serge has taken to wearing disguises. Let's get this thing off your head and see what you look like now."

Mahoney pulled the top off the disguise. He jumped back. "It's not Serge!"

"What's *he* doing here?" said Jeff.

"You know him?"

Jeff nodded and got out his camcorder.

CHAPTER NINETEEN

THE NEXT MORNING

Serge and Coleman sat across from each other with sharpened number-two pencils. Serge raced through his employment application. He reached the end and signed boldly. Coleman was still at the top of his own form, tongue out the corner of his mouth in concentration, printing his name. He was almost able to stay inside the boxes. He held it up to Serge and smiled. "How's that?"

"Coleman, your name doesn't have a 3 in it."

"Where?" Coleman turned the page around. "The *e* goes the other way?"

"Most of the time. Why don't you let me finish it for you?"

Coleman slid the page across the table. "Thanks. That was too much pressure."

Serge licked the tip of his pencil and whipped through Coleman's form in record time. He got up and went looking for The Man.

Soon they were seated again, this time in a cramped office that doubled as some kind of storage. Actually, that seemed like the primary function. A man in a white, short-sleeved dress shirt and thin black tie sat behind a cluttered desk and reviewed their applications. He scratched his chin. "You sure you're in the right place?"

"Definitely," said Serge. "I was *this close* to being a syndicated columnist, but it's all who you know. I told my partner, Coleman, that this was the next-best thing. Does your insurance cover substance abuse?"

The man raised his eyes over the top of the forms.

"Not us," said Serge. He made quote marks in the air with his fingers. " 'Hypothetically.' We have a friend who's trying to straighten his life out, but he's not trying very hard. Can barely spell his name anymore."

"Who's that?" asked Coleman.

Serge elbowed him.

The man went back to the forms. "We would prefer he complete a program first."

"Of course," said Serge. "I understand perfectly. OSHA regulations. The last thing you need is some new guy ripped out of his skull and burning down the building with everyone inside, horrible screaming, pounding on illegally locked exit doors: *'For the love of God, let us out! The skin's flaking off my body!'* Who needs it?"

The man placed the applications in the middle of his desk and shrugged. "I still don't get it. You're the most overqualified applicants I've ever seen. Why would a pair of tenured college professors want to work here?"

"The economy," said Serge. "Everyone's taking a beating out there. It's summer recess, so we thought we'd pick up a little extra scratch. My psychiatrist says I need structure."

"You're under psychiatric care?"

"Everyone at the university is. It's a career move. You're supposed to talk about it at the cocktail parties. Ever work in academia?"

"No."

"Don't start. Total snake pit. Everything's publish or perish. And you should see what gets published! *Quasi Oligarchies and the Keynesian Feminist: Recipe for Orgasm or Armageddon?*"

"It's your decision." The man began marking up a time sheet. "You can start this afternoon if you'd like."

Serge jumped up. "You're kidding!"

"We can wait till tomorrow if you have plans."

"No," said Serge. "I mean, I was just imagining a more complex process. The convening of a collegial body, vigorous debate, behind-the-scenes deal making, a protracted series of secret ballots while we wait outside for the puff of white smoke."

"To work *here*?"

Serge ran around the desk and hugged the man off his feet. "Thank you! Thank you! Thank you!" He put the man down. "Coleman, did you hear that? We have jobs!"

"Poop."

They headed out of the room. Serge turned in the doorway. "We'll be the best employees this place has ever seen. You won't be sorry!"

The man smiled politely and went back to his time sheet. "The jury's still out."

NICK SHAVERS

"Everyone has a role to play."

That's what they said about the New Journalism, and it was never more true than in the case of Nick Shavers. He definitely had a role. It kept changing.

You haven't heard about Nick yet, at least by name, but he's been around.

Nick was a pioneer and, later, one of the first casualties of a virulent industry movement that swept to prominence in the late twentieth century. *Convergence.* Media conglomerates were already in an acquisition frenzy, so why not pool information? The problem began when they also started pooling *personnel:* TV stars writing stories, newspaper reporters appearing on air, and everyone scooping themselves on the Web.

At least that's how the mergers worked in concept. But after all the spot-welding was done, the results looked more like an abstract sculpture with no moving parts. The only apparent benefit was cost savings. It was judged a smashing success.

Nick Shavers was one of the most recognized faces in the central Florida market, where he'd enjoyed a long, steady run as midday anchor at Florida Cable News, just a heartbeat from the prime-time anchor slot that was the obvious career progression in his mind alone.

Nick's problem lay in a universally denied but well-known secret of television news: age discrimination. Shavers was the best argument in its favor. As they say, certain people grow old gracefully. But there was something a little too Vegas in the way Nick went about it. His rug was too dark, dentures too white, lapels too lounge-act. He came off like one of those guys in a late-night infomercial for a sports book offering the guaranteed LSU lock. In fact, that's how Nick moonlighted until the station told him it wasn't dignified for a future prime-time anchor.

"Okay," said Nick. "When do I get the position?"

"Be patient. Your time's coming."

He was patient. The station moved into Gladstone Tower. They came to see him.

"We've got good news."

"Prime time?"

"Better."

They explained what they had in mind. It didn't sound better. He'd leave the anchor desk and return to the street for live remotes. Then he'd race back to the building and write stories for *Tampa Bay Today*.

"But I don't know how to write."

"That's what editors are for." The station's director glanced around and lowered his voice like it was just between him and Nick. "You know, those anchors who are *convergence*-ready will be most attractive for advancement. This is the future."

"Why me?"

"You're the best candidate." Because the future was unknown, and Nick was expendable.

And that's how Nick ended up back on the beat. It wasn't so bad once he got there. People began recognizing him from TV. "Hey, Nick!" "What are you doing out here?" "Did you bang the boss's wife?" He nodded and waved cheerfully. "Thank you. Thank you very much. . . ." The recognition awakened something in Nick, and it showed in his work. He tackled every assignment with the same fresh zeal before rushing back to write articles that hit the copy desk like sacks of rotten fruit.

"What the hell's this?" asked an editor.

"My downtown-redevelopment story."

"It's unreadable."

"That's what they said *you* were here for."

" 'Irregardless' isn't a word."

"It isn't?"

The editors resigned themselves and rolled up sleeves. Nick watched over their shoulders as they unconvicted suspects and fixed names of major streets.

" 'Penultimate' doesn't mean the ultra-ultimate."

"It doesn't?"

The editors grumbled to higher-ups. It wasn't just Nick. It was all the TV personalities. Their stories took more time to fix than if the paper's regular reporters had written them in the first place. Then there was the big increase in corrections: "Please disregard Tuesday's 'Home Tips.' The described wood-stripping method releases a fatal vapor."

But it worked the other way, too. TV management was livid. Print reporters didn't translate to the small screen. Stiff, caught in headlights, out of their element, like watching a painfully obvious transvestite trying to pass. Except transvestites know how to dress. The countless reshoots and extra time in the editing room was killing them. "This can't go on!"

The suits responded that it would, indeed, go on. The respective editors were instructed to do whatever it took to make it work. So they hired more staff to handle the increased efficiency.

Corporate bean counters noticed the hemorrhaging bottom line and passed up the word. An urgent all-hands memo came back down: *Unconverge!*

But it was too late. The inbreeding had already fucked up the bloodlines. Some freakish journalism hillbillies were wandering around. Like Nick.

They pulled him off the street. But his old midday anchor chair now held a buxom Florida State intern. The TV station told the newspaper they could keep him.

"We don't want him."

"Neither do we."

"But he can't write."

"So make him an editor."

Nick was put in charge of seven reporters, who promptly ambushed the maximum editor.

"He's screwing up all our stories!"

"It can't be that bad."

"He's inserting errors! Did you see my story on the gulf's natural-gas reserves?"

"No."

"He changed all the references from 'gas' to 'gasoline.'"

The reporters were backed up by other editors until it was mutiny. The Gladstone people had no choice. They called in the management of WPPT-FM.

"But we don't want him."

"Everyone has a role to play."

"Does he know anything about radio?"

"He won't have to do radio. Marketing came up with an idea. Shirley, tell them. . . ."

The radio people didn't like the idea.

They called Shavers in for a talk.

He didn't like the idea.

"But, Nick, it's another promotion."

"No it's not."

"We'll still call it that. You get to keep your job."

The next morning Nick sat at his desk with nothing to do but ignore his colleagues' snickers. A news clerk walked by and un-capped a washable marker. Red dashes extended the tracking path of the latest hurricane. The WPPT-FM assignment editor handed Nick a piece of paper. "Thirty minutes. Mayor's press conference on emergency readiness."

Nick bitterly snatched the form. He stood and wiggled into the large, feathery parrot head.

CHAPTER TWENTY

TAMPA BAY TODAY

Listless editors assembled for the budget meeting in a silent culture of defeat.

Spread across the conference table were copies of the competition's morning editions. Front-page articles above the fold: Party Parrot hospitalized by state agent. Large photos of EMTs stretchering the colorful bird from a medevac helicopter at Tampa General. Tubes, wires, oxygen. The head was off, Nick's left eye large and purple and swollen shut.

"I told you something like this would happen!" said Tom. "Setting up that serial-killer meeting was the most ridiculous idea I'd ever heard."

"Calm down," said Max. "At least Jeff's safe."

"But Nick's in the hospital with brain lesions!" exclaimed the WPPT station director. "They say the extra padding in the parrot head is the only thing that saved his life!"

Tom stared daggers across the table. "What on earth were you doing sending the parrot in the first place?"

"Me?" the station director shouted back. "It's all your fault!"

"How's it my fault?"

"Your boy Justin told him to go. What the hell was *that* about?"

The metro editor's head snapped to the side. "Justin!"

"Me?"

"You told him to go!" said the radio director.

"What? I didn't— . . . I just casually mentioned the story Jeff was working on."

"That's not how Nick put it at the hospital before going into a coma," said the director. "You told him you were passing an assignment from me. Big publicity stunt."

"Must have been delirious," said Justin.

"Gentlemen!" exclaimed the maximum editor. "What's done is done. Let's move on."

"That's it?" said the metro editor. "You're not going to do anything?"

"Okay, new rule: From now on, no crashing serial-killer meetings by the Party Parrot."

"This is a madhouse," said Tom. "I'm pulling Jeff off this story."

"You'll do no such thing," said Max. "McSwirley's boosted circulation to an all-time high. And this Agent Mahoney is an absolute gold mine. Tell him we'll protect his anonymity no matter what. McSwirley will even go to jail if subpoenaed."

Someone with a visitor's badge approached the table. "Jeff McSwirley?"

"Right here."

The man handed him a stamped document. "You've been subpoenaed."

"I think I can fix this," said Mahoney. "I'll waive confidentiality and agree to go on the record."

"It's better if you remain confidential," said the maximum editor. "I'd like McSwirley to go to jail."

THAT AFTERNOON

"You son of a bitch!" Serge yelled down at the man in the driver's seat. "I'll kill you! You hear me? I'll rip your stinking head off!"

The frightened motorist threw his car in gear and hit the gas. Serge leaned out the drive-through window and splattered the car's trunk with a cheeseburger. "I'll seriously mess you up!"

Serge felt a tap on his shoulder. He turned around. "What do you mean I can't work at McDonald's anymore?"

THE NEXT DAY

Lunch-hour lines at all the cash registers.

"Welcome to Burger King. May I take your order?"

Next register: "Welcome to Burger King. May I take your order?"

Next register: "Fuck McDonald's. May I take your order?" Serge felt a tap on his shoulder and turned around. "What?"

Serge and Coleman walked along the side of the highway on fast-food row.

"That is embarrassing," said Serge. "I feel like Chuck Connors in *Branded*."

"What happens now?" asked Coleman.

"We've run out of options," said Serge. "The only thing left is selling our blood."

Serge and Coleman walked away from a beige, one-story building of no architectural design. Whiskered people milled around the entrance with brown paper bags.

"Unbelievable," said Serge. "You can't even sell your own blood."

Coleman cupped his hands over his mouth. "I don't smell alcohol."

"They didn't have to smell it," said Serge. "You crashed into that rolling cart!"

"Someone left it in my way. Then everybody grabbing me and screaming. Complete overreaction."

"Coleman, all those bags of blood ruptured on the floor."

"What do we do now?"

Serge dropped his frustrated weight onto the curb and stared across the street at a convenience store. "Let me think. . . ."

DANIELLE

CHAPTER TWENTY-ONE

GULF COAST PSYCHIATRIC CENTER

A female psychiatrist repeatedly clicked her pen open and closed, betraying a rare moment of impatience. "Serge?"

"What?"

"I think it would be better if you turn your chair around. It's hard talking to your back."

"But I like facing the clock."

"Serge . . ."

"If you insist." He got up and rotated the chair.

"Did you follow up on my suggestion to look for a job?"

"Of course. Me and Coleman both."

"How's it going?"

"Great." Serge picked at a leather armrest. "We interviewed with the *Times,* the *Tribune* and *Tampa Bay Today.*"

"Which one hired you?"

"Almost all of them. They promised to keep our résumés on file just before we were thrown out. It's such a clique."

The psychiatrist frowned. "So you haven't been hired at all?"

"Oh, no," said Serge. "We've been hired. Twice. McDonald's and Burger King."

"You're working *two* jobs?"

"No. I resigned from both over creative differences. What I'd really like is the job where that guy flies the ultralight each year, leading those endangered migrating cranes with the defective on-board navigation. I saw a picture of it in the newspaper: this giant V formation following the kite-plane like it's a big papa bird. That's the job for me, except I don't know where to apply. Do you?"

"No. Listen, I'd like to—"

"Nobody seems to know. But I'm starting to think something's fishy about that gig, because all the people I ask about it down-town just want to get away from me. Except the arrogant lawyer types with their Guccis and four-dollar coffees who think I'm panhandling and tell me to 'get a job,' like in that Bruce Hornsby song, and I say, 'Hey, fella, I got a job. It's called stalking.' I'm kidding, of course. Well, *half* kidding, because I can't tell you how mad that kind of cruelty makes me. But then it gets funny, because I start following them around and they get all jumpy, walking faster and faster, checking over their shoulders while I make wacky faces, until they finally toss the coffee in the street and run into a building where they don't even work. This is what I'm up against out there in the job market. It's enough to make you chuck it all and live under the overpass with the other guys, except that's a clique, too."

"So you've just given up?"

"When have you ever known me to give up?" said Serge. "That's when I read about these big patriotic corporations dedicated to a drug-free America. I said to myself, that's a worthwhile calling, because I see the damage every day. Coleman. Must be a million job openings for people to watch in the bathrooms so nobody cheats. I started phoning companies to inquire about their policies, and a consistent trend began to emerge. It's mainly hourly-wage employees that get tested. Never the board of directors and defi-nitely not shareholders. I asked if someone made a mistake. They said, What? I said, Since I'm sure they were sincere about the drug

scourge, there must be some kind of slip-up not including shareholders, but they all reacted like I was some kind of crackpot. I
said, If it's a manpower issue, I'd be happy to volunteer and even
spring for the paper cups at the annual stockholders' meeting, and
then the line usually went dead. Boy, did I feel disillusioned. Turns
out they weren't interested in principles at all. It was really about
insurance costs and the ability of wealth to make working America
dance like organ-grinder monkeys. We may not have a drug-free
country yet, but we're well on the way to a dignity-free country.
After I realized that, my next move became a no-brainer."

"Which was?"

"Be an employer. Coleman and I started our own consortium.
Then we hired ourselves. I began reading the *Wall Street Journal*
and watching Lou Dobbs to see how it worked. Naturally my first
move as CEO was to outsource both our jobs. As wage slaves, it
was either move to Indonesia or get fucked up the ass again. But
as majority owners of voting stock, we couldn't have been happier at how our company was keeping the boot down on labor."

"I know I'll regret asking," said the doctor, "but what exactly
does your company do?"

"Nothing at all. It's the Enron model. Can you tell me what
they did? No. Can you name one store where you could buy an
Enron gizmo? I think not." Serge crossed a leg and leaned back
smugly. "That's something else I learned from the financial shows.
If you're impatient and want to shoot straight to the top—that's
me in spades—make sure your company doesn't lift a finger. Fac-
tories, office buildings, customers: just slows you down."

"You're doing nothing?"

"And better than anyone else! Growth is off the chart. Another week, we do a little insider profit taking, dissolve the company and make off like bandits with the retirement accounts of
our former employees, which is also us, so the big gains cancel
out. I'm still trying to figure a way around that last part."

"You didn't fill your prescription, did you?"

"Bet you couldn't tell."

"I'm writing another one. And I'm sorry to say I'm more than a little disappointed by your lack of vigor seeking employment."

"Worry not. I've got something lined up."

"Make-believe jobs don't count."

"This isn't like the others. We landed real jobs."

"What is it?"

"Convenience stores. Delivery and pickup work. Actually, just pickups."

"When do you start?"

"Next week."

Gulf Coast Psychiatric Center was located far from the coast in an old part of central Tampa called Seminole Heights. For mystic reasons, certain parts of every city attract clusters of new-car dealerships. Lincoln-Mercury, Chrysler, BMW. All bunched together in a row, duking it out every Saturday morning with balloons, snapping pennants, blaring radio-station vans and the aroma of grilling hot dogs.

Not here. This was the string of "Bad credit? No problem" used-car lots with barbed wire and a clientele of recent graduates from the bus stop. Also, used-furniture stores. Used-appliance stores. One place just sold used doors. Another rented TVs and wrote bail bonds. They occupied the ruins of undesignated historic buildings falling down around the middle of a previously thriving garden district sliced open by the interstate. Lower-rung yuppies who couldn't afford the Hyde Park section of town were fixing up circa-1925 bungalows, with mixed results.

The neighborhood's only professionals were the good doctors practicing out of the psychiatric center, which rented the second floor of an art deco movie house on Florida Avenue. The main theater downstairs was now the meeting hall for a high-turnover lineup of inspirational seminars, multilevel-marketing scams, narcotics support groups and itinerant congregations featuring rousing choirs and bass guitars.

The rent was ridiculously low, and the psychiatrists could barely afford it. Theirs was a partnership of necessity: two men who'd just completed medical suspension for writing themselves OxyContin prescriptions, and a highly capable woman swimming her way to the financial surface after a marriage that was so bad she'd left him with everything just to get away.

The woman had previously worked at a state hospital in north Florida and treated Serge after an involuntarily commitment. That was years without contact. Now look what the cat dragged in.

"If you don't mind, I'd like to further explore your violent urges."

"Shoot."

"Can you give me an example of a time you controlled your temper?"

Silence.

"Did you hear me?"

"I'm thinking. . . . Okay, yeah, a decade ago. I drove up to Crystal River, one of those nature places I like to visit when the city's about to make me explode. I bop on out to the manatee-viewing platform. Absolutely beautiful. Those gentle giants rolling around without a care. I'm calmer than I've been in months. I take a few photos, hang out some more, grab a tuna sandwich from my fanny pack. Then these two L. L. Beaners arrive. One sets up a huge camera on a monopod like they use at NFL games; the other's carrying a high-end tape recorder and extends this big, furry microphone over the railing. I smile and say hello, but they ignore me. I figure no big deal and take a few more photos. Suddenly: '*Shhhhh!*' I turn. The guys are staring. 'Your camera's disturbing the manatees.' I say, 'What'? He says, 'We're *scientists*. These animals are easily stressed.' He looks at his pal and mumbles something, and they chuckle. And then, get this: *He* starts snapping photos! I say, 'Hold it, Dr. Dolittle, *you're* taking pictures.' He says, 'We're *scientists*. Our photos help them. It's the public that's disturbing the delicate balance.' Now all my pressure gauges are in the red zone."

"Like your face is getting now?"

"Exactly. I'm right back in the city. These fuckers are going on and on about preserving the natural harmony, but I'm onto their game. They really came down to that manatee-viewing platform to rumble."

"You said this was a story of restraint?"

"That's right. Incredible discipline. I was flashing on some pretty gruesome stuff. . . ." Serge began making a vigorous up-and-down pumping action with a fist. ". . . Fuckin' stabbing the motherfuckers over and over! . . ."

"Serge . . ."

His face deepened to purple, fist thrusting faster. ". . . More stabbing in the chest! . . . And down here in the balls! . . . And up here in the eyes! . . ."

"Serge!"

"What?"

"You paint quite a picture. I get it."

"I wanted to chop them into bite-size bits and feed them to the manatees."

"But you didn't?"

"No, they're herbivores. The manatees."

"I'm sure it was more than that. I'm proud of you. You made a choice."

"That's right. I left them unconscious on the viewing stand and went home and took ginseng."

"You attacked them?"

"That's the part that cracks me up. Kept talking about *we scientists*, knowing all about animal behavior. Whoops!"

"But that's not restraint."

"Did I stab them?"

"You need to find a way to control your anger."

Other side of the wall: "You need to find a way to release your anger."

"But I don't feel angry," said McSwirley.

"Something has to make you angry." The doctor reviewed his notes. "What about this other reporter, Justin Weeks?"

"He hates me."

"You're a likable guy."

"I try to be. But I've been landing some big stories. He used to be the star."

The doctor nodded. "You stole his show."

"Didn't mean to."

"Nothing to feel guilty about. Sounds like the guy's a prima donna."

"That's him."

"He has to make you angry."

"Not really."

"But you said he makes fun of you in front of the staff."

"Doesn't bother me," said Jeff.

"Not even a little bit?"

"No, but I take pride in my work, and he undermines my performance. I don't like that."

"And *that* makes you angry?"

"No, I just don't like it."

"Give me an example of how he undermines you."

"Well, we were sharing a byline on this one story. Police investigation, so there was beat overlap. He did most of the legwork, and I'm writing it up, because I write better. The next day the top editor gets a screaming phone call from the chief. The story bollixed the results of an internal-affairs case, practically convicted a lieutenant of lewd conduct. They call me and Justin in. I'm not worried, because that was Justin's half of the story. I tell them I just copied from his notes. Then Justin shows them his notes, and it's exactly the opposite of what was in the paper. I get blamed. Big correction runs. Had to apologize in person at the cop shop."

"What happened?"

"Thought I was losing my mind. I never make mistakes like that. The next day in the elevator, Justin shows me two pages of notes. Identical copies, except he changed that one fact and switched them on me. He sticks the pages back in his pocket and tells me to stay out of his fucking way."

"You should have told your superiors."

"I did, but who ever heard of such a preposterous thing? They didn't believe me. *I* didn't believe me, and I saw the notes."

"What happened?"

"Got in even more trouble. Said they were surprised at me, lying to shift blame out of professional jealousy."

"That made you pretty mad, didn't it?"

"No, just frustrated."

"But you must have been at least a little angry. Like in the elevator. Probably wanted to slug him."

"Not really."

"No anger at all?"

"I don't think so."

"That's not good."

"I thought keeping your temper was positive."

"Usually, but under the proper provocation it's perfectly normal to get angry. In fact, it's quite abnormal not to."

"You want me to lose my temper?"

"That's not what I'm saying. It isn't about acting out; it's about having the appropriate feelings for the circumstance. Then you deal with them in the proper way. If you let it bottle up inside, it can lead to problems down the road. You've probably written articles about people who one day just detonate."

"Many times."

"Neighbors always say how nice and quiet the guy was."

"You think I'll go postal?"

"No, that's extremely rare. The more common result is depression, which I'm beginning to see clear signs of."

"What should I do?"

"You belong to the Y?"

"No."

"Join. Swim laps. Work out on a punching bag, pretend it's Justin. Then leave it at the gym. Or do something else."

"But I don't feel depressed," said Jeff. "I don't think there's anything building up in me."

"You were in here crying for the first twenty-five dollars," said the doctor. "Something's going on."

"Something's going on," said the female doctor in the next room. "While telling me the story about those scientists, you were reliving the rage like it happened five minutes ago. You allow the transgressions of others to replay in endless, obsessive loops inside your head."

Serge looked over his shoulder at the clock. "Is that what's happening?"

"You have to cut the loop. Learn to block out the background noise of hostile thoughts."

"How do I do that?"

"Give them a name."

"How about 'bad monkey'?"

"If that works for you. The important thing is not to let the 'bad monkey,' as you put it, enter your Happy Place. I'd like to try an exercise."

"Go for it."

"Are you mad at anyone right now?"

"Yes."

"Who?"

"We don't have that kind of time."

"Pick one."

"Those scientists. They're still pissing me off."

"That's the loop I'm talking about. Here's what I want you to do. Are those thoughts of rage in your head right now?"

"Loud and clear."

"Take control. Tell them to get out of your Happy Place."

"What?"

"Just say it."

"Get out of my Happy Place?"

"Use the name."

"You've got to be kidding."

"I couldn't be more serious. Please say it."

"Get out of my Happy Place . . . bad monkey . . . ?"

"Louder! With feeling!"

"Get out of my Happy Place, you bad monkey!"

"There you go. You turned your aggression on the negative thoughts. How do you feel?"

"Stupid."

"Try it again. Even louder this time . . ."

Gulf Coast Psychiatric Center, Office Number Three.

Agent Mahoney lay on the sofa reading a dog-eared paperback from the fifties. The cover had a steno pad and a snub-nose. *When Secretaries Go Bad.*

The doctor sat across from him, slumped and nodding off from the pills Mahoney had given him to provide peaceful reading time.

The walls were a bit thin.

"Bad monkey! . . ."

Mahoney sat up quickly and looked around. It began to rain. He lay back down and opened his book.

Office Number Two.

The psychiatrist raced around setting out pails. "Sorry. Roof leaks. But the rent's so low." He hurried back to his seat. "Where were we?"

"Justin."

"That's right. You mentioned these things he does to you."

"That's just Justin."

"It's not Justin. It's you. I want to find something he did that actually made you mad, and then we'll try an exercise."

"But he's just obnoxious."

"There has to be something."

"Let me think. . . . Oh, yeah. How could I forget? I almost got mad."

"Almost?"

"Yeah, he really went over the line this one time. We have these tour groups that come through the office. Reporters rotate and give little goodwill speeches in the auditorium. You know, civil service of journalism, duty to the community. I hate public speaking as it is."

"Most people do. Common fear."

"The auditorium's packed to capacity. I'm already soaked with sweat. Then I get diarrhea. But there's no time. I'm up right after Justin. He's at the podium, and I'm holding my speech, trying to get in some last-second rehearsing. I start mouthing the words, and suddenly I can't believe what I'm hearing over the sound system." Jeff stopped and looked around. "Did you hear that?"

"What?"

"Like someone yelling 'bad monkey.' "

Office Number One.

"I don't want to play 'bad monkey' anymore," said Serge.

"But you were doing so well."

"I feel silly. Can we please talk about something else?"

"All right, but I want to return to this later." She reviewed notes from earlier sessions. "You mentioned last time an interest in religion. How's it going?"

"I went to confession."

Genuine surprise. "You're kidding."

"That part didn't go so well. In fact, I was just about to give up on the whole faith thing when I decided to research its history. Am I glad I did. I almost made a serious mistake. I love religion!"

"You do?"

"Unbelievably violent. I can't get enough. They practically have to kick me out of the library every night at closing time. Take murder. Most of the major brands have a regulation against it. But when it's cage-match time against another denomination, let the party begin! . . ."

"Serge . . ."

". . . The key is to yell how excellent God is when you're waxing dudes. That's the get-out-of-hell-free card. And the methods! I'd heard the terms—'drawn and quartered,' 'burned at the stake,' 'disemboweled'—but it was so long ago it's like bubonic plague: We can all laugh about it now. Then I saw the pictures in some of those library books. Holy shit! Well, not real pictures, because they didn't have photography back then, but apparently the easel used to be as ubiquitous as the camera phone, because all the painters just happened to be strolling by—'Dum-de-dum. What a rough night. Mental note: Never drink with Vikings and . . . Oh, my God! What are they doing to that guy over there? I have to get this on canvas!' . . ."

"Serge . . ."

". . . I saw this one painting of some poor schlub who was probably just sitting in the park feeding the birds one day and happened to look up—'Wait just a minute! Could it be that it's the *earth* that revolves around the *sun*?' But some devout people were standing nearby, and two minutes later the guy's strapped down: 'Leave my intestines in there!' 'Sorry, God is stupendous'—"

"Serge!"

"What?"

She turned to a fresh page on her notepad. "Maybe you need to take a break from religion."

"Why?"

"It seems to be having a violent influence on you."

"Isn't it supposed to?"

"So Justin's finishing up his speech," said the doctor. "What happened?"

"It's really embarrassing."

"Probably not anywhere near as bad as you think you remember. Please continue."

"Okay. He's still talking, and I'm looking at the copy of my own speech that I'd been rehearsing, and suddenly I realize Justin's saying the same words. He stole my presentation out of the computer system! Then he finishes, and on his way off the stage he hands me the speech: 'Want an extra copy, asshole?'"

"How'd you deal with it?"

"Threw up on the podium."

"Wow. That's embarrassing."

"And made in my pants." Jeff covered his face. "I felt so humiliated."

"And angry?"

"Just humiliated."

"That's not good. You're fighting yourself on the inside. You have to find a way to get the fight out."

"You want me to get in fights?"

"Absolutely not. But it's dangerous if you keep letting the internal pressure build. It's like not being able to perspire. There are actually people like that, weird condition."

"I can perspire."

The doctor looked at the clock. "Hour's up. Before we meet next week, I want you to go to the gym like we discussed. In the meantime I'll write you a prescription." He clicked a pen open.

"They make anger pills?"

"No. This is the good stuff." He handed Jeff a slip of paper.

McSwirley read the script. "Isn't this what Rush Limbaugh was taking?"

"Give me half and I'll comp you a session."

"But that's illegal."

"Don't worry. My code of ethics doesn't allow me to tell on you."

Across the hall a door opened. Serge thanked the doctor and bounced down the stairs in excellent spirits. He left the building and headed up the sidewalk full of hope.

"Hey, look everyone! It's a crazy guy coming out of the shrink's office!"

Serge turned and saw a gang of day laborers taking the day off. He pointed at his chest. "Me?"

"Yeah, you, Looney Tunes!" yelled the biggest. *"Bats in the belfry?"*

Serge took a quick skip-step like a cricket player, weight and velocity behind the first punch. "Bad monkey . . ." Wham, wham, wham. ". . . Out of my Happy Place!"

CHAPTER TWENTY-TWO

LANDFALL PLUS TWO

Coleman grabbed the dashboard. "Watch out!"

"I see it," Serge said evenly, cutting the wheel. *Scree-eeeeeeeech.*

Coleman bounced off the door panel and turned around quickly to look out the back window. "What the hell's a washing machine doing in the middle of the road?"

"What about a hurricane do you not understand?"

"The part where we were supposed to stay in the eye, like you promised."

"If you didn't smoke so much dope, you'd have better judgment and not listen to me. Even *I* don't know what I'm going to do next. Caveat emptor."

"What's that mean?"

"'Non-Latins bite.'" Serge executed more evasive maneuvers around mid-road debris, briefly two-wheeling. The H2 lurched back down onto its suspension.

"I can't take it anymore," said Coleman, trembling to light a joint.

"If you want to get out of this, you need to pay attention to the laptop. What's our position?"

Coleman's hand still shook as he pointed at the screen. "Looks like we're near the east side of the eye. Or is it the west?"

"Which is it?"

"I can't tell."

"Jesus, Coleman! Is it the *right* side?"

"My right or your right?"

"Just turn it toward me! . . . Ooooh. That's not good."

"Serge!"

"Might as well turn that thing off and save the battery."

"We're going to die! Look at that wind!"

"Forget the wind," said Serge. "There's all kinds of stuff you never heard of that you should be worried about."

"Like what?"

"Like some hurricanes we've had in the past—most of the death toll was from snake bites."

"Dang it, Serge! Why'd you have to tell me that?"

"Because it's a fun fact." Serge held out an empty travel mug. "Coffee me."

Coleman unscrewed a thermos and poured. Serge chugged the entire mug in one long pull. He began tapping the steering wheel. His head bobbed. "God*damn*, this is a great hurricane! I'm really starting to groove on the baby! Can you feel it? I can feel it! Coleman! Feel it!"

Coleman grabbed the dash again. "Refrigerator!"

"Woooo-hoooo!" *Screeeeeeeeech*. They came out of the wild swerve. Serge reached down under his seat for a small tin barrel. He placed it in his lap and opened the lid.

"Where'd you get Charles Chips?" asked Coleman.

"They sell 'em in bags now. So I had to get my own can and glue the bag around it." He popped a chip into his mouth and bobbed his head. "I'm ripped on this 'cane! Isn't she great? This is the best moment of my life! I couldn't be in a better mood!"

Muffled noise from the backseat. Serge grabbed a .45 automatic by the barrel, turned around and gave a wicked butt-crack to the forehead. "Shut the fuck up!"

"Serge, you're going to kill him if you keep hitting him that hard."

"*He's* killing my storm buzz!"

Coleman reached for the potato chips. "Can't believe we already got another hurricane. We're barely finished with the last one. That's three right on top of each other."

"And two more on the way, plus that tropical depression off the Canaries they're starting to watch. Living here has turned into some kind of demented Lucille Ball skit where cream pies come down the conveyor belt too fast."

Mumbling from the backseat.

"Shut the fuck up!" Crack!

Serge turned back around and wiped blood from the pistol grip. "Why can't he be pleasant like the other guy back there?"

"Serge, I don't think the other guy can talk."

"The perfect traveling companion."

"I still don't understand it."

"Understand what?"

"Whenever I'm on road trips with other guys, we usually *lose* people and possessions along the way."

"So?"

Coleman pointed at the backseat. "You always *gain* shit. There's those two new guys, your guitar, portable amp, that old bullhorn you strap to the roof, the electrical equipment and all that other stuff that I don't even recognize."

"Hurricanes are unpredictable that way." Serge extended the empty travel mug toward Coleman. "Coffee me."

"But you just had a cup."

"Do I count your joints? Coffee me!"

"Yeah, but you know how you get—"

"Coffee me!"

Coleman nervously opened the thermos and poured.

Serge chugged the mug dry.

Coleman saw veins pulse in Serge's neck. "Uh-oh." He fastened his seat belt.

The vehicle began accelerating, Serge punching the wheel. "I love this hurricane! I know all about her! Want to know all about her? You really don't have a choice: She bloomed a low-pressure trough near Trinidad, went tropical over Kingston, in the Caymans hit the magic seventy-four-miles-per-hour maximum sustained winds to be classified a category one. Category two starts at ninety-six, three at a hundred and eleven, and so on. You have to know the numbers. Do you know the numbers? I know the numbers. But now I have to learn the Greek alphabet, too, even though there are plenty of perfectly good names left, like mine, but they never use it. Scientists! Blow their brains all over their precious fuckin' viewing platforms. She weakened briefly crossing the mountains of western Cuba, then hit warm Gulf waters and howled back to life, barreling straight for the Keys. You've never truly been Florida-initiated until you've had to evacuate from the Keys. I did. Five years ago. Mandatory. Kicked out of my motel, then I hear this music—'Trying to Reason with Hurricane Season'—I go next door to a Buffett convention. Fucked-up sight. Panicked hotel staff running everywhere, fastening shutters and pulling in pool furniture, dodging Parrot Heads getting utterly hammered, dancing to calypso bands and taking flying palm fronds to the face. I'm thinking they're nuts to stay. Of course *I* was staying because I was determined to witness history. Yes, sir, there was absolutely no way anyone was going to drag me off that island! A few minutes later, I got bored and left. I was the last car out before they closed U.S. 1 behind me. What a rush! A hundred miles all to myself, racing fate. Then more surrealism. I'm crossing the Seven-Mile Bridge, and you know picturesque Pigeon Key under the old span?"

"No."

"Very popular with weddings. Guess what? They're holding a wedding! I can't believe it! The white tent had torn loose and was floating up Moser Channel, but there she was, the anti–runaway bride, leaning sharply into the wind, veil whipping horizontally, determined to get hitched at all costs. Good for her. I reached Homestead and the turnpike. They always suspend toll collecting during evacuations, and the woman in the booth is windmilling her arm, frantically waving me through like a third-base coach sending a runner home. Another Florida rush!"

Backseat mumbling.

"I'm talking up here!" Crack.

"Sofa!"

Screeeeeeeeech.

"But the storm never hit Key West. Veered at the last second for the Dry Tortugas, which wouldn't have meant anything, except for 'wet foot, dry foot.' What's that, you ask? I'll tell you. Hey, I'm out of coffee. Fuck it—we're going anyway: The Tortugas are a scattering of seven tiny islands seventy miles west of Key West, home of Civil War–era Fort Jefferson and a migratory-tern rookery. Only accessible by boat or seaplane, so nobody's there except a few park rangers and camping ornithologists. Until 'wet foot, dry foot,' the federal immigration policy on Cuban refugees. Get picked up at sea by the authorities, you're repatriated to Havana. Set one foot on dry U.S. land, it's celebration time with the Miami relatives. For years the human-smuggling boat captains and Coast Guard had been playing cat and mouse the entire length of the Keys. Then brainstorm. Nobody was guarding the Torgs. Most Americans don't even know the islands exist, let alone that they're part of Florida. But the captains did. The little islands filled with refugees, who had to be evacuated to the mainland ahead of the storm. Hmmm, wonder if, like, a gust of wind blew one of them into the water, if they'd have to be taken back to Cuba. I should have been a lawyer. Anyway . . ."

The black H2 continued speeding west on State Road 72. Danielle had made her walloping landfall two hours earlier in Sarasota. Only getting worse. Monsoonal rain manhandled the vehicle. Debris everywhere, Serge practically in a constant slalom. Coleman alternated between off-green and death-pale.

Abruptly, a bright sky. The rain stopped.

"Coleman! Look! We're in the eye! We made it!" Serge punched him in the shoulder. "Be happy!"

Backseat noise.

"Shut your fuckin' piehole!" Crack!

"Serge, you really can't keep hitting him like that."

Serge put the pistol down. "You're right. Then I won't be able to have any fun with my special plan." He began scanning the side of the road. "I know there's a pullover somewhere along here. . . ."

Two miles later they reached the locked entrance gate to My-akka River State Park, and Serge eased off the highway. He opened his driver's door. "Coleman, come on. Help me unbolt this seat in back."

"What do you have in mind?"

Serge told him.

"But that's crazy."

"It's been a crazy day."

CRAZY DAY, EIGHT HOURS EARLIER

A black H2 sped south on the Tamiami Trail and crossed the Sarasota County line. Perfect interception path with the next hurricane, six hours from projected landfall. Coleman shotgunned a Busch. "Serge, you've seemed down ever since you left that synagogue."

"Because I had such high hopes." He changed lanes around a wide-load manufactured home. "Most faiths are on high-pressure membership drives, but back there it was just question after question."

"Like what?" asked Coleman.

"Like why I wanted to convert. I said, 'Because there are no rabbis on TV asking for all my money.' The rabbi said, 'That's it?' I said, 'And I have most of Lenny Bruce's albums.'"

"What happened?" asked Coleman.

"He smiled and gave me some books to study and said I was welcome to come back if I still felt moved."

Coleman glanced at the pile of hardcovers between them. "Looks like they weigh a ton."

"They did. And you know me—I love to read, except when it's assigned like in high school and the Brontë sisters almost made me slit my own throat. I asked the rabbi, 'Don't you have some kind of emergency fast track? Maybe we can substitute titles. I've read *Portnoy's Complaint*; can that count?' But he said not really. I'm so bummed."

Coleman looked out the window at trees beginning to bend. "Does this mean you're giving up the religious search?"

"Just the opposite." Serge patted a King James Bible in his lap. "I now realize what my soul's been yearning for."

"What's that?"

"Fundamentalist Christianity."

"Now you've really lost it."

"See?" said Serge. "Typical reaction to liberal bias. The Holy Rollers' only sin is bad PR, which stems from an underdeveloped sense of humor. There's where I come in. I've been working up some jokes. I'm going to get huge laughs at one of their revivals. "

They pulled off the highway.

"Why are we stopping?"

Serge parked in front of a pawnshop. "I just realized I need an electric guitar."

Twenty minutes later they headed back to their vehicle, pushing a pair of brimming shopping carts.

"I thought you just wanted a guitar."

"I can't control myself in pawnshops," said Serge. "The product line is irresistibly bent. Magician bouquet, beekeeper hat, bagpipe patch kit, Third Reich gravy boat, world-class dragonfly collection. Once I saw a Super Bowl ring. That was back when crack was big."

He opened the rear of the H2 and began unloading the carts, mostly boosted car audio components and raw ingredients from gutted speaker systems. He finished packing and slammed the doors. Only one thing was left in the carts. Serge grabbed the used

Stratocaster and thrust it triumphantly over his head. "Coleman, you drive. I need to practice for my tour." He climbed into the passenger seat, cradled the instrument and began strumming.

Coleman looked at Serge, then the guitar, then Serge again. "What?"

Coleman reached for another beer. "I didn't say anything."

"You were going to mention the age thing."

"No I wasn't."

"I'll have you know I've been into the guitar for years. Used to borrow my friends' all the time." Serge twisted a tuning knob. "Decided it was finally time I got one of my own. Ain't she a beauty?"

"I didn't know you played the guitar."

"Are you kidding? I can play with my teeth, and behind my head, and duckwalking like Chuck Berry."

"What songs do you know?"

"Oh, I don't know any songs yet. You have to start with the basics—" Serge cut himself off. He couldn't believe what he saw on the other side of the parking lot. "Sweet mother!"

"What is it?" asked Coleman.

"I thought it was just an urban legend. . . ." Serge was out of the car in a flash, sprinting across pavement. "*No! Stop! Stop! Stop!*"

A Mercury Cougar backed out of a parking slot. On the roof: an occupied baby seat.

"*Stop!*"

The Cougar headed for the exit. Five miles an hour, ten, fifteen . . . but the acceleration was smooth and there was no braking. The seat stayed perfectly in place.

"*No!*" Serge was fifty yards away now. The Cougar had eased up to a stop sign, waiting for a pause in traffic. Serge just *had* to make it, pouring on the speed, calves cramping from oxygen depletion. "*Wait!*"

A space on the highway opened up; the car began to go. Serge reached the Cougar and lunged. He snatched the baby seat off the roof and fell backward with it safely in his arms.

The driver got out. He looked kind of familiar, but Serge was still panting too hard to speak. He finally caught his breath and unwrapped the pink blanket in the child seat. A mechanical voice: "Mom-my." Serge stared puzzled at the lifelike doll, then looked up.

The driver was grinning.

Serge stood quickly. "What the hell's going on?"

The side panel of a nearby van flew open. A camera crew jumped out. The Cougar's driver pointed derisively at Serge and smiled wider: "*Gotcha!*"

Now Serge recognized him. The talentless host of the jokester series *Gotcha!*, one of the most popular shows on Neville Gladstone's cable network.

Coleman drove up in the H2. "Way to go, Serge. For a second I didn't think you were going to make it."

Everyone else laughed. Someone slapped Serge on the back.

Coleman became confused. "What's going on?"

"It was all a joke," said Serge.

A camera zoomed in. "And the joke's on you! *Gotcha!*"

"Yeah, you got me good, all right," said Serge. "But I'm kind of busy, so if you'll just give me that videotape."

"What?"

"The tape you shot. I'd like to have it, please."

The crew laughed louder. "Are you crazy? It's the property of the show. We *Gotcha!*"

"I'm sure your parents are proud." Serge walked over to the H2 and reached inside. He returned with a large automatic pistol. "Now, if you wouldn't mind, I'd like the tape."

It instantly appeared in Serge's hand. "Thank you." He waved the gun. "Over there."

"W-w-what are you going to do to us?"

"Nothing. You're free to leave."

They made a break for the van.

"No, not you," Serge told the Cougar's driver.

"What do you want me for?"

"I'd like to pitch an idea for an upcoming episode. Hilarious prank. Won't take long."

The rest of the TV crew watched in shock as Serge forced the show's host into the Hummer at gunpoint.

Coleman climbed into the passenger seat. "Where to now?"

"The City of the Arts."

CHAPTER TWENTY-THREE

SARASOTA

This drowsy little Gulf Coast community has a reputation for three things: art, art, art! On every downtown corner, museums, galleries, opera houses, theaters. The city seal even has a statue of David. You've probably heard about it because of protests from residents upset that the doors of their police cars have nut-sacs. Then they elected Katherine Harris to Congress. But none of that could impede this city of the future, currently in the throes of a construction spree. And not just mansions and country clubs. Due to the advanced average age, Sarasota can never get enough hospital rooms. So it was no surprise when the ribbon was cut on a new, state-of-the-art medical complex just east of the interstate. And it was even less a surprise when, one month later, cops had to hold back the mob of picketers. That's right, a second feeding-tube case. It could just as easily have happened somewhere other than Florida, but then again, no. . . ."

"Serge," said Coleman. "Who are you talking to?"

"I wasn't talking."

"Yes you were."

"I was? Wow, that's embarrassing. I never notice when I'm

doing that, but I guess other people do, because they point or give me extra room on sidewalks."

"What were you talking about?"

"I've got this constant narration in my head. Actually, several, which is why the plot is sometimes hard to follow."

"Look for a liquor store."

"The second feeding-tube case of which Serge spoke was a young man involved in a surfing accident. The board was thrown clear, but the safety cord yanked it back. . . ."

"Serge, you're doing it again."

". . . Unlike the previous case in Pinellas Park, kin were not divided. All agreed what was best. The flap came from bused-in outsiders, who marched around the parking lot and made the bedside family listen to megaphones. . . ."

The hurricane bore down from the Gulf of Mexico.

But that didn't stop the mayhem outside Sarasota's newest hospital. Waving signs, bullhorns, opinions. A Florida Cable News semi-truck sat in the back of the parking lot. It hummed with generators and electronics-cooling equipment. A thick maze of cables ran from the truck to an adjacent flatbed trailer.

The flatbed held an anchor desk. It was the kind ESPN uses for outdoor pregame shows at the Orange Bowl. Except on the front of this desk: HARD FIRE. The trailer was already surrounded by an expectant audience of devoted fans. The program director opened the door to the semi and yelled inside, "Forty minutes!"

An assistant jogged over with a broadcast schedule. "Got a problem. We're short on the panel."

"How'd that happen?"

"Don's stuck in evacuation traffic. What do I do?"

"Earn your pay. Get a replacement."

"Where?"

"I don't care. Just fill the seat." He looked at his watch. "Thirty-nine minutes."

Then it went out over the radio: A voluntary evacuation for Manatee and Sarasota counties had just become involuntary.

A lone vehicle rolled down an empty residential street near the shore of tony Siesta Key, an antique bullhorn lashed to its roof: "Today's evacuation order is brought to you by Rain-X. Apply a single coat to your windshield and the worst downpour slides right off. Rain-X, for when you're too stupid to evacuate on time. . . . Last chance to leave. A bad one's on the way. Fun Fact Sixty-three: Castro once accused the U.S. of trying to steer hurricanes toward Cuba by seeding clouds with silver iodide. . . . Still not too late to evacuate. Except the 1949 storm had a twenty-four-foot surge in Belle Glade. That's the middle of the state. So where you going to run? . . ."

Serge continued working his way across town, sounding the alarm, until he reached the packed parking lot of a spanking-new hospital, megaphone still blaring: ". . . Praise the Lord! Praise the Lord! . . . Did you know that hurricanes are called willy willies in Australia? . . . Praise Jesus! He's the only one who can save us now! *I see a bad moon a-risin'! . . .*"

"Wow," said Coleman. "Look at the size of that protest!"

"This is my comedy forum."

"You're going to try your jokes *here*?"

Serge took off his tropical shirt and slipped into the custom T-shirt he'd made just for the occasion. "Let's rock."

The current speaker had the crowd in a zealous froth as he finished reading a letter from the president. "Thank God for our commander in chief!"

Serge and Coleman walked up to a line of speakers waiting behind the podium. A man approached with a roster. "Name and affiliation?"

"Serge A. Storms. Operation Holiness."

The man ran a pencil down the page. "Don't see you on here."

"Agent just booked me this morning. It's okay. I really am holy." Serge pointed at his T-shirt: I'M AGAINST WHAT YOU'RE AGAINST.

"Good enough for me. You're up fourth." He walked away.

The mob grew more raucous with each succeeding speaker. So did the wind. A minister ripped a photo of Michael Moore to wild applause and left the podium. Serge was up. He climbed the steps and accepted the megaphone.

"Thank you for letting me speak to your club today. Hey, I got a joke for you. . . . Take my wife—off the feeding tube—please. . . . *Rim shot!*"

The crowd's roaring died down. *What did he just say?*

". . . Yes, sir, we're all here for a very important cause. 'Persistent vegetative state,' 'poor quality of life.' Based on that, most of the people I'm looking at right now would be put down. . . . But seriously, folks . . ."

The audience quieted further and exchanged puzzled looks.

". . . Hey, I got another joke for you. . . . What did Jesus say to one of the thieves on the next cross? . . .'Tough room.' . . . *Badabing! . . .*" He tapped the microphone. ". . . Hello? Is this thing on? I can hear you breathing out there . . ."

The crowd recovered from silent astonishment and began rippling with growing anger. Gusts whipped Serge's hair.

"I see I'm losing some of you. Okay, I'm no comedian. But I know what I believe. And I believe what *you* believe! I agree with all of you two-hundred percent!"

The crowd started coming around. A few shouts of encouragement.

"At first I thought you religious types were completely full of crap. . . ."

Losing them again.

". . . But then I got into it. Religions are like countries. The people are wonderful; it's governments that give the bad name. You're some of the most decent citizens we have to offer, and the country needs you now more than ever! Our political process is broken and toxic. Forget terrorists; left to our own devices, we'll eventually rip ourselves apart from the inside. So here's my solution: no more arguments. We start agreeing on everything. I consider you all part of my American family, and here's *my* family values: You don't quarrel with loved ones, even that one wing of every family who makes you hide the jewelry on Thanksgiving. To quote F. Scott, 'The test of a first-rate intelligence is the ability to hold two opposed ideas in mind at the same time.' So I'm a pro-life-choice NRA gun-control nut who wants schools to pray for the separation of church and state. For the love of God, I just want all of us to start getting along! What do you say? . . ."

"*Drop dead!*"

"I agree," said Serge.

The yelling spread quickly.

"*I think he's got something . . .*"

"*No he doesn't! . . .*"

"You're both right," said Serge.

The organizers decided it best to get him off the stage before he could divide people further.

On the other side of the parking lot, a program director opened the door to a semi trailer: "Ten minutes." He closed the door.

Moments later the door opened again; the crowd cheered as TV personalities walked to the flatbed and took seats behind the anchor desk. Staff attached lapel mikes and powdered foreheads to cut sheen.

Five minutes.

An assistant ran up to the anxious program director. "I found someone to fill out the panel."

"Howdy," said Serge. "Operation Holiness."

The director noticed Coleman. "Two guys?"

"Like Evans and Novak," said Serge. "More like Penn and Teller, because Coleman doesn't say much. At least nothing that would carry any weight at a state dinner."

The director turned to the assistant. "What's his shtick?"

"He agrees with everyone."

"Perfect. He'll be the opposition." The director checked his watch, "Three minutes. Get them up there."

They had just clipped Serge's lapel mike when the director counted down from five on his fingers, made a fist, and pointed at the center chair.

"*Good afternoon, everyone, and welcome to a special on-location edition of* Hard Fire. . . ."

The crowd erupted.

"*We're here in beautiful Sarasota for another day of feeding-tube protests . . .*"

Bigger applause. Someone blew a sports-arena airhorn.

"*But first, this just in: The federal circuit court has ruled that the feeding tube must be removed . . .*"

Booooooooo!

"*And now I'd like to introduce our all-star panel. Let's hear it for the front-runner in the Thirteenth Congressional District, the Reverend Artamus Twill . . .*"

Coleman cracked a beer beneath the desk. Serge checked his Eight Ball.

The program proceeded along scripted lines, Twill up first: "*. . . The other side has clearly demonstrated that they are the Party of Death Worshippers. . . .*" Serge kept opening his mouth to get in an edge-word; he kept sitting back. Eventually someone had to take a breath between attacks, and Serge was able to blurt it out. The first time he said it, he was dismissed as one of the kooks the show invites for the regulars to gang up on. But then he said it a second time. And a third. The crowd began to jeer. The other panelists could ignore it no longer:

"I agree."

"*Sir,*" said the host, "*if you're just going to get into the spirit of the proceedings—*"

"I'm completely serious," said Serge. "We desperately need to come together for the greater good of the nation."

"*But what about the slogan on your T-shirt?*"

Serge looked down. I'M AGAINST WHAT YOU'RE AGAINST. He looked up. "I was trying to be agreeable."

The host turned. "*Artamus?*"

"We're treading on dangerous ground. Agreeing is a secular Trojan horse for inclusion."

"I can respect that," said Serge. "Everyone's entitled to their opinion."

"No they're not."

The host tapped a pencil. "How can you be from Operation Holiness and espouse such anti-religious propaganda?"

"But I'm very religious," said Serge.

"Which denomination?"

"I agree with all of them."

"That's even more anti-religious."

"How?"

"You're a moral relativist."

"What?"

"You have to choose!"

"But they're all great. I glean the best from each. It's just that every one I've tried leaves me with a couple of questions."

"You know who invented questions? Satan."

"That was just a question," said Serge.

"What are you trying to say?"

"That's another one."

"Why, you little—"

"Okay, okay. I really do have a religion." Serge pulled his T-shirt off over his head, turned it inside out and put it back on, displaying a new slogan: I'M PROBABLY WRONG.

"That's your religion?"

Serge nodded. "Like those early snap judgments I made against organized faiths? Way off the mark. They're all based on unconditional love, and I was an idiot not to see it. As for my own spiritual journey, aggressively doubting myself keeps me curious and yearning, which only brings me closer and closer to God. It's just something I feel inside. I can't explain it."

"Because you're wrong!"

"Exactly!"

Panelists had to shout over the crowd's growing hostility.

"Impostor!" "Heathen!" "I'll bet he's against the feeding tube!"

"Just the opposite," said Serge. "I'm so in favor of it that I propose inserting a *second* tube. Then we'll have an extra to remove for the federal court. Everybody's happy."

On it went, jeers growing louder until they were deafening. The crowd charged. *"Get him!"* The rest of the TV people cleared off the flatbed and locked themselves in the semi. Serge suddenly found himself surrounded. The mob scrambled onto the platform. Shoving broke out. Coleman's shirt got ripped. "Serge, you have to do something!"

"Okay, I think I got it. It worked at Woodstock for Country Joe and the Fish. But this is a slightly different audience, so no guarantees. . . ."

Someone grabbed Coleman in a headlock. "Just do it!"

"All right." Serge cleared his throat and grabbed one of the microphones. "Give me an *F*! . . ."

Up in the hospital room, a growing roar came through the walls. The protesters were even noisier than usual. One of the relatives from the bedside vigil peeked through the blinds.

"Something's going on out there."

"Look," said another relative. "It's on TV."

"That guy on the flatbed is leading the crowd in some kind of chant."

"What are they saying?"

"I can't make it out."

Down in the parking lot, Serge had reversed his fortunes one-eighty, whipping the crowd into a revivalist fury. Serge repeatedly pumped a fist skyward in rhythm with his new mantra: *"Fuck the devil! Fuck the devil! . . ."*

A camera from Florida Cable News caught a chanting, eighty-year-old woman off guard. She covered her mouth and giggled. "Normally I'd never condone such language, but the devil just won't listen to reason."

The wind snuck up. People lost hats and picket signs. The

crowd parted for Serge and Coleman, but it was slow progress back to their vehicle with all the handshakes and autographs. Then the clouds let go, and everyone scattered for safety. Some were able to make it to their cars. Others took refuge in the emergency room.

Serge crawled the last few yards to the H2.

"We can't drive in this," said Coleman.

"I know." Serge threw the vehicle in gear. "We need to park against the leeward wall of the building. It'll block most of the wind."

On the hospital's seventh floor, an attorney appeared in the doorway. He didn't have to say anything. The Eleventh Circuit had spoken. The family stepped aside for the doctors. It didn't take long. The presiding physician spoke quietly. "It's in God's hands now." In scientific terms, that meant seven to fourteen days.

Twenty minutes later a hospital administrator entered the room. "Storm's here. It's time to go down to the shelter."

Orderlies transferred the patient to a stretcher and wheeled him down the hall to a special oversized elevator. Police escorted the family down a regular one. The power went out, and the emergency batteries kicked in.

The head nurse joined the family hunkering down in the shelter. She looked around. "What's taking those orderlies so long?"

STATE ROAD 72

A black H2 sped away from the entrance to Myakka River State Park. White orderly uniforms on the floorboards.

Coleman cracked a beer. "I can't believe we kidnapped the feeding-tube guy."

"Know what you mean," said Serge, carefully monitoring the cloud wall to stay within the eye. "This is worse taste than *Weekend at Bernie's*."

"Then why'd you do it?"

"Because it's even worse taste to exploit him for political careers. I couldn't stand to see him in the middle of that travesty. Plus, the federal court just ruled he can't be fed anymore."

"What's that mean?"

"Brings up an interesting legal question," said Serge. "If we're caught, will we be in more trouble if he's alive or dead?"

Coleman turned around in his seat and snapped fingers in front of a vacant face. "His family must be worried sick."

"Been thinking that, too," said Serge. "I screwed up. We have to return him." He slowed and executed a wide U.

"We're heading back into the hurricane?"

"Land weakened it to a category one, but you should still belt yourself."

Coleman clicked a buckle shut. "At least your heart was in the right place."

"Who knows about the human brain?" Serge gave it the gas. "Maybe he's picking this up on a subcortex level. I know if I was in his condition and ready to check out, I'd definitely appreciate it if someone drove me around on a cool road trip."

The advancing black eye wall was straight ahead. Under a mile, closing fast.

Horrible screaming.

Serge looked up at the ceiling. "I wish he'd stop that. He's going to make me have an accident."

"Think I should check on him again?" said Coleman.

"Good idea. Make sure he's safe."

Coleman climbed out and sat on the lip of his rolled-down window. Eye wall a half mile, still closing. He reached and tested the rope that secured the unbolted rear car seat to the roof rack, a larger version of the child seat on the Cougar's roof. He checked a second line holding the TV host in place. "You okay?"

"*Aaaaauuuuuuuuhhhhhhhhhh!*"

Coleman came back inside the passenger compartment and rolled up his window.

"How is he?" asked Serge.

"I don't think he likes it."

"Too late. Hundred yards." Serge accelerated to seventy. Collision course. "Hang on. She's really going to whip."

They punched through the violent wall. Serge fought the steering wheel. There was a loud *kerchunk*. Serge and Coleman looked up. Something banged down the length of the roof, and then it was gone.

Coleman turned around and looked out the back window. "Ooooooooh. He skidded on his face."

Serge grinned. *"Gotcha!"*

Nursing staff and relatives scrambled through the hospital in panicked search parties. One of the groups turned the corner on a hallway that had already been checked. They froze.

In the middle of the corridor, a young man was sitting up on a stretcher. "Am I hungry!"

They ran him down to the lab for a battery of tests. "I've never seen anything like it," said one of the doctors, reading a printout. "The only possible explanation is this brain scan indicating a recent overload of sensory stimulation."

The young man wolfed down a submarine sandwich. "I just had the weirdest dream."

A doctor came over and took the sandwich away.

"Hey! I was eating that!"

"Federal court order. We're not allowed to feed you."

CHAPTER TWENTY-FOUR

MIDNIGHT

A hand in a surgical glove wrote under the blue glow of a silent TV. No danger being discovered by handwriting experts this time, because the latest letter was being written in a made-up alphabet. Shapes and hieroglyphics and other symbols borrowed from Russians and Navajos. The sheet was folded, slipped into an envelope and addressed in the usual manner.

THE MORNING AFTER

Fifteen miles south of Sarasota. The shore was overcast. Tourists combed the beach for shells. Some fished from the giant twenty-four-hour pier. Others cracked oysters in an oceanfront restaurant named Sharky's.

People filled the water, but nobody was swimming. They stood up to their waists, working diligently with long metal poles. A lanky man raised his pole and shook the mesh basket at the end. He pulled something from the bottom, turned toward shore and waved it in the air. "Coleman! I got one! I got one! . . . Coleman . . . ?" Serge splashed his way toward the beach.

Coleman felt light taps on his cheeks. "Coleman?"

"Mmmmmm." Coleman slowly pushed himself up in the sand. "What happened?"

"You passed out again. Look what I got!" Serge stuck a giant gray fossil an inch from Coleman's face. It was pointy and serrated. Serge pulled it back. "Been hunting this baby for years. Now my collection's complete!"

Coleman peeled matted seaweed off his arms. "An old tooth?"

"Not just any old tooth!" Serge rubbed it like a genie bottle. "*Carcharodon megalodon*! The Holy Grail!"

Coleman brushed sand off his tongue. "*Car*-what?"

"Prehistoric ancestor of *Carcharodon carcarius,* the great white shark, but up to five times as long. Some say eighty feet."

Coleman noticed all the people in the water. "What are they doing?"

"Another Florida hurricane tradition. We're in Venice . . ." Serge swept an arm over the beach like Caesar. ". . . Fossil capital of the state. I've filled coffee cans with all kinds of tiny teeth: mako, tiger, bull, blue. Once I stepped on a mastodon vertebra. But until a few minutes ago, no *megalodon.*"

"Why not?"

"It's the fossil capital, which means it's pretty much fossiled out. Everyone rents these metal tooth-hunting baskets from a concession on the side of the restaurant and picks the place clean. But hurricanes are your big chance. They churn up the sea bottom, bringing a new shipment of teeth to the surface. And now I got mine! Let's celebrate!"

Coleman lay back down on the sand and closed his eyes. "I celebrated in advance, in case something good happened."

Serge grabbed him by the arm. "Let's go to Sharky's. I'm buying."

They reached the side of the restaurant. Serge returned the

rental basket and thrust his tooth in the face of the kiosk man. "I rule!"

"That's nice." The man refunded Serge's deposit.

"Can I get quarters? I'd like to buy a newspaper. A lot is going on in our times. Miss a day and you could go years thinking Buddy Hackett's still alive. What if you ran into his family and said something inappropriate?"

Serge received his change and grabbed a paper from the row of boxes next to the rental fishing poles. They entered the restaurant from the beach side, and a waitress led them to a patio table in the wet-bathing-suit section. "I got my tooth!"

The waitress smiled politely and handed out menus. "I'll be right back to take your order."

"I'd like to order now. What do people usually have when they're celebrating The Tooth? You probably get this all the time. Anything on the menu, like the Congratulations-on-Your-Tooth Platter?"

"I'm kind of new here. . . ."

"Sorry, I'm being a bother. You're busy with a full room of customers. I promise not to monopolize your time. Let's just say I'll try, because sometimes I can't help it, especially if I've had coffee." He closed the menu and handed it back to the waitress. "Just bring me coffee."

Coleman returned his own menu. "Beer."

The waitress left, and Serge carefully propped the tooth atop the napkin dispenser for maximum display. "There. I can sit in awe." He spread out his newspaper and . . . A fist pounded the table. The tooth fell. "Motherfu—!" Heads turned.

Coleman unwrapped a not-for-individual-sale packet of saltines. "What is it?"

"Article on my most recent masterpiece. Mahoney's taking advantage of the tragedy to plant more ugly rumors about me." Serge kept reading. The fist came down again. "*Impotent!* That's it! I can't let this go unanswered!"

"What are you going to do?"

"Write a letter to the editor."

"But you already wrote one."

"I can write as many letters as I want. You're thinking of manifestos. There's a one-manifesto-per-serial-killer limit."

"Manifesto?"

"Everybody has a manifesto," said Serge. "You, me. Yours is probably short. The point is that everyone else doesn't have an insecure need to call attention to themselves: *Look at me, I killed a bunch of people, please publish my manifesto.* On the other hand, all communities have a hard-core base of unstable, rambling letter writers who are actually encouraged so newspapers can fill pages for free. I'll need to stay clear of coherence." Serge waved for the waitress. "Can I borrow a pen?"

TAMPA BAY TODAY

The first budget meeting of the morning. Editors dribbled in. An identical Xerox lay on the table in front of each chair.

The maximum editor arrived. "Another letter?" He picked up his copy. "What are all these weird symbols?"

"An alphabet Serge made up," said Mahoney. "We've already sent it to the FBI. Their top cryptographers are working round the clock."

"And?"

"No luck. We'd like you to publish it in case one of your readers can crack the code."

"But if the best experts can't—"

"That's how they untangled messages from the Zodiac Killer," said Mahoney. "These two teachers figured it out at their breakfast table."

The metro editor pointed at a spot near the bottom of the page. A straight line intersected a squiggly one. "This symbol's bigger than the others."

"Probably his logo. The Zodiac did that, too."

A news clerk approached the table with an envelope. "Sir, this just came."

"Another letter?"

"Drop it on the table!" said Mahoney. "Nobody touch it!" He reached into his jacket for tweezers and a clear evidence bag. The letter was gently unfolded and slid into the plastic.

McSwirley leaned for a better look.

"That same Eye of the Storm guy?" asked Metro Tom.

"Don't know," said Jeff. "It's a completely different style."

"How can you tell?"

"It's written on the back of a seafood place mat."

"It's the same guy, all right," said Agent Mahoney. "Serge. His personality's splitting."

"Let me see that thing." The maximum editor pulled the bag toward him and pushed reading glasses up his nose.

Dear Letters to the Editor,
Impotent! Why, I'll have you know this cock still gets hard enough to bash your fucking skull in! By the way, nice redesign job with the sports section. Much easier on the eyes.

Look, I know the confidential source is Mahoney, and I understand you have to play ball to keep the leaks coming, but is name-calling really necessary?

Speaking of names, a word to parents: Stop using alternate spellings for your kids. Aimee, Eryn, Bil, Derik. You're only costing jobs. The whole customized-coffee-mug and key-chain industry. An entire generation is being robbed of their roadside-Florida-souvenir heritage. "Daddy, why don't they ever have my name? I see something close, but it's spelled different." "Sorry, honey, we decided to be pricks."

Next: state government. You know that official Hurricane Preparedness Program last year when all storm supplies were exempt from sales tax? The first two weeks of June. *Preparedness*. The first two weeks *of hurricane season*. The answers are all right in front of you, but Americans tend to overanalyze. Like during the space race, NASA spent fifty thousand dollars developing a zero-gravity pen that didn't skip. Know what the Russians did? Pencil. Think about it.

—S

CHAPTER TWENTY-FIVE

SARASOTA

A few miles above Venice, the Tamiami Trail takes a pair of jogs as it swings past Marina Jack's and the bridge to Bird Key, home of lifestyle pace-car and AC/DC front man Brian Johnson. The road continues north toward the international airport as part of something designated 'Florida Scenic Highway,' a route singularly characterized by a dense concentration of endangered mom-and-pop motels clinging from the fifties. Many had already been demolished, while others were converted to a variety of mixed-density operations selling live bait and sex toys. The most tenacious kept the neon buzzing: the Seabreeze, the Sundial, the Cadillac, the Galaxy, the Siesta, the Flamingo Colony. . . ."

"Serge," said Coleman, "you're doing it again."

". . . In the middle of this stretch is a small, easily missed concrete building set back from the road in a nest of palms and island vegetation. Above the front door, in Tahitian lettering: BAHI HUT. What do you say we take a peek inside? . . ."

"Serge, we're already inside. You're talking to yourself at the bar."

". . . The lounge's interior was aggressively dark and Polynesian. Wicker, bamboo, tiki gods, wooden surfboards. The kind of place criminals might hatch schemes in early episodes of *Hawaii Five-O*. I advised Coleman to try the hut's signature drink. He ordered two. . . ."

Ten minutes later Coleman had paper umbrellas in his hair over both ears. He caught the bartender's attention and held up an empty glass. "Another mai tai."

"Sorry, you've already had two."

"So?"

"That's the rule."

Coleman turned. "Serge . . ."

"Shhhhh!" He was hunched over a newspaper. "I'm concentrating."

"But the bartender cut me off, and I only had two drinks."

"Were they mai tais?"

"Yeah."

"That's the rule."

"What?"

"You're in the venerable Bahi Hut." Serge scribbled. "Most people drive right by. A lot of the locals don't even know, but it holds a dear spot in the hearts of all knowledgeable Floridaphiles."

"What's that got to do with the rule?"

"Also affectionately known as the Bye-Bye Hut, from the potency of their infamous mai tais. Hence the self-imposed two-drink ordinance."

Coleman grabbed one of the umbrellas from his hair, opening and closing it. "What's so special about them? I don't feel a thing."

Serge turned the newspaper upside down and marked something else. "Give it time."

"What are you doing?"

"Being interrupted." Serge rotated the paper and made another mark.

Coleman leaned over Serge's shoulder. "Another letter from the killer?"

"This one's in code. Police are stumped, so they're asking the public's help."

"But if the police aren't able to solve it, how can the public?"

"That's how they cracked the Zodiac Killer's letters. The solution came from a married couple in California. They sat around the kitchen table one Sunday morning and tried to figure it out as a lark instead of fiddling with the crossword."

"How'd they do it?"

Serge unfolded a Florida road map and aligned it over the newspaper page. He held both up to a dim lamp above the bar. "The teachers assumed the guy was a megalomaniac, so the first symbol had to be 'I.' They also correctly guessed that the word 'kill' would be big, and they looked for symbols that repeated twice. Sure enough, the symbol for 'I' preceded most double characters. Now they had three letters, which they plugged in everywhere else, and it quickly unraveled from there."

"That's what you're doing?"

"Don't need to. I've already cracked it." Serge used the lamp as a guide and carefully slid the map across the newspaper. "Now I'm just working on this big symbol at the end."

"How'd you solve it so fast?" asked Coleman.

"The second I saw it, I immediately recognized the length of each stanza. Of course you'd have to be a state-history buff."

"What are stanzas?"

"What this thing's written in." Serge stood. "Get your shit together. We have to head back to Tampa."

"What for?"

"Start our new jobs tomorrow. I promised my psychiatrist."

"I don't want to work."

"I don't want to work either, but we need some mad money for the next storm." Serge threw a couple of fins on the bar.

There was a meaty thud. Coleman picked himself up from the floor. "Whoa, the drinks . . ." Coleman waved for the bartender again. "What was in those things?"

Serge and the bartender in unison: "It's a secret."

TAMPA BAY TODAY

A news clerk ran into the budget meeting. He waved an envelope. "Sir, one of our readers cracked the killer's code!"

"Let me see that," said Max.

"Drop it on the table!" yelled Mahoney. "Nobody touch it." The tweezers again.

Everyone crowded around. "Well, I'll be," said Metro Tom. "It's the state song."

Someone couldn't resist a little singing. "*Way down upon the Suwannee River . . .*"

"And this thing at the end wasn't a logo at all," said Max. "It's a location." A tiny cut-out square from a Florida road map was taped over the symbol. "See? He used the edges of the paper as compass points and looked for a spot where the Suwannee crossed a bridge at that angle. Even the bends in the river match up. . . . It's signed 'Serge.'"

"One killer cracked the other's code?" said Max.

"There is no other killer," said Mahoney. "The guy's coming apart, writing letters back and forth to himself."

"How can you be so sure?" asked Tom.

"You think this is all a big coincidence?" said Mahoney. "What are the odds that nobody could decipher the code except the other lunatic sending us letters?"

"Now that you mention it . . . But what does the message mean?"

"My gut says the location of the next body."

CHAPTER TWENTY-SIX

TAMPA

I hate work," said Coleman.

"That's why they call it work," said Serge.

The buddies had gone blue-collar. The collars were attached to uniform shirts with red cursive stitching over the pockets. Coleman's said "Eddie." Serge's said "Willie."

They walked across the parking lot toward a convenience store. It was one of those places where the architecture and shape of the sign told you it used to be a 7-Eleven. But the neighborhood had evolved, and not in a direction sought by the 7-Eleven people. So it was now one of those freelance convenience stores that sold *Hustler* and rolling papers and was called something like Zippity-Grab-N-Dash.

They had been on their new job for twenty minutes, and Coleman had been griping for thirty.

"Why do I have to push the handcart?"

"Because I have the clipboard."

"Why do you get the clipboard?"

"Because I'm the supervisor."

"Says who?"

"Whoever has the clipboard gets to be the supervisor."

Coleman pushed the cart a few more feet and stopped. "Wait. . . . Are you saying that if I had grabbed the clipboard this morning, I could have been the boss?"

"Yes, but the question's academic. That's the difference between us. You didn't know to grab the clipboard; I did. It shows I have managerial skills."

"It's just a clipboard."

"Therein lies the irony. You can buy them anywhere, but they possess magic powers. It's like a camera. Walk around an airport or bank lobby taking lots of pictures and people lose their minds. They think you're up to something unauthorized, and then it's confrontation time again in Serge World. A clipboard's the same but different. You attract an equal amount of attention, except this time the employees keep their distance because a clipboard means you could be someone important from The Home Office."

"Sounds like bullshit."

"Try it sometime. If you ever need a psychological edge, walk into a place and start writing on a clipboard. Messes up the staff. Their minds retreat to the fear corner: Are they cutting back on personnel? Did they see me take that money from the register? Sometimes a bolder employee might come up and ask rhetorically if he can help you. You say no, then read his name tag and write it on the clipboard." Serge opened one of the glass entrance doors to the convenience store. "After you."

Coleman pushed the handcart inside. "How'd you first discover the power of the clipboard?"

"By accident." Serge stopped to inhale crisp air-conditioning. "Started carrying one around all the time because I was constantly having breakthroughs that would slip my mind before I could reach a writing surface. Was in a Kwiki Lube getting my oil changed, and I'm staring absentmindedly and jotting stuff. The manager walks up and asks, 'Can I help you?' I say, 'You already are. You're changing my oil.' He points: 'You have a clipboard.'

I say, 'Correct.' He says, 'What are you writing?' I say, 'Societal observations.' He says, 'What kind of observations?' I say, 'Like, people who work in lube shops get all the supermodels.' He says, 'What are you? Some kind of wise guy?' So I wrote down his name *and* snapped his picture. Then I was asked to take my business elsewhere. I said, 'Fine,' and walked away."

"What about your car?"

"Oh, I wasn't really getting my oil changed. I was casing the place for a robbery." Serge approached the convenience store's front counter. An immense woman with drawn-on eyebrows and ten piercings around the rim of each ear restocked an overhead cigarette rack while talking on her cell phone.

Serge smiled big.

The woman purposefully looked away and laughed into the phone.

"Greetings!" said Serge. "Hate to interrupt a business call!"

The laughter stopped. Into the phone: "Hold on, someone wants something. . . . No, someone else. . . . I know, it never stops. . . . Yeah, I'm at work. . . ."

Serge continued smiling and tapping fingers on the counter.

". . . No, he's not going away. . . ." She reached up and slammed the plastic Winston rack shut. "Give me a sec. . . ." She covered the phone and gave Serge an inconvenienced look. "Who are you?"

"The new guys."

"I haven't seen you before."

"We're new." Serge looked back at Coleman. "Take note. That's why she's behind that counter."

"What'd you say?"

"I was telling him I can see how you got to be back there."

"What's *that* supposed to mean?"

"It's a neutral statement, personally subjective, like a psychiatrist's butterfly inkblot. If you feel bursting with success, take it as a compliment. If not, consider it a cultural intervention."

She squinted with cranial discomfort. "What are you talking about?"

"Exactly. And that's the question you have to answer for yourself." He set the clipboard on the counter. "I need you to sign this."

"What is it?"

"I don't know. They just said you're supposed to sign it. You don't have to, but then I'm forced to tell them you wouldn't cooperate."

She scribbled her name. "I don't want any trouble."

Serge took the clipboard. "Sometimes it just finds you." He headed toward the back of the store. Coleman pushed the handcart past an end-cap display of two-liter Mountain Dews. "Where am I going?"

Serge rounded the last aisle. "Over there."

Rubber wheels squeaked across the unwaxed floor.

"Why do we have to work anyway?" said Coleman. "We were doing just fine."

"Only six more shopping days till the next hurricane," said Serge. "I've had my eye on a number of things. . . . I'll tilt this back, and you slide the cart underneath. On three: one, two . . ."

Coleman placed his right foot on the handcart's axle and pushed the bottom lip forward. "You sure are buying a lot of gadgets lately . . . and guns."

"I know where you're going."

"Up this aisle?"

"No, the age thing again. This spending spree has nothing to do with that. There's just a bunch of stuff I've been holding off on until I was mature enough to control my spending. . . . I'll push and you tip the hand truck back until the weight's balanced on the wheels. On three . . ."

Coleman tilted the cart.

"Serge . . . it's heavy."

"You got it?"

"Not really."

"Watch out! You're going to drop it!"

". . . Help."

Serge grabbed the handles just before Coleman was pinned to the floor. "Here, let me. You have to find the center of gravity. Hold it at this angle and let the cart do the work."

Coleman got the hang of it and began pushing. "I'm not criticizing. You deserve your new stuff. . . ."

"We're back on that?"

"I'm just amazed at it all. You got the limited-edition shotgun, the limited-edition pistol with engraved velvet case, the Glock, the derringer, the Mauser, the new laptop with DVD and GPS, a digital camera that also takes movies, a movie camera that also takes photos, a BlackBerry cell phone that takes photos *and* movies, a satellite radio, a Taser, another iPod when the old one was still perfectly good—"

"The new model has twenty more gigs. I require maximum memory allowed by law."

"Plus all your hurricane stuff: titanium flashlights, crank-operated weather-band radio, fifty-in-one pocket tool, personal executive defibrillator, foot-pump siphon in case you need gasoline from someone else's car—"

"Hold up. How can you remember all that?" asked Serge. "And you're over your syllable limit."

"I'm higher than a fuck."

"Wonderful. You're going to be a real prize to work with. Why'd you go and do that when I told you what we had to do today?"

"Because you told me what we had to do today. I always get high before work. I hate work. It makes it go easier. For the first minutes. Then it intensifies how much I hate it for the rest of the day. You know anything with five-minute shifts?"

"West-side blow jobs."

"I hate work."

"Everyone hates work. That's why they do it. They think the more they work, the sooner they get to stop. But it's all a big lie because they don't figure inflation. And *someone* keeps raising the Social Security age. But I'm under no illusions about my deal with the devil. I need stuff, therefore I work. It's a paradox beyond my control."

"What's a paradox?"

"Like, 'We sentence you to death because thou shalt not kill.'"

"I thought you were *for* the death penalty."

"I am," said Serge. "So instead I'm against public displays of the Ten Commandments. I just might be the only person in America with a consistent position on those two."

Coleman uprighted the cart.

"What are you doing?"

"Taking a break."

"We just started. You haven't gone halfway across the store."

"I'm winded."

"Shouldn't have stayed up so late last night."

"I know, but I got really stoned and started playing with some of your new shit. Now I understand why you dig it."

Serge became deadly earnest. "You didn't break anything, did you?"

"No. It was all was working fine when I was done. Especially the Taser."

"You used my Taser?"

"It's pretty cool."

"What on?"

"What do you mean?"

"You said you used my Taser. What did you use it on?"

"What do you think? Myself."

"You *Tasered* yourself?"

"I couldn't find my pot. That's how I came across the Taser. I was going through your dresser looking for my weed—"

"Wait. Why were you looking in *my* dresser?"

"You'd have to be a pot smoker to understand. When you lose weed, it could be *anywhere*. Then I found the Taser. You know me: I'll try anything once. *Zzzzappppp!* Good thing I was sitting down. After I stopped twitching, I had to wipe all the foam off the front of my shirt."

"At least you learned your lesson."

"Actually, I kind of liked it."

"And I thought you couldn't surprise me anymore."

"Killer rush. Bright flashes, sonic hallucinations . . . So I decided to give your defibrillator a whirl."

"What!"

"Fuckin' great."

"But that's for heart attacks! If you're not having one, it can *cause* one."

"I was responsible. I kept it on the lowest setting."

"Coleman, you're special."

"Really?"

"As in 'Olympics.'" Serge approached the counter again. The clerk was still on her cell. She saw them coming and turned away toward the window. ". . . Those boobs are *not* real. Because I just know. . . . You're right, they can't afford it. But they'd already planned on declaring bankruptcy, so first they maxed out the credit cards on a home theater and tits. . . . No shit. Pretty sophisticated financial planning. . . ."

"Yoo-hoo!" said Serge. "I'm back."

She covered the phone. "What do you want now?"

"You have to sign."

"I signed before."

"You have to sign again. One in. One out."

"The old guys never made me sign twice."

"We're the new guys."

She cradled the phone against her shoulder and wrote quickly. Serge took the clipboard and pushed the front door open.

Coleman grunted against the weight of the handcart. "I get the clipboard tomorrow."

MIDNIGHT

A nondescript pickup drove quietly through the Interbay section of peninsular Tampa, just north of the Air Force base. It turned onto a dark residential street featuring more pickup trucks with bumper stickers announcing political grievance and morning radio preference.

The truck passed the padlocked chain-link fence around a rented two-bedroom ranch house with brown water stains and absentee landlords. The house was dark except for the blue glow from a back window.

The room was a fire hazard. Stacks of yellowed newspapers almost to the ceiling. Under the window was a desk, and in the chair sat a man with surgical gloves. The latex appeared luminous in the dim light of a twelve-inch TV with snowy picture tube and no sound. The hands folded a single sheet of stationery and creased it smartly. It was slipped into an envelope that was already addressed:

JEFF McSWIRLEY
STAFF WRITER
TAMPA BAY TODAY . . .

The envelope's adhesive flap was moistened from a finger bowl and pressed shut. The man stood and walked to the back wall, completely covered, a floor-to-ceiling bulletin board of taped and thumbtacked items. It started with faded newspaper clippings. Hundreds of them. Variety of topics, but one thing in common. The byline. Jeff McSwirley. Most were heavily marked up in ballpoint. Triple underlining, emphatic circles, intense marginalia. The articles progressed chronologically, left to right, eventually reaching the present: Tuesday's report on Serge. More circles than usual on that one. Then came the photographs. Hundreds again. McSwirley again. The big blowups were from his newspaper tenure, but others went back years, to grade school.

A blue light flashed.

It was the glint off a rising meat cleaver that caught the TV's reflection. The blade came down heavy through the middle of the biggest photo, splitting McSwirley's face and wedging into the drywall. The man walked back across the room and sat again in the chair. Gloved hands reached down and tightened Velcro straps on his sneakers.

CHAPTER TWENTY-SEVEN

TAMPA BAY TODAY

Copies of the latest letter sat in front of each chair around the conference table. Nobody spoke.

> Dear Jeff,
> I'm very disappointed in you. I thought we were friends. But you have been stupid, Jeff. You are more interested in publicizing the weak, hollow, absurdness of this pretender you call Serge. That makes me angry, and you don't want to make me angry, do you, Jeff? I know you don't, so I am now forced to instruct you. I don't want to do what I have to next, but this is all your fault, Jeff. You leave me no choice. Before the moon reaches its final quarter, my full power will be revealed in all its glory.
> —The Eye of the Storm

"We have to take him off this story," said Tom.

"Nothing doing," said Max. "In fact, we need to get him rolling on this letter right away."

"I can't."

"That's an order!"

"No, I mean I really can't," said Tom. "He's not available."

"Why not?" asked the maximum editor. "Where is he?"

"You know."

"Still? I thought that was just one day."

"No, it's not just *one* day!" said Tom. "I told you we needed to do something."

"Then do it."

The metro editor sat across a table from McSwirley. A Plexiglas divider between them. A small speaker in the middle.

"Get me out of here," said Jeff. "I don't like jail."

"Easy, kid. We have our best lawyers working on the subpoena." Tom gave the reporter a quick once-over. "Jesus, you look like hell."

"I've barely slept. I got this creepy cellmate. Every time I nod off, I wake up and he's standing over my bed watching me. I ask him what's going on. He doesn't say anything and just climbs back into the top bunk. I doze off and wake up, and there he is again. . . ."

"It'll be over soon."

". . . At mealtime, they take my food. I'm not even thinking about a shower."

"The attorneys say they can get a hearing. They'll release you until then."

"That's it? That's all the paper had to do?"

Tom nodded. "You'll be out in an hour."

"You could have done this the first day?"

"Max . . ."

McSwirley put his head down on the table. "I can't take it anymore."

One hour later, downtown Tampa was filled with news trucks and TV cameras, all pointing at the front entrance of the jail.

"*There he is!*"

Cameramen pounced. Editors shielded McSwirley and fought their way through the mob. The Party Parrot jumped in the background.

"Has the serial killer contacted you again?"

"Will you reveal your secret source?"

The metro editor pushed away microphones. "Please! He's been through a lot!"

"Are you next on the death list?"

They rushed Jeff across the sidewalk to a waiting sedan and shoved him inside. Doors slammed. Cameras converged on the back window.

"Why are you crying?"

The sedan sped off.

Yet another emergency budget meeting was under way when Jeff and his editor burst into the newsroom.

"McSwirley's safe," said Tom.

Everyone cheered.

"Glad to hear it," said the maximum editor. "We need to get him back on the story."

"He just got out of jail!"

"It's the damn *Tribune* and *Times*," said Max. "Have you seen their websites teasing to tomorrow's editions? Both have scoops on Serge and an accomplice applying for jobs. They're running sample columns he wrote." The editor stood and began pacing. "Why didn't they apply here? What are we, chopped liver?"

"Actually," said Tom, "I think they did."

Max slammed both palms down on the table. "What!"

"Week ago. Pretty sure it was them. One was nuts and the other was drunk. Had security throw them out."

"Damn it! You should have hired them!"

"Just when I think I've heard everything . . ."

"At least we'd have writing samples to counter the competition," said Max.

"They did give us writing samples."

"They *did*?"

"Two columns. Pieces of paper folded in tiny squares. But it was just babbling."

"Please tell me you kept them in their application file."

"I didn't keep an application file. I told you, they were crazy."

"You threw the columns out?!"

"I didn't say that. Security has 'em red-flagged in their 'future threat' file in case we ever have to turn anything over to police."

The maximum editor snapped his fingers. "Get me security."

Five minutes later, a uniformed guard arrived with a manila folder. Max removed a heavily creased page. "This is the 'God Talk with Serge' column the *Trib*'s running. We can't use it." He tossed it aside and grabbed a second sheet. His lips moved as he read. "Say, this isn't half bad."

"Now I *have* heard everything."

"No, really," said Max, slowly rotating the page to follow the writing in a circle around the margins. "You're right: It's rambling, but in a good way, like Kerouac. . . . What's this hurricane road-trip business?"

"Said he wanted to do a Kuraltesque profile each week showcasing sites of historic Florida landfalls."

"Well, we're definitely into hurricane coverage, so it's relevant."

"You're not actually thinking of running it as a real column."

"We'll pull our human-interest guy for tomorrow," said Max. "He's through anyway. Did you read that thing about his dog?"

"But this is highly unethical!"

"Look," said Max, "we won't say it's an official column. We'll just run it in the column position and let the public decide." The maximum editor snapped his fingers again and handed the page to a news clerk. "Type this into the system. Slug it for Jerry's space."

"What title should I give it?"

"Use the one it's already got."

"Yes, sir." The clerk walked across the newsroom, planted himself at a computer and began tapping:

The Art of the Night Tour

© by Serge and Coleman, all rights reserved. This means you.

Hi. Serge and Coleman here. Our first column—boy are we excited! They finally let us graduate from Letters to the Editor, and it couldn't have come soon enough. We were sharing the page with a bunch of kooks! I met this one guy who used to work for an editorial page, and he said the big inside secret is how many turds they get in the mail. I'm thinking metaphorically, and he's says no, real logs. Some are gift-wrapped for surprise effect, others just squeezed off into the box. Most don't include letters or notes because, I'm guessing, you know, "Enough said."

So let's get to it!

Am I proud to be a Floridian! Storm-resilient! Practically the whole state's been hit, so I thought we'd make a round-robin and start geographically in Pensacola. Coleman and I had a chance to visit after the last hurricane. FYI: Even though I'm doing all the writing, don't sell Coleman's contribution short. He's like my muse—cracks me up all day long! You know that one friend we all have? Coleman's that guy, exponentially. Like, how some idiot will get his hand stuck in a jar? Coleman got his *head* stuck in this big glass candy bowl. I'm reading a book on the sofa and hear him come in the room, and I say, "Hey, Coleman"—without looking. He says, "Hey, Serge," but his voice has reverb like it's coming out of a toilet. I turn around. "Coleman! What are you doing with your head in a big glass bowl?" "I don't know." "How can you not know?" "I woke up, and there it was." He goes in the kitchen, and I'm reading my book again, and he comes back and asks to borrow my car keys. Then he's gone a half hour and returns with three bags from the grocery store, and there's a tap on my shoulder. "Serge, I can't get it off." I say, "What?" He says, "I tried ignoring it, but I need it off now." Thanks again, Coleman. The book had just gotten interesting: This guy's been stabbing people with icicles, so the murder weapons melt. I'd mentally blocked off the afternoon to make icicle molds for the freezer, because it's Florida and the book's in Alaska. I tell Coleman to sit at the kitchen table, hold still and close his eyes. He says, "What are you doing with that hammer?" Then it's a big chase around the house, and somehow he slips out the front door, and we're running down the middle of this busy street in downtown Pensacola. We'd driven up there after Ivan, staying with one of our few friends who still had a roof, doing what little we could to pitch in. The mettle of that place! People think St. Augustine is the oldest city, but it's just the oldest *continuous* city. Pensacola was founded earlier, except there was an interruption. You guessed it: hurricane. And here they were, persevering once again, days without sleep, shoveling debris, and then Coleman and I go running by with a glass bowl and a hammer. Apparently this was just the comic relief they needed. The whole street broke up! We ran around this tree several times until someone took pity and mashed sticks of butter up into the bowl, and it popped right off. The sun was setting, and before I knew it, they're all chanting "Night Tour! Night Tour! Night Tour!" Said they want to show us the *real* Pensacola. Coleman's head is still lathered with butter, and we tell him where he can meet us later, but he doesn't want to get left behind, and another friend breaks out a case of these special beers we didn't recognize. Maudite, La Fin Du Monde. Coleman asks, "What's this?" The guy just grins. "It'll kick your

ass." Turned out to be triple-strength import beer, and
Coleman had like four right away, and we drove across
town to Sluggo's, an ambitiously subterranean dive that
shunned profits and catered to artists and anarchists.
Coleman's getting free beer at the bar because they think
he's an expressionist working in dairy products, and I get
talking to the regulars, who say the dunes are up to your
nipples in the Flora-Bama Lounge, and people are going
snow-blind from sand drifts. I explain that Pensacola
sand is so bright because of a geological break with the
mainland, which is Georgia red clay, but the barrier islands are quartz. Trivia bonus: Because those pristine
beaches are such tourist cash cows, there's actually a law
against transporting red clay across the bridges. I laugh
about it, because where's the profit in that crime? Then
another friend yanks me off my stool and says, "You
gotta see the Knoll Room." I say, "What?" but he just
drags me into this back room with ripped Naugahyde
cocktail booths and flickering *Twin Peaks* fluorescent
lights. And you know how if you're in a supermarket and
see something out the corner of your eye and freak a half
second because you think someone's snuck up on you,
but you spin around and it's just a life-size cardboard guy
advertising something? That's this room on steroids, giant cutouts everywhere. Then it hits me. Those grainy
home movies of the Kennedy assassination. This is the
cast from the Grassy Knoll: Funny-Sunglasses Lady,
Mother and Daughter, Umbrella Man, Windbreaker
Dude, Overpass Guy. My friend says some artist kind of
got into the JFK thing. I say, "Some story." He says,
"That's not the story. During the fortieth anniversary of
the assassination, the artist loads all the cutouts in his
car and drives to Dallas, where he sets them up on the
knoll in their same positions, and the cops grab him." I
say, "What was the charge?" He says, "I don't think

there was one. Sometimes society just steps in when the weirdness level gets too high." Then we go back to the main bar, where everyone's collecting empty paint buckets and assembling search parties to look for red clay, because, you know, they're anarchists. We grab Coleman and split and find ourselves driving along the railroad tracks in the middle of bombed-out nowhere, and the only light is coming from this bohemian coffee joint called the End of the Line, which is popular on the hobo telegraph, because all these people keep jumping off boxcars and coming in, and on the other side of the tracks is a giant field and the civic center where they hold the big rock concerts, and after gigs Judas Priest apparently likes to walk across fields and railroad tracks, because there's a picture of them on the wall playing an impromptu set by the cappuccino machine. Everyone in our group but me is completely gassed, shouting "Night Tour!" again, so we leave on foot, and our group has grown by several hobos, and we walk for miles past the cemetery and all the way to Palafox Street to see if anything else might be open. But nothing is. Then: "Where's Coleman?" We retrace our steps. "Coleman? . . . Coleman, where are you?" A door opens, and these young people are helping Coleman and one of the hobos keep their footing. "Coleman, where'd you go?" He says he and his newest buddy found the only open downtown bar, where they sat at the counter and ordered beers. The guy behind the counter gave them strange looks but served anyway. Then Coleman notices these two hot chicks on a sofa staring at them. Not in a good way. He looks around, and it's one of those chic, foo-foo minimalist bars with no cash register and a theme he's never seen before. It's almost like . . . somebody's apartment. They were so fucked up they just walked into these people's pad demanding beer. And got it. Then we hitched a ride with unlicensed contractors out to the beach, where police lights flashed and people were getting handcuffed with pails of red clay, and then we're trying to find a way back, and the gang got scattered, and me and Coleman spot a pink-neon "Open" sign a mile away and finally reach the strip club to use a phone, and there's only one customer and four dancers sitting around a card table eating pizza. We wait outside a half hour, and when our taxi finally gets there, he drives right by. The lone customer comes out and stands next to us. I say, "I hope you're not waiting for a cab," but he says he has his own ride and do we need a lift? Then we're in a station wagon with his mom, and a cockatoo jumps on my shoulder and starts squawking "Eat me" in Spanish, and we came home the next afternoon. And that's pretty much the hurricane history of Pensacola.

CHAPTER TWENTY-EIGHT

TAMPA

Loud knocking on the door of a motel room across from Busch Gardens. Actually, it wasn't knocking. Someone was kicking the door. "Open up! It's heavy!"

Coleman checked the peephole and undid the chain. Serge came in with a giant square of plywood.

Coleman found one of the many opened beers he'd forgotten around the room. "Where have you been?"

"Getting supplies."

"How'd you find plywood? TV said all the stores were out because of the storms."

"That's why I never go to stores. I hate lines. If there's any kind of wait at all, I last about as long as the pope on the uneven parallel bars. So when I need plywood, I use another of my Florida hurricane-survival secrets."

"What's that?"

"Steal it from construction sites. There's still a line, but it's shorter."

Serge ran back out the door and returned with a portable drill and car audio components from the pawnshops. He made another trip, and another, more and more components: amplifiers, equal-izers, signal boosters and pieces of speakers.

Serge hoisted the plywood and placed it over the room's single window. "Coleman, grab this side."

"But I'm drinking a beer."

"Coleman! I can't hold this whole thing and drill at the same time!"

"Okay, okay. I'm coming." He drained the rest of the can and gripped the edge of the wood. "Heavier than it looks."

"Had to go with three-quarter-inch, or she'll crack for sure." Serge drilled pilot holes and sank concrete-boring bolts.

"It's slipping," said Coleman.

"Hang on. I'm almost done."

"Serge, why are we staying in another dump? I understand when money's tight, but we got all that cash from our new job."

"You just want a minibar."

"No, really. I wouldn't mind staying at a fancy place for once."

"Me, too. But I'm making a stand against hypocrisy." Serge revved the portable drill. "Luxury hotels are like keyhole views into the secret world of conservatives."

"What do you mean?"

"Who owns the most expensive hotels? Who stays there? As a rule, super-rich conservatives." Another bolt countersunk into the concrete. "And what do wealthy neocons like to do more than anything? Stick their noses in our bedrooms. Wait, that's number two. Take our money's number one."

"What's that got to do with hotels?"

"They act all sophisticated and elegant in the lobby. Then they get to the privacy of their rooms." Serge fed another bolt. "You should see the pay-per-view adult movies—not even an attempt to change the titles for appearance."

"They all watch dirty movies?"

"Only some, but the rest aren't complaining, even though they know about it. They're too busy interfering with *our* sex lives. Remember Ed Meese?"

"No."

"Reagan's attorney general, who strong-armed the Southland Corporation. That's why the lunch-bucket crowd can't buy *Playboy* in 7-Eleven anymore, while the big party donors are up in their five-hundred-dollar suites watching *Amateur PTA Moms Backdoor Entry, Vol. III*." One final twist from the drill. "There. Done. You can let go now."

"Serge?"

"What?"

"I thought you were supposed to put the plywood on the outside of the window."

"This isn't for the hurricane. It's for my guitar."

"I don't follow—"

"I'm tired of that dinky amp. I've decided my career needs a big sound. That's why I've been collecting all these components from pawnshops. And now I have the final pieces to build the largest amp I'll ever need. Maybe a world record."

Coleman turned around. "Where?"

"You're standing in it." Serge began unscrewing stereo woofers.

Coleman looked at his feet. "I don't see anything."

"The *room* is the amp. Ten thousand watts if this motel's fuses don't blow first." Serge arranged heavy chunks of metal on the bed.

"How can a room be an amp?"

"Easier than you'd think. It's just a matter of scale. Take what would make a regular amp and multiply it by cubic volume." He unwired a speaker harness. "There are two kinds of amps. The ones that breathe and the airtight. Those are called acoustic suspension. That's why I needed the plywood. The first note on my guitar would have blown the window all over the parking lot."

"So that's why we're staying at this motel instead of your house. I thought it was to hide out."

"Landlords are picky about drilling a bunch of holes." Serge drilled a bunch of holes. He began mounting metal chunks. "These are the magnets that drive the speakers. Figure sixty ought to do it. The pawnshops had way more than I needed—lots of starving musicians out there. I'll also have to mount some of the magnets *inside* the walls, for Dolby noise reduction and proper high-end fidelity during my incredible Eddie Van Halen solos. That's what the jigsaw is for."

It took most of the day. The mounting went well, but Serge had to parallel-wire all the components, and Coleman kept tripping over cables.

"Look out!"

"There's no place to walk."

"We're leaving soon anyway. Just sit on the bed and watch TV."

Coleman clicked the remote. A stenciled title came on the screen. "Cool. Our favorite show."

". . . *Welcome to another installment of* Florida's Funniest Surveillance Videos, *where we open tonight's program in Tampa.* . . ."

Coleman watched black-and-white footage of two men and a handcart. "Hey, Serge. We're on again."

"Which one?"

"Convenience store."

The choppy video now showed the two men wheeling a small ATM out of the store. "*Our crooks were so brazen they even stopped to have the clerk sign for it.* . . ." The screen switched to a follow-up interview with the employee. "*Why'd you let them take the cash machine?*"

"*They had a clipboard.*"

Coleman glanced toward a corner of the room and the jimmied-open ATM. "I can't believe we got away with that so easy."

"I can," said Serge. "Once again, validating Serge's Key to Life: Always act like you deserve to be here."

By nightfall, the room's floor was an intricate web of wiring. Serge plugged in no fewer than eight power cords. "I think she's ready." He grabbed his guitar case. "I've been practicing *Goats Head Soup.*"

"Great album." Coleman cracked another beer. "Let 'er rip."

"Not here," said Serge. "It isn't safe. We have to clear the blast zone."

"How are you going to play from that far?"

Serge held up a rectangular box the size of a garage-door opener. "Pawnshop again. Transmitter, like all the great guitarists use so they can leap around in concert. I've decided my stage persona needs lots of jumping. . . . Let's go. Watch your step."

"Can I be a roadie?"

The sun was setting as Serge climbed up on top of the H2. It was parked at a closed Laundromat two hundred yards from the motel. "Roadie, guitar . . ."

Coleman handed it up, and Serge looped the strap over his neck. He turned the transmitter on.

Coleman raised his right arm and flicked a Bic lighter. Serge began strumming.

DUH-DUH! Da-da-dah, . . .

A million dogs barked. Car alarms whooped everywhere.

"Wow, it really does sound like the Stones," said Coleman. "And freakin' loud!"

DAH-DAH! . . . "Told you it would work. Now time to really crank the volume!" Serge twisted a knob all the way up and began bounding around the Hummer's roof.

DAH-DAH! . . .

CHAPTER TWENTY-NINE

TAMPA

Footage from McSwirley's jail release played throughout the day and into the night. It was on in bars, department stores, newsrooms. One TV sat in the back of a ranch house with a rusty chain-link fence.

Hands in latex gloves held a newspaper. The guest column by Serge and Coleman. It was ripped to shreds, then confetti. Yelling from the television made the person look up. There was McSwirley again, surrounded by a million cameras and shouting reporters, getting all the attention.

"Please!" said the metro editor. *"He's been—"*

A brick went through the TV.

TAMPA BAY TODAY

The phone rang for the hundredth time.

"Metro, McSwirley. . . . No, I'm sorry. I'm not doing interviews. . . . I just don't feel like it right now. . . . I know I've become part of the story. . . ."

He hung up, and it rang immediately.

". . . I'm sorry. No interviews. . . ."

Justin Weeks waved urgently from the next desk. "I'll do an interview."

"Hold on," Jeff told the caller. "Someone wants to talk to you. I'm going to transfer."

Another phone rang. "Hello? This is Justin Weeks, McSwirley's partner. I've been working on the same story. Actually, it's really my story and— . . . I see. . . . I see. . . . I understand. . . . If you change your mind . . ." Justin hung up.

"What happened?" asked McSwirley.

Weeks pretended to look for something important on his desk. "They only want to interview you."

The scene repeated chronically into the night, phone ringing and ringing. McSwirley not wanting to talk to anybody. Nobody wanting to talk to Justin.

Jeff finally got up and stretched. "I'm going to the break room for a soda. Want anything?"

"I'm good," said Justin.

"Can you get my phone while I'm gone?"

McSwirley was smiling in the photograph. It was the mug shot from the occasional weekend column he wrote for the paper. The picture rested in the middle of a trembling hand. The other hand dialed a phone. The photo was crumpled into an angry ball and tossed away. The phone began ringing. The hand cupped around the caller's mouth.

A reporter turned toward a ringing phone. He got up and walked to the next desk.

"Metro, Weeks. . . . And who are you with? . . . What? . . . No, really. Who are you? . . . You're joking. . . . You think you know who the killer is? . . . You'll only talk to McSwirley because of how sensitively he handles his stories? . . . No, McSwirley's not here. In fact he won't be back for days. . . . Wait. Don't hang up. I'm his partner; I'm even more sensitive. He learned all that from me. . . . Why don't *I* meet you instead? . . . Okay, wait a sec. Let me grab a piece of paper. . . ."

McSwirley rested with an arm braced against the front of a vending machine. He scanned selections. Little red "out of stock" lights next to everything he wanted. Only one flavor left at the bottom. No wonder it was still available. Darn. McSwirley smoothed out a dollar bill and stuck it in the machine. It whirred and came back out. He stuck it in again. It spit back out. . . .

Justin grabbed a coat and switched off his computer. McSwirley returned to the newsroom, sipping a grape Fanta. "Where are you going?"

"Out." Justin slipped an arm through a coat sleeve.

McSwirley looked toward his desk. "Anyone call while I was gone?"

"Nope."

The phone rang.

Justin tensed.

"Metro, McSwirley. . . . Where? . . ." He grabbed a pen and began writing. "I'll meet you there."

"Who was that?" asked Justin.

Jeff grabbed his own jacket. "Agent Mahoney . . ."

Justin relaxed.

". . . On his way back from the Suwannee River. Found two more bodies."

"At the river?"

"No, one there and one here. I'm on my way to the second location."

The reporters rode the elevator down together and left the building in opposite directions.

CHAPTER THIRTY

EAST SIDE OF TOWN

Police cruisers filled a motel parking lot on Busch Boulevard. The Pink Seahorse.

Mahoney was just getting out of his car when Jeff drove up in an oil-dripping '84 Fiero.

"ID the body up at the river?" asked Jeff.

Mahoney nodded. "Another child molester."

"How'd you find him?"

"Molested."

They headed toward a room with an open door and crime-scene tape.

"That motel sure is pink," said Jeff.

A sturdy officer ran out of the room and got sick in the bushes.

Mahoney and the reporter went inside. A tangled mat of electrical cords across the floor. In the middle was the victim, still tied to a chair. Blood from every natural opening. No wounds. Jeff caught a brief glimpse and reflexively jerked away. "Oh, dear God!"

Mahoney leaned for a closer look. "A Hip-Hop Redneck." He stood back up and handed Jeff a hankie.

"Thanks." Jeff wiped his mouth. "What the hell happened?"

"Not sure," said Mahoney, surveying the crime scene. "But it reeks of Serge."

An officer entered the room who did not look like the others. He was Dipsy the Hippie Cop. Used to be one of the sound guys for the Grateful Dead. Now he was a police audio tech with a house on the beach, thanks to his skill at turning inaudible bugs and wiretaps into crystal, convicting evidence.

"Whoa!" said Dipsy. "Someone's been busy!"

"You know what happened?"

"Abso-fuckin'-lutely," said Dipsy. "I definitely want to rock with these cats."

"So you going to tell us?"

"Biggest amp I ever saw," said Dipsy, admiring a relay junction. "Even tops that insane thing Phil Lesh made us carry around in '73."

"Amp? Like in *guitar* amp?"

"Acoustic suspension to be precise." Dipsy chomped a granola bar and inspected magnetic drivers attached to load-bearing studs. "Nice work, too."

"I can't believe it killed the guy," said a homicide detective.

Dipsy checked connections to one of the signal boosters. "I'd be more surprised if it didn't. Sound waves are incredibly powerful. Just because they're invisible, people don't realize . . ." He gestured at the blood-spattered electronics. ". . . This was fishing with dynamite."

"But how is it possible to build an amp this big?"

"It's more than possible; it's easy. Just multiply components and wattage by the cubic volume of the room." He stuck an empty snack wrapper in the hip pocket of his cutoffs. "Reminds me back in '62 when me and the brothers at Sig Ep built this ridiculous speaker from eight Heathkits and an abandoned refrigerator. That thing was insane!"

An H2 drove past a motel parking lot full of police cars.

"Looks like they found your amp," said Coleman. "What do you think happened to the guy you left inside?"

"The Hip-Hop Redneck?" Blue lights flickered off Serge's face as they passed the motel. "He got to hear my first concert."

"Don't you think it was too loud for him?"

"Normally, but you heard his car stereo in traffic. He'd already established that he prefers his music too loud."

The H2 reached the corner, and Coleman looked back. "They're wheeling a stretcher out of the room. It's covered with a sheet."

"Another pioneering feature of my upcoming tour," said Serge. "Forget the front row and backstage passes. For the right price, you can sit *inside* the amp. Of course, you hemorrhage to death from the sound concussion, but *it's only rock 'n' roll!*"

MEANWHILE, ON THE SOUTH SIDE OF TOWN

Justin Weeks drove slowly through a decaying neighborhood. Potholes, growling rottweilers, no streetlights. He squinted at dim house numbers.

His car neared a dead end. It stopped in front of a rusty chain-link fence. He checked the address on his scrap of paper. Matched the mailbox, darkest house on the block. Justin got out. He opened the squeaky front gate and walked stiff-legged to the front porch.

Knock-knock-knock. "Hello? Anybody home?"

No answer.

Justin glanced around and tried the knob. Unlocked. He just *had* to scoop McSwirley. The door creaked open. "Anyone here?" He kept calling as he walked through the unfurnished living room, then the empty dining room. In the kitchen he found a light switch. Roaches made a jail break from a pile of spent TV-dinner trays.

Justin worked his way around the rest of the mounting garbage. Empty tuna tins and Chef Boyardee cans, jagged lids bent up, some still with forks inside from when they'd been eaten cold. "Jeee-zusssss Christ . . ."

Weeks continued canvassing the house, with no sign of life. Only one room left in back. The door was closed. A sign: No Trespassing! Anyone else would have split right there. No, they never would have gone inside in the first place. But that was the thing about Justin. He was smarter. . . . Knock-knock. "Anyone in there?" He knocked again; the door was ajar and slowly swung open on its own. "Helllloooooo? . . ." Justin's hand felt along the wall again and flipped another light switch. That's when he saw it. His jaw fell, and an electric tingle danced up his spine. *"Oh . . . my . . . God . . ."* He was looking at The Wall. He didn't hear the car drive up.

Justin found himself unconsciously stepping forward in fascination. His eyes first went to the largest photograph of Mc-Swirley. The one with the meat cleaver through the forehead. Then the others: college, high school, family. He turned to the newspaper clippings, moving through the years until the most recent coverage of Serge. One had a double byline, McSwirley and himself. The article was covered with handwriting. Bold, all caps, in thick, blood-red marker: WE DON'T LIKE JUSTIN. WE LIKE McSWIRLEY.

The door behind him creaked shut.

Justin spun. "I . . . uh . . . the door was open. . . . I'm sorry. . . . I have to go. . . ."

Quick footsteps toward him. Justin raised his arms to fend off the crowbar. Then the lights went out.

There was a stereo on a shelf in the corner. Latex hands inserted a CD and turned the volume all the way up.

The music brought Justin around. He stirred and raised his head.

". . . Talkin' 'bout the Midnight Rambler. . . ."

Justin raised his arms again in defense. "Noooooooo!"

The chain saw roared to life. The business end hung in the air for a breathless second. Then it came down with an unmistakable gnarling sound.

This was clearly the work of a madman. Everyone knows it's not safe to run a gas engine indoors.

ESTEBAN

CHAPTER THIRTY-ONE

TAMPA BAY TODAY

One hour before sunrise. A lightning storm of xenon camera strobes lit up the main entrance to Gladstone Tower. Photographers from the crime lab and the newspaper elbowed for shooting space.

The chief of police was on scene with all the brass. Only a couple gawkers so far, winos crawling from alleys. But that would seriously change with the morning rush hour. "Get a sheet around the whole thing," said the chief. "We don't need everyone seeing this."

All across town, sleeping newspaper editors rolled over in bed and fumbled for ringing phones. "Hullo? . . ."

Twenty minutes later. Unshaven journalists streamed into the newsroom. Every coffeemaker in service. It started getting light outside. The earliest emergency meeting yet at the oval conference table.

"Where's McSwirley?" demanded the maximum editor. "We need him on this!"

"Don't you care at all about his safety?" said Tom.

A news clerk held a phone receiver. "Still getting his answering machine."

"What about his cell?"

The clerk shook his head. "Must be off."

"Keep trying!"

Features raised a pen. "Is it true there are pieces of Justin all over the sidewalk?"

Sports raised a pen. "I heard the parts were arranged to spell 'Hi!'"

A pen from Business. "Did they really dot the *i* with his head?"

The news clerk: "Still no answer."

Max's face fell into his hands.

"Let's not overreact just yet," said Tom. "There's still a good chance Jeff's on his way in right now. You know how he likes to get here early."

A green '84 Fiero exited the Lee Roy Selmon Expressway in the predawn half-light. It rumbled over the metal grating of the Brorein Street Bridge. An Ivy League rowing team had clandestinely pulled up to a seawall on the Hillsborough River and begun spray-painting their school name below the Radisson.

McSwirley didn't see them. He was distracted by the countless red and blue lights flashing through the downtown canyons. Jeff came off the bridge and began zigzagging across the grid of one-way streets to Gladstone Tower. The closer he got, the brighter the lights. He made a final turn onto Kennedy Boulevard, and police barricades forced him to loop around the block to get to the parking garage.

A cell phone rang at the conference table. Metro Tom pulled it from his jacket, immediately recognizing the numeric display. "It's McSwirley!" Everyone hushed. Tom pressed a button "Jeff! Where are you?"

McSwirley drove slowly through the second parking deck,

looking for a free spot. "In the garage. I just saw a bunch of police out front. Anyone covering it? If you want me to check it out—"

"No! Don't!" said the editor. "Get in the building as fast as you can! We're all up here waiting for you."

The maximum editor snapped his finger at an assistant. "Call security. Get some people to the garage!"

"You're at the office awfully early," said McSwirley. "I thought I was going to get the overnight reporter. Something big must be up, eh?"

"Just get in the building!"

"Oh, no!" said McSwirley.

"What is it?" shouted Tom. "What the hell's happening?"

"I thought I found a spot, but it's a motorcycle."

"Are there people nearby?"

McSwirley looked around. "Nope. . . . Hey, I found a space! . . . People?"

"You need to find *people*! Get in the building!"

Jeff climbed out of the Fiero. "What's going on?"

"We'll tell you when you get inside. Just hurry!"

"Okay." Jeff closed his phone.

Tires screeched. Jeff turned around. Serge jumped out of a black H2, waving a pistol. "Hurry up! Get inside!"

Jeff stumbled backward.

Serge rushed forward, excitedly gesturing at the reporter with the gun barrel. "You're not safe here!"

Jeff kept backing up.

"What's your problem?" Serge lunged and grabbed the reporter by the arm. "We have to get you out of here. Something bad's happened. Just heard it on the radio."

Jeff went limp, and Serge had to drag him the rest of the way. Coleman opened a back door.

"Up you go!" Serge boosted the reporter inside and slammed the door. He climbed into the driver's seat and peeled out. They screeched down the exit ramp.

Two security guards strolled into the quiet garage, looked around and shrugged.

Max stared at his wristwatch. "What's taking him so long? It's only a couple minutes from the garage."

Sports raised a pen. "Something bad must have happened."

A news clerk held a phone. "Security just found his car abandoned in the garage. The driver's door was left open."

A cell phone rang. It almost flew out of Tom's hands as he answered. "McSwirley! Where are you? . . . What!"

"What is it?" asked Max.

The metro editor covered the phone. "He's been kidnapped. The killer jumped him in the garage." He uncovered the phone. "Are you all right? . . . Thank God! How are you calling? Are you locked in the trunk or something? . . . Serge *told* you to make the call? Why would he do— . . . He wants everyone to know you're all right? . . . What? Could you repeat that last part? . . . Okay, I'll hold." Tom covered the phone again. "He's putting Serge on." Tom uncovered the phone. "Serge? . . . Listen, you touch a single hair and I swear I'll kill— . . . Huh? . . . What do you mean you're taking over Justin's old job? . . . *You're* McSwirley's partner now? . . . No, wait! Don't hang up!"

The metro editor slowly closed his phone.

"What's going on?" asked Max.

The metro editor turned with a blank face. "They're working on a story."

CHAPTER THIRTY-TWO

FOUR DAYS LATER

Editors sat solemnly around the conference table at *Tampa Bay Today*. Hope fading.

"He's probably dead."

"Don't say that!"

"But you saw that crazy police chase on TV."

"I still can't believe they got away from all those helicopters."

Someone staggered through the newsroom's entrance.

"It's McSwirley!"

"He's alive!"

They stampeded over.

"You're white as a sheet!"

McSwirley looked like he was about to faint. "I need to sit down."

"Get him a chair! . . . McSwirley, you need anything?"

"I could use a soda."

"Get him a soda."

"Not grape Fanta," said Jeff.

They crowded around.

"Are you okay?"

"What happened?"

"How'd you escape?"

"Everyone, back off!" said Metro Tom. "Give him some air!"

"I didn't escape." Jeff rested forward with elbows on knees. "They let me go."

"Let you go?"

"Just down the street. Said they'd watch until I was safely in the building."

"Did they hurt you?"

Jeff shook his head. "At first I was scared they would, but they actually turned out to be pretty nice."

Mahoney combed gel into his hair. "Stockholm syndrome."

"I don't get it," said Max. "If he just let you go, why'd he grab you in the first place?"

"To save me from the killer."

"But *he's* the killer," said Tom.

"He doesn't think so," said McSwirley.

"Split personality," chimed Mahoney. "Told you."

A news clerk handed Jeff a grape Fanta. "All they had."

McSwirley took a big guzzle. "He said I was the next target."

"Why does he think that?"

"Recently watched *The Mean Season* again—he has this thing for Florida movies."

"I don't remember that one," said Tom.

"Me neither," said McSwirley. "But Serge knew all about it." He flipped open his spiral notepad. ". . . MGM, 1985. Based on *In the Heat of the Summer* by John Katzenbach, son of former attorney general. Serial killer contacts reporter. Filmed at the *Miami Herald*, but they called it the *Journal*. Climactic location shots in the 'Glades . . ."

"McSwirley . . ." said Max.

". . . Freeze-frame and you can see Pulitzer Prize–winning crime reporter–turned–novelist Edna Buchanan as an extra in one of the newsroom pans. . . ." He turned a notebook page. ". . . And Mariel Hemingway shouldn't have shown her knockers—"

"McSwirley!"

"What?"

"That's all very informative, but how does it make you a target?"

"The killer goes after Kurt Russell at the end."

"Completely cracking up," said Mahoney. "Not much longer until he makes the crucial mistake."

"Serge told me your plan to flush him out won't work," said Jeff. "I got the feeling he doesn't like you."

"I'm crushed." Mahoney opened his own notebook. "Did he mention anything else about me?"

"He said 'fuck' a lot. And 'cocksucker.'"

"Just thank God you're safe," said Tom.

"He wants me to write an article," said Jeff.

"Article?"

"Set the record straight. Even stopped at a Walgreens to buy me supplies so I could get it all down." He held up the bulging spiral book. "Craziest story I ever covered. You're not going to believe what happened."

"So what happened?"

"It all started after they grabbed me in the garage. . . ."

AFTER THEY GRABBED HIM IN THE GARAGE

A black H2 sped north on the Nuccio Parkway.

Serge looked back over the seat. "Honor to finally meet. I'm a huge fan. My name's Serge, although you probably guessed that, being a crack reporter."

McSwirley's color drained.

Serge pointed across the front seat. "I'd like you to meet Coleman."

Coleman made a quick salute with a joint. "Yo."

They turned right onto Seventh Avenue. McSwirley found his voice. "W-w-what do you want from me?"

"Want from you?" said Serge. "Nothing."

"Then why'd you kidnap me?"

"We didn't kidnap you. We *saved* you."

Coleman exhaled a big hit. "We're like your heroes." He offered the joint to Jeff.

McSwirley shook his head. "Saved me from what?"

"You seen TV this morning? Listen to the radio?"

McSwirley shook his head again. "I just got up and came right in to work."

"Oh, my God!" said Serge. "That partner of yours? Justin? Dead! Real nasty, too."

"Justin's dead!"

"Chopped up good. Chain saw." Serge sped up to run a yellow. "Lots of pieces, blood splattered all over the place. His severed head . . ."

Coleman finished another hit. "Serge . . ."

"What?"

"I think you're upsetting him."

Serge looked in the rearview. "What are you crying for? You're safe. We rescued you just in time."

McSwirley's blubbering got worse.

"Don't cry," said Serge. "Please don't cry. . . . How about this: Justin only got a boo-boo? Happened to be inoperable."

Through sobs Jeff finally managed heaving words. "I . . . can't . . . take . . . this . . . anymore!" Then more wailing.

"Of course you can take it!" Serge began playing with one of his new guns. "You're a great reporter! I've read your stuff. Pithy, precise, incredible turns of phrase, a human touch most could only dream of. I hate to speak ill of the dead, but you were carrying that Weeks guy. So I wouldn't be that upset."

McSwirley sucked in sniffles. "It's not him."

"What is it then?"

"Everything. All those people I've interviewed. Their sad faces . . ."

"Listen," said Serge, "I'm sad, too. I just don't cry. Except at the end of *Million Dollar Baby*. Who didn't? Coleman, how were you after that movie?"

Coleman exhaled. "Torn the fuck up."

"There you go," said Serge, cocking his pistol. "A lot of people are sad. There've been a bunch of murders lately. Absolutely gruesome. Not to mention everything else in the world. Watch CNN any length of time and you'll slash your wrists to your shoulders. The important thing is appreciating what little you've got for the short, miserable time you're sharing this godforsaken hellhole of a planet with those *motherfuckers . . .*"—waving the gun near the ceiling—"*. . . douche-bag scientists and their fucking manatee-viewing platforms—*"

Bang.

Serge looked up. "Dang. Now I'll have to patch that. See, Jeff? We all have our problems."

"Serge . . ." said Coleman.

"What?"

He canted his head toward the backseat.

"Why are you crying again?" said Serge. "I'm trying to cheer you up. Look out your window! There's a birdie! Isn't he cute? Just chirping away! Happy to be alive, blissfully unaware he's someone else's meal, if the mercury poisoning doesn't get him first. Then it goes right up the food chain. Brain damage. Blindness. Coma and slow death. The key is not to think about it. Don't look at the birdie."

"I'd like to get out now, please."

"And let you fall into the hands of the killer?" said Serge. "We're more loyal than that. Hey, look again! There's the landmark Columbia Restaurant. Try the paella, or the 1905 salad. That virgin olive oil they use!" Serge kissed his fingertips. "Know why it's called the 1905 salad? That's the year they first opened. Very historic. Over a hundred years in the same spot. And you know what that means? Everyone who ate those first salads: all dead."

The H2 made a left at the corner and accelerated for the interstate.

"Please," said Jeff. "If you want to save me, just take me back to the paper. They have guards."

"That was my first plan," said Serge. "After I saw the predawn TV report on Justin, I said, 'Coleman, you know what this means?' But Coleman's a slow starter in the morning, so I was essentially talking to myself. I said, 'McSwirley must be next. We have to get to him before the killer does.' So we staked out the garage, because it was the logical place for a psychotic to lie in wait, but luckily we got to you first. Then I was going to drop you off at the front door and watch until you made it safely inside. But the place was crawling with cops. Never seen so many flashing lights. That's why I don't chop bodies. Raises eyebrows."

"So you really didn't kill Justin?"

"There you go!" said Serge, slapping the dash. "I knew you were tough. Ever the reporter! Notice how you tried to slip in that investigative question? Good for you! No, I didn't kill Justin. That was disgusting. Whoever did that is screwed up. . . . Go ahead, ask all the questions you want. Except the ones where, if I answered, I'd have to kill you."

"Can I get out now?"

"Already answered that one. Next question."

"Where are we going?"

"Don't know. Where do you want to go?"

"Back to the office."

"But it's a beautiful day. Besides, you need a secret place to hole up now that you're a target. Why don't you stay with me? I can be pretty hard to find when I want to."

"I don't think so."

"I'll put you down for a maybe. Give it a few days. Doesn't work out, we shake hands. But in exchange for our free trial period of protection, I'd like to ask you a favor. Only reasonable."

"I thought you said you didn't want anything from me."

"I lied. Felt you needed to get to know us first and realize we're

not like all the other people who just want something. So here's
what I want: You know that unnamed source of yours?"

"I'm not allowed to reveal sources."

"It's okay. I already know it's Mahoney."

"How'd you know that?"

"I didn't. Only suspected. I just tricked you into telling me. So
there goes Mahoney's theory of me losing my edge. I have another
favor to ask. Actually, it's a favor *I'm* going to do for *you*."

"What's that?"

"Justin's dead."

"I know."

"You need a new partner." Serge turned all the way around in
the driver's seat and smiled his widest.

McSwirley looked perplexed. "Who?"

"Me!"

"*You* want to be my new partner?"

"Always dreamed of working for a paper. And have I got a big
story! Giant inside scoop!"

"What's that?"

"Me again!"

"I don't know. . . ."

"Bet your editor would agree. There's a newspaper war on.
Where's that cell phone you've secretly been trying to dial?"

"But I wasn't—"

"It's okay. I'd be trying, too. Call him right now. He'll be so
excited!"

CHAPTER THIRTY-THREE

TAMPA

Word swept Gladstone Tower.

"McSwirley escaped from the killers!"

"He's telling the story!"

Employees from all departments raced down stairs and elevators, streaming into the newsroom from every direction. They surrounded McSwirley's chair in a hush.

"And that's when you called me on the cell phone?" asked Tom.

McSwirley nodded.

"What happened next?"

"He wanted to show me the Vinoy Hotel in St. Pete, where Gehrig and Hemingway hung out. But cops spotted us on the other side of the bay."

"That's right," said Max. "The big chase across the bridge with all those helicopters."

"We saw the whole thing on TV," said Tom.

McSwirley opened another soda. "Thought I was dead for sure."

"So did we," said the maximum editor. "I had someone start your obit."

Jeff looked up.

"Nothing personal. We have deadlines."

"But, Jeff, how on earth did Serge get away? There must have been five choppers."

"I couldn't believe it either." McSwirley opened his notebook. "Never heard so many sirens. . . ."

Sirens screamed across the choppy surf. A dozen squad cars raced onto the Courtney Campbell causeway with more right behind. A police helicopter swooped over the middle of the bridge and the black H2 speeding east.

"Jeff! Isn't this exciting? Are you getting it all down in your notes?"

"We're going to die!"

"Eventually," said Serge. "But not today." He leaned forward in the driver's seat and looked up through the windshield.

"There's no way out," said Jeff. "You have to surrender."

"There's always a way out."

Two news helicopters came in low out of the setting sun and joined the chase. Colorful emblems on tail rotors: ACTION 2, EYE-WITNESS 5.

McSwirley rolled down his window and waved an arm at the sky. "Help!"

Serge hit the electric switch, raising Jeff's window. "Better get your arm in."

McSwirley retrieved it just in time. "We're doomed!"

"Have faith." Serge changed lanes and whipped around a bakery van. More whapping blades overhead. A green-and-white sheriff's helicopter joined the blue one from Tampa police. Another direction: Florida Cable News. The thick air traffic negotiated an impromptu formation chasing the fugitive vehicle.

McSwirley's cheek was against the glass, eyes upward. ". . . Three, four. . . . Serge, there are five helicopters now! Nobody can get away from five helicopters!"

"I'm not worried about the helicopters." Serge checked the flashing lights in his rearview: police cruisers hampered by slow-moving bridge traffic a mile back at the hump. "We still have a solid lead on the land vehicles. That's all that counts." Serge reached the end of the bridge and made a skidding right turn across three honking lanes.

Whap, whap, whap. Helicopters all over them.

"Not worried about the helicopters?" said McSwirley. "But that's how everyone gets caught, even if they lose the police cars. You've seen TV chases. It's all over once the choppers have you."

"Because those are idiots who don't even plan their next breath."

"You have a plan?"

"Watch the doctor operate. . . ." Serge cut the wheel and threw McSwirley against the door. They made another last-second turn onto a just-appeared exit ramp. Serge curled into the cloverleaf, pushing the H2's low center of gravity to the centrifugal edge. He came out on a straightaway and floored it.

McSwirley looked out the window. Whap, whap, whap. "They're still there. Even closer."

Serge didn't answer. He was in the zone. All the patrol cars even farther back now, hopelessly out of the running. Just the helicopters. But they were glue.

McSwirley got an idea. "Serge. If you give up peacefully, I'll put in a good word. I'll write a sympathetic article explaining your point of view."

"You will?"

"Definitely. The readers will rally—"

"Excellent," said Serge. "Trying psychology. I hate people who just accept their fate, even when they have to. You'll be a lot happier if you started accepting yours."

Whap, whap, whap.

"Serge, trust me. This will work. I'll write a whole series. All the hardships in your life that led up to this."

"I've had a great life," said Serge. "What about you, Coleman?"

"No stems, no seeds, I'm a pig in slop."

McSwirley tried the slightly different strategy of abject panic. "You'll never get away with this! You'll get the death penalty! . . ." He hyperventilated and pointed up. ". . . The helicopters!"

"What helicopters?" said Serge.

"The ones—" McSwirley stopped. The whapping was gone. He spun and looked out the rear window. Five tiny helicopters hovering in a stationary line a mile back. "What just happened?"

"All those idiots in TV highway chases," said Serge. "Some drive for hours across multiple counties, when the answer's obvious." The H2 passed under a green information sign for rental-car drop-off. "Wherever I go, I always make sure I'm aware of the nearest federal airspace." Serge stopped at a crossing gate. A machine spit out a ticket. Serge grabbed it, and the gate arm raised. They entered long-term parking at Tampa International Airport. "Even police helicopters in hot pursuit can't penetrate federal airspace without permission. Losing a suspect is nothing compared to endangering a commercial flight on final approach. They're required to hang back and radio for FAA clearance, which only takes a few minutes to coordinate with the tower, but it's all the time you need to duck into the overhead concealment of a parking deck. . . . You getting this down? You need me to stop and spell anything?"

"You plan for helicopter pursuits?" asked McSwirley.

"All the time. Learned it from a secret agent, standard spycraft, except it's usually used prophylactically to sterilize your trail before a chase has a chance to start. I've got to work on that."

"You know a secret agent?"

"No, I watch secret-agent movies. Except it wasn't in the movie; it was in a deleted scene. And it wasn't *in* the deleted scene; it was in the director's commentary about it *not* being in the deleted scene, which explained why it made no sense, and that's the reason they *wanted* us to think they cut it out of the movie. But they couldn't fool Serge!"

"What do you mean?"

"Don't even think of selling me a DVD and expect to sneak covert messages by in the bonus material."

"But, Serge, I don't think they were—"

"And here's a convenient parking space! It must be our lucky day."

Serge skidded into a spot on the fourth level of the Lindbergh deck. "Everyone out!"

"What are you doing?" asked McSwirley.

"Switching cars," said Serge. "It's the obvious next move. Come on, Jeff, get into this story. Hey, did you know that in the parking diagram on Tampa International's website, they misspelled Lindbergh's name? Instills that confidence in flying." Serge reached a nearby vehicle of similar color and appearance. "We're in luck! A Hummer!"

"It's just like our other car," said Coleman. "Only bigger."

"One of the advantages of frequent travel." Serge slid a thin strip of metal inside the rubber seal of the driver's window. "All kinds of free upgrades." The door popped, and the burglar alarm whooped; Serge silenced it with a yank on a twenty-amp fuse and secret wire deep under the steering console.

Coleman climbed in. "I didn't realize you liked Hummers so much."

"It's one of those love/hates," said Serge. "As a guy, I can't resist; as a student of cultural collapse, I can't resist. Born a death machine in the First Gulf War, became a soccer-mom car, and now we have Hummer stretch limos."

"I've seen those," said Coleman. "They're everywhere."

"As a society, you just have to plead no contest. The introduction of the Hummer limo is an airtight case that your civilization has finally become bullshit on stilts. . . . Where's Jeff?"

McSwirley was halfway across the deck, sprinting as fast as he could for the exit.

"Jeff!"

"What's he doing?" asked Coleman.

"Probably has to use the bathroom. Get in."

A half minute later, the SUV's wheels squealed down the cork-screw exit ramp connecting the garage's various decks. They reached level two. Coleman pointed. "There's Jeff."

McSwirley was about to pass out but still running as hard as he could down the spiral ramp. Serge pulled up alongside and rolled down his window. "Need a lift?"

The black Hummer eased into a toll-booth lane. Serge grabbed the three-day-old parking ticket off the dash and tossed it on the floor, then substituted the fresh stub he'd taken from the machine upon arriving a few minutes earlier. "Neat trick, eh?" said Serge. "I'm about to save this car's owner a lot of money."

"Let me go," said Jeff. "I'll yell. The woman in the toll booth will hear me."

"Yeah, but then we'll have to take her with us. On the other hand, she's pretty hot. Maybe *I'll* yell." Serge pulled up to the window.

McSwirley grabbed his shoulder from the backseat. "Don't! No other innocent people! I'll go with you."

Serge paid and accepted his receipt. "You sure?" he asked Jeff. "I'm a sucker for toll-booth uniforms."

"I'm sure," said Jeff.

"All right, then . . ."

A voice from the booth: "Is everything okay?"

"Why?" said Serge.

"You got your change, but you're not moving."

"Just having a discussion," said Serge. "We're kidnapping people for this road trip. Want to be abducted? It's lots of fun."

She noticed Serge's ice-blue eyes. A slight blush and smile. "You guys in some kind of fraternity?"

"No, they wouldn't have us. We weren't enrolled, and Coleman drank all their beer. . . . Last chance. That parking-attendant outfit has it going on."

"Look, I got people backed up." She wrote something and handed him a second receipt. "Here's my number."

The Hummer sped south on Interstate 75. "Jeff, we've got

quite a drive ahead. Why don't you start that exclusive interview with me?"

Jeff's arms were folded in protest. "My stuff's back at the office."

Serge hit a blinker for the next exit. "We can get Jeff some stuff, right, Coleman?"

"Look for a liquor store."

CHAPTER THIRTY-FOUR

GLADSTONE TOWER

The newsroom mob around McSwirley was bigger than ever.

"She really gave Serge her number?"

"He's not bad-looking," said Jeff. "But mainly there's this cha-risma. It's amazing. Women just . . . You'd have to see it."

"Did he ever call her?"

"Actually—"

The maximum editor suddenly noticed the size of the audience. "Doesn't anyone have anything to do around here? Get back to work!"

The audience grumbled as it dispersed.

"Enough storytelling," said Max. "First deadline's in three hours. We need to start getting this into the system."

Tom and Jeff headed over to the metro desk. McSwirley took a seat and began typing . . .

WALGREENS

Jeff had his pens and notebook in a shopping bag, and Serge had Jeff by the arm. "Will you please stop trying to signal people? I know you're just showing initiative, but it's getting old."

They reached the parking lot.

"It's only a matter of time before you're caught," said Jeff. "This may be a different car, but it looks too similar."

"I won't get caught." Serge reached into his own shopping bag for a can of shaving cream.

A black Hummer raced south across the Manatee River Bridge. Shaving cream down the door panels: JUST MARRIED.

Serge glanced sideways at Jeff, now sitting up front in the passenger seat for prime-time interview access. "Ready when you are . . ."

Jeff just gazed out the window at the raised span of a railroad bridge.

"What's the matter?" asked Serge. "Did I forget something?" He looked at the plastic drugstore bag near McSwirley's feet. "Spiral notebook, pens, microcassette recorder, extra tapes, disposable camera for my updated mug shot. The shadows in the ones the police took make me look like I don't groom on schedule."

McSwirley watched a pleasure craft motor back to the Bradenton marina.

"Don't be like this," said Serge. "You're a great reporter. How can you resist this exclusive? I mean, *everyone* wants to talk to me. Detectives, mainly. That's why I've cultivated my recluse mystique."

"I'm too nervous." Jeff held out a palm. "See? I'm shaking. I don't know what you're going to do with me."

Serge was taken aback. "You think I'm going to kill you?"

"I honestly don't know. All those others . . ."

"They were jerks," said Serge. "You go through life throwing elbows, you take your chances."

"You're saying that now," said Jeff. "But you're clearly insane."

Serge faced the road ahead. "That stings."

"I'm sorry."

"Don't apologize. I've been doing some soul-searching lately. And I've come to admit it's true. But you have to understand, mental illness is like cholesterol. There's the good kind and the bad. Without the good kind, less flavor to life. Van Gogh, Beethoven, Edgar Allan Poe, Sylvia Plath, Pink Floyd—the early *Piper at the Gates of Dawn* lineup—scientific breakthroughs, spiritual revelation, utopian visions, zany nationalism that kills millions. Wait, that's the bad kind."

Jeff's bottom lip began to quiver.

"Hey . . ." Serge gave him a playful punch in the shoulder. "I'm not going to let anything happen to my buddy. What can I do to earn your trust?"

"Let me go."

"You'll just have to trust me."

Jeff wiped his eyes. "Then tell me where you're taking me. What are your intentions?"

"You know the category-three hurricane off Belize that's hooking this way?"

McSwirley nodded.

"Figured we'd hit historic high points down the coast—Snook Haven, Spanish Point, the Edison Estate, Cabbage Key—and still have plenty of time."

"For what?"

"To pick up the hurricane. If the track holds, we'll grab it just below Naples and ride her straight across the Everglades on the Tamiami Trail."

"You're going to drive in a hurricane?"

"Perfectly safe. We'll stay in the eye."

Wind suddenly gusted into the side of Serge's face. He turned and lunged toward the open passenger door, grabbing Jeff from behind by his belt. He yanked him back inside. "Jesus, you call *me* crazy? We're going seventy!"

McSwirley lost it again. "I can't take this anymore."

The door marked MARRIED flapped on the downside of the bridge. "Coleman, would you mind getting that?"

"What?"

"The door!"

"Oh. That's *wind* I'm feeling. I thought it was peyote kicking in again. The early rushes sometimes cause confusion." Coleman reached for the handle and pulled it closed. He offered a red drink over the seat. "Jeff, want some of my Hurricane Punch?"

Serge: "Just say no."

"Yikes!" Coleman dove onto the backseat floor and covered his head. "Tell me when the dragon people are gone. Especially the one with the pincers."

"What's he talking about?" asked Jeff.

"Who knows?" said Serge, throwing a disapproving glance Coleman's way. "I hope *you're* not into drugs."

"I smoked a little pot in college."

"How are your chromosomes?"

"I don't know."

"Hopefully we caught it in time," said Serge. "Just don't accept any left-handed cigarettes at those wild newspaper parties I keep hearing about. If your kids come out with heads like jack-o'-lanterns, you'll never be able to forgive yourself. . . . Now, how about that interview?"

"I'm not really in the mood."

"Come on. It'll occupy your mind."

Jeff listlessly reached into the bag and opened a notebook in his lap. He stared at the page. He closed the notebook. "I can't get over my nervousness."

"You just need to warm up properly," said Serge. "Like people in the Kinsey study who had to fuck in front of all those researchers aiming lab instruments at them. Instead of a ruthless killer, pretend I'm some non-threatening feature subject and open with softball questions: 'What inspired your new fragrance, Serge?' Then, after getting your feet wet, we slide into the shallow graves."

Jeff opened his notebook again. "Maybe you're right."

"Maybe not."

McSwirley clicked his pen and hunched over. "If you could trade places with anyone else in the world, who would it be?"

"Good question! Let's see. . . ." Serge tapped his chin. "Okay, I got it. I remember in *Easy Rider* where someone asks Peter Fonda the same question, and he says, 'I never wanted to be anyone else.' So I guess my answer would be Peter Fonda. . . ."

Jeff finished writing. "Question number two . . ."

Miles and hours flew by. The interview continued. ". . . Childhood memories?" said Serge. "Let's see. The Captain Jack fishing show from the Blue Heron Pier, *Sunrise Semester,* Miller beer ads in Spanish—they were only on before seven A.M. The Spanish we had back then got up early. Jai alai of course, the civil-defense siren every Saturday at noon, Fourth of July parades on Flagler Boulevard, the fortune-telling scale at Riviera Beach Drugs. When I was four, my parents wouldn't let me have a dog, so I caught one of those lizards that were everywhere, tied a piece of kite string around his neck and took him for walks. Called him Rex. . . ." Serge reached over and shook Jeff's shoulder. ". . . Wake up. We had all kinds of classic TV ads back then. You're too young, but there was Radio Free Europe and the lazy eye. Guess they cured that. And the one where a drug pusher brings a briefcase to the playground: 'Gather 'round, kiddies, the man with the goodies is here.' Televisions had tubes back then that you tested at Western Auto. Planes were hijacked to Cuba all the time—that's a cheerful one. Hurricane Betsy washed the freighter *Amaryllis* aground on Singer Island, and it became a popular surfing spot because of the wave break . . ." He shook Jeff again. ". . . Got a cap gun and cowboy hat at my birthday party. Then my next-door nemesis made a false move during pin the tail on the donkey. We began pushing, and he stuck the donkey-tail pin in my arm. His mistake. You don't bring a donkey-tail pin to a gunfight. I slapped that pointy little birthday hat off his head and pistol-whipped him good. Then I remember parents arguing and a bunch of cars screeched away from our house. The next year, I turned six. . . ."

The sun drew down in the western sky. They entered swamp country, and development dwindled. Then a break in the trees that seemed to go on forever. Hundreds of single-wide trailers packed tightly together in a bright, white-gravel lot. "That's Camp FEMA," said Serge. "Where all the people displaced by Hurricane Charley went to live." They crossed the Caloosahatchee River. Soon another break in the trees. "And there's the arena where the Florida Everblades play. Isn't that far out? A minor-league hockey team in the Everglades! Someone was either a visionary or a fool. It's a fine line, like Herzog pushing that ship up a steep mountain in *Fitzcarraldo,* which is also the perfect metaphor for marriage. I used to be married. Technically still am. Separated. Her name was Molly. So it goes. She had this thing about guest towels. You got a girl? My advice: Choose carefully. You're still young, but I know all about women. I have total insight into their nature. Go ahead, ask me about women."

"Uh, what about women?"

"They're absolutely impossible to figure out, so don't even try. Everything you need to know about them is in that Carly Simon tune."

"Which one?"

"'You're So Vain.' She sings an entire song obsessing about this dude. Then, during the chorus, he's suddenly getting shit for thinking the song's about him. But it *is,* every word. Now the poor guy's confused, probably just wants to eat his dinner in peace. But no, she starts yapping about him again, and then he's *wrong* again for thinking she's yapping about him. . . ." Serge's knuckles became white on the steering wheel. "If you ever get in a relationship, the key to fighting is, never respond. Don't take the bait. You'll still get shit for not answering, but it's a smaller pile. Just let them win, because they always win anyway. That's the big secret to women: They're genetically built to win. We're built to watch TV. Better to forfeit at the beginning instead of letting it fester into a three-day thing. Just thought of something else I loved to do as a kid. Remember when you drank a lot of fluid without eating breakfast and ran outside to play? And you could hear it sloshing around in your stomach? The first time it happened, I stopped and thought, *What's this? Maybe I can make it happen on purpose.* So I ran real fast in a circle. And it worked! Slosh, slosh, slosh. . . . Coleman, remember making stuff slosh in your stomach as a kid?"

"Fondly."

Serge looked to his right. "Jeff, what about you?"

"Nope."

"You're joking! We'll just have to fix that!" Serge hit his blinker. "There's a rest stop."

Ten minutes later a large family from Wisconsin quickly gathered belongings from a picnic table and fled to a station wagon, glancing over their shoulders.

"Run, Coleman!"

"I'm running."

Serge raced in a tight circle in the parking lot. "Faster!"

Coleman ran in his own circle. "I'm going as fast as I can."

"It's sloshing! It's sloshing!" Serge invited McSwirley over with a wave of his gun. "Jeff, come on! Join us! You don't know what you're missing."

Jeff began running.

"Faster!"

Jeff ran faster.

"Faster! . . . Jeff, you're veering off. . . . Why are you running into the woods?"

CHAPTER THIRTY-FIVE

TAMPA BAY TODAY

Deadline loomed. It would be a race. The firsthand story about McSwirley's kidnapping still had a ways to go. Jeff hovered behind the metro editor, staring intently at a computer screen.

"That's everything?" asked Tom.

"No, there were lots of stops on the way back for photos and souvenirs, and he made graphite rubbings of the hurricane monument in Islamorada and the gravestone of someone called 'Mr. Watson.' I don't know who that is, but Serge said he was 'a real asshole and got what was coming.' Then he spit on the rubbing and threw it away."

"From the Peter Matthiessen trilogy," said Tom. "Predatory pioneer in the 'Glades murdered by practically the whole town. . . . I'm adding it."

Another burst of typing. "This is all great stuff. Absolutely incredible." The editor's fingers slowed. He defined a paragraph and pasted it closer to the top of the article. "Just some minor reorganization and we're done. I'm moving up the part where they tortured you."

"When?" asked Jeff.

"Making you drink a huge amount of fluid and run in circles."

"I think that was supposed to be for fun."

The editor typed "alleged." "That covers us." A blinking cursor scrolled down the screen. "I love this next part. Thought someone was dead for sure."

"So did I . . ."

EVERGLADES CITY

A black Hummer exited I-75 just before the toll booths at Alligator Alley. It picked up the Tamiami Trail and drove deeper into the swamp.

A flashing amber light lit up the caution sign with the silhouette of a panther. Vultures collected on the side of the road, pulling long things from the belly of a fourteen-foot gator squashed by a mosquito truck just before dawn.

"Note the fence on both sides of the road," said Serge. "That's to keep wildlife out of traffic. Except people keep underestimating gators. You haven't lived till you've driven through the Everglades during mating season and seen one climb an eight-foot chain-link. Gives you a new perspective on those roadside gator attractions with little petting-zoo fences. . . . Jeff, you getting this down?" Serge looked sideways at McSwirley. The notebook was closed. He looked back at the road. Fingers tapped the steering wheel. "Jeff, you're going to have to stop trying to escape."

"So you can kill me?"

"Why do you keep saying that?"

"Because you keep pointing that pistol at me."

"Because you keep trying to run— This is going nowhere. What about the interview?"

"Don't feel like it."

"I was just trying to teach you how to have a little fun."

"By forcing me to drink a bunch of water and run in pointless circles at gunpoint?"

"For your own good," said Serge. "Like parents make you eat

foods they know you'll love. Far too quickly we grow into jaded adults and lose our appreciation for silliness."

"Coleman threw up on me!"

"The circle thing doesn't work as well with beer. . . . Here's our turn . . ."

The Hummer hooked south on Highway 29, a sparsely traveled route even deeper into the swamp. A half hour later, they came to the end of the road. The end of the state. Everglades City.

"Jeff, fact-o-whirl time. Turn on your tape recorder." Serge pointed out the windshield. "Everglades City is possibly the only place in America to get arrested. The whole city. Blame geography: The Thousand Islands region of southwest Florida is perfect smuggling country. You don't even have to try to hide in the endless mangrove channels; you have to try not to get lost. And back in the day, those channels were busy. There's but a single land route in and out, the one we were just on. Couple decades ago, a convoy of sedans with blackwall tires heads down that road. The Coast Guard blockades from the sea. Federal warrants. Of course, nobody does that sort of thing anymore."

The Hummer pulled onto the grass. The air was eerily still. They got out and stood in the middle of a wide-open green space that marked the center of the isolated community. Too quiet. All animal life had headed for higher ground. That included people. Serge made a slow pirouette in the field. His eyes started at the radio tower, then the boarded-up sportsmen's inn with yellow-and-white striped awnings, a pioneer bank of Federalist architecture, Gator Express convenience store, extra mooring lines on the few yachts still at the pier, brilliant azaleas, fiery poincianas, the radio tower again. He stopped. "Where'd everyone go?"

"The hurricane," said Jeff. "Evacuation orders."

"Yeah, but you have to understand the strain of people who live down here," said Serge. "They *never* evacuate. . . . Must have been Wilma. Incredible photos. That radio tower looked like it was in the middle of a lake."

Coleman gawked up at the steel structure. "What do we do now?"

"Find a place to stay." Serge retrieved a tire iron from the back of the Hummer.

"But everything's closed," said Jeff.

"Not for long."

They followed him across the street. Serge stuck the iron in a doorjamb and threw his weight. No luck. He pushed harder and grunted.

Coleman twisted a jay in his lips. "It doesn't usually take you this long to get in a place."

"Because it usually isn't a bank." Serge heaved a final time. The door popped with a loud crack of frame damage.

"We're robbing a bank?" said Jeff.

Serge shook his head. "Staying in one. I have this rule about always knowing the coolest shelters. Welcome to the Bank of the Everglades, National Register Historic Places." He started back to the Hummer. "Built 1923 by Barron G. Collier, namesake of this county. Barron envisioned Everglades City as the west-coast metropolitan rival to Miami, and the bank was to be his cornerstone." Serge gestured across the spartan landscape. "As you see, Miami sleeps well. . . . Let's get our gear."

Serge opened the SUV's rear doors. Jeff grabbed a bag and looked up at the granite-block bank. "It's so bizarre out here in the middle of the swamp."

"That's how I chose it. If anything's left standing, it'll be this bank. We'll ride out the brunt in the vault." They returned through the front door, and Serge dropped his duffel bags in the lobby. He clicked on a flashlight. Jeff tugged his sleeve. "If you planned this, how would we have stayed in here if the people hadn't evacuated?"

"We would have paid. In fact, I'm going to anyway." Serge pulled bills from his wallet and set them on a brochure-cluttered table.

"Now I'm confused," said Jeff.

"Why are you whispering?"

"Sorry. *I'm confused!*"

His voice ricocheted around the lobby.

"I didn't mean to yell."

The flashlight's beam found a thick metal door, open, with exposed tumblers. Serge entered the smaller room. "It's not a bank anymore. It's a bed-and-breakfast. The breakfast part is served in this vault." The beam swept ancient walls. "Imagine the history. It's like I'm in a temple. You should come in here and check it—"

McSwirley grabbed the edge of the heavy vault door, quickly swinging it shut. Just before it latched, an arm stuck out. Serge pushed it back open. "Jeff, stop fooling around. You don't want to play with something priceless like this." Serge test-swung it a few inches. "Could use some WD-40." He let go of the door and—

"Coleman!"

"What?"

"Put that money down!"

"Serge, this is a lot of cash."

"Drop it!"

Coleman cringed and replaced the currency. "But there's nobody here."

"Precisely. Whenever you break into a place, it's the honor system."

"We could use the money," said Coleman.

"So can the innkeepers. This is about historic preservation. Who knows what will happen to the bank if they go under?" Serge marched everyone back outside again. The sun was now deep orange near the horizon. He reached into the Hummer and grabbed a long leather case.

"What's that?" asked Jeff.

Serge unzipped the end of the bag, exposing a fine wooden stock with zebra grain. "My new shotgun. Isn't she beautiful? Remington twelve-gauge limited edition." He pulled it the rest of the way out of the padded case. "Can't tell you how much I've been dying to try her out. Coleman?"

"Think I'll hang back in the bank and unpack."

"You sure? It's lots of fun."

"I'm kind of tired."

"Okay, but don't take the money."

Coleman winced.

Serge rested the shotgun's barrel on his shoulder. "Well, Jeff, looks like just you and me. Come on, this is going to be a real treat."

"Where are we going?"

Serge racked the first shell into the chamber and began walking. "See those isolated mangroves next to that channel leading into the swamp? You can really get lost in there . . ." Serge stopped; no second set of footsteps. He looked back. "Jeff, what are you doing? Get up here."

"I don't want to go."

"What's not to want? Nature, playing with big guns?"

Jeff remained paralyzed.

"I get it," said Serge, poking toward Jeff with the end of the barrel. "You think I'm going to dump your body out there just because it's the perfect place?" Serge turned back around and resumed walking. "Don't be silly. Now, come on; we're losing light."

They reached the shore, countless stalagmite roots sticking out of the muck from black mangroves, jungle-gym roots grabbing down from the red. A stout, refreshing breeze bent branches. The disappearing sun flickered through green and yellow leaves.

"Are we hunting?" asked Jeff.

"No, I never kill animals. That's mean." The wind steadily increased, disrupting their hair. "That's the beginning of the low-pressure system. This is so excellent." He raised the shotgun forty-five degrees and pulled the trigger.

Kaboom!

Serge cupped a hand around his right ear to enjoy the flat Everglades echo. *Kaboom, kaboom, kaboom, kaboom . . .* "I love the sound of shotguns at sunset."

He raised it again.

Kaboom!

Serge repeated until the five-shell magazine was empty. He reloaded and handed the gun to Jeff. "Now you try. But hold her tight. You got a tiger by the tail. That first one's going to surprise your shoulder."

Jeff awkwardly raised the barrel. "Like this?"

"You got it." Serge stared up at the sky. "Let 'er roar!"

Serge waited. No kaboom. He turned. The Remington was aimed in his face.

"I told you to stop screwing around." Serge grabbed the barrel and swiped the weapon out of McSwirley's hands. "First rule of gun safety is never point at anyone unless you're going to blow their head off."

Jeff looked at his shoes. "Sorry."

Serge demonstrated again.

Kaboom!

"Like that." He handed the gun back.

McSwirley raised it a second time and, after a period of summoning will, slowly squeezed the trigger.

Kaboom.

The gun fell to Jeff's side. He rubbed his shoulder. "Ow."

"Told you. Try again. It gets easier."

He tried again. The bonding continued for the rest of the ammo box. The wind blew harder. Leaves filled the air. A small branch let go.

"We better get back," said Serge. "She's picking up."

A stinging rain arrived just as they reached the bank's front steps. Serge closed the door behind them and braced it with an antique rolltop desk. More furniture was piled at the windows, leaving only a small slit for storm monitoring.

Knock-knock.

"What the hell was that!" Serge leaped and grabbed his pistol. "You guys expecting anyone?" They shook their heads. Serge peeked out the slit. "Damn. How could I have forgotten?" He set the gun down. "Jeff, remember our little secret. You don't want to endanger any innocent people."

Knock-knock-knock.

Serge began sliding the desk. *"Hold on! Give me a minute. . . ."*

TAMPA BAY TODAY

The metro editor stood and yawned. "This is the perfect place to stop. Great job, McSwirley."

"Stop?" said Jeff. "But there's more to the story."

"Max wants us to stretch it into a series. Five parts, maybe more if Serge gets back in touch. Then we'll call it an 'occasional' series." The editor turned off his computer. "This is the ideal spot to leave the audience hanging. We'll tease to the sex in Part Two to keep 'em reading."

CHAPTER THIRTY-SIX

THE NEXT MORNING

You know how in old movies or the *Superman* TV program they'd segue to dramatic news hitting the street by showing the front page of a newspaper spinning out of the darkness? Then a brass section crescendos as the paper stops spinning, a gigantic headline across the top? Okay, picture that.

A copy of *Tampa Bay Today* spins out of the black: KIDNAPPED REPORTER INTERVIEWS MURDEROUS MONSTER.

An epidemic of empty news racks. Store clerks, all day long: "We're out."

Everywhere in town, everyone standing, sitting, walking with newspapers, quickly flipping pages, gripped by every word of Jeff's account. They couldn't get enough, so they got more Jeff on Florida Cable News: "He wants the job of that guy who flies the ultralight to lead endangered cranes back home. . . ."

Citizens on the frayed edge of society wrote letters to the editor like never before. One particular message was being composed by shaking hands in latex gloves: volcanic anger over the attention *he* should be getting instead of Serge.

The paper's operators were swamped with calls over the series, registering offense over the sex in Part Two and high approval for the murder in Part Four.

PART TWO

Serge quickly closed the door behind the newest member of the hurricane party.

"It's really blowing out there!" said the tall brunette. She pulled a scrunchy from her ponytail and dropped an overnight bag.

"Jill, the gang," said Serge. "The gang, Jill . . ."

Coleman raised a beer. "Howdy."

"Hey, I know you," said Jeff. "You're the woman from the parking-garage booth."

"I called her with your cell," said Serge. "You kept falling asleep toward the end of our interview."

Jill looked around the dark interior. "I thought you said you had a reservation?"

"They must have wimped out when they heard the storm was coming."

"But we are safe, though. Right?"

"Of course," said Serge. "I never take risks."

"Why is that guy shaking so bad?"

"Jeff? It's just from the realism of the kidnapping experience."

Jill grabbed a brush and combed out wind tangles. "Is this one of those offbeat businesses? Like Michael Douglas and Sean Penn in *The Game*?"

"Exactly," said Serge. "Someone paid a bundle for this. It's his birthday!"

"Happy birthday," said Jill.

"Thanks," Jeff said rigidly, eyes shifting back and forth. *Don't endanger innocent people.*

Serge became anxious. "Where's your uniform?"

"In my bag. I changed at a rest stop."

"Whew! You had me worried."

"You really weren't kidding about the uniform?"

Serge raised his eyebrows. "Can you put it on?"

The wind continued picking up. Rain hammered the windows. Jill emerged from a back room. "How's that look?"

"I lost my parking ticket," said Serge, attaching a coal miner's light to his forehead. "Let's go look for it in the vault."

Coleman cracked another beer and followed. "I haven't seen the vault yet—"

He was grabbed from behind. "What?"

"I think they want to be alone," said Jeff.

The first few fidgeting hours passed, with faint sounds of the growing violence outside. Coleman found an aerosol can of furniture polish and sprayed his legs. "Sure you don't want any Hurricane Punch?"

"No thanks." Jeff sat on the floor and swayed nervously. "Why are you spraying your legs with Pledge?"

"Protecting myself from those evil elves with the blow darts in that corner." He tossed the can to Jeff. "Better cover yourself good. I think they're planning something."

Jeff set the can down. "I'll take my chances." He nervously jumped again at another burst of sound echoing from the vault: high-pitched shrieking and machine-gun trivia.

"... *Harder! Faster! Don't stop!* ... *Eeeeeeeeeeeeee!* ... *That's eleven!* ..."

"... *The Beatles toured the aftermath of Hurricane Dora in '64 before a concert in the Gator Bowl.* ..."

The storm wore on. The inside of the bank became quiet. Serge finally returned to the lobby, wearing only gym shorts. A tennis towel hung around his neck.

Jeff pointed with dread toward the silent vault. "Jill ... ?"

"Asleep."

Jeff sighed with relief. "I don't know how you can possibly have sex at a time like this."

"Are you kidding?" said Serge. "Hurricane sex is the best! Another long-standing Florida tradition. Newspapers always run stories nine months later about the baby booms. Puppy booms, too."

The ceiling creaked, and they looked up.

"It's time," Serge said solemnly. "Follow me."

He led them into the vault. Walls flickered with dozens of candles stair-stacked all over the place like a mountain temple in Mongolia. Coleman looked down at a fast-asleep Jill. "How do you always make them snore like that?"

Serge was busy readying the vault fallout-style. He carefully arranged military rations, jugs of water, batteries, Band-Aids. A nine-volt weather radio was on low volume, breaking the stagnant air with a steady, mechanical voice. ". . . *The following is an update from the National Weather Service. A hurricane warning remains in effect until noon tomorrow from Cape Sable to Cape Haze. Hurricane watch from the Dry Tortugas to the mouth of the Anclote River. . . . Next update at 2300. . . .*"

They broke out a case of MREs, and Serge snatched a heating pouch away from Coleman.

"Hey!"

"I haven't forgotten last time." Serge grabbed one of the jugs. "Just a *little* water."

Jeff wasn't waiting. He sucked the contents straight from a cold plastic pouch.

"You must be starved!" Serge leaned his own pouch against an activated heater. "Most people hate this stuff."

Jeff ignored him, ravenously scraping the inside of the pouch with a camouflaged spoon.

"Serge," said Coleman, "any more Tootsie Rolls?"

"Bunches. Here." Serge did The Guy Toss. Coleman caught one, and the rest bounced off his chest. He fired a joint and peeled a candy wrapper. He had no further needs.

". . . *Sustained winds one hundred and five miles an hour, gusting to one-twenty. . . . Naples Inlet, eight-foot swells. . . .*"

Something that sounded bad smashed against the outside of the bank. Serge handed Jeff a second, steaming pouch. "They're better warm." Jeff attacked it like the first.

"Careful." Serge yanked his hand back. "You almost took one of my fingers."

"Funny, I didn't feel hungry before. Now I'm famished."

"Nerves. It means you're finally calming down." Serge tore open his own pouch of lasagna-shaped soy trickery. He propped himself against the vault wall next to McSwirley and dug in.

" . . . *Peace River six feet above flood stage.* . . ."

Into the night: spooky gales, percussion of outside debris, the vault thickening with humidity. Candle wax pooled, and Jill snored. Coleman was passed out again in another of his trademark chalk-outline sleeping positions. Just Serge and Jeff and the weather-radio robot: ". . . *Category four. Sustained winds one hundred thirty-two.* . . ."

Three A.M., still hopelessly awake. Soaked T-shirts came off. Bare chests trickling with sweat. Jeff's started to heave.

"What's the matter?" asked Serge.

"Trouble . . . breathing. . . ."

"Asthma?"

Jeff shook his head. "Panic thing. Sometimes I cry. Sometimes it's this."

"Please don't cry. I can't take that."

"Just suffocating this time."

Serge lit a new candle and planted the base in hot wax. "Didn't want to say anything, but I've noticed you're a little on the tense side. Might want to cut back on the sodas."

"Might want to cut back on getting abducted."

"We're going backward again," said Serge. "I told you, this isn't a kidnapping."

"What is it, then?"

"Okay, *technically* it's a kidnapping. But it'll go better on your breathing if you think of it as protective custody."

Jeff grabbed his heart.

"Maybe this will help," said Serge. "You know the gopher tortoise?"

"What?" Shallower breaths.

"Gopher tortoise. Florida protected species. Burrows these underground tunnels near the beach, some forty feet long. That's why a lot of wildlife survive hurricanes. When instinct tells them a big blow's on the way, they head down the tortoise holes. Opossums, raccoons, big snakes—constrictors and venomous . . ."

Faster panting. "What's that got to do with me being kidnapped?"

"Everything," said Serge. "Most of the animals are mortal enemies. But mystically they call a truce while hunkered down waiting for the storm to pass. Like Foghorn Leghorn and that dog punching out their time cards. So even if I was going to kill you—which I'm *not*—you're perfectly safe tonight. The Law of the Tortoise Hole."

Jeff took his hand off his heart.

"It's passing?" asked Serge.

Jeff took a deep breath. "Sorry for snapping at you."

"No, you're within rights. This is a lot for anybody."

"It's not this. It's—"

"It's what?"

Jeff put up a hand for additional time. A little more oxygen first. That's better. "I saw *All the President's Men.*"

"Good choice. Relevance?"

"It's what inspired me to be a reporter. Wanted to make a difference. Investigate corruption, right injustice, empower the powerless."

"So? We all used to believe a bunch of naïve horseshit." Serge saw Jeff's expression. "Oops, you still believe it. Sorry. I was thinking of something completely different."

"Are you mocking me?"

"I'm good," said Serge. "Go. Proceed . . ."

Jeff took another full breath. "They told me in school I might have to start on the cop beat. Didn't give it much thought back then. But after a couple of months . . . all the death . . ."

"I get it now," said Serge. "You saw too many bodies. Understandable."

"No," said Jeff. "I haven't seen a single one."

"Then what's the deal?" asked Serge. "No bodies, no problem."

"The survivors. They're even worse. I *wish* I saw bodies."

"Transferred grief." Serge nodded. "You struck me as empathetic."

"I think about them all the time. A lot of them scream."

"I'm sure they do. Very traumatic finding out."

"Not when they find out."

"When?"

"When they answer the door and you say you're a reporter. Runs about fifty-fifty. Half want someone to talk to; the rest feel like they're being victimized again—and *you* feel like you're doing it to them. You feel like shit."

"They ever take a swing?" asked Serge.

"That's one of the first things you learn: Right after knocking, *off the porch*."

"Hard way to make a living."

"Supposed to average three months. It's been three years. This mom jumped off an overpass. Very public, very messy. I argued against the assignment. Her husband was too distraught when he answered the door. Just shook his head. But some teenager inside heard me and started shrieking hysterically. Her daughter . . ."

"That's a tough one," said Serge.

". . . The wife of a park ranger washed away in floodwaters trying to save a kid's dog. They were still hoping, but mainly it was recovery detail. She's waiting at home for the call either way. Instead she gets a call from me. I had to hold the phone at the end of my arm. Half the newsroom heard her. Kids who couldn't get out of burning houses. Others beaten to death by live-in boyfriends. What are the moms thinking bringing these guys home? The medical reports don't pull punches. Too strong to print, but *you* have to read them . . ."

"Jeff, maybe you should stop."

". . . Five-year-old who accidentally killed himself. Shotgun left loaded in a closet. Three hours later I'm standing in this cabin out in the country, Legos still on the floor . . ."

Serge decided it best to let him vent. On and on. Serge had never heard such a cavalcade of sorrow. A forum apparently was what Jeff needed. He eventually tired and stretched.

Serge looked at his watch. "You should get some sleep."

"I'm too awake."

"You were yawning."

"I know. I've been having trouble sleeping ever since taking the cop beat—completely tired and completely awake at the same time. Ever happen to you?"

"All the time. Like now. The air is still. Still air freaks me out."

"Still air?"

"To sleep, I need air movement and white noise. A fan or A/C. It puts the brakes on my thought locomotive. If the air's still, my mind bounces all over the place, and I'm up for hours flipping the pillow. Did I turn off the oven? Are the doors locked? Is my heart beating correctly? If not, then what? Was I impolite to that clerk? What exactly *is* a hubcap diamond star halo? When did I forget that cinnamon toast was an option? Then I'll notice a bright dot inside my eyelids. But when I try to focus on it, the thing drifts to the side. So I'll rotate my eyeballs and coax it back to the center again, and it drifts again and . . . Jeff . . . *Jeff?*"

He was snoring.

CHAPTER THIRTY-SEVEN

TAMPA BAY TODAY

The budget meeting. Everyone congratulated McSwirley.

"Incredible work on the series!" said an elated Max. "The second part sold even more than the first. We've doubled our press run for tomorrow."

A man in a blue-and-red baseball cap approached the table with a large, flat box. "There a Jeff McSwirley?"

"Right here."

The man set the box down and read the receipt. "Large combo with cheese bread."

"But I didn't order a pizza," said Jeff.

"It's okay. Guy downstairs at the back door already paid. Said something about a surprise for your hard work."

"Cool!" Jeff grabbed the cardboard lid.

"*Nooooo!*" Mahoney dove over the table. He snatched the box out of Jeff's hands, dashed across the conference room and slammed it down into the saltwater aquarium. "Nobody move!" He flipped open his cell and hit speed dial. "Bomb squad?"

Metro Tom arrived at the meeting. "Sorry I'm late. . . . Jeff, don't worry about lunch. My treat. Got a pizza coming."

"It's already here."

"Where?"

Jeff pointed behind a tiny skeleton popping out of a treasure chest.

A man in a blue-and-red baseball cap approached the table. "Jeff McSwirley?"

"Right here."

"Large all-the-way, dipping sticks."

Jeff opened the lid.

"Hold it," said Tom. "What's this?" He peeled a greasy page off the top of the pie.

"What is it?" asked Max.

Tom's eyes shot toward him. "We have to cancel the series!"

"Why? What's that thing say?"

" 'Cancel the series or Jeff dies.' It's signed 'Serge.' "

"Serge doesn't like the series?" said Max.

"No, he loves it," said Tom. "But the note says he watched *The Mean Season* again last night and thinks it might get the other killer pissed off at Jeff."

"There *is* no other killer," said Mahoney. "Don't you get it by now? He's the same guy. He's gone around the bend."

"Either way, we have to stop the series," said Tom.

"Nothing doing," said Max. "We're running it."

"You can't!" said Tom.

"Excuse me," said Jeff.

"I'm running it!"

"No you won't!"

"Excuse me . . ."

"Yes I will!"

"You won't!"

"I will!"

"Excuse me!"

The editors turned.

Jeff's hand was raised. "May I say something?"

"Definitely," said the maximum editor. "You wrote these incredible articles. What do you think? We should run them, right?"

"Sir, I don't think I'm in any danger from Serge."

"What do you mean?" asked Tom.

"I don't think he and the other killer are the same guy."

"Of course they are," said Mahoney.

Jeff shook his head. "I spent four days with Serge. At first I was scared to death; then I got to know him."

"And you don't think he's crazy?" said Mahoney.

"No, he's nuts, all right," said Jeff. "But there's a method to the madness. As bizarre and erratic as he may seem, I discovered a consistent underlying moral code."

"You felt safe with him?"

"Not remotely," said Jeff. "But I was worried about his impulsive risk taking. I'd stake my life that he'd never intentionally harm me."

"I ain't buying it," said Mahoney. "Schizos sometimes only show one face to certain people. I've been studying him for over a decade, not four days."

"It's moot anyway," said Tom. "We're not going to press."

"Sorry," said the maximum editor. "Even if I wanted to, it's physically impossible to cancel the series."

"Why's that?"

"Already raised ad rates. That would mean a refund."

PART THREE

Hurricane Esteban's early effects had been making themselves known for six hours now, but the slow-moving eye had stalled over the Gulf, gathering strength before landfall.

Serge was up early in the vault, monitoring developments on his battery-powered TV. The attention centered on the Naples shore.

". . . Naples is Florida's last major city on the bottom of the west coast. During the 1980s, it wore the mantle of America's fastest-growing statistical area. Development had since jumped the interstate like so many wildfires that sweep the region. Gated communities, upscale shopping centers, country clubs. From the air Naples inspires the question, who plays that much golf? . . ."

"Serge," said Coleman. "You're doing it again."

". . . But there would be no tee times today. Sand traps were water hazards, and the clubhouse staff raced to hack down coconuts before they could become cannonballs. Esteban had just been upgraded to the fiercest of the record-threatening year, each new televised landfall increasingly populated with agenda-sluts occupying respective spots along the beach at trade-show intervals. The usual TV cast of human wind socks now competed for space with feverish preachers, doomsday prophets, has-been folksingers, self-published psychics and T-shirt vendors. The Reverend Artamus Twill, from Church City, Virginia, was down on the beach with his congregation, eyes closed and heads bowed. Twill raised his right palm in stiff-armed opposition toward the crashing surf, praying for God to stop the hurricane or at least make it swerve into the wickedness of Fort Myers. . . ."

Jeff woke up. "Who's Serge talking to?"

". . . There was a second congregation from Sarasota, who had become rudderless and depressed since the feeding-tube guy started making commercials for Subway sandwiches—until finding a new cause and flipping their picket signs over for fresh writing space. . . . There was the research team, previously developing Neville Gladstone's suborbital rocket ship, which had been diverted to create an anti-hurricane machine that was now moored two miles offshore on an oil barge: fifty 747 Pratt & Whitney turbofan jet engines mounted in concentric circles and pointed skyward to create an opposing updraft that theoretically would dissipate steering currents into the upper troposphere. . . ."

Jill woke up. "What's Serge babbling about?"

". . . Sunrise was a half hour ago, but you couldn't tell. A steady drone of gas-powered generators lit the beach in floodlights. There had been some notable overnight microbursts, but disappointed reporters currently idled in a lull between storm bands. Make no mistake, the hurricane would soon be the genuine thing, but right now it was still theater. Channel 7 came back from a commercial for personal-injury lawyers. '. . . *Joe, can you pan to that flying napkin? . . .*' Then small waves became large. The reporters donned bright slickers with their stations' logos and color schemes flapping in the growing gale. Rain cut loose. Hoods went up over heads, goggles with watertight seals. More strength. Correspondents leaned into the wind. A Florida Cable News cameraman zoomed in on the Sarasota congregation: '*Fuck the devil! . . .*'"

"Does he talk like this often?" asked Jeff.

Coleman cracked a breakfast beer. "So often I barely notice anymore."

". . . Finally it got real. Honolulu-size waves pounded the historic fishing pier. A pizzeria awning cut loose, frame and all, gaining altitude like a box kite. Rookie reporters would have been worried, but not these veterans. They'd developed a system. As long as the lightest TV personality was okay, they all were. That happened to be the five-foot-three, ninety-pound correspondent from Channel 2. She was placed in the path of hurricanes because she was hot! . . . Then she was gone. A forceful gust sent her eight feet up. She landed flat on her stomach, screaming and clawing the slick grass for traction, but the wind was too strong and sent her skimming like an air-hockey puck until she was finally yanked to a stop at the edge of the seawall by her rock-climbing harness. A winch on the Channel 2 van began reeling her in. The tidal surge raced toward shore. It pitched the anti-hurricane machine up on its side. The barge took flight, fifty full-throttle jet turbines propelling it in crazy, random loop-de-loops in the sky before barreling toward shore inches above the surf, scooping the Reverend Twill off the beach and splattering him into a three-story oceanfront mansion. . . ."

Serge turned toward Jeff and Coleman.

They were staring back.

"What?"

"You were doing it again."

"No I wasn't."

"Yes you were. You said the Channel 2 chick just went."

"I did?" said Serge. "Wow. Then there's not much time. We have to be out the front door before the second guy goes."

Jeff pointed at the TV. "The second guy just went!"

"Which one?"

"The Party Parrot. . . . Oooooh, he got hung up on the jetty."

"Oh, shit." Serge grabbed a duffel bag. "Move it!"

Their gear was already assembled in the bank's lobby for a quick break. Serge threw open the door and raced outside with Jill and Coleman. Three quick trips and the Hummer was loaded again. "Jeff, come on!"

An echo from the vault: "I'm not going."

"Damn it." Serge ran back inside.

"Ow! Ow! Ow! Let go of my ear!"

"Get in the car!" Serge boosted Jeff into the backseat with Coleman. He climbed up front with Jill and floored it. The Hummer sped past the radio tower and out of Everglades City.

Serge's calculations had been spot on. He reached the Tamiami and picked up the eye. Clear sailing. Jeff's chest heaved again.

"What's the matter?" asked Serge. "We're out of the weeds."

That was the problem. Too many weeds. Up till now visibility had been poor. But the recently opened eye and low Everglades horizon gave Jeff an unobstructed view of his predicament. He twisted around, completing a 360-degree panorama of the perfectly defined, cottony gray wall. "We're in the middle of the hurricane!"

"Isn't it great?"

"We're going to die!"

"You're shit-dwelling too much," said Serge. "I've covered everything. We're monitoring all crucial coordinates with a laptop and GPS receiver."

"Who is?"

"Coleman."

"No he's not."

Serge turned around. "Coleman, where's the laptop?"

"I thought you had it."

"Coleman! You're the navigator!"

"Must have left it at the bank."

"But our lives depended on that computer! We're flying instrument-blind!"

Jeff's chest heaved again. "Serge, what does this mean? What's your backup plan?"

"No backup plan," said Serge. "Isn't it great? Anything can happen now! If we survive, life will taste that much sweeter."

"Oh, dear Jesus!" yelled Jeff, struggling with the child-locked door handle. "I have to get out of here!"

Jill looked up from Serge's lap. "Do our lives really depend on that?"

"No, I'm just fuckin' with Jeff," whispered Serge. "Go back to what you were doing."

"Oh, my God! We're doomed!"

"Jeff, take your hands away from your face. You'll miss everything. Crossing the Everglades is one of the coolest things you can do in Florida, like an astronaut looping around the dark side of the moon. Totally on your own out here, no tether, farther, deeper, back through a billion years of amphibian genetic memory, *his brain is squirmin' like a toad*. Look! There's the Ochopee post office, nation's smallest, and here's an authentic Micosukee Indian village . . ." They passed a cluster of thatched chickee huts with Yamaha dirt bikes and a Camaro out front. ". . . And there's an airboat concession. I love airboat rides! It's the only way to truly appreciate the 'Glades. You don't realize it because all the reeds create the illusion of land, but this artificially dredged causeway is in the middle of a hundred-mile-wide slough, inches to feet deep, 'River of Grass,' God rest Marjorie Stoneman Douglas. Sure wish we could take an airboat ride! But that's the drawback of riding the eye: Most things are closed, like the Skunk Ape Research Center coming up on your right. Best three-dollar tour value in Florida."

Coleman looked out the window. "They have a skunk ape?"

"No, just skunk ape T-shirts and baseball caps and a bunch of snakes they let you pose with for photos." Something else went by the window. "I can't believe it!" Serge slammed the brakes.

Jill sat up. "What is it?"

"We're in luck!"

The Hummer pulled into a narrow gravel parking lot. "Every-one out!" yelled Serge. He raced down to a dock on the edge of a drainage canal. An oversized tourist airboat sat lashed to a rustic pier. A stocky older man with leather skin was on the knees of his Levi's, tightening a knot on a mooring cleat.

Serge ran up to him and grinned. "We'd like an airboat ride, please."

"Are you crazy?"

"Crazy about the Everglades! How much?"

"We're closed." He threw an arm skyward. "The hurricane. I just came out in the eye to make sure these lines were holding up."

"I guess you're right," said Serge. "We'll come back another time. You won't be going anywhere. I mean that as a plus, not the other."

The man pulled hard on a second rope. Serge turned and spoke reverently to the others. "You're in the presence of history. He's making knots The Old Way. . . . Sir, what kind of wild-animal fur did you fashion that line from?"

"Nylon."

"I have another question, sir. . . ." Serge stopped and chuckled to himself. "Listen to me. 'Sir.' Using the White Man's tongue. You're probably a big chief. Proud ancestral name like Thunder Foot, Standing Bear or Recumbent Intestinal Parasite."

The man stood. "Sylvester."

"Gang," said Serge, "I'd like you to meet Chief Sly."

"I don't know what you're planning," said Sylvester. "But if you're going to take shelter, you better do it now. The back wall of the eye's almost here."

"Did you hear that?" Serge asked the others. "His keen native senses alert him to the slightest changes in weather. Amazing phenomenon. Science can't explain it."

Sylvester pointed. "It's right there."

They turned and looked straight up at the growling wall. Sylvester headed back to the concrete souvenir store. The others ran for the Hummer.

CHAPTER THIRTY-EIGHT

TAMPA BAY TODAY

Another codependency budget meeting.

"I won't stand for this," said Tom. "I demand you cancel the series!"

"Are you starting again?" said Max.

"I'll call New York—"

Three photographers in twenty-pocket safari vests sprinted past the conference table. The last slowed briefly. "You might want to see this."

"What's happened?"

Moments later an elevator opened on the ground floor. The budget meeting stampeded across the street to the garage.

A fire truck foamed down the parking space under a charred chassis.

McSwirley stepped forward on unsure legs. "My Fiero . . ."

"See now?" Tom told the maximum editor. "We have to stop the series!"

"Sorry," said Max. "I'd love to help, but Part Four just went to press."

Another spinning paper:

KIDNAPPED REPORTER UNABLE TO STOP MURDER.
HERO OR ACCOMPLICE? YOU MAKE THE CALL!

PART FOUR

With only seconds to spare, they dove into the Hummer and raced away from the airboat concession.

Jeff's eyes were locked on murderous blackness out the back window.

"Don't worry." Serge uncapped his thermos. "The storm's not that fast. In a few minutes, we'll be miles out in front again."

The eye tracked sure and steady. Not the Hummer. Serge kept pulling over for landmarks. Locks and dams. Back in the car. Back out. Shark River, overlooks, historic markers, restaurants with swamp cuisine. In, out, in, out . . .

"Shotgun!" yelled Coleman.

Jeff ended up in back with Jill.

"So you're a newspaper reporter?"

Jeff had difficulty pulling himself away from the eye wall. "Huh? . . . What?"

"Newspaper reporter," said Jill. "I heard you up there doing the big interview. I thought I recognized him."

"You *know* who he is?"

"It's that guy, right?"

"I'm not supposed to say anything," Jeff whispered. "And you shouldn't say anything either. For your own protection."

"Don't worry. The secret's safe with me." She smiled and shook her head. "Imagine that. Me, Jill Ribinski, on a road trip with him."

"You're happy about this?" asked Jeff.

"Of course. This is going to be in *Rolling Stone,* right? I just *love* his music."

"Who exactly do you think he is?"

"You know. *That guy.* I don't remember his name, but I knew he looked familiar."

"When?"

"Back at the airport garage. Recognized him right away. But I couldn't remember where. First I thought I might have seen his picture in a newspaper or the post office. Then I noticed the guitar in the front seat, and it hit me! Just in time, too, or I wouldn't have been able to give him my phone number."

"Listen," said Jeff, "I'm not sure you understand what you've gotten yourself into—"

"You sound just like my girlfriend." Jill glowed with the recollection. "As soon as you left the parking deck, I called her and said, 'You'll never believe who just came through my lane! . . . No, guess again. . . . No, guess again. . . . No. . . . Okay, I'll just tell you—it was *that guy*!' She said, 'Stay away from him. You know, the whole lifestyle thing.' "

"You have no idea."

"It's worth the chance. How could I not with those ice-blue eyes?"

"You're really attracted to him?"

"Oh, *definitely*! There's a bit of an age difference, but I can go for that. I think my parents saw him back when he was just getting started. Of course, they saw *everybody*. Wait till I tell them!"

"You might want to hold off."

Jill slid closer to McSwirley. "You can trust me. Tell me some inside stuff about him."

"Trust *me*," said Jeff. "I really can't."

"R-i-b-i-n-s-k-i."

"What are you doing?"

"Spelling my name for your article. He and me—we're an item now. You know, back in the bank and"— grin—"the front seat. People will want to know all the intimate details about his love life. You tell me stuff, I tell you. Deal?"

"I'm not supposed to reveal any personal—"

"His cock is incredibly huge."

"Call me crazy, but I can't begin to imagine how I might fit that into an article."

"I was just establishing trust. I'm dying to know more about him." She smiled adoringly toward the front seat. "You never know how they're going to be in person. Sometimes it's a big disappointment. But he's so down to earth—and humble. He has yet to mention a single word about his body of work."

"That's him."

"What's the current project? Is this like a back-to-his-roots trip?"

"You could say that."

"I knew it! He must be working on a comeback."

"You could say that, too."

She covered her face and almost cried. "I can't believe it. He's going back to the studio. After all these years! And I'm going to be there by his side! . . . Me! Jill R-i-b-i-n-s-k-i."

"Don't want you to get your hopes up," said Jeff. "One thing I can tell you for sure is, we're not going to a recording studio."

"That's where you're wrong," said Jill. "I was *with* him. I believe in his dreams."

"I'm telling you," said Jeff. "You've got the wrong picture."

"We'll see."

The Hummer passed a modern, freshly constructed school and a cluster of civic buildings with red, black, and yellow tribal symbols. A modest but clean middle-class neighborhood went by. "Makes you proud to live in America," said Serge. "They're diligently tending the flame of— Hold it, what's this?"

"What?" said Jeff.

Serge pulled onto the shoulder of the road. "Back there, loading his car."

Jeff turned around. "The guy evacuating?"

"Pretty late to be evacuating," said Serge.

"But *we're* evacuating."

"We're not taking a plasma TV."

The Hummer crossed a small bridge over a drainage canal and rolled slowly down a side street skirting the back of the house.

Serge furtively grabbed his pistol. "Jill, honey, would you watch the car? I have to visit a sick friend."

"That's so nice of you."

"Won't be long." Then, to Jeff and Coleman: "Come with me. Stay as quiet as you can."

"What are you doing with that gun?" asked Jeff. "What's going on?"

"Martial law." Serge checked the chamber. "I *hate* hurricane looters."

They crept along the bushes on the side of the ranch house. Coleman bumped into Jeff, who stepped on the back of Serge's shoes. "What if he's armed? Let's leave."

"Shhhhh!"

A man walked out the front door, straining under a stack of stereo components featuring the new two-hundred-watt JVC integrated amp. Serge leaped from the shrubbery. "Drop it!"

Electronics smashed to the concrete.

"I meant, freeze! You're under arrest!"

The man looked Serge over. "You're no cop!"

"I just deputized myself." He waved the gun. "Back inside."

They entered the living room, and Serge closed the door. "Take a seat on that couch." He began pacing. "I just don't understand looters!"

"They sell the shit to pawnshops," said Coleman. "Make money."

"Coleman! Put that down! You're not taking anything in here!"

"But, Serge . . ."

"You don't even know what it is."

Coleman pulled the object from his windbreaker. "Sure, it's a— They still give you money."

Jeff pointed at the floor. "Look at all these dead bugs."

"Because of that can."

"What can?"

"Aerosol. Middle of the floor on that newspaper." Serge kept the gun on the man as he reached the wall, turned around and paced back the other way. "Looters are the lowest. What would be an appropriate punishment?"

Jeff picked up the empty can. *"Bug bomb?"*

"Another Florida hurricane tradition," said Serge. "You're going to be gone anyway and taking the pets with you. Perfect time to bug-bomb." He scratched his nose with the gun barrel and faced the man on the sofa. "Now, what *am* I going to do with a cockroach like you?"

"Serge, shouldn't we be in a hurry?" said Jeff. "The storm . . ."

"It's a typical twenty-mile-wide eye going an average twelve miles an hour. We got here on the front side. You do the math."

Jeff wandered into the next room doing the math. "There's a bug can in here, too—and in this other room. . . ." His voice trailed down a hallway. "Another one in here. . . ."

"Jeff, I'm trying to concentrate!"

McSwirley came back into the living room with a half-full twelve-pack from Sam's Club. "They bought more cans than they needed."

"Jeff! I can't think!"

The looter's eyes squinted over his duct-taped mouth. He looked up at a formless face that was framed dark against the contrasting bright blue sky. Serge's features began filling out as the sky dimmed. The eye was passing. The captive struggled with rope-bound hands and feet, wedged into the well of his car's trunk among all the loot.

"Jeff, come here."

"I don't want to."

"Buck up!" Serge waved him over. "Remember that tsunami in Asia? Fascinating fact: Virtually no animals died. They all cleared out. *They* knew what was going on. But humans have lost touch with nature and become susceptible to misadventures in bad weather, like our friend here." Serge spoke into the trunk. "If you were more in tune with our planet, you might have run a better chance with this hurricane. Enjoy the silverware . . ."

Serge had something in his hand. He pressed a button. Hissing. A canister landed on the captive's chest and rolled under his armpit next to a deep fryer. Serge grabbed another canister. Another hiss. It hit the man's stomach. Another canister. Another. The trunk was alive with the aerosol chorus.

Jeff jumped back. "Serge! Jesus! Please, don't do this! I'm begging you—"

"I saw the same disconnect when Frances headed for Tampa. So I zipped down to Bayshore Boulevard for the A-view, and a million other cars were already parked along the balustrade. I said, 'Coleman, look at all the idiots out in this storm.' . . ." Serge tossed the last can and smiled at his hostage—*"Sorry, lost another loan to Ditech"*—and slammed the trunk shut. ". . . Then something I'd never seen before: The storm had sucked the water halfway back, dry bay bottom for hundreds of yards, all these fools scrambling over the railing to run around in the muck. Luckily a hurricane isn't as fast as a tsunami, and they all got out before the bay flooded over the seawall, and the boulevard filled with kayaks. . . . Jeff, you're crying again. What now?"

Jeff blubbered and pointed.

"Why are you upset?" asked Serge. "This was your idea."

"No it wasn't!"

"Take praise when it's due."

"I just showed you the extra cans. I didn't want *this*!"

Tendrils of ominous vapor seeped from the trunk's seals. Kicking sounds through the fenders.

"But it was your core concept," said Serge. "You got the ball rolling, so take credit, or at least responsibility."

"Give me the keys," said Jeff. "I'm going to get him out. There's still time."

Serge reached back and hurled the keys as hard as he could

over the roof of the house. He hopped up and sat on the trunk's hood. "Now deal with your actions."

"These aren't my actions!"

"Jeff, Jeff, Jeff . . . knock off the innocent act."

"It not an act! Maybe we can get him out with a crowbar."

"It's in the trunk."

Jeff whined and grabbed his head.

"Tell the truth," said Serge. "Didn't it piss you off that this asshole was preying on the good people of this state in their hour of crisis?"

"But this isn't the answer!"

"Don't be a denial-chimp. Admit it! He made you mad!"

"Okay, I was kind of mad."

"And you know the type of person I am, right?"

Jeff nodded slowly, trying to figure where Serge was going.

"Why do you think you brought me those cans? You subconsciously wanted this."

"I didn't! I swear!"

"Somewhere deep inside. Think about it. . . . Don't answer right away."

Jeff opened his mouth and stopped. *Oh, my God, was it possible? Did I actually intend . . . ?*

Serge smiled. "We're really not that different, you and me."

"Yes we are!"

The trunk lid banged under Serge. He leaned down; "I hear you knocking, but you can't come out!"

The trunk eventually became still. Vapor gone. Eye wall closing. Serge consoled Jeff on their way back to the Hummer. Jill was in the front seat reading *Spin* and rocking out to personal headphones. She took them off when the doors opened. "Jeff! What happened to you? You're crying!"

"His mother died," said Serge.

"That's horrible," said Jill. "I'm so sorry!"

"It's okay," said Serge, starting the engine. "Happened years ago, and he didn't like her."

The Hummer headed east on the Tamiami Trail. It shot under a flashing yellow light at Dade Corners, the agricultural cross-roads where the Everglades dovetail into the first rural traces of inland Miami. A normally brisk truck stop was empty except for a single car parked behind the diesel pumps. A brown Plymouth Duster with stolen Indiana plates. Someone in the driver's seat watched the Hummer go by. The Duster pulled out of the truck stop and headed east on the Tamiami Trail.

CHAPTER THIRTY-NINE

TAMPA BAY TODAY

demand you stop the series!" said Metro Tom.

"Is there a broken record in here?" asked the maximum editor. "We've already been over this."

"We got another letter."

"What's it say?"

" *'The Fiero was just a warning. It would have been so easy if I wanted you in it.'* "

"Okay, we'll buy him a replacement," said the managing editor. "It's the least we can do. Spread out the deductions from his paycheck."

Six photographers with jumbo lenses sprinted past the conference table. The last slowed. "You might want to scramble some reporters."

The metro editor drove McSwirley over in a Cutlass. They parked next to fire trucks. Nothing to do now but roll up the hoses. The lot was leveled. Jeff got out of the car and stared in shock at the smoldering embers. "My house!"

McSwirley's landlord drove up. "My house!"

The metro editor spotted a fire inspector walking back to a white sedan with a rack of red lights on the roof.

"Excuse me," said Tom. "I'm a friend of the person who lived there. Do you have a cause yet?"

"The explosion or the fire?"

"Explosion?"

The metro editor was livid on the phone to Gladstone Tower.

"Sorry," said Max. "I'd love to help, but Part Five just went to bed."

Soon another spinning paper hot off the presses:

SURFING THE EYE WITH SERGE: BEE GEES GOT BUM RAP.

PART FIVE

Ocean Drive. Esteban still blowing, but mostly epilogue. Scraping branches and rolling trash cans. Future site of another street cleanup. This one with busted neon tubes, twisted wrought iron and South Beach flair. Serge could have spit. The pastel façade of that postcard hotel row blown out like a special-effects movie finale.

The long run across the 'Glades had sapped the storm back down to a category one when it exited Miami and disappeared into the Atlantic. The Hummer's tires rolled through chic debris, headlights piercing a gray mist. Otherwise quiet and empty. Nobody in sight except the vague form of a topless sunbather on ecstasy staggering toward the beach.

"Will you take me home now?" asked Jeff. "You promised."

"Just one more stop," said Serge. The Hummer passed a municipal garage on Collins. Two blocks back, a new set of headlights. Brown Plymouth Duster. Both vehicles swung around the Fontainebleau and continued north through Surfside and Bal Harbour.

"Where are we going?" asked Jeff.

"Criteria," said Serge.

"Uh, okay," said Jeff. "How about a place where there's a lot of police and I'll be safe?"

"No," said Serge. "That's the *name* of the place. Criteria Studios."

"What's that?"

"You've *never* heard of Criteria Studios?" said Serge. "My God, this is your lucky day! Opened 1958, tiny underdog sound studio that hit the map when Jackie Gleason moved his show to Miami and the orchestra needed a place. Since then, everyone's recorded there. The Stones, James Brown, Aretha, three hundred plus gold and platinum albums; you'll see them covering the walls."

Jill elbowed Jeff in the backseat. *"Studio."*

The Hummer took a left onto Sunset Isles Boulevard and crossed a bridge over Biscayne Bay. "Shhhhhh! Listen!" said Serge. "You hear that? I heard it!"

"Hear what?"

"The bridge. That clackety-clack sound."

"So?"

"You don't recognize it?" said Serge. "Think of where we are! I'll give you five clues. No, three. No, one. Fuck it: I can't wait. I'll just tell you. It's the opening guitar riff!"

"From what?"

"Now you're being deliberately dense."

"Honest, Serge, I don't—"

"The year: 1975! The place: Miami! The magic: Bee Gees! . . . Illustrious Brothers Gibb in town to let Florida soak into their *Main Course* LP being recorded up the road at Criteria. Barry had to take the Sunset Isles Bridge to work every day—the same one we're on right now!—and he starts humming along with that clacking bridge sound. Genius strikes! Hit song! 'Drive Talkin',' because he's driving to work with his lunch sack and all, which was later changed to—you guessed it!—'Jive Talkin'.' Boom! Completely new sound for the band, which was slumping post 'Lonely Days.' The single's shipped with a blank label to radio stations worldwide. Nobody knew what to make of it. Who *are* these fresh princes? Shoots to number one! Bee Gees back on top! Next stop *Saturday Night Fever,* music history! And it all started on this bridge with that sound you're hearing! Can't you dig it? Jeff, dig it with me! Everybody sing! *J-j-j-jive . . ."*

The Hummer made another left at Northeast 149th Street and pulled up behind a building on the 1700 block. Serge grabbed his guitar case and portable mini-amp with rechargeable battery. He led them down an alley. Soon another door was getting jimmied. Serge smiled at Jill and glanced toward his crowbar with a chuckle. "The place is so old and historic my keys always stick. But I won't let them change a thing!"

The door finally popped. Jill followed Serge inside, leaving Jeff in her gloat cloud. Serge stopped in the middle of the studio and began setting up. Jill sat cross-legged at his feet. "That little thing's your amp?"

"Left my big one in a motel room," said Serge. "I'm going for the Professor Longhair, 125th Street dirty atmospheric sound. . . . Jeff, you ready to capture this first blistering track?"

"I don't know how to run a sound board."

"Use that microcassette you got for interviews."

"But the sound quality will be terrible."

"Even better. We can charge more, like Dylan's basement tapes." He turned to Jill. "Can you hear it?"

"Hear what?"

" 'Layla.' Clapton cut it here. Right where you're standing. Clapton is God. Are you religious? I've decided to follow Clapton now. Those legendary chords are stuck in these walls." Serge grabbed his Stratocaster by the neck and twisted a knob. "He's been a major influence on me ever since."

Jill's eyes grew larger. "You *know* Clapton?"

"Of course," said Serge. "Everyone does."

"Maybe in *your* circles."

"We do have a bit of an age gap."

"Wow," Jill said to herself. "Clapton . . ."

Serge strummed a stripped-down E chord. *"Layyyyyyyyy-laaaaaa . . ."*

Crash.

Amp went over. Guitar strings scraped unmusically. Jill Ribin-ski dove on top of Serge, tearing open his shirt. "Fuck me right now! Right where Clapton played!"

"Only if you call me 'Slowhand.' "

"Fuck me, Slowhand!"

Coleman strolled over and helped Jeff stare into a corner. "So you're a reporter?"

Out in the alley, a brown Plymouth Duster pulled up next to a Hummer.

Jill lay flat on the historic carpet. Completely wrecked. Perspiration beaded along her upper lip. "That was the best— . . . I must have come twenty times!"

"I had one," said Serge.

Coleman and Jeff continued admiring framed albums in the corner. "Frampton. Righteous . . ."

Unnoticed, the front door creaked open. A shiny automatic pistol came through the crack.

"Clapton also chose Criteria to lay down the classic *461 Ocean Boulevard* album." A guitar plug went back into a small amp. Serge cranked up treble, gain, distortion and everything else that had a knob. "The album's famous cover was photographed just up the street at . . . well, the address is on the cover. Took a certain luster off *that* scavenger hunt."

Coleman stared at more gold records: "So, Jeff. Ever see any dead bodies?"

Serge ceremoniously perched himself atop the tiny amp and hunched over his venerable Strat. "And now, ladies and gentlemen, the tenth and final cut from that 1974 tour de force, Clapton's finest song ever: 'Mainline Florida'!" Serge thrust his right arm high in the air, threatening to tear tendons. Defenseless guitar strings waited helplessly below. He let his hand remain at the peak an extra-long moment to give the crowd what it wanted and needed. "The big opening chord, coming right up. . . ." A mandolin-style pick twitched in his fingertips, still up there. ". . . Almost time. The big chord. Get ready. . . ." He reached with his free hand for another knob. ". . . Just a little more feedback. . . . Nearly there . . . and . . . Hold it, one more second. . . ." Another knob twisted. ". . . Readyyyyy . . . Readyyyy . . . Okayyyyy . . . Now!"

Serge's hand crashed into the strings.

An explosion of sound.

The guitar went silent.

"What the hell?" He grabbed the Strat by its solid-wood body and shook it in front of his face. "I just bought this fuckin' thing. . . . Maybe it's the amp." He bent over and looked down between his legs. He stuck a finger through a bullet hole in the speaker fabric. He looked up. "Molly!"

A redhead aimed her pistol. "Who's that tramp?"

"Who's Molly?" asked Jill.

Serge pulled his own gun. "My wife."

"Your wife!"

Molly shot again, the bullet whistling past their ears. Serge grabbed Jill's hand. "Come on!" He returned fire as they took cover behind the mixing board.

Molly angrily turned the gun on Jeff and Coleman. "Were you in on this?"

Jeff put his arms in the air. "I'm the hostage."

Coleman put his up. "Sorry about your guest towels."

A tight pattern of bullets flew past Molly and lodged in acoustic tiling. Another slug shattered a million-selling Bob Segar disc. Serge was usually a better shot, but Jill kept hitting him. "Your *wife*?"

"We're separated."

"You lied to me!" Whack.

"Can't it wait? We're in a firefight."

"No, I want to talk about this right now!"

Molly assumed a one-kneed shooter's crouch and emptied her clip into the mixing board. She ejected the magazine and re-loaded. "You two-timing son of a bitch!"

"Honey, I'm cutting an important album." Serge dumped shells from his own gun. "Don't be a Yoko."

Jill whacked him again. "You're too busy to talk to me, but you can find time to talk to her!"

The spouses emptied another set of clips at each other, hitting nothing.

Molly reloaded her magazine again. "You're so vain!"

Jill jumped up and grabbed her purse.

"What are you doing?" said Serge. "Get back down here!"

"Don't shoot!" Jill yelled across the room. "I'm leaving. He's all yours."

Molly ceased fire and headed for the mixing board. Jill cocked her chin and marched for the door with sashaying hips that spoke a language found only in Mafia wiretaps. The women snarled as they passed each other. Molly resumed fire, advancing on Serge's defensive position. Bang! Bang! Bang! Serge covered his head. Platinum album pieces rained. He reached for another clip. Out of ammo.

"Hold it!" yelled Serge. "This is crazy. Remember all the good times?"

"Don't try to sweet-talk me!" Bang! Bang! Bang!

"You must be getting your period."

Bang! Bang! Bang!

Serge recognized the distinct hollowness of the nine-millimeter boom. Sixteen in the clip, one in the chamber; counting under his breath. . . . Molly was almost on top of him with no sign of mercy. Bang! Bang! Bang!

Serge stood and smiled. "Baby!"

She pulled the trigger. Click, click, click. "You bastard!" She threw the gun at him. He ducked. Ted Nugent took one for the team.

Serge dashed around from behind the sound board. She began pounding him on the shoulders. He grabbed her wrists. She struggled, but Serge was too strong. "There, there. It'll be all right." Molly's face fell into his chest. Serge stroked the back of her sobbing head. Their bodies began to entwine with raw animal desire. . . .

Ten minutes later, postcoital recovery. They reclined in a pair of swiveling sound technicians' chairs behind the mixing board. Molly fanned herself rapidly. "Whew! You've gotten better! I must have had twenty!"

Serge looked at his fingernails. "I had one."

"Where did we go wrong?" asked Molly.

"People change," said Serge. "Happens to a lot of marriages. And you tried to kill me with dynamite."

"I needed your attention." Molly twisted a strand of her flaming red hair. "You always put your career first."

"I blame society," said Serge. "How'd you find me anyway?"

"I *know* you," said Molly. "We lived together, remember? After reading in the paper how you stole a car and rode through that other hurricane, I knew you couldn't resist this one. Only a single route across the lower 'Glades. I just staked out Dade Corners. Child's play."

Serge smacked his forehead. "Duh! . . . Just glad none of the cops figured that out."

On the Sunset Isles Bridge: "Son of a . . . !" Mahoney twisted a lug wrench on the bolts of a flat tire.

Molly swiveled idly in the sound tech's chair. "I obviously know that idiot Coleman, but who's the other guy?"

"Jeff?"

"Said he was your hostage."

"He's fixating."

"He's kind of cute."

Serge stuck two fingers in his mouth and made a shrill whistle. "Jeff!"—a big circling motion with his arm—"Get over here! I want to introduce you to someone."

Jeff ambled over with those goofy strides.

"Molly, this is Jeff McSwirley. Jeff, my wife, Molly."

"Pleasure to meet you," said Jeff. "He's told me a lot about you."

"Like what?" asked Molly.

"Nothing," said Serge. "He's just trying to be polite."

"No, I want to hear."

"Not you specifically," said Jeff. "Marriage advice in general. You just happened to be in all the examples."

Serge chuckled anxiously. "Like I said, nothing."

"No," demanded Molly, "I want to hear the rest."

Serge gave McSwirley The Look.

"Well," said Jeff. "He told me to always forfeit on purpose so I can watch TV. The Carly Simon song really is about the guy."

"No it's not," said Molly.

"You're totally right," said Serge. "It isn't about him. Jeff, guess what? Molly thinks you're cute. Isn't that right, Molly?"

Jeff's face turned red.

"Back up," said Molly. "What's this forfeit business he's talking about?"

"I don't remember," said Serge.

"Domestic arguments," said Jeff.

Molly spun on Serge. "You were just forfeiting all those times?"

"Me?"

"I thought you had come around to my point of view."

"I had."

"No you hadn't. You just forfeited. Nothing was ever re-solved."

"Honey, a forfeit's absolute. You win! Happy? Isn't that what it's all about?"

"Not if you're just giving up without accepting my position." Molly walked over to her purse. "That doesn't count. You're still harboring secret shit in your head."

Serge glared at Jeff. He clenched his eyes shut and thought a moment. He opened them. "You're right, dear. I was wrong. For-feiting is bad." He took a couple of steps and picked up his guitar.

"You're just forfeiting again . . ." Her hand came out of the purse with a pistol.

Serge swung the guitar by its neck.

The Stratocaster's sleek body clipped her forehead with a sick-ening melon thud, sending her shot through the watercooler. She went down like a sandbag. Serge leaned over. "You win again."

"Jesus!" Jeff screamed. "What's wrong with you? Why'd you do that?"

Serge pointed down at the .25-caliber, pearl-handled auto-matic curled in her left hand. He kicked it away.

Jeff became woozy and steadied himself against the wall. "Is she dead?"

"Just unconscious." Serge unplugged his amp.

"This is too much for me," said McSwirley. "I mean, first she tries to shoot you, then you have sex on top of a mixing board, then you club her in the head with a guitar?"

"See, Jeff, that's the thing," said Serge. "You've never been married."

THE NEXT DAY

Lunch hour. Downtown. Starched shirts in crosswalks. Verizon people in manholes. A black Hummer drove along the river and eased into a fire lane in front of the Tampa Museum of Art.

"There she is," said Serge.

Jeff peered out through the top, tinted edge of the windshield. Sparkling glass and metal. Gladstone Tower. Jeff looked at his driver with disbelief.

"What?" said Serge.

"You kept your promise."

"Of course I kept it. Did you ever doubt I'd bring you back?"

"I . . . I'm not sure," said Jeff. "I can't believe everything I've seen in the last four days. Seems like four *years*."

"We're friends for life. If you're ever in trouble, just remember our contingency rendezvous site. I'll be there in a flash."

"I guess I should thank you."

"Get the fuck out," said Serge. "You're holding me up."

Jeff was taken aback.

Serge smiled. "Go on, Scoop. Your exclusive's waiting. Just spell my name right. . . . Here, take this."

"I'm not taking that!"

"You'll need it."

"What do I need a gun for?"

"Generally, because it's Florida. Specifically, because someone's trying to kill you."

"I'm not taking it."

"Take it or I don't let you go."

Jeff gingerly accepted the gun between his thumb and index finger like he was dangling a scorpion. He opened his door and stepped onto the curb. He turned around. "I . . ."

The Hummer sped away.

Jeff crossed the street and entered a sterile lobby. He took the elevator to the newsroom.

"Look!"

"It's McSwirley!"

"He's alive!"

HURRICANES #5 AND #6

GASTON
AND ISAAC

CHAPTER FORTY

GULF COAST PSYCHIATRIC CENTER

Serge sat in the headlights of a woman's withering stare.

"What?"

The doctor looked down at her notes. "You know. . . ."

"Not a clue."

"I don't think I can treat you anymore."

"Why not?"

"I have to ask you a question, and I want you to tell me the truth."

"Go for it."

"After our last session, did you attack someone outside the clinic?"

"Me?"

"He's in intensive care. Fractured skull, teeth knocked out."

"Someone was attacked?"

"They heard the assailant yell, 'Bad monkey!' It's the phrase you were using in here minutes before."

"The weirdest thing. Since our last session, I've noticed a bunch of people on the street yelling that all the time. Usually just before they beat someone."

"Look—and don't say anything! Just shut up!—I think you did it. But confidentiality prevents me from breaching these sessions, and 'bad monkey' seems to be your sole connection to the assault. The only ethical way I can go to the authorities is if I believe you're deliberately planning a future crime, which I don't. I don't believe you plan anything . . ."

"Ouch."

". . . My only other option is to Baker Act you under Florida law, which is a seventy-two-hour involuntary psychiatric confinement if I think you're an imminent threat to yourself or others, which I don't. You're a *long-term* threat. So the final option is the one we have here. You're not under commitment anymore; you're coming to me of your own volition, which shows at least a minimal desire to deal with the problem. If I break off treatment, you'll probably flee back into the woodwork, and who knows when you'll strike next?"

"Remind me to send my kids where you went to school."

"I'm serious. For us to proceed from here, you must give me a vow of sincerity."

"Like Linus in the pumpkin patch." Serge grinned. "Nothing but sincerity as far as the eye can see. . . . But you have to do the same for me."

"What do you mean?"

"I need to be able to depend on your confidentiality. I got a little shook when I saw all those police officers out in your hall."

"They're for another patient."

"What did he do?"

"Can't say anything." The doctor relaxed and opened her notebook. "I'm glad we had that talk."

"Water under the bridge."

"So what's on your mind today?"

"Oh, it's incredible!" Serge reached into his pocket and pulled out a tracking map. "Have you been following the weather?"

On the other side of the wall was a hallway. Two policemen stood in front of a door. Behind the door was another office. Its two chairs were empty.

Jeff stood in the middle of the room. "I don't want to do this."

"You have to learn to express your anger," said the psychiatrist.

"But I don't feel angry."

"That's the problem," said the doctor. "You should."

"This is stupid." Jeff turned around. "I'm sitting back down."

"No, stay right there! What kind of man are you?"

"Okay."

"See what I mean?" said the doctor. "You let everyone walk all over you. There must be lots of pent-up anger. I can feel it."

"I can't."

"Let it out."

"I don't want to go through with this."

"Do it!"

"Can I just yell instead? *I'm mad as hell!* There."

"That was faking. I want you to hit me."

"I won't."

"Pretend I'm Justin. Hit me! As hard as you can!"

"How can you bring him up? He's dead!"

"So what? He was an asshole. He treated you like crap."

"He's dead! Stop talking about him like that!"

"Why? Makes you angry?"

"No."

"Loser! Worm!"

"Stop saying that!"

A third police officer arrived in the hallway. He had a cardboard take-out tray with three lattes-to-go.

"Thanks, Jim." An officer removed a plastic lid and blew. "What lottery did we win to get this assignment?"

"No kidding," said another. "This is a tit."

"It's not ease," said the third officer with the tray. "It's a question of dependability. I got a friend at the nuclear reactor: A simple three-dollar part that has a ninety-nine-percent success rate but *cannot* fail costs three *hundred* if it's separately tooled and inspected for a ninety-nine-point-nine-nine-nine confidence rate. We got a high-profile murder witness who's also a newspaper reporter."

"Big deal."

"It's not a big deal right now, but it will be if we so much as let him stub his toe."

The first cop looked toward the office. "Wonder what's going on in there?"

"Let's listen."

"Okay."

They put their ears to the door.

"Don't say that!" said Jeff.

"Pussy!"

"Stop!"

"Hit me!"

The division commander reached the top of the stairs and entered the hallway. "What the hell are you doing?"

Three officers straightened. "Nothing."

On the other side of the door: "Okay, I'll hit you. . . ." Jeff reached out and gave the doctor a playful tap on the shoulder. "How's that?"

Wham! Jeff went tumbling across the floor. He sat up in shock and rubbed his jaw. "You punched me in the face!"

"You hit me. What the fuck were you thinking?"

"You told me to." Jeff held a hand under his nose. "I'm bleeding."

"See what happens when you don't express your anger? It allows people to provoke you into unsafe responses."

Jeff got to his feet. "I'd like to leave now."

"Our hour's not up."

"Don't worry. I'll pay for the whole thing."

"Sit down."

"Okay."

"You did it again!"

"Sorry."

"What's your *problem*?"

Jeff held the side of his face. "I think I need to see a dentist."

"Does it hurt?"

"Yes!"

The doctor jotted on a pad. "Here's something for the pain. I'll stop the clock, and you fill it down the street right now. We split fifty-fifty."

On the other side of the wall was a third office. It had a long couch. The couch was empty.

Mahoney was in the middle of the room, hopping on the balls of his feet. "The next night was the big Dempsey rematch at Soldier Field—"

"I don't want to do this," said the doctor.

"Come on, stand right there," said Mahoney. "One of my canaries was working the vig off some trouble boys with five large on the Manassa Mauler. . . ."

"This is stupid."

"Don't move or you'll get hurt. . . . It was a brutal combination in the third round." Fists sliced the air with the sound of wind.

"You almost hit me!"

"You moved." Mahoney danced backward. "Tunney counters with a jab. The crowd's on its feet. The wiseguys smell something hinky. Big Jack gets him in the clinch—"

"Let go of me!"

"The referee breaks it up. Jack reacquaints himself with his legendary right cross."

"Ow! Jesus! My nose!"

"You moved."

"Damn it!" The psychiatrist sat down and tilted his head back. He pulled a hankie from a pocket and shook it open.

"You don't want to spar anymore?"

"You're insane!"

Mahoney walked over to the doctor. "Let's just keep this between us." He reached into his pocket and handed the doctor a Baggie of scored tablets.

"What's this?"

"Something for the pain. . . . And there's the bell!" Mahoney trotted back and sat on the edge of the couch, hooking his arms over imaginary ring ropes. "Cut me, Mick."

"Smile!" said Serge.

The psychiatrist blocked her face. "What are you doing?"

"Taking your picture for my address book." Serge fiddled some more with his BlackBerry. "These new phones do *everything*! I had no idea."

"Can we get back to—"

"Hold on." Serge navigated the touch screen.

"No! Put that away. It's disrespectful."

"Couldn't agree more. I hate phones . . ." Tap, tap, tap. ". . . For years I made a commitment never to answer them, because ninety-nine percent of all phone calls are bullshit. Everyone wanting something from you, like to talk. But you never get those calls from people forcing you to accept lots of cash for no reason, unless you have one of those special magic phones. But the people at phone stores won't sell you those. Oh, no, they're keeping them for themselves. And I *really* hate cell phones. They should be treated like farts: Keep it short and take a few steps away from the herd to establish a courtesy zone."

The doctor's cell phone rang. "Sorry, thought I'd turned it

off. One second." She looked at the display. A text message: GUESS WHO?

"Serge!"

Serge tapped his screen. "How about we don't talk and instead text-message the rest of the hour? . . ."

"No!"

". . . I dreaded the thought of getting my own cell, but the cut-throat competition of the wireless industry has created all kinds of special offers you can't refuse. Like mine. This guy set his phone on the counter in Starbucks, and before he knew it, I was halfway down the block."

"Serge! I want you to get off the phone right now!"

"*Alllllllll right*. I'll get off the phone." Tap, tap, tap . . .

"You're not doing it."

"I'm not on the phone anymore." Tap, tap. "I'm on the Internet now." He held up the screen. "Color Doppler radar." He turned it back around. Tap, tap. "I have to keep monitoring the weather. Something historic is about to happen. And I need to buy a new guitar amp."

"Why?"

"My wife shot the shit out of my old one. Women never understand your hobbies."

CHAPTER FORTY-ONE

THAT AFTERNOON

A sparse crowd filled a downtown bar at the corner of Franklin and Cass. At later hours it would be popular with newspaper reporters, office workers and students from the nearby University of Tampa occupying Moorish buildings and flophouses. But not now.

Coleman walked through the open front door and waved for the bartender. Serge grabbed a stool and unlatched a velvet-lined drafting set. The first beer arrived in a frosted mug, and Coleman didn't let it hit the counter. "I love midday drinking."

Serge studied map coordinates. "I thought it was the all-inclusive plan with you."

"This is a bonus." Coleman drained half the mug. "You know how when you're in some downtown joint in the middle of the day, and the sun's really bright, and you look out the window like right now and see all those people on the street who are still working? But you're already in a bar? Makes me feel like I've gotten a lot accomplished."

Serge shifted on his stool for the ever-elusive right position. He shifted another way. He shifted back and scratched his neck rapidly like a beagle. Coleman ordered a second beer, plus a backup in case the bartender became too busy with the other three customers. "What's the matter?"

Serge shifted again. "What do you mean?"

"I know you. Something's wrong."

Serge looked over his shoulder at the bar's interior. "It's the Hub."

"But you love the Hub."

"I did back when it was on Zack Street. Since 1947. Sacred place, like if that corner restaurant in *Seinfeld* was a bar. But now it's over here; it's the *new* Hub."

"So?"

"That's like the *new* Dead Sea Scrolls." Serge unfolded a tracking chart. "I'm losing all my touchstones at an exponential rate. The Chatterbox, the Moon Hut, the Pelican Diner, the Big Bamboo gutted by fire . . ."

"Then why'd you insist we come here?"

"I love the Hub." Serge walked the needle points of an engineering compass across quadrants. He raised his tracking grid to the light. "Unbelievable."

"What?"

"The biggest climax a hurricane season's ever seen." He set the grid back down and scribbled more calculations. "National Weather Service is clearly keeping the public in the dark to avert pandemonium. But if my new figures hold up, we'll be riding into the history books."

"Serge, I think I know that guy over there."

"Which one?"

Coleman pointed toward the poolroom. Three bikers waited their turns with cue sticks. A nonbiker leaned over the table and sank a striped ball, then took a step and lined up an intricate bank shot. The head of his costume sat on a shelf next to the bowl of chalk.

"It's the Party Parrot!" said Serge. "I *love* the Party Parrot!"

"What's he doing in here?"

"Let's go find out."

They picked up their drinks and headed toward the billiards.

"Nick!"

"Who are you?"

"Your biggest fan!" said Serge. "I didn't know you were the Party Parrot."

Nick stroked through the cue ball. A scratch. "Damn." He reached for his bourbon and chugged the whole thing, almost taking a fall when he slammed the glass onto the counter.

Serge grabbed his drumstick. "Easy there, fella. Better slow down."

Nick collapsed into a chair. Feathers floated to the floor. "I can't take it anymore."

"Take what?"

"All these hurricanes. I'm getting killed out there." Nick raised a wing. "Try swimming in this fucking thing."

"I saw them pumping your stomach on TV."

"The storms are coming so close together they don't even have time to fix my costume." He held up the other wing. "Look at this shit. I'm baled together with chicken wire and duct tape." Nick flapped for the bartender. "Refill!"

Serge grabbed the wing again and lowered it. "Get a grip. Just tell them you want off storm coverage."

"I can't. They'll fire me. I'm out of options."

"I have an option," said Serge.

"You do?"

Serge lifted the parrot head from the shelf and walked around to the other side of the pool table. "Here."

"What am I supposed to do with this?" asked Coleman.

THAT NIGHT

A door opened. Efficient people marched inside without small talk. The door had a number on the outside: 1037. More and more people entered the motel room, like it was a clown car. Politicians, detectives, lawyers, editors and, finally, McSwirley. The door closed.

The officer assigned to protect Jeff remained outside. Someone phoned room service. McSwirley flopped down onto a cushy bed.

Detectives made the standard sweep of the room. A lieutenant peeked out the tenth-floor window. Delta landing lights in the night sky. He pulled the curtain tight. The hotel was one of the upscale high-rise jobs that circled Tampa International and catered to important business travelers. The oversized clock radio said 12:05.

"Jeff, outstanding work today!" The maximum editor grabbed the TV's remote and began clicking through an on-screen menu of in-room movies. "We might be talking Pulitzer."

Jeff closed his eyes. "I just want to sleep."

A United flight from Hartford roared overhead.

"Good. Get your rest." The maximum editor pressed the remote again, now into the gentlemen's titles. "You have a big day tomorrow. Everyone is very pleased with your performance. That's why we sprang for the classiest hotel in town. All the richest people stay here."

Jeff was distracted by the TV menu. *Twats on Fire*. ". . . I'm sorry? . . . You were saying?"

"I was saying how far you've come." The editor tossed the remote aside and walked over to the bed. "We'd like to reward you." He reached inside his jacket and produced a small gift box. "It's not much. We have a tight budget. Actually we don't, but it's not for reporters. Here. A token of our thanks."

Jeff accepted the box without sitting up. He removed the lid. "Letter opener?"

The editor nodded with gravity. "Real silver plating."

"Says 'Gladstone Media' on the handle."

"You're family."

"Thanks."

"Don't you worry about a thing," said Max. "We got police outside your door, and I'll be staying in the next room."

"You don't have to do that," said Jeff.

"I don't mind," said Max. "There are some movies I want to watch."

Another roar over the hotel. Metro Tom looked up at the ceiling. "Who picked this place?" He pulled back the curtain. A string of headlights on the Courtney Campbell causeway. One light was higher than the rest, an inbound Southwestern. Another rumble as it flew over. The editor closed the curtain.

"How's he going to get any sleep with all that racket?"

They looked back at the bed: Jeff snoring, letter opener still in hand.

"Think we should turn down the covers?"

"Let him sleep." Tom gently slid the letter opener from his fingers and set it on the nightstand.

The editors left the room and said good night to the police officer. The cop took a last look inside and closed the door.

Four A.M.

A TV glowed in the dark: MSNBC replaying excerpts of the McSwirley interview on Florida Cable News. Hands in latex gloves clicked the remote control over to CNN. McSwirley again. Fox. McSwirley. It was like that all night, every channel.

An interviewer held out a microphone. *"Does the Eight Ball tell him to kill?"*

A fist punched the wall. The gloved hands reached down and tightened Velcro straps on a pair of sneakers.

CHAPTER FORTY-TWO

THE NEXT MORNING

A JetBlue flight roared overhead.

Jeff sprang up in bed. The room bright as noon.

The noise passed. McSwirley sought his bearings and remembered where he was. He threw legs over the side of the bed and trudged for the bathroom. Something on the dresser stopped him. A single sheet of hotel stationery with large, forceful handwriting. He picked it up.

Think you can hide from me? Are you enjoying all the attention I should be getting? You just don't learn. So I'm forced to teach you another lesson. Have a nice day.

Jeff began trembling so badly he couldn't read the sign-off: *Eye of the Storm.*

Banging on the door. "Police!"

Jeff jumped and dropped the note.

The door crashed open. In they poured with guns drawn. Body armor and black helmets. "On the floor! Now!"

They didn't really give him the chance. Jeff's face ate stain-resistant carpet. His arms were twisted behind his back for the cuffs.

"What are you doing?" yelled Jeff. "What's going on?"

"You're under arrest!"

TAMPA BAY TODAY

The newsroom was a hive of morning industry. People running in conflicting directions. Photographers in flak jackets grabbed shoulder bags. Reporters broke out extra emergency scanners and laptops. Editors raced back and forth with already obsolete bulletins. They posted a news clerk full-time at the big washable map of Florida. Someone handed him a note; he drew another dash with his Magic Marker.

Murmuring department heads took seats at the conference table.

"Where's Max?"

"Still at the hotel."

Metro Tom took charge. "Just have to start without him. This is too big." He turned toward the wire editor. "Those numbers still holding up?"

"No. They're higher. Latest update from Coral Gables just reclassified it."

"But how is that possible?" said Tom. "It was just a tropical depression yesterday. Supposed to sputter out near Eleuthera by the weekend."

"This weird weather cycle the last few years," said the wire editor. "We're in uncharted waters."

Tom looked across the newsroom at the washable map. From the Gulf of Mexico, a series of red dashes placed category-three Gaston on a dependable northeastern track across the state. The news clerk moved to the other side of the map and made a new set of northwest dashes, straightening out the wobbling path of a previously aimless system, now Isaac. Projected to slice across the state from the opposite direction.

Tom took off his glasses and rubbed the bridge of his nose. "Two hurricanes at once?"

"Still anyone's guess where they're going to cross," said the wire editor.

"What happens when they do?"

"Nobody knows."

Another news clerk ran up to the conference table. "Sir, the first storm. We have landfall in Port Charlotte. It's on TV."

Tom replaced his glasses. "I've seen enough landfalls."

"You haven't seen this."

Department heads rushed downstairs to the main control room of Florida Cable News. The crowd was already four deep at the monitors.

"Oh . . . my . . . God . . . !"

The roomed hushed. Just swirling wind from the audio feed. And that image on the screen, the same one seen in homes and businesses across the state.

A mighty cheer went up in the electronics section of a department store. *"I've never seen anything like this!"*

Stranded fliers in a Gold Member lounge. *"He's really getting into it!"*

High fives in a sports bar across from the hockey arena. The reason was on the overhead sets: A man in a parrot costume staggering across the beach, swinging a fifth of Jim Beam by the neck. He tilted his head way back and jammed the bottle into the beak.

"Man, when the Party Parrot parties, he goes all the way!"

The bird stumbled a few more steps toward the surf and defiantly flung the bottle into the gray storm. The bottle flew back and bounced off the costume head with a small explosion of feathers.

"What's he doing now?"

"Not sure. Looks like he's reaching down for something."

"I think it's his zipper, or whatever those costumes have."

"No, he can't! . . . He wouldn't! . . ."

"He is! . . ."

It became the defining image of an era, a single iconic moment releasing years of latent hurricane frustration from an entire region.

"He's waving at the storm with his—"

Another breathless news clerk ran up to the metro editor. "Sir . . ."

"Not now."

"But it's McSwirley."

"What about McSwirley?"

FIFTEEN MINUTES LATER

Sedans screeched up to an executive hotel north of the airport. Suits sprinted past the valets.

The tenth-floor hallway:

McSwirley's arms remained fastened behind his back. Rugged police hands pinned his neck against the wall. "Don't move."

Jeff could see into the next hotel room, because the door was open. And not because maids were cleaning. Police photographers, fingerprint dust, blood. On the floor, protruding from behind the bed, two legs.

A detective crouched and stepped under the crime-scene tape across the doorway. He held a clear Baggie to Jeff's face. "Recognize this?"

"My letter opener. Where'd you find it?"

The detective's head swung toward the open door. "That guy's chest. Return to sender."

"Max is dead?" said McSwirley.

"You ready to confess?"

"I didn't do it!"

He grabbed Jeff by the front of his shirt. "Why, you slimy—"

A jet roared. Elevator doors opened at the end of the floor. Expensive shoes walked briskly down the hall. Mayor, police brass, editors.

"Uh-oh." The detective released Jeff and began reading his rights.

"What the hell's going on here?" yelled the chief. "Why is that man handcuffed? You're supposed to protect him, not—"

"Sir," said the detective. "There's been another murder. We found his letter opener in the victim's heart."

"I didn't do it!"

The detective raised the Baggie again. "Got a good set of prints. Bet it matches our guy here."

"Of course my prints are on it," said Jeff. "I handled it last night."

"That's right," said Tom. "I saw him. There's got to be an explanation."

"There is," said McSwirley. "Go look in my room. There's a—"

Another officer came out of Jeff's suite with another clear evidence bag. Inside: a single sheet of hotel stationery.

"That's it!" said McSwirley. "That's the note! It's from the killer! He's framing me! He was in my room!"

"That's not possible," said the first detective. "We had a guard posted all night."

The police chief looked at a uniformed officer standing quietly in the background. "You were here all night?"

"Yes, sir."

"See anyone?"

"No, sir."

"And you're sure you didn't leave? Not even for a second."

"No, sir. I mean, yes, sir. I mean I took a smoke break. A couple of 'em. But just for a minute. There's no way—"

"You're suspended pending dismissal! Get out of my sight!"

The officer left quickly. The chief turned toward the detective with the note. "Let me see that." He read it quickly and handed it back. "You just found this?"

"It must have slipped behind the dresser . . ." said the detective.

". . . when I dropped it," said Jeff.

"Uncuff him!" shouted the chief. "Now!"

"Yes, sir."

The bracelets came off. McSwirley rubbed his wrists.

"Find another hotel," said the chief. "Triple the guard."

"Yes, sir."

CHAPTER FORTY-THREE

PEANUT ISLAND

Coleman moaned and raised his face from a cold, unfamiliar concrete floor. Like most mornings.

He heard music. Different from what he was used to at this hour. A military sound, drums and bugles. He sat up and took off the parrot head. "Serge? . . ."

Coleman thought it was Serge, but he couldn't be sure, because Serge was backlit by the portable hurricane spotlight that he had set up to backlight himself. It was next to a boom box on top volume: "Hail to the Chief." Serge's hands were on his hips. He wore a leather bomber jacket.

"Serge, is that you?"

"Shhhh! I'm letting the moment build. I'm almost there."

"Almost where?"

"Nineteen sixty-two."

The ceiling was a low arch of corrugated government metal. Coleman pushed himself up from the floor and looked around. Row of lockers, utilitarian desk, cylindrical escape tube leading deeper somewhere else. The place had a cave quality, like they were underground, because they were. Serge stood in the middle of an official design painted on the floor.

The seal of the President of the United States.

"What the hell is this place?"

"Another perfect spot to ride out a hurricane," said Serge. "I know them all."

"Looks like some kind of shelter."

"JFK's nuclear bunker from the Cuban Missile Crisis. We're on an old fill island in the middle of Lake Worth inlet, just a few hundred yards from the shore of Palm Beach, where the Kennedys used to winter. They secretly built this place after he was elected."

"But I don't understand," said Coleman. "If this really was the president's shelter . . . I mean, the security. How did we possibly get in here?"

"Easy. And it's not the first time." Serge tuned a portable TV to storm coverage. "Used to camp out here with my Little League team in the early seventies. Back then, the bunker was literally abandoned. Bunch of rust, broken locks. We snuck in all the time and told ghost stories in the tunnel. A few years later, some of the kids replaced the ghost stories with marijuana."

"Doesn't look abandoned now."

"They finally realized the history they were about to lose and fixed her up. But it's still just a little exhibit with nothing really to steal, so there isn't much security to speak of. Even less since it's still temporarily closed after damage from Hurricane Frances."

Coleman tried to reattach tape to the parrot's beak, but it drooped again. Serge turned off his music. "We'll wait for the eye, then make our break."

"Serge?"

"What?"

"How did I get down here?"

"I carried you again."

"Thanks."

Serge pointed at the tiny TV and its twin, split-screen radar sweeps. "Don't thank me yet."

TAMPA BAY

Hotel number two. Actually, *motel*. It was on the Gulf of Mexico, one of the old roadside deals being drooled over by condo developers. Single story, vintage aqua neon, art deco office with wraparound corner window. Middle of the Treasure Island strip. The Surf, the Sands, the Satellite.

McSwirley checked the closets and under the bed. He locked the locks a tenth time. He tested the makeshift length of broomstick the motel's owner employed to burglar-proof sliding windows since the state had taken the downturn. He looked out the glass at foaming waves, hovering gulls and the ancient ruins of a shuffleboard court. He closed the curtains tight, then unlocked the locks and went outside to make sure nobody could peek in.

Three cops reclined in patio furniture and sipped coffee. "What are you doing?"

"Checking to make sure nobody can peek."

Laughter. "Relax, kid." The cops weren't in uniform. Instead, they wore undercover tropical shirts and shoulder holsters to fit in with Florida.

Jeff went back inside. Locks bolted. He sat on the foot of the bed and listened to his heart. That just made it louder. He turned on TV for distraction. *Law & Order*. Maid finds a body in a motel room. He changed the channel. A phone rang. He leaped from the bed. "Jesus! I can't take it! . . . Okay, breathe slowly. It's just your cell. . . . *Hello?*"

"Jeff, it's me, Serge . . ."

"Aaaauuuhhhh!!!"

"Jeff! What's the matter? . . ."

Two police officers with headphones sat in a van across the street. "This is the call. We got him now."

Jeff slammed the phone down.

One of the officers in the van took off his headphones. "Did he just hang up?"

Across the state, Coleman looked at Serge. "What's the matter?"

"The line went dead. Our pal must be in trouble!"

"Try him again."

"Already dialing."

The other officer in the van pressed headphones to his ears. "Hold on. Got another incoming call."

Jeff apprehensively opened the phone.

"Jeff! It's me, Serge! Are you in danger?"

An officer took off his headphones. "He fuckin' hung up again!"

Rrrrinnngg!

"Jeff!" said Serge. "Whatever you do, don't hang up!"

Click.

Headphones went flying across the van. "Son of a bitch!"

Jeff paced feverishly. An idea stopped him midstep. He grabbed the handle of his overnight bag and hoisted the Samsonite onto a bed. Manic digging through socks. There it was: one of the camcorders Gladstone Media had issued all its reporters for intrusive tragedy footage. He found the adapter and plugged it in—"Please, please, please . . ."—still worked. He set the tape speed on superlong play and looked around the room until he saw it. The perfect spot. He slipped the video camera under a spare blanket at the top of the closet. He hit "record" and left the door ajar. There. If he didn't die, at least he was going to have some answers.

Jeff turned off his cell phone and crawled under the covers. Sleep came like dental gas.

CHAPTER FORTY-FOUR

SUNRISE

The Gulf of Mexico had hurricane sky.

A sharp knock on a motel room door. "You okay in there?"

Jeff sat up quickly and looked around. *How long have I been out?* His checked his watch.

Another knock. "Jeff, answer me!" Then muffled conversation: "Think we should go in?"

The door opened a crack. The cops turned and broke off discussion. "There you are. We were worried."

Jeff rubbed his eyes. "I'm fine."

"Okay. Tell us if you need anything. We're ordering later. Mexican place."

Jeff stretched and yawned. "I'll let you know." He closed the door and shuffled toward the bathroom. He froze.

A sheet of paper on the dresser.

I thought we were friends. . . .

Jeff dropped it without reading the rest. He ran to the closet and reached under a blanket. The camcorder was still there, undetected. Jeff rewound the tape and began watching the tiny monitor. Just an empty room except for McSwirley lying still in bed. He skipped forward through the tape. Nothing, nothing, nothing—stop! What was that? He rewound. The part he'd been looking for. Someone entered the frame and began writing a note on the dresser. . . . Grainy, low light. Hard to identify. Jeff slowed the tape and brought the monitor closer to his face. *There we go, come on, please turn around.* . . . The person in the tape turned around. Terrified recognition flooded Jeff's body. Legs buckled. He grabbed his cell phone and turned it on to call the paper. It rang in his hands.

"Jeff, it's me, Serge. We have to meet right away. I know they're listening, so I'll speak in code. Remember that fail-safe contingency place I always talked about?—"

The phone broke apart on the terrazzo. Jeff ran out the door.

"Jeff," said one of the cops. "Where are you going?"

Jeff kept running toward the beach.

The cops looked at each other. "What's he doing?"

"Think we should chase him?"

"If we like our jobs."

They leaped from patio chairs and took off across the sand. "Jeff! Wait up!"

ST. PETE BEACH

St. Pete Beach used to be called St. Petersburg Beach, but the name was too long for certain government computers, which lopped off "Beach" and sent subsidy checks to the nearby municipality of St. Petersburg. So they shortened it to "Pete," an idea that didn't sit with the locals.

Another idea they hadn't warmed to was the closing of the Pelican Diner. The vintage chrome eatery sat a seashell's throw from the Gulf of Mexico, one of the last authentic 1940s nighthawk joints. It was dispiriting to see the diner empty and decaying. There hadn't been a customer in years. Until today.

Agent Mahoney sat alone in the last booth reading the morning paper. He knew he'd been inside Serge's head a little too long, and his gut told him to back off, but Serge was so close! He could feel it in his bones like the approaching weather. Mahoney took a swig of coffee and checked his slender Elgin wristwatch with the alligator strap. Time to make the final plans. He studied the newspaper's latest tracking chart and added some notes with a fountain pen.

To Mahoney the diner wasn't depressing at all. In fact, it was full of people: men with fedoras and packs of Lucky Strikes, others in sailor uniforms, coeds ordering milk shakes. What wasn't to be happy about? World War II had just ended!

Mahoney waved for the waitress. She arrived chewing gum. He ordered a cup of joe and asked about the pie.

Tourists walked down the sidewalk, past a chain-link construction fence with No Trespassing signs. They spotted the lone man in the back of the diner talking to himself. Someone phoned the police.

Mahoney looked up from his paper. That waitress sure was taking a long time. His police walkie-talkie sat on the table next to the ashtray. It squawked with the report of the intruder in the Pelican Diner. *That's where I am.* He stood and pulled his pistol. The other customers nudged each other and pointed in alarm. A couple of mugs near the front of the diner pushed hats down onto their heads and ran out the door.

The walkie-talkie continued squawking. Mahoney looked down. *Wait, what's a strange, futuristic device like this doing in the forties?* Mahoney glanced up again. All the people had disappeared. The lights were off. Dust, cobwebs. He looked out the diner's window. Tourists gossiped and gestured, until they saw the gun, then they ran. The walkie-talkie crackled again. This time the call was from a heavy-breathing cop running down the beach less than a mile away.

Mahoney put on his own hat and rushed out the door.

Three out-of-breath officers in tropical shirts hustled back to the motel, getting their stories straight how they'd lost McSwirley.

"He must have run track in high school."

They arrived at Jeff's former room. A dark line of clouds advanced from the south. A burnt orange '61 Coupe de Ville skidded into the parking lot.

Agent Mahoney ran toward them, flashing a badge. "Where's McSwirley?"

"Got away."

"How'd you manage that?"

"He had a big lead."

"We almost caught him . . ." said another officer.

". . . But then he jumped in a cab in front of the Thunderbird. He used to be a big track star, you know."

Mahoney went through the open door of Jeff's room.

"Hey! You can't go in there!"

Mahoney made a quick recon sweep. He read the note on the dresser without touching it.

"What's that?" asked one of the cops.

"Just evidence. Nothing you needed to have noticed." A tiny, flickering screen caught Mahoney's eye. He walked over and picked up the still-running camcorder dropped on the bed.

Mahoney rewound it. The screen was blank for the longest time. He fast-forwarded. Nothing. More fast-forwarding. . . . Stop! A shadow crept into view. It began writing the note on the dresser. Mahoney held the screen closer. *Come on, turn around.* The person stopped writing and briefly looked back toward McSwirley's bed, an ambient light catching the side of his face. Mahoney's jaw dropped. "Oh, my God!" The camera bounced on the bed.

"What is it?"

Mahoney ran out the door and jumped into his Coupe de Ville. It started to rain.

CHAPTER FORTY-FIVE

MIDDLE-OF-NOWHERE, FLORIDA

A rented green Taurus sped east through a driving rain. The wipers couldn't keep up.

Jeff punched the steering wheel. *"No! No! No! No!"* He looked down. The speedometer said ninety. His foot pressed harder for more fuel. "Dear God! Please help me!"

Jeff had taken the cab to the airport, where he'd swapped it for the rental. Police quickly got the description, but Jeff was already halfway across Polk County in the belly of phosphate country, an even greater pursuit distance when category-three storms are factored. The nearest person to catching him was in a burnt-orange Coupe de Ville ten miles back on State Road 60, chasing a hurricane hunch.

Gaston had continued its predicted track, cutting northeast across the state from the Gulf of Mexico, now up to an ambitious twenty-two miles an hour. The storm's increased speed had taken a bite out of Jeff's safety cushion. If its course held, in less than an hour it would bisect Lake Wales Ridge, the north-south spine of peninsular Florida and the closest thing to a mountain range anywhere in the level state.

Then it got interesting. Forecasters at the National Hurricane Center issued an urgent update. On the other side of the state, Hurricane Isaac had taken a last-minute jog after barreling in from the Atlantic and raking downtown West Palm. Latest projection: Lake Wales Ridge.

The Taurus's rubber wipers tore loose and took flight. Metal scraped glass. The steering wheel pressed into McSwirley's chest as he strained for visibility. The junction sign at U.S. 27 told him he was almost there. The Taurus swung north.

Serge checked his watch. "What's taking him so long?" He was under the concrete overhang of a tourist-attraction snack bar. The overhang wasn't engineered for rain that went sideways, let alone up. Serge peered out through the haze at the loose definition of a seventy-eight-year-old tower on the highest point of the ridge. He heard someone coming and pulled his piece. "Jeff! Is that you?"

A human form gradually took shape in the swirling leaves. It was running toward the concession, across an open, rain-lashed field dotted with oaks and palms. Serge tucked the pistol into his belt. A soggy McSwirley ran under the overhang and chucked the skeletal remains of a shredded umbrella.

"You made it!" said Serge. "Thanks for coming."

"Serge, I have something important to tell you—"

"It'll have to wait," said Serge, grabbing Jeff's arm and pulling him to relative safety. "It's about the killer."

"But, Serge, I know who the killer is—"

"Shhhhhh! I think I see someone else coming." Serge pressed against the side of the snack stand and shielded Jeff behind him. He drew his pistol again and peeked around the edge of the building. Another form took shape in the distance.

"But, Serge, the other killer! I saw the tape—"

"Not now," said Serge. "I think I see the other killer. . . ."

Coleman went through his usual checklist upon awakening: *Where am I? What's happening? Why am I wet?*

Sometimes Coleman would wake up in motion, like now. He raised his head. The view was dark except for two small circles of light a few inches from his face. What he saw through the eye-holes in the parrot head told him that the costume was acting as a kind of Niagara Falls barrel. He slowly floated somewhere.

"This is new."

Serge squinted into the storm. The form became identifiable, growing larger as it covered the last hundred yards. A soaked Mahoney rushed under the overhang and angrily threw a wooden umbrella handle against the wall.

Serge stepped out from the side of the building. "So if it isn't my old pal Mahoney."

The agent spun toward the voice and drew his weapon, but Serge already had the drop and shook his head. "You're not that fast."

Mahoney set his pistol on the ground.

"Kick it to me."

Mahoney did.

Serge picked it up and stuck it in his pocket. "What are you doing here?"

Mahoney wrung out his sopping hat. "I discovered who the other killer is."

"Who?"

Serge recognized the cold piece of metal the moment he felt it against the back of his head. A deep voice behind him: "Drop it!"

Serge set his pistol on the ground. "Jeff, have you lost your mind?"

"Yes," said Mahoney. "That's what I was trying to tell you."

McSwirley jabbed the back of Serge's head with the gun barrel. "Get over there with Mahoney."

Serge walked a few feet and stood next to the agent. "Where'd you get the gun?"

"You gave it to me when you dropped me off," said Jeff. "Remember? You told me I'd need it."

"The bright side is, I was right again," said Serge. "But I still don't understand what's gotten into you."

"Jeff's the other killer," said Mahoney.

"No way!" said Serge. He turned to McSwirley. "Right?"

Jeff hyperventilated. "I can't take it anymore! All the death, human cruelty, murder victims and their relatives . . ."

"I didn't want to mention anything before," said Serge. "But you need to get off the self-pity jag. It's kind of icky."

"Fuck you!" yelled Jeff, flashing with rage and waving the gun. "You think this is self-pity?"

"Just the whining and crying and the rest of your personality," said Serge. "But other than that—"

"Shut up! There's nothing to pity here!" Jeff's face twisted into something Serge hadn't seen before. "You think I'm feeling sorry for myself because I have to talk to those people? *Oh, poor, poor me, all these sad stories. I have it so hard.* No! *They* have it hard! I have nothing to complain about. This isn't self-pity!"

"What is it, then?"

"Self-loathing! I shouldn't even be knocking on those fucking doors. I'm revictimizing them."

"I was almost right," Mahoney told Serge. "Strong split-personality vibe. Except it wasn't you. It was Jeff."

"Shut up!" McSwirley stretched out his shooting arm. "This is it."

"This is what?" asked Serge.

"Thanks for all you did for me. I know you've got your problems, but you genuinely cared."

"Jeff," said Serge, "just put the gun down. We can talk this out. Remember all the yuks on the road?"

"Too late. I didn't know what I was going to do until I got here, but now it's clear."

"What is?" asked Serge.

"Mahoney's the closest one to catching you, and he's never going to give up. So I'm going to do you a favor."

"Jeff, listen to me—"

"Before I shoot myself, I'm going to shoot Mahoney. Then you'll be free. Just give me the word."

"But I don't want you to shoot Mahoney."

"Why not? He's vowed to bring you in."

"We all have our roles to play. Mine's to instruct jerks. His is to catch me. That's how it works. He's one of the good guys."

"Okay," said Jeff. "Then I'll shoot him because *I* want to. Then I'll shoot *you*."

"He's lost it," said Mahoney.

Jeff covered his ears with his hands. "Shut up!"

Serge lunged for the gun, but Jeff quickly took his hands down and aimed again. "Don't even try it!"

Serge backed up. All manner of debris was flying now, like if compost heaps were used for a ticker-tape parade. They were on the downstream side of the building, temporarily shielding them until the hurricane's rotation switched. The field began to flood. Water lipped over the concession's patio.

"Your choice," said Jeff. "You tell me to shoot him, you live. You don't, I kill both of you."

"It doesn't have to end like this," said Serge.

"What's the matter? Suddenly you don't like death? It's not so much fun anymore, is it? Now you know what *I* have to go through."

"Jeff, look," said Serge, "that night in the vault, all those things you said. If I'd known it was this serious—"

"Shut up!" Jeff covered his ears again. "Stop telling me that!"

"Okay, I'll shut up."

Mahoney nudged Serge. "He's not talking to you."

"Who's he talking to?"

"The voices," said Mahoney.

"Shut up! Shut up! Shut up!" Jeff stomped his feet in the rising water. "I'm going to kill you!"

"Jeff," said Mahoney, "don't listen to the voices."

"I was talking to you that time," said Jeff.

"Sorry," said Mahoney. "It's getting kind of confusing."

"Could you start using names?" asked Serge.

Jeff extended his pistol arm again. "I almost admired you. But you don't have any backbone at all. I'm shooting Mahoney first, just so you can see it before you go. . . . Time to die!"

CHAPTER FORTY-SIX

LAKE WALES

The entire nation clung to every update from the National Hurricane Center. It was on all the stations. Nobody ever imagined such a thing. Because it had never remotely come close to happening.

The eyes of two full-blown hurricanes were about to crisscross in the middle of Florida. Then what? Would the storms keep going? Would they cancel out? Would they join together in some kind of hurricane supernova?

The intersection was less than thirty minutes away. If the networks could reach the epicenter in time, their footage would be historic. Satellite trucks raced toward the middle of the state, converging on Lake Wales Ridge.

The rising water reached Serge's shins in a riptide. He pleaded with Jeff, but it was hard communicating in the deafening collision of storms. Lightning crashed, mini-twisters spun across the flooding ridge, birds drowned, frogs could fly. Drama on a biblical level.

Jeff reached the end of his tether. He stiffened his arm and cocked the pistol. A finger began pulling the trigger.

"*Noooooooooooo!!!!!*" Serge jumped in front of Mahoney.

Another shout: "*Ahhhhhhhh!*"

A giant bird cascaded around the side of the building in the floodwaters, slamming into the back of Jeff's legs. A pistol flew into the air and splashed. Serge and Mahoney dove and grabbed four legs, saving Coleman and Jeff from being swept away. Then they huddled against the side of the building where the current was weakest.

"That was close," said Serge.

"Don't move."

Serge turned toward the barrel of Mahoney's gun.

"I'm faced with a problem," said the agent. "You saved my life again."

"So stop screwing up."

The sky suddenly grew light. They raised their heads toward the parting clouds. The eyes were crossing.

Mahoney began backing off the patio into a drizzle.

"Where are you going?" asked Serge.

"This meeting never took place," said Mahoney. "But the debt's paid in full. There'll be a next time." He ran off into the mist.

Serge watched him disappear and turned to Jeff. "Now, what are we going to do about you?"

Jeff lowered his head and sniffled. "Please kill me."

"Jesus," said Serge, putting an arm around his shoulders. "Nobody has to kill anyone. And we have some lovely parting gifts."

The news trucks began arriving on the crest of Lake Wales Ridge, just in time to catch the last of the eclipsing eyes. A Florida Cable News correspondent jumped out with a microphone.

"*This is Blaine Crease, the first on the scene at the historic crossing of the hurricane eyes. I'm standing at the foot of the equally historic Bok Tower, dedicated in 1929 by President Coolidge—*"

Crease and the cameraman were distracted by a sound. It was music. Except it wasn't the melodic, sixty-bell carillon usually heard from the marble-and-coquina tower. More news trucks arrived. The noise grew louder. Nobody spoke. Just a bank of cameras trained on the top of the edifice, broadcasting live to the nation. The noise became even louder, now competing with the rear wall of the twin eye, moving in fast. Wind snapped and rain stung. Then they all saw it.

Atop the bell tower, Serge stepped into view with his Stratocaster and battery-powered mini-amp. His right hand slammed guitar strings. *DUH-DUH! Da-da-dah, da-da-dah, da-da-dah, DUH-DUH!* They all recognized it now—the unmistakable opening hook from "Jumpin' Jack Flash."

"I was born . . . in a cross-fire hurricane! . . ."

The eyes began parting, and everyone took cover.

EPILOGUE

TAMPA: WESTSHORE BOULEVARD

Serge wielded a razor-edged knife.

"Please, don't! . . ."

Serge shook his head. "I can't help myself."

"Listen to reason! . . ."

"Stop arguing and give it to me!"

Witnesses watched in horror.

Serge sat with a big cloth napkin tucked into his collar. The knife was clenched in one fist, a fork in the other, both pointed upward in the ready position. Serge slammed the butts of the cutlery on the table. "Bring me another one!"

"And another scotch," said Coleman.

"Yes, sir." The waiter ran off.

Coleman poured ice water over the liquor-seasoned cubes in his cocktail to get the extra. "I've seen you eat before, but never like this."

"Hurricanes bring out my appetite." Serge grabbed a roll and butter. "Besides, this isn't about eating."

"What's it about?"

"Paying tribute to The Legend."

A large group of onlookers continued to gather where Serge was seated at the bar. The waiter returned and set a plate in front of him. A forty-eight-ounce Angus steak the size of a doormat. "You don't have to go through with this."

"Nobody ever *has* to be the best." Serge went to work with the knife. "You just get the calling. And when you hear it, you better listen. It's something me and The Legend understand."

"But your name's already going up on the wall." The waiter pointed toward an honor roll of engraved brass plates. "You already ate one of those monster steaks."

"I'm eating two."

"But nobody's ever eaten two. Nobody's ever *dared*."

"Did Shula win just one Super Bowl?"

Coleman held up an empty glass and jingled ice cubes in the international refill signal.

Serge continued cutting meat. "I used to think Clapton was God, but now I realize the transmission was garbled. *Shula* is God. Luckily, a lot of other people are experiencing the same revelation, and these churches have begun springing up all over the country."

Coleman looked around at the scores of autographed football helmets and jerseys. "Serge, we're in Shula's Steak House."

"They want you to *think* it's a steak house." Serge popped a chunk in his mouth. "That's because all new religions face persecution at the beginning. Like when the apostles had to sneak around the Roman Empire flashing secret gang signs or they'd be martyred." Serge turned to a group of traveling telecommunications salesmen at a nearby table. He held a fist close to his chest and gave them a furtive thumbs-up. He winked and whispered, "Shula."

Coleman grabbed the football off a tee in the middle of the table and read the menu on its side. "What's this eating-contest business?"

"It's not a contest. It's a sacrament. Consume an entire mondo Shula steak, for a modest tithing of eighty-five dollars, and get your name written in the Book of Eternal Life. There are thirty thousand souls so far."

"How do you know?"

"It's on the Internet. A man named Taft Parker has eaten a hundred." Serge stuck the fork in his mouth. "But one at a time."

Coleman set the football back on the tee. "You seem to be in a great mood."

"I'm on a roll: excellent hurricane season, got away from Mahoney—again—and I found the religion I was searching for."

Coleman idly stared at a team photo of the undefeated '72 Dolphins. "Funny, I can't stop thinking about Jeff."

Serge chewed and sawed at the same time. "That kid was *fucked up*. If I'd had any idea, I never would have let such a dangerous person in our car."

"What do you think's going to happen to him?"

"Nothing," said Serge. "Mahoney and I took care of that."

"You talked to Mahoney?"

Serge nodded and swallowed. "On the phone. You wouldn't believe the freakish stuff he was able to piece together. *Jeff* didn't even believe it."

"Like what?"

"Mahoney took him back out to where his house burned down. Found all these crazy charred remains in a back room. Hundreds of photos and clips, or what was left of the ones the firefighters had been able to hit with the hoses before they burned up completely."

"How's that weird?"

Serge bit another chunk off his fork. "Jeff didn't remember any of it. Said his landlord kept this one back room locked all the time."

"Why would his landlord do that?"

"Coleman, catch up. It wasn't his landlord; it was Jeff's alter ego. Mahoney said he's studied a lot of split personalities, but never a case where one identity was stalking the other. Jeff really did hate the other Jeff—or at least what he had to do for a living. Writing all those creepy letters to himself. Pretending his cell phone was vibrating in the state park for a make-believe call, then phoning Justin from the newspaper's break room to set up his murder. Although I have to give him credit for that Suwannee River code."

"But you said nothing's going to happen to him?"

"Felt sorry for the poor kid. So Mahoney's agreed to leak a cover story that I confessed to all of Jeff's crimes. Nobody needs to be the wiser."

"He's just back on the street wandering around?"

"No, I wouldn't do that to society. He's a real sicko." Serge stuck another bite in his mouth. "We're getting him the help he needs. He used to see a psychiatrist, but apparently not a very good one. So I hooked him up with my shrink. At first she said her calendar was booked solid, but I made her an offer she couldn't refuse." He set down the fork and picked up the menu football. "Coleman, go long. . . . On three! . . ."

Coleman went long. "I'm open! I'm open. . . ."

Crash.

GULF COAST PSYCHIATRIC CENTER

A phone rang. "Excuse me," said a female psychiatrist. "I keep forgetting to turn this thing off." She looked at her cell phone's display. GUESS WHO?

She looked up at the chair across the room.

"Smile!" Jeff snapped her picture with his own phone.

"Jeff, please. We have some serious issues to—"

McSwirley began fiddling with another device. "Thanks for seeing me."

"Thanks for coming."

"Serge said you were booked solid but that he made you an offer you couldn't refuse."

The normally unflappable doctor began stuttering. "I . . . I . . . There . . . uh . . ."

Jeff looked up and grinned. "I won't tell anyone. You make a nice couple."

She blushed brightly. "I . . . You have the wrong . . ."

"Said he must have lost his mind fooling around with those young chicks. You're what? A couple years older than him? That fits. He told me one of his mottos: 'Intelligence and maturity are always sexy in a woman.' . . ."

She blushed more, this time with an involuntary smile.

". . . Said you could name vice presidents and everything." Jeff hoisted a gym bag onto his lap and began rummaging. "Also told me he'd gotten over the aging thing, so he gave me all his midlife gadgets. Look at this great stuff! Plus a bunch of guide-books . . ."

"Jeff?"

". . . Old souvenirs—said he bought some doubles by accident—more gadgets . . ."

"Jeff!"

"What?"

"Slow down!"

"But I'm so excited about life."

"I can see that." The doctor checked her notes. "Your mood has greatly improved. You were really depressed the first time I saw you. In fact, there's something completely different about you." She stopped and watched Jeff unfold a portable keyboard for his BlackBerry. Tap, tap, tap. "Jeff, you're . . . confident."

"I guess so." Tap, tap, tap.

The doctor quickly flipped back through her file. "When was the last time you cried?"

Tap, tap, tap. "It was back . . . I don't remember."

"Amazing. I've rarely seen such rapid progress."

"Serge said you'd be able to help me." Jeff stowed the PDA and resumed searching through his bag. "No disrespect, but it wasn't working with that other doctor. Whatever happened to him?"

"Went to prison. Jeff, do you have any plans?"

"Great big ones." He pulled something out of the bag. "The

newspaper gave me three weeks off, and I've decided to do a little traveling. Actually, a lot."

"Very positive," said the doctor. "Where are you going?"

Jeff held up a musty 1939 edition of the WPA guide to Florida. "Everywhere!"

"I'm very happy for you—but a little concerned about you being alone right now."

"Oh, I won't be going alone. Someone's coming with me."

"Who?"

"My girlfriend."

"You have a girlfriend?" The doctor wrote something quickly. "Very positive, forming human bonds. That might account for the sudden self-confidence. . . . What can you tell me about her?"

A horn honked outside.

"She likes to honk the horn," said Jeff.

"That's her?"

McSwirley got up and walked toward the window. "We're leaving for Key West right after this session." He cranked open the glass and waved down at the flaming redhead parked at the curb in a brown Plymouth Duster. "Just a minute, dear."

"How'd you meet?"

"Covering a story." Jeff walked back to his chair. "Told me I was cute."

"What's her name?"

"Molly."

"That's a nice name. How's it been going?"

"Great! We fight all the time!"

"How is *that* great?"

"Because Serge taught me how to deal with women."

The doctor assumed a skeptical look. "How do you do that?"

"Forfeit. Tell 'em whatever they want to hear and move on with enjoying the miracle of life together."

The horn honked again. Jeff bent over and tightened the Velcro straps on his sneakers.

"But that's deceptive," said the doctor. "You're not being honest and working through your true feelings."

"You're right. I won't do it anymore." Jeff stood and headed for the door. "Are you able to have multiples?"

"What?"

Honk.

Jeff pointed. "I better be going."

THE EVERGLADES

Serge had finished his work; now it was time to play. He parked the Hummer and headed across a long, narrow field.

Someone met him in the middle, and Serge handed over a roll of hundred-dollar bills from a boosted ATM. "Will that be enough?"

The man moved his hand up and down, gauging the weight. "More than enough. You sure you want to do this?"

"Never been more sure of anything in my life. Until the next thing."

"You've used one of these before?"

"Million times. We set?"

"Ready when you are." The man walked back to his pickup truck, an empty trailer hitched behind it.

The field sat along the edge of the swamp, just north of the panther-crossing signs and toll booths at the western end of Alligator Alley, a rapidly developing section of Florida known as Golden Gate. But it wasn't completely spoiled yet. A great blue heron stalked needlefish in a marsh along the perimeter of the clearing. Ibis, spoonbills, snowy egrets. Crickets buzzed, gators lounged. The sunset over Naples was all you could ask for. One of those wavering crimson balls.

Serge turned and gave Coleman the backslapping guy hug. He held him out by the shoulders. "Take care of yourself while I'm gone."

"How long till you're back?"

"Three days, three years, who knows?" Serge sat down and buckled crisscrossing straps over his chest. "I just set events in motion and let them go where they want."

Coleman grabbed the edge of a long metal blade. "Now?"

"Now. But get those hands back or it'll chop 'em right off."

Coleman pulled down fast. An internal-combustion engine burped smoke and chugged to life. The blade circled herky-jerky for the first few rotations, then spun invisibly. Serge donned goggles and a long scarf.

Before all the encroaching construction—back when this was still a nearly impossible-to-reach outpost—the narrow field had been a grass landing strip for pot-bale Cessnas. Smugglers ran out at night with generators and strands of Christmas lights to mark the runway.

"Remember the key to life," Serge shouted over the engine. "Always act like you deserve to be here."

"What?" yelled Coleman. But his pal was already bounding across the field. Coleman shielded his eyes and watched the ultralight plane lift off. The pilot's right arm thrust into the air.

"*Shula!*"

The racket flushed a flock of endangered cranes from the brush. They took flight, forming a perfect V formation and following Serge into the setting sun.